FENCING
WITH
THE KING

DIANA ABU-JABER

FENCING WITH THE KING

A Novel

W. W. NORTON & COMPANY
Independent Publishers Since 1923

Page 153: Mahmoud Darwish, excerpt from "Sonnet V," from *The Butterfly's Burden*, translated by Fady Joudah. Copyright © 2007 by Mahmoud Darwish. Translation copyright © 2007 by Fady Joudah. Reprinted with the permission of The Permissions Company, LLC, on behalf of Copper Canyon Press, coppercanyonpress.org.

For information about permission to reproduce selections from this book, write to Permissions, W. W. Norton & Company, Inc., 500 Fifth Avenue, New York, NY 10110

For information about special discounts for bulk purchases, please contact W. W. Norton Special Sales at specialsales@wwnorton.com or 800-233-4830

Manufacturing by Lakeside Book Company
Book design by Brooke Koven
Production manager: Julia Druskin

Library of Congress Cataloging-in-Publication Data

Names: Abu-Jaber, Diana, author.
Title: Fencing with the king : a novel / Diana Abu-Jaber.
Description: First Edition. | New York, NY : W. W. Norton & Company, [2022]
Identifiers: LCCN 2021042897 | ISBN 9780393867718 (hardcover) |
ISBN 9780393867725 (epub)
Classification: LCC PS3551.B895 F46 2022 | DDC 813/.54—dc23
LC record available at https://lccn.loc.gov/2021042897

W. W. Norton & Company, Inc., 500 Fifth Avenue, New York, N.Y. 10110
www.wwnorton.com

W. W. Norton & Company Ltd., 15 Carlisle Street, London W1D 3BS

1 2 3 4 5 6 7 8 9 0

For Scott and Grace, my all.

To the memory of Victoria Allman, fearless, beautiful friend.

*To the memory of Ghassan Saleh Abu-Jaber, fencer,
father extraordinaire.*

Fencing with the King is fiction, a work of imagination, but in the way of so many novels, that imaginary world takes its inspiration from aspects of the real world. My family is descended from Jordanian Bedouins and Palestinian city dwellers, from refugees and long-established gentry—and their movements through time and history were echoed in several of the plot points of this book.

My father's life was divided into the time before and after his arrival. His family history was the stuff of legends, and as a child, it was at times almost impossible for me to tease apart legends from truth. My great-grandfather Ameen opposed the Ottoman rule in the Levant and helped protect Armenians fleeing the Turkish genocide, sometimes hiding them in his grand house in Jerusalem.

As the Turkish army retreated, they decimated the crops and there was famine across the Levant, so my great-grandparents and their family eventually made their way to Jordan to stay with distant relatives. My young grandfather, Saleh, fed and sheltered them and eventually he married their daughter—my grandmother Anissa. My grandparents were renowned for their hospitality—their beautiful historic home was filled with musicians, poets, academics, and politicians. Not long after they were married, then-Emir Abdullah came to their house in al-Salt, Jordan, and stayed for three months. Saleh protected him during this politically fraught time until

Abdullah made his way to Amman and was declared the King of Trans-Jordan.

My father was indeed one of King Hussein's fencing partners— and reputedly the "favorite." Several of my relatives were high-ranking politicians and diplomats and I did have an uncle who lived in a cave. But the characters in my novel do not represent any of those actual individuals; they are the products of my imagination, with lives and personalities that are theirs alone. Like reflections in a cracked mirror, the events of this story are fabrications and the characters are their own people.

FENCING
WITH
THE KING

CHAPTER

1

Al-Mafraq, Jordan, Saturday, October 28, 1995 •

THE SCREAM FELL from the sky. Amani watched the falcon pause in midair, fold its wings and dive.

"Too fast to measure," the man beside her remarked. "Extraordinary things."

She fanned herself with a program, smearing ink on her hand. "So, this is—a race?"

He nodded. "The four hundred meter."

Under the open-air warm-up tent, trainers milled around, forearms lifted, hooded falcons balanced on leather gloves, showing off. The birds looked heavy and monumental, like imperial beings. Amani and Gabe were allowed to watch from the warm-up tent which smelled of hay and bird shit. There were photographers, wealthy tourists in suits, necks slung with camera equipment. Servers with trays walked through a sea of conversation. Amani accepted a glass of something nearly transparent; it smelled grassy and felt light in her mouth. She would have given her last dollar for an ice cube. Somewhere on the risers under the sun, amid a sea of white dishdashes and keffiyehs, sat the King.

"Don't they believe in water?" her father asked.

"They?" Hafez looked bemused. Someone edged in front of Amani and took a picture of her uncle. She shuffled backward.

"All day and all night in those airplanes—it's like crossing the Sahara," Gabe said.

"I'm well aware." Hafez lowered his nose to his glass. "This vintage is from the palace sommelier." He looked up in the direction of the royal entourage: it was the third time Amani noticed him doing this. She took another swallow: it was warm.

"If there's time later, I'll introduce you." He smoothed back his shock of white hair and nodded toward the King.

On the competition field, a man in jeans, T-shirt, and creased red keffiyeh jogged backward across the swept ground, swinging bait on a long tether.

"Okay, what's that thing?" Amani pointed. "Fill me in here."

"Feathers," her father said. "Feathered incentive."

The falcon flashed past the bait, flew in a narrow ellipsis, returned for another attempt. The man lowered the bait and swung it along the earth before the bird descended.

"It's duck wing," the man beside her said. "And that field is now falcon territory." Wind rumbled along the roof of the tent and everyone lifted a hand against the dust. His brown eyes had a green light to them, the irises shone with flecks. He took something from a boy and offered it to Amani. A little paper cup of tepid water.

She thanked him profusely, swallowed it in one gulp, gave a second cup to her father.

"You have it," Gabe said. "I can wait."

"Dad, just—have this. Please?" She turned back to see the boy already returning with two more tiny cups.

"No, no." Hafez shooed the boy. "Don't drink that. Ya' Allah.

He's getting that from the animal hose." Hafez gestured to someone in the crowd; minutes later, his driver appeared with frosted glass bottles of Evian. "Samir can find anything," he said, handing them to Amani and Gabe. "Five-hundred-dinar donation to get into the trainers' tent and they can't give us decent water."

Falcon-oriented discussions circulated all around: she heard that Sheikh Majed had bought out first and business classes on Emirates Air to fly his eighty falcons to Jordan on the arms of their trainers, the Abu-Dhabi Falconers Club. The birds had needed passports to travel internationally. "Required—to protect against smuggling," one of the trainers said. "It's easier for a falcon to get a UAE passport than for me." Behind him, a silk banner rippled, inscribed in Arabic and English: *In Commemoration of the Sixtieth Birthday of King H. of Jordan.*

She swiped an arm across her forehead. Her eyes felt gritty. Heat waves warped the air and she couldn't shake the sense that the ground was creeping underfoot. They were at a desert camp in Al-Mafraq, sixty-eight kilometers north of Amman, on the edge of the Jordan valley. Ivory-colored swells of dust filled the air, hitting the back of her sinuses. In the distance rose a sparse, shaggy landscape, everything dried to the same colors, the trees pointed, rows of spindly firs like last survivors. She felt as if she had walked through fiery curtains to get here.

Throughout their long trip, her father had sat gray-faced, pale with sweat—she'd thought he was anxious about flying, but he looked much the same today. They'd landed in Amman at two a.m. Saturday morning, then Hafez had appeared at nine a.m., banging on the front door, calling, I'm here! He had plans. He'd walked in and clapped his arms around his youngest brother. "And your lovely wife?" he'd asked. "We won't be seeing her?"

"It's her busy time," Amani said. "School started last month."

"You Americans. You know what they say?" He smiled broadly. "Arabs have family, Americans have work."

She laughed a little, uncertain if she should feel hurt or flattered.

Driving to the falconry exhibition, they'd passed hillsides scattered with low buildings, roadside vegetable markets under tents, hand-lettered signs for petrol, sizzling high tension towers. Beige cinder blocks. The entire country appeared to be under construction. "Welcome to Jordan in October!" her uncle said expansively, twisting around in the front passenger seat, slapping the arm of his driver, who didn't flinch. Dizzy with jet lag, Amani wanted to crawl back into bed, but her uncle was an undeniable force. He was determined that these birds be watched and admired. "Thirty years I don't see my favorite niece unless I take three airplanes to get to Syracuse," he said. "Now it's my turn."

One of the trainers approached Amani. He held an immense gray falcon on his forearm. Its merciless eyes like onyx and flattened head made Amani think of gryphons. It clicked its curved beak open then closed, then shifted, spreading and closing its black enamel talons on the glove. The trainer spoke little English but he held out his bird and Amani understood that he thought she might like to pet it. She pointed to her chest. "Me?"

Hafez chuckled. "Be careful—they can smell fear."

The trainer said something. "He says this is a sweet bird," her father translated.

"Ah, a cozy falcon." Hafez smiled, jingling his pocket change. "Charming."

"Your grandfather owned a falcon. . . ." Gabe told Amani.

"He did?" She glanced again at the gray bird. "You never told me."

"Several actually," Hafez said.

"But this one, it was devoted to him. He always said that falcons aren't affectionate, but that bird. . . . It was a good animal. It let me stroke its head. I wrapped up my hand with a dishrag and carried him around."

"Damnedest thing," Hafez said complacently. "Ugly as a buzzard."

A couple of the trainers started talking to Gabe, gesturing. He lowered his head, laughing. Hafez cut in with some remark and Gabe lifted his eyes. He stopped laughing. The men looked at Hafez, who was still smiling. Amani turned to the speckled falcon and tentatively lifted the back of her index finger to its breast. Under its feathers, she felt the soft tap of its heart.

Gabe started walking out to the competition area.

"Dad?" Amani stepped forward. "Hey, Dad? Where you going?" She and the trainer went to the end of the tent where sunlight fell in a sharp slant. The temperature had risen steadily and the seats were emptying. "I don't think you're supposed to be out there!" The air was thin, the sky like solid glass.

The man with the flecked eyes also moved to the tent's edge. "What's he doing?"

"Brother, y'akhi, you are lost?" Hafez yelled. He was smiling but he stopped at the shadow's edge. Watching her father, Amani felt a twinge of uneasiness.

Out in the field, someone handed Gabe a creased leather glove: he slipped it on his left hand. A trainer with an amber-colored falcon came to the start of the field and waved to Gabe. He released his bird and it flapped to the flagpole beside the risers. It landed, its head ticking with tiny movements. Gabe raised his glove, gave a low whistle, but the bird remained in place.

Gabe lifted the glove again, holding his hand out. He shook it a few times, index finger curved, and gave another whistle. With a sound like snapping sheets, the falcon lifted from its perch, sailed, head level, talons outstretched: it landed on Gabe's hand. Amani clapped, startled, delighted. "Look! Look your baba!" the trainer beside her said, his own falcon ruffling and resetting. "Is in the blood," the man said. "The history. You know? The birds scent it. They know he is real Bedu." Her father was laughing out in the field. Someone whistled. He tossed the bird into the air and it swooped back toward its trainer.

Her uncle had clapped as well, but then crossed his arms. There was an empty section in the risers where the King had been seated. Seeing her uncle, something in her chest softened. When she was a child, she had liked to imagine that suave, educated Uncle Hafez was her actual father. He recited poetry and spoke with presidents and traveled the world. Oh, she did love her father, but Gabe kept to his woodshop and barely knew how to read English. Uncle Hafez did such marvelous things, helping to govern a kingdom, steering the world in the direction of peace. And he spoke up for the Palestinians and other dispossessed people—at a time when few others dared to.

When Amani was in college and worried about what to major in, he'd told her: Follow your voice. You love to write, yes? So, you will do that. As soon as she made that decision, her anxiety dissolved.

Now she watched her father with the birds. People, even parents, could continually surprise you. She sensed the tilting pull between the brothers—was this what it was like to have a sibling?

Amani trotted out to claim her dad. Gabe smiled, shaking his head at himself. Then he halted, eyes lifting above Amani, his lips parted, his expression stopped. Amani slowed down. An instant later, she heard wings, an uproar of feathers. She turned to see two slim black talons extended. She shrieked, lifting her arms, the bird's grand wings outstretched, beating furiously, as if to carry her away. The trainer sprinted over, shouting in Arabic, and grabbed his bird. Two welts were torn through her cotton shirt and into her shoulder. She tried to catch her breath, to laugh, but when she saw a bright crimson stripe run down her arm, her knees buckled.

A mistake, she thought as she hit the ground. I'm not supposed to be here. I shouldn't have come. Then the other one was at her side, the first man who'd talked to her, lifting her head, pressing a bandage to her shoulder. "My God, I've never seen one of them do that before. Like you'd called to it."

She tried to laugh. "Did I call it to come eat me?"

"Whatever you were saying," he said. "He heard you."

CHAPTER

2

AMANI WOKE in a twist of cold bedsheets. She had no idea where she was. It felt as if she hovered two inches over her skin and her ears were filled with flat, unnerving silence. A radio clock said 6:02 but it seemed too early for the milky light in the windows. She pushed up to sitting and felt a pulse of pain.

Two serrated red marks punctuated her shoulder.

That moment—the explosion of feathers, talons, strokes of blood—came rushing back.

She sank into the bed, eyes closed, curled on her good side, remembering that one of the trainers had produced a first-aid kit and bandaged her wounds. "Never turn your back on a falcon," he scolded, as if she should have known this. "Trained or not! And with all this loose hair! To him you looked just like prey. Like a baby sheep."

She'd apologized repeatedly. Yesterday was a miasma of faces and images, of exhaustion so powerful her bones seemed to be melting. Her uncle Hafez had stood slightly apart looking disappointed.

She drowsed, then woke again when voices reached her through the floor.

It was her father's other brother, Farouq. He and his son Omar greeted Amani as she came down the stairs. Kissing her twice on each cheek, Farouq said, "You've been anointed—is this the word? Appointed?"

"Ha. I barely feel it anymore," she lied, and moved her shoulder. Then she flopped on the couch beside her uncle.

"Yo, cuz." Nineteen-year-old Omar started carrying their suitcases upstairs to the bedrooms. They'd arrived so early yesterday morning they'd just deposited their bags in the entry and stumbled to their beds. Now she heard Omar drop one case on her father's bed then roll hers into the next room. She considered following him upstairs to unpack, but couldn't stand. Half of her still seemed to be somewhere over the Atlantic.

"You are sure? I can get the tabeeb to look at that, easy," Farouq said.

"Baba, don't harass her," Omar said as he came back down. His English was flawless. "Amani fights eagles, jumps over bridges. She does it all."

Gabe was slumped in the armchair, withered against its brocaded upholstery. He closed his eyes. Yesterday after the falconry show, Farouq's driver had taken them home. In the backseat of the car, Gabe had touched Amani's bandaged shoulder and mumbled, "I knew we shouldn't have done this."

Unsure if he meant seeing the falcons or coming to Jordan, Amani had put her hand over his and squeezed.

Now she looked at Farouq with a limp smile. "I'm pretty sure we disgraced ourselves. Totally embarrassed Uncle Hafez."

"Oh, what of it?" He lifted his chin. "I personally am un-embarrassable. I don't believe in it—getting embarrassed."

"That's true," Omar said.

"Yeah, well, this was pretty bad." Amani settled back. "And of course the King had to be there. Well, at some point he was there."

"So? The King is everywhere." Farouq flitted his fingers then looked around. "Bella put food for you in the fridge. Coffee. We'll send one of the girls to help with cleaning, cooking. Anything."

They were in a bustling part of town called Shmeisani, their guesthouse just next door to Farouq. The small, two-story villa was surrounded by dark irises and leggy roses. At the front gate, a stone faun stood guard: it held a pan pipe in its left hand, its hoof bowed forward as if inviting passersby to dance. Amani hadn't registered it when they arrived; now she gazed from the window at its lightly draped backside. Directly to the south loomed Farouq's rectangular house with its marble columns and archways. Real estate, he said, was his favorite hobby. In the distance, Amani could hear a buzz of traffic.

Uncle Farouq—older than Gabe and younger than Hafez—had spent just two years in the States finishing his degree, but he was wealthier than either of his brothers. He seemed to have an innate talent for making money. Already he was strolling around the front room, circling a brass table, discoursing in his careful English on co-import agreements and wonderful new free zones, which opened the way to an American coffee franchise he'd been waiting to launch. "See, the whole idea here is to show the Jordanians how many very good things come from the West! Not just Nike and Michael Jackson. The more stable Jordan is, the more the people with their big pockets come to us. Everybody wins." He started to talk about development in the valley, explaining the difficulties of wastewater treatment, desalinization and minefield removal, but then seemed to forget about English and shifted into Arabic.

"Mumtaz! Y'akhi, mabrook," her father said. Congratulations. "Amazing news. I wish I could invest in you." He closed his eyes again. Amani sat on the arm of the couch beside him and patted his head. There were two new mobile phones on the coffee table—gifts from Farouq. After years of subpar telephone service, flip phone mobiles had started to appear, making phone-line infrastructure unnecessary. Providentially, her uncle had bought stock in Motorola.

Amani always suspected there was something slightly compromised about her middle uncle—as if he might switch allegiances—to companies, people, anything—according to whichever option was most profitable. Farouq was shy and funny and she was fond of him, his fragile English, his big round belly and nose, his retiring nature—but Hafez was still the one she admired most.

Farouq went on as if he and Gabe didn't phone each other regularly. Once Farouq got started on resettlement space and fish farming, Amani retreated into the kitchen. They were staying a month, but her aunt Bella had filled the cabinets with enough bread, fruit, vegetables, and cheeses to last a year. Omar came in and dropped into a chair at the kitchen table. "I couldn't believe it—when Baba said you guys were coming. And six weeks!"

She found a jar of Nescafé and unscrewed it. "Well, it's pretty cool, don't you think? A fencing match with the King? I never even knew my dad used to fence."

"Very cool. No question. Super cool, actually. Uncle Gabe can do anything."

She spooned coffee into two cups. "But it's true, I did have to sort of—convince him to do it. I really wanted to come."

"Yeah, so like, why is that exactly?" Omar propped both elbows on the table. "I mean, I guess I could see, like, a long weekend, maybe. But a solid month? In this place?"

Amani poured hot water into the cups and considered her younger cousin. "Why, what's so terrible about here?" Omar had grown up in Amman, but his parents sent him to summer-long horse camps in the Catskills and surf camps in Southern California and Hawaii. He'd spent Christmas breaks in Syracuse with Amani and her parents. Omar was drawn to her father, his hearty, masculine nature, in the same way that Amani had been drawn to Hafez's erudition. Gabe taught Omar how to use a chisel and plane; they built a bookcase together. And even though Amani was twelve years older, Omar had somehow decided on their friendship years ago—she supposed it was because the two of them had been born with the same halfway identities—between parents, between countries.

"Ha, you live in the *States*. You can do whatever you want. You can actually make stuff happen there. Here, it's like sit around, eat, smoke shisha, gossip, yell about politics, rinse, repeat. I'm getting myself out of here as soon as I get my shit together." Omar accepted a cup. "For real, I can't even figure out why you want to come here in the first place."

"A lot of reasons. Like, it's heritage. You know. Identity?"

Omar stared at her.

Amani found cream in the refrigerator and brought it to the table. "A free trip to another country? Parties and sightseeing and hanging out with the King? Wouldn't you go for it?"

When he continued to stare at her, she studied a rectangle of light on her cup of coffee for a moment. "Well, and then for another thing, I found this, sort of like, a blue letter."

"A blue . . . ?"

"That's how I think of it. I'm not sure if it was a poem or what exactly. Dad thinks his mother wrote it. I don't know. But I got into it. Maybe it's dumb." She shrugged lightly. "I just really wanted to find some . . ."

Before she could say more, her father and uncle came in looking for coffee and the conversation shifted away.

LAST AUGUST, her parents' phone rang so late at night, Amani knew it had to be a relative. Sometimes their calls came once a month, some for her mother, more for her dad, sometimes night after night—hours of gossip and politics—certain aunts and uncles seemed to hold Gabe responsible for American foreign policy. But on this night—Gabe told her later—a deep, British-inflected voice had said: "I'm calling on behalf of King H Bin H, ruler of the Hashemite Kingdom of Jordan."

"Hafez?" Her father laughed, and held the phone in both hands. Amani watched through her bedroom doorway. She'd moved in with her parents after she and Bill divorced; for months she'd been saying that she would find her own place. As soon as she heard her father say *Hafez,* she felt a familiar admixture of alarm and excitement. She imagined the transatlantic static haze that swept over the line, shrinking then expanding his voice, rattling it like metal coins. "Is that you?" Her uncle didn't call as frequently as the others, preferring instead to squeeze in appearances at the Syracuse airport, usually on his way to DC or New York.

"Gabe," Hafez had boomed. "Listen to me," he said. "Don't say a word, y'akhi. I have an invitation for you—amazing, amazing. This is the kind you can't refuse."

After the call, Gabe beckoned to Amani. Francesca was working in her office—a desk in the corner of their bedroom, bent over a pile of paperwork. Amani could just make out her mother's eyes in the lamplight, a sheath of hair over one shoulder. Francesca tapped her pen and smiled patiently when she heard her brother-in-law's name.

It seemed Gabe and Francesca were to be honored guests. The King was about to turn sixty and there would be a month of birthday celebrations and events. They'd been offered a suite of rooms at the Four Seasons, but of course they might prefer Farouq's guesthouse. In exchange, Gabe was asked to participate in a kind of educational fencing exhibition—a bit of public reenactment and reminiscing with His Majesty. Everything paid for, easy, comfortable.

"Supposedly this comes from the King himself," Gabe said with a wry smile. "Hafez said the King remembers me. He swore he'd asked for me by name. Can you believe that?"

"If Hafez swears to it," his wife said drolly, "then I'm not sure I do believe it."

Gabe kept shaking his head, laughing in disbelief.

"I didn't know you *fenced.* And with the King!" Amani sat on the edge of their bed. Thirty-one years old yet her parents still surprised her. "Why didn't you ever talk about it?"

Francesca glanced at her husband. "You know that's not your father's style."

"Is it a midlife crisis?" Gabe mused. "Do kings get those? At sixty?"

"I suppose it's a king's prerogative," Francesca said. "Really, though, it's somewhat mad."

"Jordanians love parties. They're the national pastime."

"All this in October?" Francesca tapped her pen some more, put it down. She was the principal at St. Anselmo's in North Syracuse. "It's my worst time—mid-fall, before the holidays. I could never get away." In addition to student retention, behavior problems, and placating the parents, Francesca worried over the school itself. Housed in an old brick and ivy building, St. Anselmo's was beset by plumbing and structural problems that required almost continuous repairs.

"Oh, of course not. Neither of us can. I've got all kinds of things coming up. The kitchen remodel for the Hudsens. And Hafez wants us there for a *month*—or longer. He's got all kinds of plans. I can't close up shop for that long."

"Come *on*, you guys!" Amani looked from one to the other of her parents. "You'd turn this down?"

"I wish I could go. Really I do." Francesca's eyes turned to Gabe's. "But your father could take you. . . ." Francesca was an immigrant like Gabe, though she'd come over as a young teenager. She'd retained just the trace of an accent. Gabe told Amani he'd seen the faraway spaces in her mother right from the beginning—the edge of Sicily, its rocky white shores. Now they listened to her pen tap. "You never take time off, habeebi. You don't have to oversee every project." She smiled. "It's—what? Thirty-five years you haven't been back? Don't you think you're ready?"

"No. I already told him no," he said firmly.

To AMANI, Jordan was illicit; a story to which her father had never returned. Once, Francesca had said, "You know that your father's mother is from Nazareth?" Her father frowned as if trying to remember something. Whenever the news was on, the screen crossed with the image of young boys whipping rocks at soldiers, Gabe left the room. But this time, he said, "Mismar. It was a little place—just south of Nazareth." That was all he said. It was a part of them, and yet her father didn't speak of it. Apparently she wasn't meant to either. And because of this, she wanted to talk about it all the more. It was like an energetic call; it came from inside herself—secret, silent, and elemental.

She wasn't surprised that he had turned down the invitation. Yet, in the days that followed, she kept thinking about it.

It wasn't practical, she told herself. It wasn't even necessarily a good idea. She needed to stay home and rebuild. Save some money. Try to salvage her career. Bill, of course, was a lost cause. She'd felt shocked and betrayed by the demise of her marriage. An only child, she'd grown up feeling like a third wheel beside her sweet, beautiful parents. She was good at being alone, she hadn't ever expected to risk getting married. Kind, soft-spoken Bill had proposed three times before she relented. Six years ago, newly married, she'd written her collection of poetry as easily as if in a dream. It won a big literary prize, and she'd been offered a tenure-track position. Bill read all her work. He said he'd never cared about poetry before. He said her words spoke straight to him. That he'd never known words could do this.

But something happened—as if she'd awakened during a dream of flying. Molecule by molecule, things in her life began to erode: so slowly at first, it was almost impossible to determine where it started—the ice in the air, how her imagination had seemed to grow brittle. Amani felt silenced and distracted when she sat down to write—her thoughts vibrated in tiny collisions. Over the past three years, her disintegration had increased: the word "free-fall" kept coming to her, the image of a parachutist right before the chute opens, arms spread in right angles, body flattened against wind. She and Bill separated: she'd learned that he'd had a fling with another contractor—a blond electrician named Emily. He blamed Amani for this: he said he'd been lonely in their marriage; that poets were in love with the sound of their own voices. Remembering, she felt breathless, her insides still cramped with pain. It wasn't the best time to ask him to critique her work, and then she did. Like pressing her thumb on a bruise.

"I'm serious." Bill's eyes were grave. "You're a great writer, Amani, but don't write about this stuff—nobody wants to read about Arabs. Why do you always like to make things even harder on yourself?"

This was what her mother also said Amani did—made things harder. She gently reminded her daughter of her favorite motto—the "Principal Principle," she called it: *Stop struggling.*

Amani still hadn't learned how to do that.

A WEEK AFTER Uncle Hafez's call, her father brought out his knife. This occurred about once a year, around the time of his birthday. Il Saif was like an honored guest he kept in a drawer, showing it off on special occasions. Gabe sometimes spoke of its great age and worth, how it had traveled between countries, how it had been his father's favorite knife. This time, she'd asked to hold it. Turning the blade, she'd felt a soft pulse in her fingertips.

The next morning, Amani went into the kitchen and noticed Il Saif carelessly left on top of a pile of ads and fliers. That was Gabe—forgetting a priceless heirloom on a stack of recycling. She returned the knife to the leather satchel under his desk, then paused. Inside the satchel were the few mementos her father retained from his earlier life—a few aerograms from relatives, a book of poetry, a handful of blurry snapshots, a larger black-and-white image of her grandparents and their three little boys, its bottom corner torn away at the edge of Gabe's hand. Amani picked up the book and opened it: the pages were almost translucent. It had a bronze cover inscribed in Arabic calligraphy. Her father said he couldn't remember exactly where he'd gotten it from, but he'd always liked the cover. He rarely read anything but the newspaper. She sat in the rolling chair and ran her finger over the embossed letters on the cover. There was a catch in the gilt-edged pages: it opened to a sheet of blue paper. She paused and rubbed the corner of one eye. Prying the paper out with thumb and forefinger, she opened it carefully. There were lines of handwritten Arabic in black ink, and between each line, in pencil, appeared to be an English translation in a spidery penmanship upright with a few smudges and erasures and gaps. The ink and pencil had pressed a ghost of writing through to the opposite side of the page. She sat on the edge of the chair and read:

> *I've lost interest in the night.*
> *Stones taken beyond the clouds become stars.*
> *Now I know this happens with children as well. Take them*
>   *beyond the clouds and they grow wings.*
> *Abandonment, planets, moons,*
> *Stepping backwards into the black.*
> *There is no child*
> *More beloved than the one thrown away.*
> *A دير near قلعة are the last known places.*
> *But I was too afraid to look.*
> *And one must always take the risk.*

The English handwriting was small, curling, and neat: a little like her father's penmanship. He was fluent in conversation but his written English wasn't this good. It seemed more private than a poem, somehow—more like a whisper. She read it again as she stood, walking to her father's workshop behind the garage, a shiver starting along her arms. "Dad?"

"Sweetheart." Gabe removed a piece of plywood from his circular saw then pushed the safety glasses back on his head. He wiped sawdust away from his cheek with his upper arm. Amani felt a pulse of nerves as she handed him the paper. He glanced at it and picked up his readers from a shelf. His eyes traveled across the page, his fingers shifting. At last, he lifted his gaze.

"You left your knife out. Out on the kitchen counter," she said in self-defense. "When I went to put it back, I took the book out of your bag. This was stuck inside."

Gabe looked again at the page. He ran fingers over his forehead.

"Looks like it's been in there a long time," she said.

Gabe's voice was thin. "It was in that old book of mine?"

"It was hard to see. It was stuck to one of the pages."

His eyes traveled over it.

"Did Uncle Hafez write that?"

"No." Gabe's eyes stayed on the page. "My mother." The sight of his curved back and bowed head cut through her. "Your mom?"

Finally, he lowered the paper. "I don't know. Yes, I think so. She wrote a lot. Always. When she ran out of things to read, she would write. She did that. Wrote in Arabic and then in another language." He stared at Amani. "Before she came to Jordan, the nuns taught her English, French, some Latin." His fingers wavered near his brow. "She's in your face."

Other relatives had mentioned this resemblance: usually her father just gazed at her for an extra beat. She waited for him to say more, then she pointed. "It looks like there are two words here that she couldn't translate . . . 'A—something—near—something—are the last known places'?"

Gabe squinted at the paper, his lips moving silently over the two Arabic words. He struggled with written words, whether in English or Arabic: Amani's mother, who began her career as a reading specialist, had told her she thought he was dyslexic. "This word, *deir*, is like rest place? I can't think of the English."

"You mean resting place? Like a grave? Or a cemetery?"

He thought a moment, frowning, then turned back to the paper. "Well, this word—this is castle—*qal'ah*."

"Do you think she left it there for you?"

Gabe placed his hand over hers. He looked uncertain, turned his head as if to shake it, then stopped.

"*I* do," Amani said slowly. "I mean—I think *someone* put it in your book." She touched the impression of the pen on the paper, its depth and shapes like Braille.

"Before I left," Gabe said. "It's been there, all this time."

Amani brought the letter back to her room and sat on the edge of her bed. Her notebook was open on the comforter, the pen on top of it, a paragraph of handwriting with a pen slash through it. She felt a kind of pressure on her chest, as if someone had placed an enormous magnet there. She'd proposed it before, but Bill had never wanted to travel to Jordan; he used to say it wasn't safe. But she wanted this trip. In that moment it felt like her existence depended on it. The leaves made a rattling sound outside her window: these were the last moments before fall, she could almost taste it, the way the green would fade away and leave the shells. It was such a terribly beautiful time of year.

That night, she went back to her parents' bedroom. Her mother was at her desk and her father sat on the bed reading the newspaper. He lowered it and looked up.

"Is it too late?" she asked.

"Too late?" Gabe glanced at Francesca.

"For what, darling?" her mother asked.

"Uncle Hafez," Amani said. "Is it too late to tell him yes?"

CHAPTER

3

HAFEZ MUNIF HAMDAN, senior advisor to the king, crossed his arms over his stomach and felt the lines of his face sinking. Nothing was right. He'd invited his niece over for teatime, but they'd just found another leak. His office was in the King's diwan, second floor of the R Palace, and now the place would be crawling with plumbers and who-knew-what. The palace was flanked by the velvety sapphire lawns of the Royal Compound, roses imported from Normandy, white stone steps leading to a stone edifice nearly medieval in its ghostly beauty. But inside? His office had leaking corners and celery-colored shag carpeting selected by an office assistant in the early '70s. Did they truly expect him to host international guests when his office was in ruins? The pipes moaned and whistled during meetings, and Rafi and Mrs. Bosa—Hafez's white-haired secretary—gave each other looks and Mrs. Bosa murmured how castles come with ghosts. During downpours, one could actually see the water stains darkening below the crown molding like some sort of spiritual taint.

Mrs. Bosa tottered in in her sagging pantyhose and flat shoes to scold him about the convention, and the project exchange meeting with the Moroccans, and the speech to the Soroptimists—all three at once—and would he be fulfilling any of his obligations today? From his desk, he gazed up at her. "Please, Mrs. B—didn't you bring more ma'moul cookies? With the dates? Not even one?"

She regarded him over her half-glasses. "Hafez, what did the doctor say? Already you forget?" She came to stand beside him, pulled out his drawer, jammed it into his stomach, and extricated a slip of paper, slapping it down on the desktop. RX: METFORMIN, the written diagnosis: Al Sukkari. Diabetes.

Hafez wiped a hand over his face. Ah yes. The sugar. No more sugar. And what was the point of teatime, then?

He was supposed to be up the hill, at the Royal Cultural Center, attending the MENA Conference. It was a big deal—an economic summit to collect politicians and money people from all over, engage banks and business councils and entice private investors. Which was meant to forward the cause of peace and stability. But Hafez already felt exhausted, nearly drugged, his mind loosening in a provocative way where things were starting to buzz and vibrate. Ever since he learned his brother would return to Jordan, he'd felt the start of some sort of dissolution, a profound disorientation. He struggled to make himself focus on his work. It was an especially critical time. For months, the streets of Amman had been busy with men in jumpsuits repainting curbs, scrubbing the building fronts, lining the medians with trees imported from Turkey and Iran, workers shaking out the young, green canopies like opening umbrellas. Luxury hotel gift shops carried buttons that said WE MENA BUSINESS and MENA SPIRIT OF 1995. Investors had arrived from across the Middle East, Europe, Asia, and the Americas. Hafez had watched all this industry with dismay and a sense of inevitability.

He'd managed to make a stop at the morning's plenary session. There were Qatari sheikhs, Saudi financiers, pharmaceutical importers, electronics importers. Yasir Arafat was wheedling his way around the media. Warren Christopher and his entourage. The Israeli prime minister. Boris Yeltsin was around somewhere. The managing director of the International Monetary Fund opened his arms and shouted, "The Middle East is open for business!"

Afterward, Hafez had dutifully distributed his card, lined up days and days of meetings—then looked at the docket and envisioned it: business suits, shined black shoes, broad smiles, hands held out, stretching to infinity. He'd snuck out before lunch. Let them meet with each other.

"Hello!" Rafi Al Bustani appeared in the office door in his suit with the shiny elbows and thready cuffs. "Look who I found downstairs!"

Amani appeared from behind the man: tall and olive-skinned with such regal bones, scrolls of black hair and eyes gleaming as if her soul had surfaced there.

Hafez stood quickly, banging against his desk drawer. "They were supposed to announce you," he said. He'd wanted her to see how impressively visitors were presented.

"Oh, I know," Rafi said. "But she was already waiting when I came in, so I just brought her up." Smug.

Hafez enfolded his niece in a hug, kissed her thrice on each cheek. "Come, please, please. Welcome to central command."

"How gorgeous. I can't believe this is where you work. I mean, look at these ceilings!"

He nodded at the ceiling, pointed out woodwork. "The stone was quarried from Ma'an and this window glass—over here? A replica of the stained glass in Al-Aqsa Mosque."

Rafi brought in a good chair and Mrs. Bosa fluttered over Amani, bringing American coffee and a plate covered with ma'moul, baklawa, and other sweets.

Hafez helped himself to the ma'moul, white powder cascading down the front of his suit. His secretary gave him a fierce look. "Mrs. B, you've surpassed yourself."

The old woman sniffed sharply.

"Oh, you love me." He tried to kiss her fingertips, but she pulled away.

"Laa'." No.

He brushed at the front of his jacket, smearing sugar. "At the King's dinner, I would like you to put my niece up near the head. She's a very big-deal poet. Did you know she published a collection?"

Pink rose into Amani's cheeks. "Oh, Uncle."

"How lovely!" The old woman's eyes glowed.

"Here. Look." He picked up the slim volume with its dark cover. "I keep this on my desk, right here." He positioned it in the corner. Amani had mailed it to him years ago. He wondered if her father knew she'd done that. He hoped not. At first, he'd felt slightly shocked by the poems—they were unruly—without formal structure, in that way that was so typical of Americans. But the voice in the book—because there was very much a *voice*—was especially troubling, so rough-edged. Unnuanced. But the more he read and reread, the more he appreciated what she'd accomplished. Its passion was its strength—ambitious and too intimate, unvarnished and fascinating. He came to feel that her poems—about love and the body—were beautiful. Like songs from a pure spirit.

"Near the top. I've made note." Mrs. B wrote on a pad. "And her father as well, yes?"

"Her father, certainly." He brushed again at the sugar. "But not together. Put him toward the back."

Mrs. Bosa nodded, carefully returning to her office. Hafez turned to his niece and clapped his hands on his knees. "Finally! I get you to myself."

"Ta-da." She held her hands up.

"And your wounds?" He tapped his shoulder. "All is well? No lasting damage, I hope."

"No, no—nothing, I'm fine." Her cheeks flushed. Reflexively, she put one hand on the talon marks hidden under her blouse. "My pride's a little scarred, but it should make a full recovery."

"Miserable buzzards," he muttered.

"It wasn't anything. I was being an idiot."

"Tell me what you're working on. Is there a new opus? I want to hear everything."

"Oh." She cleared her throat lightly. "I'm in—sort of a formulation stage right now."

"Formulation, yes. I am king of formulation. It's my favorite stage. If only one could just skip the rest of it. If you need ideas, let me know. I have all sorts of ideas for books, poems—yours for the taking. Free of charge!" He folded his hands. "Tell me, what can I do for you while you're in Jordan? What are you interested in?"

Amani studied the walls for a moment. Shifting her weight to one side she crossed her legs. "Of course I want to know all about this country, certainly. I think, if anything, though, I want to learn more about the family—"

"Ah!" Hafez straightened. "Your grandfather was extraordinary— from a very old and distinguished line. The Hamdans are descended directly from Huwyatat Bedouins—settled in this area for centuries, pre-dating modern Jordan—and own vast tracts of property throughout the Jordan valley. . . ."

"And my grandmother?"

Hafez smiled. "Not much to know. She raised a family, she died early—like most of them in her generation. No. But now, your *grandfather* would make an excellent subject for a book—"

"I'm sure," Amani said—a bit dismissively, he thought. "But I'm sort of fascinated by Natalia. People tell me I look like her." She paused as if waiting for Hafez's confirmation. "And she was also a writer, I guess?"

Hafez offered Amani the tray of sweets before taking another. "Hm, she liked to say al 'aql zeena. This means"—he spun his fingers meditatively—"'your mind is your beauty.'" Now Amani gave him a smile. His mother had also said an arrow of truth should dip its point in honey. A proverb for every occasion. What good did it do her? Not to mention the ferocious way she had of looking at her children, as if she might gobble them up. Too much love. She ran hot and cold. Staring, swinging to indifference, wandering in her forest of books. And her tiresome admonitions: *You must read, you must carry your past with you. Keep your home in your head. They can't take your education away.* Too much, too little. No wonder he'd favored Munif—a drunk, a bully, but at least his father was relatively whole.

"I promise, very soon, we will talk and talk. I'll answer all questions," he assured her.

Glancing up, Hafez noticed Mrs. Bosa at the back of the room, scowling. He wiped the sugar from his lips. Deep in his bottom drawer was a letter from the director of employment asking him to sign off on a two-percent raise for Mrs. Bosa. It had been there for weeks. He loved Bosa, the old witch—truly. But a shift in money meant a shift in attitude, however minor. It upset his balance. It was a principled stand—nothing personal. When one of the undersecretaries came asking him for donations to yet another baby present or retirement gift, instead of giving cash, he'd write a line or two of advice and toss that into the hat.

Money changed everything, and Hafez preferred that certain things not change: houses, policies, people. In this sense, his needs were simple and he asked for little. Tokens. His father's knife, a bit of land. A sweeter world. Poetry. He patted his niece's hand, then looked at her photo on the back of her book: her eyes luminous, hung with moons. Before this visit, he hadn't seen her in years and wasn't prepared for how thoughtful, how formidable she had become, her lean, elegant face and hands. All right, there was some echo of his mother in her face. His mother as a bride, before she hunched and her expression fell into disappointment. At certain angles, he thought, Amani might even resemble him—certainly more than she did her father. With the right sort of guide, imagine who she might still become.

Beyond the windows, the late-afternoon light melted through the olive groves, turning leaves to coins. Hafez sat on the low couch after Amani left, thinking of his brother and the king, one hand resting on his chest. He should have remained a professor. He should have had children. It might have helped. He envied Gabe, he supposed—his headlong way of risking things, of living in his body. Hafez recalled the falcons, the way his brother had simply lifted his hand. He assumed it was an illusion: the birds were trained, and his brother must have held some crumb between his fingers to lure it.

Years he'd waited. It seemed at times that Hafez's life had been dedicated to waiting. The things he wanted were always right around the corner.

Then, a chance. It came about a year earlier, at the Beit Al Sousin Foundation, a cultural organization housed in a series of grand old buildings in the center of Amman. He'd walked with the king, a curator, a docent, Rafi, and several photographers. Beit Al Sousin was one of the preeminent guardians of culture and heritage, started, ironically enough, by Palestinians. Hafez had never much liked the place—he felt the spirits of old British colonialists in the air: Colonel Peake, Glubb Pasha, the Arab Legion filled with Englishmen. The great pillagers with their fanatical devotion to collecting the lives of others. Hafez also liked to collect, but he sometimes felt like one of the pillagees. Reception attendees drifted past in wisps of passing conversation: "economic subsidies . . . entities . . . double-edged sword—originated with the Arabic, *zou hadayn*—the sword of two edges . . ."

Rafi turned in circles, narrating and pointing, showing off his knowledge of regional history. The curator opened a case so the King might fondle a khanjar from Oman, its surface engraved with the names of God, twining leaves, and songbirds. Hafez thought of Il Saif, his father's knife. This was where it belonged, after all. Among

this splendid array. The region of its birth and its history. He'd
endured years of fretting: did Gabe still have the damned thing?

An unadorned object—some might even call it humble—Il Saif
was extraordinary in both its age and provenance: it had its own tree
of ownership in the records office, passed from generation to generation within the Hamdan family. The Prophet Muhammad, peace
be upon him, had owned swords of renown, including the glorious al
Mathur, passed to him by his father, covered in gold and rubies, and
the infamous al-Battar, inscribed with the names of the prophets,
once owned by King David, seized from Goliath the giant, stamped
by its Nabatean makers over two millennia ago.

Eight of these artifacts were displayed in the Topkapi Palace in
Istanbul. But perhaps there was another such treasure still at large.
That's what his father, Munif, used to intimate, lifting his knife
for his sons to admire. With its inlaid amber handle and straight
steel blade, Il Saif was rumored to have slain one of Muhammad's
mortal enemies in battle; it was even rumored to have been held
by Muhammad himself as he butchered a lamb. "Look, boys—my
hand," Munif said slyly, proudly, "upon the Prophet's." The Christian
and the Muslim.

Hafez's father, Munif, had refused to have it appraised, not trusting the unscrupulous dealers. Munif didn't care for any material
assessment of worth: how to place a value on something that tran-
scended time and money? It was the knife that Hafez's great-great-
grandfather had worn—and his father and his father—and that
Munif had worn under his robes, against the skin of his stomach.
Hafez glimpsed it whenever his father roughhoused with his sons or
when he drank too much and fell asleep with his clothing splayed.
His talisman and his familiar. Hafez hadn't seen it since he'd left for
school in the States, forty years ago.

Rafi Bustani, senior secretary level 3, dogged the men, reading
aloud from the royal calendar mounted on his clipboard. Over the
past year, the schedule had become increasingly complex as heads of
state caught wind of the plans. But it had started with their director

of publicity, along with certain media-savvy members of the cabinet, a nudge from Warren Christopher—"unity is the surest path to
security"—and Hafez himself, who knew no Jordanian could resist
a good hefleh. Together, they decided: H's sixtieth birthday would
be momentous.

These celebrations would be the proverbial syrup on the baklawa—
a symbol of their rising preeminence in the region. Global investment
money had started trickling into Jordan, following their tentative
early success on the diplomatic front. After decades of talks and broken promises, there was, miraculously, a glimmer of a treaty with
Israel. Hafez had taken one-a.m. meetings with UN special envoys,
appeared on the *Nightly News*, golfed in Kennebunkport with Dan
Quayle, engaged in diplomatic skirmishes between Amman and
Riyadh. The work was tricky and sensitive, and if one approached it
too directly, agreements floated away like a thread on the eye. Even
the Jordanian prime minister had been gently, then firmly, per-
suaded to resign because of his Palestinian origins. So many Palestinians were hostile to the peace process because they'd been screwed
and re-screwed—they saw it as a form of airbrushing away what
had gone before. Hafez appreciated this sentiment. *Never forget*, he
thought, *war is always more powerful than peace—especially for the
oppressed*. Though he wouldn't say such things aloud. King H had
decreed peace, and Hafez would support the King in all ways. Or in
as many ways as seemed prudent.

Just last summer, they'd flown to the States to sign the Washington Declaration: Hafez was there in the black jeep with the majesties,
on the way from the airport, rewriting the King's speech to the joint
session of Congress, about to officially close out on a forty-six-year
war with Israel. Hafez sat behind him on the dais, watching a line of
sweat deepen between the royal shoulder pads, soaking through his
jacket, as his king had leaned into the podium stand and thundered:
"This is the moment of commitment and of a vision."

It was a sort of culmination for Hafez as well, the top of an arc
that had started in childhood. He and the King had run on the

same playgrounds, attended the same prep schools; their family lines extended together for generations, intertwining vines. At the end of high school, Hafez had produced the highest *tawjihi* score in the country and won the national scholarship. At the award ceremony, he'd shaken hands with King Abdullah, with his turban and white beard, and the old man had nodded at Hafez and said to his grandson, the prince, then nine years old, "Remember this one, *habeebi*. Keep him close." Fifteen years later, Hafez was chair of the Political Science Department of the University of Jordan, author of the well-received work *The King and the Sword: Legends of Exile*, when his office phone rang and a deep, familiar voice boomed, "I'm in the market for a guide." He became the King's ear, his guiding spirit, his sounding board. He came to the King's chamber in the center of the night and listened as His Majesty paced the floor in a bathrobe and talked so intimately of his hopes and uncertainties that Hafez himself forgot he was there.

But things had started to change. As they do. His Majesty fell in love with that peacenik prime minister Rabin, and lately Hafez sometimes laid awake at night, grinding his molars, suspecting he was being edged out.

It wasn't just the King's birthday that preoccupied him, it was the birth of a new Middle East—a place where young people from both sides of the bridge could make new lives, where refugees would leave their tents and where soldiers would retire their guns and where Michelin-star chefs from Milan and Vienna would come and help fill beautiful, tall Euro-Arab hotels. It was a moment of possibility, and Hafez could either help make it happen or be swept aside. And then, a year ago, at the Beit al Sousin Foundation, Hafez had the audacious new thought: to set in motion an event to outshine all the others, to show the world that the King was still hale and vital, yet in touch with history and tradition. And an event with fringe benefits: instead of always chasing the knife, he could bring his brother *here*. Gabe could bring the knife. They would all be close again: reunion upon reunion. It could be Hafez's moment as well.

Rafi had trailed Hafez and the King around the grand arts center, footsteps echoing between vitrines, ticking off birthday plans—"The Saint Petersburg ballet has choreographed a special dance—it can follow the saluki races."

The King continued to nod, not a word in response, his attention glancing over the exhibit of weapons. Rafi's eyes kept returning to Hafez, a silent, hopeless plea. Hafez had stopped before one particularly seductive piece, a knife with a tooth-colored ivory handle. He'd touched the glass as he'd said, vaguely, "Will there be archery or shooting?"

Rafi looked over his notes. "The Beni-Hamidi tribes are bringing their marksmen—" he offered.

"What about the sport of champions?"

Rafi stared at Hafez, baffled. "Horseracing?"

"Rafi!" Hafez ticked his chin up. "*Fencing*, of course."

The King turned, a metal scabbard in his hands, eyebrows lifted.

Rafi began unscrolling page after page, studying the entries.

"Your Majesty used to do a little, yes?" Hafez twisted and swished the flat of his hand through the air.

Turning, the King held the scabbard up and the curator levitated it from his hands. His Majesty smiled, slid the top of one knuckle under his mustache. "That was very long ago."

Rafi lowered his clipboard. "I understand His Majesty was a superb fencer—unbeatable."

It seemed the conversation was already tapering off as the King started toward the Beit's arched doorway. Hafez said, "You sparred with my brother. Once or twice? I've studied the art myself, in school, but not like you and Gabe, in the field."

The King's attention kindled. "Gabe Hamdan. Of course, of course." He chuckled. "Gabe. We were partners. Oh, how is he? What a fencer. He and the men picked it up in just a few weeks."

"He was fortunate to spar with His Majesty." Rafi raised his voice above their footsteps.

"Still out there—in the States?"

"Always."

The stone walls of the old building admitted skimmed light. The sounds of women's laughter reached them from the courtyard.

"Your brother," the King had said thoughtfully. "He was very good. Marvelous. It was a pleasure to duel with him."

Good, not best. Hafez studied the monarch's clear profile as he hovered a moment in the doorway. "He, Gabe, he said . . ." Hafez said, his breath soft, "that His Majesty was an excellent fencer." He'd slipped his hands into his pockets.

"Excellent?" Rafi held his clipboard angled on his hip, his wrist dangling over the top. "I should think so. His Majesty won every match."

"Well, you know what they say about that—" Hafez had quipped. " 'The King always wins.' "

"That rascal," said the King, undeterred. "Gabe said that?" He chuckled, muttering to himself. "Rascal." After a moment, he turned to Rafi. "You know what? Let's do it. Why not? Let there be fencing."

Rafi glanced at Hafez. He jotted something on his clipboard.

HE BIT INTO the last cookie and looked toward Mrs. Bosa's closed office door. Amani had gone and there were no other witnesses. He slipped off his shoes and padded in socks down the Royal Hall toward the diwan kitchen. He knew where the rest of the pastries were hidden.

It no longer mattered to him what his brother did. Such things used to trouble Hafez—in the past. His brother's confidence and competence, his easy, happy life an ocean away were all a kind of affront. At times, thinking of this, Hafez felt a dark curtain fall across his mind. But things were different now: he felt the nearness of Il Saif; he saw it in Gabe's eyes. Returning to his homeland, after thirty-five years away, was an admission of defeat. Gabe had brought back Hafez's knife, as was only just. "Please bring it," Hafez had said. "Let me see it once more." And Amani. Bring your family. Was this happiness, this sense of completion? Hafez had almost forgotten. He felt the sweetness of a better, possible life. Mentorship, he thought. Even better than fatherhood. He would be a guide.

He returned to his desk with a plate of date-stuffed cookies and returned his niece's book to the shelf behind his desk. The knife was another form of art. Like fencing. Like poetry, he thought, his mouth full of sugar. Let there be poetry.

CHAPTER

EACH BIRTHDAY, Gabe visited with his mementos. First, he took out Il Saif. After the knife, he looked at the photograph of his family. The enlarged black-and-white showed them all together: older brothers Hafez and Farouq, father Munif, tall and sternly upright, and mother Natalia, her wire reading spectacles propped on her head. Her eyes that peered into other worlds. Gabe, a grubby, squinting kid on the ground. His hand was lifted as if he were holding on to something, but the corner was torn away at his fingers.

Every day that Gabe went deeper into his American life he felt the past go with him. His mother would have been ninety years old this year: he tried to look into the granular image of her face: a hazy smile, sweetness and sadness melting together.

When he came to the States, he hadn't known how the past could smuggle itself into the next generation. But then his daughter had been born with the night in her eyes, navy-black, like his mother's—her way of staring instead of crying. Visiting relatives commented on the uncanny resemblance. He was stricken, but not surprised, when Amani's marriage fell apart, nor when she moved back into her old bedroom. He felt at times as if she were aging in reverse—her eyes too large, her wrists too thin. It was his fault—there must have been something scanty or deficient in her upbringing. He'd cut himself off from family and country when he came to the States—what could he expect to offer to his child?

A week after Hafez's invitation to return, Gabe had gone to his mementos for his annual visit: the old files he kept in a satchel: his birth certificate, his passport, a bundle of letters. He reached into a back pocket and removed the velvet wrapper. Il Saif. At first glance it looked like nothing, dull pewter and age. But its beauty emerged—the pearly glimmer, soft as skin. His mother had liked to say it came from the sea, polished by naiads, that it was old as the Earth. Gabe believed in his father's knife almost as if it were enchanted—a thing to ward off danger. Holding it, he heard the voices of children again, the call to prayers rising in the late day. His mother—her soft hands over the sink, the cutting board, the broom, her furtive rush from housework to books—she called him *eyni*, my eyes; *hayati,* my life; *wardi*, my flower. To all the others he was the strong, able, uneducable Gabe. She was the one who looked into him. When he left for the States, he had promised that he'd come back to her soon.

That week, after Hafez called, when Amani walked into his workshop holding something, he'd recognized the blue paper. It was the color his mother favored, the hopeful color of aerograms. His daughter looked wrung-out; she hadn't slept well since her divorce; she wasn't eating properly. She opened the page and looked at him, curious and uncertain. And he thought he saw hope.

Gabe had called Hafez back and his brother had said, "The mountain moves! You really will? Carole—" Hafez called to his wife. "The mountain moves!"

"What is that supposed to mean?" Carole's sardonic voice was in the background.

It took Gabe a moment. "You mean you are Muhammad," he said. "And the mountain is coming to you."

But then Gabe was surprised to hear genuine emotion in his

brother's voice, as if Hafez was actually touched. He heard the ripple again as Hafez said, "It's true then? You truly will come?"

"So it seems," Gabe said.

Just before they hung up, his brother said, "And it would mean—so much—if you would bring Il Saif. Yes? I'd like to pay my respects—at least once more." There was no chance to even think how to answer. Gabe was left staring at the empty receiver in his hand.

Just a couple of flights, and here he sat, thirty-five years later. He sipped the Turkish coffee that Farouq had boiled on the stove. It was so baffling and so ordinary to sit in this guesthouse in Amman, tasting the rich bitterness, a fillip of cardamom that took him back to childhood; the housekeeper stirring the brass ibrik. He smiled despite himself, unable to think of a time he'd enjoyed a cup of coffee this much. He wanted to try to explain this to Farouq, but it was beyond him—the coffee, the disorientation of a sip, how the longer you're away, the bigger and more elusive the past becomes; a beautiful monster.

CHAPTER

5

HER AUNT'S HOUSEKEEPER had come with the family. "It's always been that way," Carole said. "Mrs. Ward, her mother, her grandmother—they were handed down. Like a legacy."

"Like a set of china," Amani said.

"Kind of," said Aunt Carole. She accidentally jostled her tea, sloshing the saucer.

Mrs. Ward entered the house with an armload of dresses wrapped in dry cleaners' plastic. "Where do want?"

"The bedroom is upstairs, please, Mrs. Ward," Carole said.

Amani tried to take them, but the woman, five feet tall, swathed in black, refused to stop. She stumped up the stairs with her load.

Amani followed her aunt's housekeeper. She took the dresses at the doorway and took them to the bed, dropping them there in a pile. "Please—sit down for a second. I'll grab the rest." She tried to slip by, but Mrs. Ward planted herself in the doorway. The housekeeper lifted her face, white hair plaited and parted down the middle; black eyeliner bled into the creases around her eyes. "I get them."

Straight from her aunt's closet, these dresses were contenders for the King's dinner party. "You didn't bring a bunch of dress-up clothes from the States. Why would you?" Carole shook her head. "Trust me—this shindig is going to drop you right into Jordanian society—such as it is. Let's make a splash." Sighing, Amani pushed back the plastic wrappers and lifted the dresses, their straps pinched between her fingers: plunging necklines, satin bodices. Valentino, Prada, Versace; there were designers from Holland and the UK, the material rich as cream between her fingers.

Amani dragged something from the pile. The material was heavy and smelled of rosewater and lemon. It dropped over her shoulders and she smoothed it with the backs of her hands before presenting herself downstairs.

"Okay now." Her aunt stood at her side, tugging and straight-ening. "Mm-hm. Now then. If you adjust the sleeve . . . just—like this—you can't see any red marks. Still can't believe Hafez had you running around with those birds. I question that man's judgment."

"I promise—it wasn't his fault." Amani's smile diminished. "I make all kinds of bad decisions all on my own."

Sadia's brows lowered. Her aunt had remarked quietly to Amani that her new maid was "a little slow on the uptake." Not a legacy servant, it seemed. "I think—this—it makes you look so old. Is that how you says it?"

"What?" Carole looked over her shoulder at Sadia and laughed. "She looks lovely. She looks elegant."

"Not *she* is old," Sadia corrected. "Dress. *Dress* is looking old."

Carole smiled.

Mrs. Ward returned from the car, trudging up the stairs with another crackling pile. Amani followed dutifully, asking if she couldn't please carry the dresses. She felt like a child begging to help the adults. Mrs. Ward ignored her and dumped them on the bed. Amani sat beside them, pushing aside the filmy wrappings. "This is ridiculous—rigging me like this. What's the point?" She rubbed the back of her neck, then glanced at Mrs. Ward. Watching, the older woman seemed to hesitate.

"My auntie keeps you busy I guess," Amani said. Peeling away a piece of the plastic wrapper, she asked the housekeeper, "Did you really know my grandparents?" She felt tentative, unsure if she was being intrusive.

The housekeeper paused then lifted her chin. "Your sitt—of course I know her. From long time."

Amani sat straighter, a ball of dry cleaner's plastic scrunched in her lap. "Sitti? You mean Natalia?"

Mrs. Ward looked at the door. "I know her," she repeated. "I keep them."

"You keep—" Amani hesitated. When Mrs. Ward lifted her eyes—lightly lidded, narrow inner corners—Amani saw a dark wire in the woman's expression, a look of feeling outmatched, acted upon. Mrs. Ward frowned and Amani felt the strain in her silence— it seemed there was more that she meant to say, but Amani wasn't certain how to read people here. She heard herself trying to reassure the woman: "It's, really, it's mish mishkila." No problem. Aunt Carole called from the base of the stairs, "Darling—have you got something on?"

Mrs. Ward's eyes changed. The older woman shook her head briefly before leaving the bedroom. Amani stared after her.

Through the wall, she heard Mrs. Ward announce to Aunt Carole she was "done." A bang as she went out the front door. From the bedroom window, Amani saw the older woman climb into the backseat of the car, where she would apparently wait for them, however long it took. Standing, Amani rummaged through the dresses and saw a tuft of something bright in the pile. She didn't want to try on any more, but Mrs. Ward had toted all that stuff up the stairs for her. She pulled a rose-colored slip dress out of the pile; it fluttered over her head. Two pieces crossed high over her chest and encircled her neck. It was weightless, like wearing a breath. She could see both marks on her shoulders—livid, upside-down V's.

When she walked out, Carole lowered her hands, and said, "Oh, how did that get in there? That's a cocktail dress."

Sadia nodded and pointed. "Thees one. Here. Thees one. Berfect."
Fine, Amani put her hands on her hips. Pink it is.

AFTER THE WOMEN drove off—Carole leaving the dresses in the
hopes that Amani might change her mind—Amani sat at the desk
in the little guesthouse office upstairs. She pushed away from the
computer screen, her elbow glancing the coffee cup so it rattled.
The office walls were covered in flocked wallpaper. Prayer beads
and framed photos of gazelles and oryx hung on the walls. She
hated the poem she was working on. She closed the screen. Her jaw
ached. She'd had a dim, unsatisfying sleep—not that different from
her usual sleep. When they'd first arrived, there had been a few
hope-filled days when she'd read and took notes and thought she'd
be able to write. But today, their sixth morning in Amman, she'd
awakened to a sense of spiraling dismay. Her father's event was on
the nineteenth, in a little over two weeks, they went home on the
thirtieth—it didn't seem like enough time to take things in, and at
the same time an eternity of family gatherings and official functions
seemed to rise before her.

Now she went back into her bedroom to stare at the pink gown.
She resented having to attend some dreary function—to be held
at the main palace no less—and was already wondering if the trip
had been a mistake. Each day so far had been taken up with visits to the homes of relatives where she and her father were served
daylong meals. Each gathering began with politely formal English
for her benefit, then gradually dissolved into Arabic. Amani's
college courses in Modern Standard Arabic seemed to have little
application here. She had met scores of cousins she'd never heard
of—nearly all of them wanting to know where her husband and
children were, though she had neither now. Her father was led off
to the rooms filled with men, leaving Amani in rooms of women
and wild kids.

When they weren't at gatherings, her cousin Omar walked them around town—Gabe in a state of disbelief over the transformation of Amman, its highways and traffic, the cranes, bulldozers, the new coffeehouses and restaurants. Much like his father, Omar talked continuously as they walked—about weight-lifting, nutrition, his personal-training business, his dream of opening a gym. Omar had been raised in Jordan, but his mother, Bella, was originally from California, and Amani seemed to see both places in his personality. Yet neither was a perfect fit. He talked as if he hadn't had someone to speak openly to in years. He asked Gabe if he would teach him how to fence—which would in turn help Gabe get ready for his match. Gabe laughed and shook his head. "It's not a real duel, habeebi. Just for show."

"Still, Amo, I want to learn it. Hafez says if you want to be civilized you have to know how to fence."

Gabe smirked. "I can teach you a little fencing. Civilized is up to you."

Omar told Amani he had asked a few relatives about the blue letter. The main response seemed to be a shrug: he was told repeatedly that their grandmother had been a sweet but eccentric recluse. Bookish. Distracted. His father said Natalia was always jotting down her thoughts, tucking them here and there: it was just the way her brain worked. There used to be blue letters all over the house. Great-Aunt Lamise tapped her temple with a finger and said, "She had a disordered mind."

AMANI WASN'T SURE she was all that different from Omar: without a country. Since her school days, she'd been haunted by a feeling that the American national anthem didn't quite include her. At one time, she'd thought perhaps her identity was bound to poetry or to writing, or that perhaps her marriage would become her home. Lately, though, she lived in the country of too much drinking and sleeping and the melancholy that seemed to hover just before the onset of depression.

Sometimes she worried that her only true country was wine.

She was seventeen when she discovered how charming it was, how it broke her free. Loosened things up. Her first drink—just a few sips, really, at a cousin's wedding—had opened her like a key within a lock. When she and Bill had first started dating, he'd kept pace—a beer for each pinot. He worked for her father as a handyman and she was a young assistant professor. There were stacks of papers to grade, her classes were demanding and the students looked bored: it was nice to open a bottle at the end of the day. She was mostly fine, getting up and going about her day, preoccupied, always, with staying on top of her work, but then Bill started to stay late at his jobs, and there were too many things to think about—committee meetings and admissions files. Sleepless at three a.m. beside Bill, turning through the radio static of her mind, she searched for the source, the thing she needed to fix, to stop the coming apart. When she drank she could settle into herself. Temporarily. She felt less unfamiliar to herself. Often, she'd found she preferred drinking to writing.

It caught up to her one day at an afternoon event, a reception to celebrate the end of the semester; student accomplishments: a graduate student had sold her memoir in a heated auction; another had a cycle of poems accepted at *The Paris Review.* The reception wasn't far from campus. Amani walked to an evening class afterward. That had been her mistake—thinking she could go from drinking to teaching. She remembered the way the floor seemed to slant as she stood at the front of the seminar room, holding the podium, asking, "Does anyone else feel that?" Remembered laughing at things that no one else found funny.

"Oh, you're too important to laugh," she remembered saying. She heard a few murmurs, caught sidelong glances. It was such a delicious growing sense of release, letting things slide away, a slow, pluming avalanche. "Oh, I forgot how important you are. How could I think I could teach you? You're so much more . . . so much . . ." When someone stood and walked out, she'd laughed, saying, "Another one down."

She winced to think how one of the older students tried to convince her to go home. She'd swatted his hand from her elbow. A couple of students whispered behind cupped hands. Amani snapped at them. "You're so, so pretty. Congratulations. None of you can write though. Did you know that? Not a single one of you special people." She'd swung her index finger. "You think you can write? You put your words down, you cover pages with it. You don't mean it though. You don't mean any of it. You don't even know *how* to mean it. And I don't know how to teach that to you."

There were swaths of that evening she didn't recall.

A week later, she'd sat down with the director of graduate studies, the department chair, and Tom Castagna, the faculty union rep, who read a formal student complaint out loud. Castagna used to work for the Syracuse Teachers' Association and he knew her mother.

The complaint contained additional outrageous statements and actions that she had no memory of. (Could she have possibly draped herself over another student and begged him to dance? Did she really tell the remaining, petrified group that her father owned a dagger and invite them to the house to see it?) It seemed that at the very end, before one of them had driven her home, she'd tearfully admitted that she didn't love her husband, had never really loved him, and yet *he'd* left *her*. Of all the things she'd said or imagined saying, this seemed to her to be the most embarrassing.

The tall leaded-glass windows illuminated shelves of American modernists and cast squares of color to the floor. "This would normally not be such a to-do," Elaine Chambers, the chair, was saying. "But you're only in your fifth year. You don't have the protections of tenure yet."

Tom Castagna held a page of handwritten notes on his lap. "Actually—only a few students've signed this complaint—"

Fred Hallensby, director of graduate studies, broke in, "They were extremely upset."

"But a minority," Tom said. "A vocal minority. We could take this to mediation."

"Oh God, no." Amani hunched forward in her chair, digging fingers into her hair. "Enough already."

"This will have to go into your file either way," Elaine said.

"The union will fight any kind of written reprimand," Tom said.

"Fine—an oral reprimand," Fred Hallensby said. "But it *will* be noted in her file, even so. I'll see to that personally."

"Amani. This isn't like you. Or, I don't think it is." Elaine looked at her over her glasses. Soft lines fanned from the corners of her eyes making her seem warm, nearly maternal. "What happened? I just don't understand this. Can you just walk me through it—just one more time?"

Amani had tried to explain twice already. There were no extenuating circumstances—no reasonable professor would ever say or do such things. She'd had many glasses of Champagne and she was unhappy—though she'd only recently sensed the depth of that unhappiness. "No," she said firmly, back straight, eyes resting on the long windows. "I'm afraid I can't."

"And why is that?" Hallensby asked. He studied the ceiling, eyes roving speculatively. "You're a *word* person, aren't you? Why is it that you can't explain yourself, Professor Hamdan?"

"Probably because I was so drunk," she said, hands on her lap. "I can't remember most of it."

They wanted remorse: she knew that. Fred Hallensby wanted shame. She felt inklings of these things, yet at the same time it all seemed so removed and abstract, as if the woman in that classroom had had nothing to do with her.

She was lucky, the union rep told her a few days after their meeting. The chair had rigorously defended her to the dean and to the provost, who had wanted to take this matter to the Graduate Grievance Review Board for a formal investigation. This time, Tom said, there would just be a "note" in her file. But when she came up for tenure the following year, it could be the deciding factor against her.

Or her odd teaching evaluations—extreme in both praise and criticism, from students in the same classes. Or the deciding factor might be her failure to produce a published work since her first book. This university was notorious for hazing their junior faculty, making tenure vanishingly difficult to attain. To be denied tenure meant losing her job. It would follow the note in her file, coda to humiliation before her students and the rest of the department.

THE FOLLOWING MORNING, Amani was again at the guesthouse desk chair, studying the blue paper. She read it for the eight or tenth time now, waiting for something to emerge. At last, she refolded it carefully along the old creases, then returned to the bedroom. The inappropriate magenta dress hung in the closet. Sadia was supposed to come by later for Aunt Carole's other dresses, but Amani scooped them up. This would be her first outing in Jordan without a family member escort. She felt alert, too vigilant perhaps, disoriented by the layout of the neighborhood. Walking along Zahran Street, she had to face backward only a few moments before a cab stopped for her. She was relieved when the driver understood her hesitating Arabic.

Sadia looked startled when she opened the door and saw Amani, the dresses' plastic wrap wafting in the breeze. "I would got them," she said reproachfully, reaching with both hands.

Mrs. Ward loomed up behind Sadia. "Your auntie went into town. At the souq a-thahab." Gold market.

Amani didn't quite look at the older woman as she said, "Actually . . . I wondered—do you have a minute?"

Sadia pulled in her chin. Mrs. Ward peered over Amani's head to the street then turned and said something in Arabic to Sadia. The younger woman left the room, scowling. Mrs. Ward took Amani into the dining room, then brought a pitcher and poured her a glass of lemonade. She appeared to be anxious, and hesitated after Amani asked if she wouldn't sit down. Pulling out one of the straight-backed chairs, she finally perched on the seat.

"Yesterday, at the guesthouse? You were starting to tell me something, I thought."

Mrs. Ward looked toward the door then back to Amani. "I hear your cousin—Mr. Omar—he is asking Mrs. Carole about a letter you have—and I think maybe . . ."

Amani let out her breath. She removed the book from her purse and saw Mrs. Ward squint at its cover. Amani spread the blue paper out on the table between them. "I found this tucked inside an old book. My dad thinks that Natalia wrote this."

A sound came from outside and Mrs. Ward stood. "I don't know. It isn't my business," she said quickly. She didn't even look at the paper. Her face was impassive, almost haughty. Neither of them spoke for a moment, listening.

Amani glanced over one shoulder. When she was sure no one was coming she said, "I thought maybe—since you knew her so well, you might be able to help me?"

The woman's eyes slipped toward the doorway then back to Amani. "No. Nothing like this." She began clearing the table.

"Because my dad—he just gets so sad when I ask about his mother. Sometimes I don't even bring stuff up because—" She lifted her shoulders, let them drop. "Sometimes I feel like I might really hurt him. And I thought maybe you . . ." Amani noticed the woman's hands on the pitcher of lemonade appeared to be trembling. She looked up at her. "I can tell you know things."

Mrs. Ward put down the pitcher silently and appeared to be thinking. Finally, she slid back into the seat. She rubbed her hands up and over her cheeks once, then lifted her face. "You remind me by her." Her voice was quiet. "Your sitt and me—like this." She held up her crossed index and middle fingers. "Our villages—at home—next to each other. People says to her, don't be so friends with a servant. But she—she is kind to all people. Children, they come to her house. She feeds them. The neighbors bring her gifts. They know if you come, bring her a book. Any kind. She read. Write. Like this one—?"

Amani nodded. "Letters? Or poems maybe?"

"I think they make her life more"—her eyes traveled around the table, searching—"tolerable. Easier."

Again Mrs. Ward's face smoothed into a kind of emotional distance. "I can't tell anyone from here about her. Mr. Hafez doesn't like this. Your uncle . . ." Her voice dwindled.

"It's okay. I won't tell anyone. You can talk to me," Amani said, but Mrs. Ward didn't respond. After a moment, Amani said, "My grandmother did mention something about children—in that note. About the child who gets thrown away?" She nudged it just a bit toward the housekeeper, who still didn't look at it. It occurred to Amani that she might not read English.

Mrs. Ward stared at the table. "Natalia. Her life, very . . ." She shook her head. "Her babies come weak. There's not enough for them. . . ." She placed a palm on the top of her chest.

"They—died? Starved? Is that what she meant by thrown away?"

Mrs. Ward looked back at the table. "I don't know that. It was before I come."

Amani sat with her fingers on the glass, condensation seeping between her knuckles. "If she really was a writer like you say, then there were other poems. Maybe a lot more—even if there was no one to show them to. Especially if there wasn't. You end up talking to yourself," she added drolly. "What happened to her writing? Do you know?"

Mrs. Ward held still, hands clasped, her face closed. Amani paused, wondering if she'd asked too much. Recalculating, she turned her glass, noticed shreds of mint threading between the ice. "So, you guys—you were so close. You must have known her really well?"

There was another sound outside, a thud; Mrs. Ward's eyes flicked then returned. "More than anyone, I think. But I can't—I push it—from my head. I have to go forward." She made a sweeping motion with her hands. "What's behind is too hard. What's behind—I mean—"

"What's behind?" Amani asked.

Sadia's voice rose suddenly at the front door, welcoming someone. Mrs. Ward got to her feet, hands pressed to her stomach. Carole came in, unwrapping a scarf, scowling at Sadia. "Why are you shouting? I'm not hard of hearing." She stopped short at the sight of Amani, who was just sliding the book into her purse. "Oh. Oh goodness." She touched her face, then smiled. "Well, hello. What—when did you get here, my dear?"

Amani stood. "I was dropping off your other dresses. I really appreciate it. And I'll have the pink one dry cleaned after the party."

Carole appeared to relax; she laughed. "Please don't," she said. Her driver came in with grocery bags on his way to the kitchen; he glanced at Amani. "They'll mangle it. I'll send the dress to Beirut." She leaned in front of Mrs. Ward and touched her lips to Amani's cheek. "Come to the terrace. Mrs. Ward can bring us lunch out there."

Amani ducked slightly, her gaze brushing over Mrs. Ward's as she moved toward the door. "I wish I could. But I really better get back to it. Got to try and get my head into work mode. I'll see you at the party later at the el-Ramadis' house." She smiled at Carole. "Can I have a rain check on lunch?"

Walking out, Amani felt a surge of guilt for pressuring Mrs. Ward—the same sort of uncertainty she'd often felt around her father's relatives. It was considered aggressive, even rude, to be too direct—it was the way of Americans. Her Arab family seemed to prefer a gentler, more oblique narrative. An arabesque. Was that why she'd become a poet? She walked briskly, mulling this over, already halfway up the lane, the pavement shaded with thin, curving trees, when she heard footsteps. Mrs. Ward was out of breath as she reached Amani and slipped something into her palm—a necklace, impressed with the silhouette of a queen. She said, "I'm happy you come. But no more. Mr. Hafez is not—" She shook her head, her words muffled. She waved once, hurrying back. Amani watched

Mrs. Ward go, clipping up the front path to the house in her low pumps, the windows hazy with light. It was too far for Amani to make out clearly through its pale drapes, but there appeared to be a face in the front window.

HER FATHER WAS still out when Amani returned to the guesthouse. She patted the stone faun between its pointed ears. Once inside, she gazed around the living area, noting the artifacts that decorated its shelves and walls, the stone pieces and medallions and figurines. In her hand was the necklace from Mrs. Ward—a gold teardrop pendant bearing the raised profile of Queen Nefertiti. She closed her hand around it. It came to her then that there were actually two countries before her: one seen and one unseen. One was in the guidebooks and the hotels and restaurants—it floated lightly on the surface of the other, the world of deep memory, the place of both belonging and dispossession. She'd come here, she realized, in the hopes that she might simply enter her father's past like an American would, walking through a door, and that the whispers, the haunted feelings would fade, finally resolved.

She could back away. It would be easier to live in the tourist's world—a visitor in a train stop. But the second one pulled at her, drawing her into the faces of the people around her. She told herself this place wasn't really meant for her. It wasn't her province. And yet she felt it calling—a long breath exhaled through her dreams, drawing her like a summons, attracting and frightening her as she entered.

CHAPTER

6

OMAR'S EYES were framed by a piece of hair falling across his forehead. He had an expression Gabe had seen on his daughter's face—an expectant look. But what for? Gabe wished he were wise. He wished he knew how to use words and could offer more of himself. Instead, he pointed to the hilly fields to their left. "Come this way. I got an idea where we can practice."

Omar's laugh was bright. "Ya bay yay! Here we go."

He still felt fragile and light-headed after a week in Jordan. But his nephew had had that hopeful look when he appeared this morning, so Gabe had slipped a note under Amani's bedroom door and dragged himself out. He and Omar climbed over a short rock wall onto the sandy dirt. A sign advertised this spot as the future home of a Bank of Jordan: a few stacks of concrete cinder blocks and some rebar. They passed the construction materials and walked up a scrubby hill. At the top, he dropped his gym bag and pulled out the case holding the foils. "I think this is it. Where we used to go. Me and the guys, when we were learning. See—the fencing pavilion is still over there? It's good to practice outside—in the open air. You'll see."

Omar shook out his arms, stretching a little, as Gabe handed him a foil. "Cool. Outdoor training. Good idea—your match is going to be outside."

Gabe said, "So, let's do basics."

A morning breeze rippled through their thin jackets; overhead, the sky was mottled with pewter-colored clouds. The air had a metallic taste that made Gabe think of snow. Omar lifted his foil. "Amo—your word, my command."

Gabe touched the length of his own foil to his open palm. He rolled back his shoulders. Perhaps he hadn't fallen apart completely just yet. He gave thanks again that he didn't sit behind a desk for a living. Lifting his foil, he called: "En garde!" then moved into the crouched stance, weight slightly forward on his right foot, his foil tipped forward.

Omar imitated him, crouching and lifting. The clouds expanded overhead, glistening and back-lit. In the distance, a goatherd flanked by a bawling flock came nearer to watch. The man wrapped his red-checked keffiyeh more closely around his face, only his eyes and nose showing, and squatted to his ankles. Shaggy, droop-eared goats milled around him, shaking off flies.

"The way it works," Gabe said, frowning, thinking through the old moves. "One attacks, the other retreats. Lunge—like this." He kicked his leg stiffly before him, landing heel first, rolling forward. "You go. But don't stab me."

Omar tried the unnatural kick, coming up a bit high, landing swiftly, his thrust coordinated with his legwork.

Gabe felt some vigor in his step; his back did seem looser. The match was on the nineteenth, scarcely more than two weeks away; between the visits and family gatherings, there was little time for training. Still, he saw his younger self in Omar—his sincerity, standing the way Gabe had stood in his uniform, solemn and important, saluting the king. Their commander had brought in a teacher from Florence who spoke no Arabic. Gabe and three other privates learned by shadowing his every move. He was an elegant, stern

teacher, and within a matter of weeks the four young men could follow him like dancing partners; after a month, they were duelists and
Gabe spoke some Italian. Now Omar rocked backward on one foot,
uncertain, but Gabe urged him forward, as Sr. Cavalli had once done
with him. "Attento alla scelta del tempo"—you must pick your time,
he used to say. Gabe smiled, remembering. He called to his nephew,
"Try again—strike, with the tip. Come, come. It's all right. See, I'll
try to avoid you." He scooped his stomach, back arching, his legs
instinctively sinking back, making himself airy, light. "Become invisible," was something Gabe learned in Italian. *Diventare invisibile!*

Watching Omar, Gabe wondered if he would've been a better
father to a son than a daughter. So often, he'd felt he was failing
Amani: it seemed she needed more—or something other—than he'd
known how to provide. Gabe and Omar lunged and parried over the
hilltop, the goatherd watching in the distance. Omar's face glowed as
he lunged and retraced, eyes wide with concentration. Gabe bounded
back and swept the foil up, while Omar charged with a yell, then
stopped, hovered. Gabe took a step, another step, a skip backward,
a skip forward. They held their foils half-extended, half-withdrawn,
their chests rising and falling.

He and Omar dodged each other, occasionally losing their footing
on the sandy dirt. Gabe stopped adjusting his nephew's form and let
him go. Sr. Cavalli used to say: *Form first, then improvisation.* Omar
stumbled and recovered, grinning, swinging wide. Gabe lunged and
his foil struck the center of the boy's chest. He jerked back, apolo-
gizing, but the boy cried, "Yella, Amo. Imshee!" They jabbed and
feinted to the cheers of the goatherd. Gabe made hit after hit and
swayed out of his nephew's reach.

The two fenced until they peeled off their jackets and sweaters,
and stood, arms limp, wrists burning, their bodies drenched and
weaving. Finally, Omar dropped his foil. "I'm dead. All done, Amo.
Dead and buried."

Gabe wiped off his head with the crook of his elbow, deeply
relieved. "Enough?" He picked up the foil and returned the equip-

ment to the case. The goatherd approached them and shook their hands one at a time in both of his, though it hurt Gabe to uncurl his fingers to do so. The man's palm felt thickened; his face was burned to mahogany. He thanked God for giving him this show, he prayed for their continued good health, and he told Omar that someday, God willing, he would be as great a warrior as his father.

Omar shook out his hands. "Yeah, inshallah," he said, "but I doubt it."

Gabe lifted one finger to the sky, now bright and cold and swept clean. He dashed it right, left, right. Remembering with the motion what it had meant to him to lift a foil. He believed that was why the King had also loved to fence. If one absolutely must fight, then let it be in defense, and let it happen with nobility, the dignity of shared danger.

Was there any way to explain this to his daughter?

The goatherd laughed with recognition and made the Z in the air as well. "The mark of Zorro!" he cried. "Today I met Zorro. Truly, God is great." He embraced Gabe, kissing his cheek.

CHAPTER

7

HAFEZ SAT IN THE BACKSEAT, hunched against the window. They drove along the open vistas leading toward the private college: the land stretched wide into striated bands of sage and bone. He was brooding about the knife, again, his thoughts soft and unguarded. He needed to be more careful. Besides Carole—perhaps more than Carole—Samir was the one Hafez confided in, revealing how he suffered and waited. Probably he said too much. Sometimes he forgot what he was talking about and where they were going. Sometimes he wanted to tell Samir, *Keep going, boy. Don't turn back.* If they kept driving, perhaps he would become the sort of person who could leave things behind, let the house fall down, let the phone ring. He was not the right sort of person, he knew that. Why did he think he could help broker a peace treaty? What hubris. Who was he? These days, hesitations and remembrances seemed to pop up in his brain like tiny traps; for example, now: the way the Dead Sea Highway opened into golden bends, making him think of the long, stony path he, his brother, and his father had once taken. But why was he think-ing of that? Ever since Gabe and Amani had arrived, he kept feel-ing an unexpected prickle, something like remorse. He had always prided himself on never feeling remorse, which was a destructive force, which only held one back.

Still, thinking of Amani lifted him—the idea of a legacy—continuation of the narrative. He thought of the Hamdan name written in cursive across the cover of her book. She was his true intellectual heir.

BEFORE HAFEZ had left the house that morning, Carole told him that his niece had dropped by.

"Very good." Hafez watched himself knot his tie in the mirrored armoire. "She could stand some guidance. I get the feeling that our Amani is a bit adrift right now. Look what happened with her and that young fellow she married. Didn't I tell you that wouldn't work?"

"She hadn't come to see me." Carole sat on the bedside.

"What do you mean?"

"I don't know." Carole pulled her cardigan a little closer. She was always chilled these days, Hafez noticed, as if her body had dried down onto its bones. And there was a vagueness to her character, an irritable detachment that he believed to be the result of unemployment. After a stint teaching nursery school, she hadn't worked at all, not for forty-plus years. No job. And no babies—which he wondered if Carole had deliberately arranged. She'd said on several occasions she didn't see herself as a mother. She wouldn't go to a regular tabeeb, but was always taking various medicaments and decoctions, consulting with the old witch selling teas and herbs on the corner.

"She was already here when I got home. I'd been out shopping. She said she'd come to return my dresses, but she was sitting in the dining room with Mrs. Ward. She practically ran out the door when she saw me come in."

Hafez touched the knot of his tie, adjusted it carefully with one hand. "She was sitting with Mrs. Ward? What on earth were they talking about?"

"I have no idea."

He lowered his hand and frowned at his face. "Are you sure they were actually talking?"

"Well. No. But it was just the two of them there."

"Probably she was waiting for you." Hafez finally turned toward her. "How long had she been there?".

"Sadia said it was maybe a few minutes, but she has no concept of time, believe me."

Hafez didn't say anything. Unsettled, he pulled on his suit jacket and touched the top of his hair, smoothing it back. He checked himself in the mirror one more time. "Let's have them over here soon."

STEERING, Samir offered a cigarette over his shoulder, which Hafez accepted gratefully. Strictly forbidden by his doctor. But neither his tabeeb nor Carole nor Mrs. Bosa were there to give them the evil eye. He cracked the window and exhaled directly into the fresh air.

Tonight's talk was for the Soroptimist Club at Al Zaytoonah College. Their charter, apparently, was to improve women's lives through education: the Soroptimist name, it was explained, meant *the best for women*. "We hoped you might say something about sustainability issues and water—like the environmental impact of the valley settlements on the Yarmouk and Jordan Rivers," the chapter director, Um-Leila, had said. "Our members are very much interested in the implications the peace treaty may have for local ecosystems."

Call it what they liked, his talk was always sixty minutes of the State of Jordan Entering the New Millennium. He would mention tonight's event to Amani—he could offer to make introductions and sponsor her membership in the club. He'd started to think it might be better if she stayed on in Amman a bit longer. There was so much opportunity for her here.

Hafez understood the female persuasion. Several of his fellow cabinet ministers wouldn't even deign to speak to the women's groups. Frustrated housewives, the finance minister, Tolal Morami, said. Let them take up a hobby. Frustrated perhaps, but Hafez saw the chip, chip, chip they made in things. After he'd returned to Jordan with his several degrees and new wife, he was delighted to encounter a new generation of Arab feminists. They might cover their heads, but they were also outspoken and educated and active. Two of the women in this group were doctors. There was a judge. An architect. A city planner. One had written a bill to outlaw the plastic grocery bags clogging the sides of the road, blowing like tumbleweeds over Mount Nebo and down into the Jordan valley.

At the university, Hafez lifted the women's hands on his curved knuckles, planted a kiss on each. The Soroptimists filed in, greeting one another, pencil skirts and red lips. A voice filled with silver lights said, "Oh, Hafez, it's you." Mrs. Waleeda, with her devastating smile-that-was-not-a-smile, stood there, sizing him up, one hand on her hip. "You're the special speaker tonight."

He obtained her hand and had barely bent over before she took it away. "I hope you'll say something about the water-conservation initiative," she said.

"I didn't know you were one of the optimistic sorority."

She sniffed lightly and turned toward the windows. "I'm not." They were in a seminar room near the cafeteria, where student workers ferried in trays of hot coffees and tea.

"Aha—you sought me out? Came here special?" He recalled the night, a few months earlier, when he and Mrs. Waleeda had sneaked away from the nonsmokers (his wife, for example, and Mr. Waleeda, for example) outside the Intiman Royal Centre for the Arts, and found themselves in such a private, moonlit corner of an open field, they couldn't resist putting down their glasses of Lebanese red and sneaking a few kisses. Oh, her tongue between his lips! Heaven. "Where did you learn to kiss like that, madame?" he'd asked.

"From my husband," she'd said, amused, and flicked her fingers through his hair. And, like that, intermission was over, and he sat, dazzled and elsewhere, through the second half of *Coriolanus*.

They hadn't talked since then. Stolen kisses were horrendously dangerous; *The Jordan Times* had a regular report on that week's honor killings and whose brother or son had executed his female family member over a rumor and then been released from prison in a matter of days. Article 340 of the Jordanian Penal Code: *He who discovers his wife or one of his female relatives with another in an adulterous situation, and kills, wounds, or injures one or both of them, is exempt from penalty.* As a child, Hafez had once seen some neighbors celebrating over the body of a young girl. She had just been strangled in front of their house by her brother for looking "suggestively" at another man. The mother had stood over the body and ululated, voice pealing, lifting her palms, extolling her son for restoring the family's compromised honor. And within this, Hafez heard the woman's disguised, piercing grief. The girl's veil had fallen aside and she lay still and open-eyed, hair spread in a glossy fan on the ground. Watching from the side of the road, Hafez felt his heart lurch in involuntary appreciation of her beauty.

And now here was Mrs. Waleeda again, looking at him with her laughing, ravishing face. He bent toward her tenderly and murmured, "I've thought about you."

"And I think of you, dear Hafez. Just the other day, in fact." She smirked. "I see you've filed a petition. With the church."

Hafez tipped his head, his smile faintly guilty. Mrs. Waleeda was assistant to the archbishop: she was lovely by any measure, but certain connections now enhanced her beauty. "How is His Holiness?" he asked.

"His Holiness sends his love."

"He does? To me?"

She lifted her chin. "His Holiness always sends his love."

Father Jacob was the head of the Christian Orthodox Church in Jordan, a small and disproportionately powerful minority. They ran their own schools, had their own monuments, celebrations, and system of justice—one of the few in Jordan that could stand up to Shariah law—or tribal justice. "Funny, I was just wondering—" Hafez hesitated.

"Your petition? There's about a hundred in line ahead of you."

He sucked the insides of his cheeks then blew out.

Of the three brothers, Hafez was the sole churchgoer: Farouq never attended mass and Gabe had converted to Islam—another of his youngest brother's whims. Irritating at the time, with its shades of family rejection, now this conversion seemed fortuitous to Hafez. He and Carole donated to the Church and had hosted fundraising events: His Holiness was frequently an honored guest at their home. Hafez had even nudged aside Mrs. Ward and cooked for him with his own hands—Father Jacob's favorite: wild bitter greens and wild mushrooms with a hint of salty broth. Nothing more. Not a speck of bread or meat. Luckily, Hafez was a good cook: he sprinkled a smidgen of sugar over the greens and at dinner Jacob asked for seconds then finished the pot. Over the past year especially, Hafez and Carole had started attending services, cultivating their souls. Carole fidgeted and played with her gloves, but Hafez always closed his eyes: was he truly alone with his thoughts in there? God? Hello? *If you're really there, Father,* he thought, and his chest rose and fell with fire, *save us.*

But now this creature was showing him the dimple in her right cheek and saying something about bumping him up in line. He caught her hand and kissed it. He continued to peek at her throughout his talk as he covered his talking points:

- Jordan, new nation/ancient past.
- Crossroads, blah, blah. Turkoman trade route. Blah, blah.
- Big city/small-town heart.
- Size doubled by Palestinian influx. Tripled now?
- Joke about Arafat and Saddam. Risky?
- The importance of strong mothers and wives.

The last bit was his add-on for the Soroptimists. He gave these talks in honor of that last remaining scrap of his soul that clung to his mother. To women. (He thought of his niece showing up like that to their house. How odd. Most likely she'd come looking for him. He would ask Mrs. Ward directly. He would ask and he would watch her eyes. What the mouth said didn't matter as much as what the eyes said.)

He glanced at Mrs. Waleeda. She smiled.

After the talk, Hafez helped Mrs. Ali carry an unused slide projector back to her car before he ambled, hands in pockets, over to the maroon BMW still parked in the far corner of the lot, alone. Only nine o'clock and the college was closed up tight.

Mrs. Waleeda had pried off her high heels and placed them arch to arch on her passenger seat. She leaned against her car in a pair of shibshibs; her bare toes sweetly curved, nails painted red. The moon glimmered, a white goblet over her left shoulder. Off somewhere in the darkness came the bleating of a goat, a tinkling of bells, the murmur of their shepherd. Hafez was sixty-nine and three-quarters, filled with his powers. As she lifted her smile, he felt like a desert stallion. What did the Bedu call them? *Drinkers of the wind.* That was Hafez. He slipped his fingers into the dark dimensions of Mrs. Waleeda's hair. He closed his eyes to kiss her.

She tented her fingers on his chest, gave the barest push.

"No?" he said piteously.

The shadow of her dimple appeared. There were just a few sodium lights around the lot, their amber glow dimmer than the stars. What did the old Bedu say? *If the moon is with you, don't worry about the stars.* He thought she was smiling: he could still see the well of that dimple. A well to fall into. She traced the outline of his face with the tops of her index and middle fingers, gently, evaluatively. "Listen, Hafez—my brother, Hassan, he's had some troubles with the Mukhabarat. He needs, desperately, a visa to the U.S."

"I see," Hafez murmured. The Mukhabarat were the meddlesome, not-so-secret-police. The word filtered through his emotional haze.

"Hassan Salhab," Mrs. Waleeda said. "He wrote that column? What would happen if the King should die. About the order of succession."

That guy. Hafez cleared his throat again. "That was short-sighted. Does he have any idea how many assassination attempts His Majesty has survived? Just mentioning the idea of his death . . . It's provocative." A journalist. He recalled Salhab's sulking presence at the diwan, the close way he questioned participants in treaty discussions, twisting their words, accusing this one or that of being too Jordanian, or worse, Israel-friendly, saying that they had swept aside the Palestinians' concerns in their eagerness for peace. Hafez still remembered Salhab's op-ed: *They have blinded themselves to the ongoing assault upon the rights and the lives of the Palestinians. How can there be peace without justice? How can we forgive and forget when the Occupation keeps Palestinians in an ongoing state of siege? How can there be security when they fear for their lives, and those of their children, on a daily basis?*

Now a coolness flowed between himself and Mrs. Waleeda. He felt it in the fingers that she pressed against his chest. "A *year* now in prison. For the crime of suggesting the King might be mortal? And for pointing out that the people might actually be involved in the transition to a new regime. I thought 'democracy' was King H.'s favorite word."

Hafez softened his voice. *Dip your arrow in honey.* "Your brother is a fine journalist. Very good. I'm certain he'll be released soon."

"Once he gets out, no one will hire him," she said coldly. "He'll be an outcast. *If* he gets out."

"I have friends," he murmured. "At the American embassy. And other helpful places. There are ways for him to begin again."

"And I have access to the petitions on the archbishop's desk." The dimple was gone now, her face smooth as an almond. "His Holiness considers me a particular confidante—did you know? A word from me and—I do have some influence." She lifted a delicate brow.

He closed his eyes. He could drink her essence from a bowl. He reached for her, but she slipped into the car. From the west, the athan crackled to life from a minaret. He watched the silhouette of her arm extend from the window as she drove away. Hafez retreated to his own BMW. Slumped in the backseat, he studied the lights glowing along the entrance to campus, the low phantom buildings, the scarcity of trees. The Turks had chopped them down to build their damned Hejazi railroad, for rail ties, bridges, and worker camps. The subsequent soil erosion destroyed habitat, emptying the land of bird life, leaving the Bedouin without twigs to cook on, a scar slicing from Damascus to al-Medina. Yet not far from that parking lot, about 1,378,000 dunams of brilliantly fertile land glimmered in the valley. Each dunam roughly equivalent to a quarter acre. These were the subject of his petition to the archbishop.

THE LAND HAD belonged to Amer Amer—a second cousin on their mother's side, recently deceased. Amer had lived with, then outlived, his mother, in a small stone house, spending nothing, casually buying land in the Jordan valley. In '48, Palestinians started flooding into Jordan and everyone wanted a patch of dirt. Meanwhile, Amer's holdings grew dunum by dunum. He lived in such a miserable little hut, no one but Hafez guessed that he'd grown wealthy—not even Farouq had sniffed him out. But Amer's mother was a simple soul who trusted in Hafez's prominence and status: not long before her death, she'd confided to him that she was worried about her son's obsession with collecting property, afraid that the government might confiscate it. The Crown paid close attention to all land deals near the border with Israel.

Hafez learned that Amer's holdings were valued in the hundreds of millions. He privately suspected Amer collected land because he'd seen his childhood home invaded by soldiers and their property seized. On the few occasions Hafez attempted—discreetly!—to ask what Amer's plans for the land were, he'd say only, in that dogged way: I don't believe in plans. He collected earth, Hafez thought, like someone who planned never to die.

Apart from Hafez, Gabe, Farouq, and a few cousins, Amer had no other immediate relatives or close friends. Even as a young boy, Hafez recalled, Amer was solitary and off-putting. Feeble. Weepy. A tattletale. Always with his head on Mommy's lap. His nose whistled.

Gabe, Farouq, and Hafez had played with Amer when they were children. Amer was wonderfully easy to torment: Hafez discovered one afternoon that he could flick tiny stones at the back of his cousin's head and the child couldn't work out where they were coming from. He had continued this game for years. When Hafez learned, about a year ago, that Amer had the sugar sickness—diabetes—and then a "minor" preliminary heart attack, for some reason he'd thought of the tiny stones game first. Then he'd wondered: And who will get all that property?

There was a second heart attack and Amer died intestate, Hafez and his siblings his nearest kin. If the inheritance was apportioned out Shariah-style, the brothers would each get a share, as well as their cousins Taiyal, Adel, Boulos, and their dead cousin Matrouk's wife, Tamim, and their children. But if it were divided according to the interpretation of the Orthodox Church, then the only ones to inherit would be the living, Christian next-of-kin.

And if the Church were to support his petition, it would follow the custom of their father's clan, in which case it would all go to the firstborn son.

He felt no compunctions over this: Hafez had been cheated once already—his father had said his eldest son would inherit his possessions—which turned out to be some clothes, guns, maps, a few musical instruments. But somehow, the most precious, the knife— somehow *that* had gone to Gabe. Hafez wanted what he was owed. He was the child of a Palestinian refugee, like Amer, terrible as it was to admit, and property—especially that which contained the long, unbroken line of the past—was the only thing that would make the dispossessed whole again.

FOR A MOMENT, it seemed to Hafez that wisps of zaatar, piss, and lavender—the scent of Amer's old house—rose in twists around his head. He jumped nearly out of his body at a knock on the window, a burst of Arabic, "Boss? You awake?"

Samir got behind the wheel and started the car. There was a lit cigarette on his lip, a fresh cigarette behind one ear and a soft pack inside the pocket of his T-shirt.

Hafez considered asking for another one. Instead, he folded his arms and said, "Those are going to kill you," inhaling deeply as he gazed out the passenger window. "And me."

"Akeed," Samir nodded. Sure. They pulled out of the parking lot.

Hafez watched the nod in his peripheral vision, then turned to his driver. "Would you ever consider taking more than one wife? I mean, if you were married to begin with. You're a good Muslim, right? Have you thought about it?"

Samir's brows lifted halfway up his forehead. He took the cigarette from his lip and knocked it off on the open window. "If you're thinking of converting, ya ustaz, there are some things . . ."

"No, no, no." Hafez rubbed three fingers across his jaw. "I've just wondered. How would one manage? Two wives? You can have up to four, correct? Ya'Allah, how does one function?"

Samir smiled around the cigarette. "Apparently, one manages."

"One manages, one manages," Hafez said dolefully. "So, in other words, four is no better than one, and possibly worse."

"Very possible."

Hafez felt for his worry beads at the bottom of his right pocket. He'd bought them rather impulsively from a souq merchant who swore they were excavated from the area of Djenné and Gao, dated to the eighth century: heavy, jet beads with one blue stone to ward off the covetous evil eye. They had a reassuring quality in his hand. Still, he tried to never let anyone glimpse them—they were so rustic, so Muslim. He slid the beads between his fingers and tried to imagine introducing Carole to her new sister. He could see Mrs. Waleeda in his bed, but not in his living room fighting for the remote.

"It's a bad business." Samir turned for a moment so Hafez could see his driver's profile, the slightly squashed nose, sensitive mouth, his cigarette the brightest thing in the car. "Wanting. The Qu'ran says four, yes. But only if each is treated equally. You can't do that. No one can do that. Maybe with money. But not . . ." Samir tapped his palm flat against the center of his chest. "You get to have only the idea of it."

Hafez's lips curved in the darkness. "So, you're tempted by the possibility, but can't ever have it in reality." Absurd religion. As were they all.

The driver clicked his tongue. "The hope is worse than no hope."

"I'm not interested in hope." Hafez threaded his fingers through the beads, their click nearly inaudible. "I've wasted too much time on hope."

In the rearview mirror, Samir's eyes wrinkled with a smile. "You don't need hope, boss, you have power."

Hafez lowered his window. He felt that power hovering just beyond his grasp. How to reclaim it? He'd been robbed. To ask for power destroyed the power; to steal it destroyed it. It had to be conferred, bestowed. Born into. Or legislated. He lowered the window all the way, a relief to feel the air rushing with cold moonlight, nets of it caught in the tree branches lining Hamra Street. The sky bowed overhead, clear all the way to outer space. What should he care about knives, brothers, women when it seemed at such moments he owned the whole city? But then he thought of those tribal chieftains, the Bedouin sheikhs he was descended from, just like the King himself. They were the true nobility of Jordan—quiet arbiters of power. He could see their shrewd faces, how they would gossip over the coffeepots, under the blowing tents. None of them would respect his ownership of the land—not really—as long as they knew he didn't own Il Saif—the soul of their family.

This was his fundamentally rooted understanding—ingrained by his father and the males of the village: that land, money, and inheritance were power. That without such power, he wouldn't be able to hang on much longer to his position as the adjudicator of peace. His influence was slipping: His Majesty had blamed the Oslo debacle on him—though the King had never said anything explicitly, Hafez knew it! Hafez should have had his ear to the ground. *He* should have been the one to observe the Palestinians jetting off to Norway—instead of that old war horse, Yasir Arafat.

He sighed and Samir glanced in the mirror. Dusty, crowded Amman sped by as they made their way at last back to the Embassy District, traffic slowing to a crawl, the trees retracting into green lace. He tented his fingers. They turned onto Khanzeer Street, which everyone called Spanish Embassy Street, the sidewalks broad in places, impassable in others where someone had decided to carve out chunks of cement and plant the spindly new trees. "Samir—your people are from—"

"I'm Beni-Sakhr tribe," he said, fist knocking the front of his shoulder. "True Jordanian."

"True Jordanian indeed." That's what Hafez's father, Munif, had always called himself. Pointing to his fields, tossing his red checked keffiyeh over one shoulder, his knife under his robes. True Jordanian. Hafez huffed a laugh and closed his window. "Well, aren't we all?"

CHAPTER

8

AMANI PEERED out the window, the Nefertiti necklace in her hand. She had written notes to herself:

> *Blue letter*
> *church & cemetery*
> *necklace*

The guesthouse office was bordered by three large windows. If she stood near the northwest window—opposite from Farouq's main house—she could see into the courtyard of the building next door that Farouq and Bella were remodeling. Its courtyard was lined with blue tiles that glittered like glass, and if she squinted it looked as if it were filled with water. All afternoon she watched men with hammers and saws going in and out through the arched entry. One of the workers had spread a prayer mat near one corner of the wall where he'd probably supposed it was private. He washed his hands, the back of his neck, his face, and wrists, then stood at the bottom of his rug, hands together in prayer. Amani lingered a moment to watch the man lift his palms to the sky, then backed away from the window.

Downstairs, a door opened and her father was saying her name. The fencing match would take place in less than two weeks and today was the third time Omar had managed to get Gabe to the gym. Gabe stood in the front door, a gym bag drooping on one shoulder and garment bags over his arm. "Aunt Carole sent more party clothes for tonight—in case you change your mind." He held the bags out. Omar slid through the entrance behind Gabe. "Your dad's a beast. You should see what he did. He destroyed. Ask him what he's benching now."

"Ninety pounds," Gabe said dolefully. "I can maybe carry two suitcases—if they don't have too many clothes."

"But when you started?" Omar chided.

She looked at the garment bags. "How fancy is this thing?" It seemed odd—a birthday dinner on a Monday—as if the King were flaunting how nothing constrained him, not even the workweek.

Gabe partially unzipped one garment bag. "Well, here's your uncle's tuxedo that I'm supposed to wear. His tuxedo number two. I don't know what's going on with tuxedo number one."

"Do people need more than one tuxedo?"

"Jordan, man," Omar said. "It's Weddings Central, every day. Hafez probably has eighteen tuxes." A sliver of something gauzy and champagne-beige tufted out of the other bag.

"I'm not trying on more clothes." She stuffed the gauze back into its bag and looked at her cousin. "You guys aren't coming? Not even your parents?"

Omar smirked. "This is for rocket-fuel society. Above our pay grade."

Rashwa and wasta, Omar had told her, that was how everything ran here. Bribes and connections. And that everyone kept score. She'd started to feel wariness over the gifts and favors that people offered. In the space of a week, two shopkeepers and a taxi driver had offered "discounts" and "special-for-you prices," then asked if she could help get them visas to the United States. Her father accepted everything without hesitation, but Amani wondered what the price of each offer might be.

"Oh, and there's this." Gabe held up another hanger. "When I was leaving, the housekeeper said for you to have it. A present."

"Mrs. Ward?" Amani reached quickly for the dress and took it up to her bedroom, peeling back dry-cleaning plastic along the way. She slipped it over her head. A white spill of silk and cotton, long bell sleeves, a high square neckline yoked with red embroidery—six pointed stars and a design like heads of wheat—repeating around the cuffs and waist. Cut for a shorter woman, it came just to her ankles, but fit perfectly around her middle and felt soft against her legs. The lower border of the skirt was also covered in red embroidery: tiny chevrons and stars. It was modest and traditional, but light as cream. A dress to float in. *Natalia*, she murmured—it had to be. *Thank you.*

Omar clapped when she walked downstairs. "Yo, goddess."

Her father's arms fell open. For a moment she couldn't read his expression. "Lovely," he said at last. "Lovely."

Then she saw herself through her father's eyes: hair combed for once and twisted up off her neck, wearing what was probably the first nice thing she'd put on since her divorce. She laughed in embarrassment. "Stop."

Her father held her at arm's length, studying the dress. "This is old-time—all this embroidery. By hand. Every village had its own style. See the stitches? My mother could tell where someone was from by her dress."

"Cuz," Omar said. "You're gonna kill."

"So . . . this belonged to Natalia?" Amani asked. But her father shook his head. "I never saw her in anything like this. She wore plain house clothes." He shrugged. "She was usually reading in the kitchen or outside with the goats."

Amani ran her hand over the embroidered yoke. She was also wearing the necklace from Mrs. Ward. Cool against her bare skin, a gold marquise-shaped pendant of Nefertiti's profile—her aquiline features, the flat, tapered headdress. Amani kept glimpsing herself in the entryway mirror, startled by the way the dress altered her appearance, elevating it, as if she'd jumped up a social class. The change seemed startling yet familiar, like a tap on the shoulder. It was like seeing someone she almost recognized.

As they waited for the driver who would bring them to the party, Amani's thoughts traveled to another image, of a faded old painting.

It was a face surmounted by a bare silver halo hung on the nun's wall. The Virgin Mary was the ideal role model according to Sister John, Amani's third-grade teacher at St. Anselmo's, because becoming a nun, she said, would be any girl's dream. Sister John was tall and willowy, the oval of her face outlined by a black wimple. Amani couldn't quite recall her facial features, just a long, pale space, a pair of pink lips. The nun told stories of heaven and saints, the warriors and martyrs, seraphim and cherubs. One day, Sister was explaining guardian angels to the class, how each baby was assigned a special guide and protector who would be with them always. When Amani raised her hand the nun paused before calling on her. Amani sometimes made observations that interrupted class. On this day, she confided, "I know who my guardian angel is." All the children turned, regarding her with interest.

Sister John smiled. "Ah, you think so? And who is that?"

"I know so. I know it! My grandmother, Natalia." She knew her grandmother was dead, so that meant she was an angel. But it was more than that: she'd often had the sense of being somehow accompanied; it came to her at odd times, descending lightly and sweetly—the feeling that there was a reassuring presence at her side.

There was an alteration on that pale oval; the nun said, "Ah yes, I can see how it might seem that way, but I'm afraid that's not quite correct." She went on to explain how the guardian stands between God and child, how they are divine agents, residents of heaven. Amani noticed that the more she insisted her grandmother was her angel, the redder was Sister's face. After class, Sister John accompanied Amani to her mother's office. Francesca had recently become assistant principal and she peered up at Sister John from her desk without speaking. She didn't stop tapping her pen until the nun had finished explaining about how wayward and recalcitrant Amani often seemed, her strange ideas, the time she told class that the communion host was made of paper, and how sorry Sister was for her loss, but angels were divine intermediaries, untainted by the physical world: Francesca's mother could not strictly be a considered a guardian angel.

"My mother?" Francesca laughed. "I hope not. According to my watch, she should be in an aerobics class in Palermo right now."

"I meant my grandma Natalia." Amani went to stand beside her mother. "*She's* my angel."

Francesca looked surprised; she touched her daughter's face. "Your daddy's mother? You think she's your angel? Well then, she is. She is your angel."

Natalia came to her in musical phrases, the lullaby with the sweet, elastic notes her father sang to her, lying curled beside her on the little bed when she couldn't sleep. Usually, he fell asleep before she did, singing and dozing so it became a dream song that accompanied the image of the face in the old family portrait, her grandmother's mystical eyes. Her father said that Natalia sang her sheep in across the fields, that her laughter was musical. He described her old village of Mismar: Amani saw the lilt of the village homes against the hillside, the women with jugs balanced on their heads, babies in their arms, their long practical black skirts and fitted, embroidered jackets, the women squatting around a tub outside to wash their clothes, children running barefoot on cobblestones, carpenters with angular saws and white keffiyehs, ivory-colored mosques with pale minarets, the men standing in the street with coffee cups, strings of pink paper lanterns hanging in a cleanly swept alley. Sweet Natalia, always kind—rising early to bring in the laundry, so her sisters wouldn't have to—blurred in Amani's mind with the *ifrit*, the fairies in her storybook, hidden within the village well, or drifting from the lantern spout, just out of sight and always sad not to be human.

Sister John lowered her head and didn't speak for a moment. Lifting her chin, she said, "I realize your husband has different beliefs— it's understandable that Amani is confused. But my job, as I see it, is to provide a clear spiritual path to my pupils. I cannot accomplish this without parental cooperation."

Francesca rolled back in her seat and crossed her arms. Amani didn't see this expression very often on her mother's face, and she was surprised to see it here with Sister. "My husband is a Muslim," Francesca said evenly. "Though I fail to see what that has to do with anything."

"It has everything to do with this," Sister John said, just as evenly.

Eyes glinting, Francesca asked, "Did you know Islam says we all have two guardian angels? I think they may have outdone the Catholics."

Sister John's face and throat seemed to tighten. "I'm sorry you find this amusing. We're talking about your daughter's immortal soul." She glanced at Amani. "The child resembles her father. She has his complexion. It's been my experience that sensibility tends to follow resemblance."

Her mother stood up quickly. She asked Mrs. Morris who worked in the front office to give Amani a coloring book and crayons. Amani sat quietly, listening to the dashes of her mother's voice through her door, wondering what was *foreign*, what was *complexion*, why couldn't her grandmother be an angel? She thought about these secrets; it seemed there was something forbidden and enticing about her father's world—something important that was meant for her but that shouldn't be. She tried to color very carefully between the lines, until she couldn't, and then she drew all over the page.

Two SMALL Jordanian flags flickered on the car's hood. Beyond the smoked windows it was difficult to make out details in the setting sun. Amani watched the streets widening, bordered by low yellow-and-black-striped curbs. They flew along Zahran Street and she sensed the city fall away from them, as if the street were a spine rising above miles of square stone buildings, arcing palms, rickety wooden fruit stands, banners and billboards, and beyond it, a dust-soft radiance.

Traffic streamed in front of and beside them, through overpasses painted with ads in Arabic and English and street signs, an enormous Colonel Sanders on the right, buildings of blue glass on the left. Rivers of glass. The traffic pouring into their street from all sides gave Amani the sense that everyone in town was headed to the same place. There was continuous honking and gesturing. Stopped at a light, she heard a crackle through the thick windows, then a soft moan: the call to prayers. They moved forward and a momentary rain sifted over the windshield.

Her father held her hand. They arrived at a checkpoint with a uniformed guard. He gave a nod as the barrier swung open. The traffic and city lights faded as they slid into an older, more formal, green space. Even in the darkness, Amani had the feeling of entering a land apart, a landscaped park opening around them. Trees, older and taller than any in the rest of the city, rose around the car, towering black silhouettes sparkling with rain. Even the night vaulting the royal court compound seemed elevated to her, the moon hanging like a goblet.

"Is this where you used to come? To fence?" she asked, noting the shapes of multistory buildings, of columns and pointed archways slipping past in the night. She knew Uncle Hafez's office was somewhere nearby, but it had all looked different by day. She wondered why she felt so anxious.

"Oh no," Gabe said. Gazing out, he smiled. "Not by a mile."

They rounded a bend and the lights turned into one slick blaze illuminating an avenue. Before them, a building was completely outlined in little white bulbs like stars and lights were strung along the entry steps. They pulled up to the grand entrance. On each step stood a uniformed guard, his red-checked keffiyeh scarf tucked and folded into black skull rings, a bayonetted rifle held at attention. Arriving guests clipped up the steps, the women in furs and heels.

Amani's father squeezed her hand. Their driver came to a stop, sprang out, and sprinted to the palace-facing passenger door. He opened it, bowing slightly, as another guard approached. Copying something she'd seen in movies, she placed her fingers on his open palm and allowed herself to be helped from the car.

A wine-red silk carpet covered the steps, extending all the way to their car door. In a crowded receiving area, guests pressed together chattering; women grabbed one another's hands, kissing each cheek, wiping lipstick traces with their thumbs. A phalanx of valets dipped through the crowd, ferrying away coats and capes. Helping women off with their coverings, the valets pushed each heavy fur up slightly in an expert gathering motion, then slid the coat away to reveal décolletage, arms glowing with the chandelier lights. A few women were dressed in lemon or plum or celadon-colored silk headscarves in varying degrees of sheerness. Many women emerged from the wrappings nearly bare. One woman wore a diamond necklace in reverse: a chain dangled down her backless dress, above the dip of her spine. Amani ran one hand along the front of her dress again, feeling underdressed.

She and her father were escorted into an exhibition hall lined with gold-framed portraits and engraved swords. For a moment she stood still, just blinking and turning. Satin drapery billowed over the windows toward a landscape of curved chairs and settees. Waiters circulated with trays of flutes misted by cold Champagne. At the back of the room, the King and Queen stood with a handful of young people whom Amani assumed were some of the King's ten children.

An older woman in a floor-length kaftan stood with the children, straightening their clothes. She noticed Amani's dress and gave her a small nod.

Amani let two trays go by, then swiftly lifted two flutes from a tray, handing one to her father. She would just hold hers, she decided, for a prop. "Do you know anyone here?"

"Nobody." Gabe pointed to one of the guests in military uniform, a chest full of medals: "I think that's the prime minister—I forget his name."

Hafez appeared. "There you are, there you are! Why are you disguised as an old Bedouin woman?" Uncle Hafez kissed Amani then Gabe twice on each cheek. Carole glided to his side. "I thought you gave her some proper clothes?" he said to his wife with a laugh. A small group stopped to pat his back and embrace Carole. Hafez introduced them to an admiral, a Luxembourgish duchess, and a black-haired starlet of Cairene soap operas. The actress stared at Amani and asked where she might acquire a gown like that.

"I wish I knew, honestly," Amani said, and glanced at Carole. "I'm pretty sure this one's handmade."

After the group dispersed, Aunt Carole stood back, lips parted, one hand on her chest. "What happened to the pink dress?"

Amani lifted one flowing sleeve. "I thought you sent this one too—Mrs. Ward gave it to Dad."

Carole's eyes ticked once around the room before she leaned closer. "No. I did not. You look like you crawled out of a tent." Her cheeks and throat were red.

Hafez chuckled and touched his wife's back. "Carole, you're giving yourself a conniption." He turned to Amani. "You look wonderful, my dear. It's called a *thawb*. It's very—correct. You'll educate this bunch about their own culture." Turning quickly, he called to some people across the room and pulled Gabe along with him.

Carole's gaze now focused on her throat. Amani put her hand on the pendant; it had slipped under the embroidered yoke. Carole reached toward her shoulders. "That neckline is all wrong." Amani felt her aunt move the top of the dress shoulders so it fell an inch lower and the whole pendant was showing. "There. That's *correct*," she said archly.

More waiters came with appetizers and Amani placed her untouched drink on a tray. A woman with stiff blond hair sailed up to Carole smacking air kisses, and Amani edged away. She moved among the guests and wandered through one stateroom after another, each filled with French furnishings, multitiered crystal chandeliers, and silk draperies. At the rear of one long chamber, positioned on a dais, were two upholstered red chairs with straight backs, gold crowns embroidered on the cushions. An oil portrait of Queen Victoria, scowling in an ornate gold frame, hung on the opposite wall.

Amani made her way to a formal salon, where the King was swarmed by well-wishers. He wore a black tux, his quick eyes radiating laughter. Two men flanked the King, standing with hands clasped, backs to the wall, still as potted plants. They were decked out in dark coats with silver trim, silver crowns on wool hats. She stopped, head tipped, studying the uniforms. A man in a dishdasha winked at Amani and nodded at the guards, murmuring, "Beware the Turks!"

"Those are not Turks—that's the Circassian guard." The voice behind her right shoulder was like a touch: she started and looked at a face she was certain she'd seen before—long, handsome jaw, warm eyes, a curved mouth. "They're supposedly the trusted loyal ones— no Palestinian intrigue," he said, lifting a chin toward the guard.

It took her just a moment to place him—the speckled green-and-brown irises. "We've met before," she said.

He gave a short bow. "At the falcons. You made quite an impression. On everyone, I think."

She shielded her face with the side of her hand and laughed. "Oh God. Please don't remind me."

"Your shoulder is better?"

"Like it never happened." She waved his concern away, wanting to change the subject. "Did the rest of the club come with you?"

"The club?" His eyebrows rose, then he laughed outright. "Oh, no. I'm not—"

She felt the heat in her temples before she could work out her mistake. "A—falcon trainer?"

Jostled by the crowd, he brushed slightly closer to her. "Only a fan. What do Americans say? A wannabe?" He had a slight accent. There was a litheness about his movements. He stood a bit close.

She tipped her head toward his so she didn't look at him too directly. "I could have sworn . . ." She laughed at herself, her skin still warm.

"No, no, it's a good mistake—I like this mistake. I like old-fashioned kinds of things. The falcons, the horses, the salukis. They're very adab." He touched his solar plexus. "You know this word? It means proper. Noble."

Another waiter appeared and the man lifted his hand. "Lovely, yes. You will have?" He took two flutes and handed one to her, then raised his glass.

Amani took a sip. She muttered, half to herself, "I was just told I looked like I crawled out of a tent."

His forehead lifted. "I've never seen anything so beautiful come from a tent."

She felt annoyed with herself—that she was so susceptible to a stranger's compliment. "So do you go around saying things like that to people?"

"Actually, I'm not sure I've ever said anything quite like that." He seemed bemused. "Certainly not to someone I've just met. Re-met."

A man in uniform paused beside them, saluted. "Captain, hello."

After he moved on, she looked at the man with his light eyes. "Should I salute?"

He grimaced and lifted his shoulders. "God, please don't." A wave of newcomers crowded the room; Amani held up her drink to avoid getting splashed. He asked, "Should we stroll?"

They walked through the salon, through an archway, into a salon with silk wallpaper and rigid Louis XIV furniture. On the ceiling was an oval mural of dancing cherubs. Stealing glances at her new acquaintance, Amani found herself noticing again the way he moved, how he seemed in control of his movements. They drifted toward a quieter corner of the room. Amani walked into a chair, banging her shin. "It's this dress," she confessed. "I'm all . . ." She squeezed her eyes shut for a moment.

He shook his head. "Palaces have that effect on people."

"I bet they do." She laughed. "I don't have much experience with them."

"Wish I could say the same," he said. "I used to teach fencing at the officers' academy—there were regular palace exhibitions. Now I run my own school." His eyes were lighter than his skin. Moving behind him, the faces of the other guests blurred into soft colors. "Eduardo Attias."

"You're here for the fencing! So am I." Amani felt happy and a little light-headed: she held on to the back of the chair. It felt as if the marble floor floated over water, tipping back and forth. Someone joined them—she looked up to see her father, watching Eduardo, curious and wary.

"Here you are! You are having fun?" His gaze moved between Amani and her glass.

She introduced her father to Eduardo, adding, "And I'm Amani. Hamdan."

"Oh, I know," Eduardo said, taking her fingers in his hand. He kissed them; she felt his breath on her skin.

WAITERS HURRIED through the room, picking up glasses, urging guests toward an arched doorway. Someone in a tuxedo took Amani to a seat at one of a series of banquet tables where mists of jasmine blossom rose from the centerpieces. Her papyrus place card was written in English and Arabic. A narrow man bent like Picasso's guitar player was being helped into the seat across the table; he was introduced to the others as Professor El-Afif, Political Science, Al Quds University. Eduardo slipped through the diners: he bowed slightly, then checked the place card at the setting next to Amani's. "Ah," he said. When Hafez appeared, Eduardo shook his hand, saying, "I wondered if I might—" He made a twisting motion with his fingers. "Make a trade?" He handed the place card to Hafez.

Amani saw only her uncle's back, but he seemed to stiffen. Eduardo snuck a look at Amani, the ghost of a smile. Hafez turned then and planted a hand on Eduardo's shoulder. "Of course. I was hoping you two would find each other. Eduardo here was on the Jordanian team to the Olympics. . . ."

"Twelve years ago?" Eduardo said with a laugh.

"He is head of the Royal Fencing Academy," Hafez went on. "Best school in the Middle East! He trains all the cadets now—they send them to him—even from Libya and Kuwait. His team is going to show off before Gabe's big event." He slapped Eduardo's shoulder. "So I am going to relinquish my seat to the better man. I know when I'm beat." He turned. "Amani is my favorite niece—I'm counting on you to keep her entertained." He stretched his neck, studying the room. "If you'll excuse me, I believe I have a wife around here."

"I guess you know my uncle. . . ." Amani said as Eduardo took his seat.

"I do. And your auntie. Your cousins. The whole family is pretty famous around here. Hafez Hamdan especially."

"Somehow that doesn't surprise me." Amani picked up her wine, allotting herself another sip. It softened her nerves. She checked the room: her father was several places away. Hafez and Carole took seats across the table from him. Hafez, half-turned, was pressing hands as more officers and men in white robes hovered over him, lowering their faces to his ear.

Waiters moved along the table, snapping open napkins. Beneath each place card was a dinner menu in French, Arabic, and English:

On the occasion of the sixtieth birthday of His Royal Majesty Talal Ibn H. Clouds of colored Baccarat crystals dipped from the ceiling. In the background, Amani could just make out the undulant chords of the Lebanese singer Fairuz. Two rows of banquet tables were lined up end to end, possibly a hundred guests in all, a waiter stationed behind each guest. Bridging the two rows was a head table heaped with pink flowers and crystal table lamps. Cavalcades of Arabic and English moved around her: under the table, Eduardo's knee tapped hers then quickly moved away.

The chamber orchestra at the front of the room began playing. A door opened at the northeast corner of the room and the King, Queen, queen mother, and a medley of young adults and children filed in. The guests stood. Filigreed pearl garland on her head, the Queen seemed to float an inch above the gathering. Originally from the States, she'd been given a new first and last name by the King and had married into three generations of stepchildren from previous wives. Amani studied her face, her marble stillness, and wondered what it felt like to be so thoroughly stripped of a past life: did she ever feel like she'd lost herself? Amani's gaze fell to her own hand resting lightly on the tablecloth. She could no longer make out the paler skin at the base of her finger where her wedding band used to be.

A uniformed servant at the right of the head of the table announced each royal family member as they took their seats. After the last royal sat, the guests did as well, resuming conversation.

Right away someone stood to make a toast at the opposite end of the room. Amani picked up her glass: along the banquet table, the sparkling glasses lifting. Her gaze intersected that of her uncle Hafez, nearer the center of the table, his eyes red-rimmed and glassy. Beside him, Carole's gaze ticked from face to face.

Amani turned toward Eduardo. "So, you know Hafez and Carole. But why did you say you know *my* name?"

Their place settings were removed by silent waiters. Another set of servers took the Champagne and poured glasses of something pink. Others brought out domed dishes that breathed a vapor of lemon when opened. A man a few places down the table stood with his glass raised: another toast was made.

"Because of your father." Eduardo rested his forearms on the table. "Everyone in our world—in fencing—has heard about the exhibition with the King's favorite. I was curious about this favorite. We're hearing all sorts of stories—the best sparring partner! But at the warm-up tent—I saw you—"

She lifted an eyebrow, turning her new glass of wine.

"And if it isn't too forward to say so, I forgot all about the favorite." He brought the edge of his glass to hers so carefully it barely made a sound.

The woman on Amani's left touched her arm. She wore a strapless black gown and white gloves to her elbows. Her eyes cut to Amani's place card then to her face. "Any relation to Hafez?"

Amani smiled. "Hafez is my uncle. Hafez Hamdan." She glanced back at her uncle and noticed he was again facing in their direction. He nodded and the woman on her left lifted her glass. She turned back to Amani. "Your dress is lovely. Oh, this is Nile cotton—it has those wonderful long fibers. And this is a Nazarene stitch, yes?"

Amani looked at the embroidered border. "Do you know the stitches for the different towns?"

"Just a few. My aunt was from Nazareth."

Amani hooked her fingers around her necklace, sliding the pendant back and forth. "I think my grandmother was from a little village—this place called Mismar—outside of Nazareth."

The white-haired professor across the table said, "Mismar. I haven't heard that name in forty years."

Amani looked over at him. "Do you know it?"

His eyes were sunken, his skin almost translucent; she could see the veins in his temples as he shook his head. "Yibna, Hittin, Alma, Mismar . . . So many vanished villages, towns, all across Palestine. I visited once or twice as a child—I scarcely remember."

The bearded man beside him mumbled something and the professor leaned closer, cupping his ear. "Pardon?"

"Nothing. No"—the other man held up a hand—"ignore me."
His accent sounded vaguely European to Amani.

The woman's eyebrows rose.

The bearded man glanced at her and his shoulders fell. He shook
his head. "It's just my random way of thinking. It's nothing."

Eduardo cleared his throat softly. "You know someone—from one
of the depopulated villages?" he asked Amani.

She didn't speak for a moment: it seemed as if the conversation
had taken a somewhat personal turn, as if Eduardo were requesting
more than dinner-party chat. "Some of my family—I think. I'm trying to research while I'm here."

"Why don't you ask your uncle?" the woman on her left side broke
in. "Hafez—he has always such an interesting perspective." Her
smile was tipped and sly. "On everything."

The old man turned back to her. "You should. It's essential to try
to learn what you can—if your family is from one of the disappeared
villages. There's not so many of us old folk around anymore. The
Palestinians have been torn out by the roots, scattered to every corner.
Us and our stories and such memories. 'Never forget'—as they say."
His voice shook.

The bearded man said lightly, "Secret histories. Even more evanescent than the written kind."

The professor looked offended. "Secret histories are precious.
Everyone knows that. The preservation of cultural history is
everything—it's a reclamation of displaced persons, of fractured
identity. . . ."

"Oh, come now—must we bury ourselves in what's past?" the
bearded man said. He sounded exhausted, as if all the air had left
his body. "Let's let go of it already." He turned to Amani. "Let yourself be young, free."

"I wouldn't know where to start," Amani said.

Eduardo chuckled and started to say something, but servers began
to move between their shoulders, murmuring, "Finished?" They
exchanged the plates with fresh ones.

Voices died away as the waiters stepped back. The King stood up at the head and lifted his arms. He welcomed them, mentioning several of the seated, including a few generals, various sheikhs, visiting dignitaries, and a foreign poet named Ben Sheltzer. The King's voice, a resonant baritone, took up the dimensions of the room. He made a joke about turning sixty, patting his nonexistent belly.

He talked about his hope for peace at last.

After so many meetings, so much bloodshed, so much diplomacy. He alluded to the suffering of the Jewish people. He alluded to the suffering of the Palestinians. What is a home? Is it in the house? The people? The land? When people are evicted from their origins, what is fractured, where is the crack? He started to say something more; his voice descended and broke, and for a moment there was a tremendous quiet as the King stood there, touching his forehead. Finally, he mentioned the recent assassination of his friend, Yitzhak Rabin. A murmur rose around the table. He called for a moment of silence.

After a pause, the King lifted his head. "There will always be naysayers and doomsayers. There will always be those more invested in war than in peace. But the will of our peoples shall not be stopped. It is a great and rushing force for good. We are living in remarkable days," he said in Arabic, followed by the English translator, a young man in wire-rim glasses who stood slightly behind the King, looking at each guest in turn as he interpreted. "The Madrid conference, the Oslo Accords. These are thrilling, unprecedented moments in the creation of peace in the region. I have given my soul to this process: the attempt to show the humanity of the Palestinians to the world whilst never forgetting the horrors of the last World War. We are seeing history unfold before our eyes. To my mind there could be no greater gift than a unified Jordan and a true and sustained peace throughout the Middle East."

Amani glanced at her uncle, warmth behind her eyes, feeling as if some light shone on the whole room. Following the others, she lifted her glass; chandelier reflections caught in the goblets and scattered against the walls. Someone called out, "Hear, hear!" There was applause and another cried, "Mash'allah."

Eventually, they returned to their seats, waiters adjusting chairs, spreading napkins. Conversation resumed around the table; the party regained its equilibrium. The two men across from Amani were already back to their conversation.

"If that's the way you think, in that case it's actually a shame," the white-haired professor was responding loudly to something the bearded man had said. The main course arrived—crown roasts of lamb redolent with saffron and pine nuts. A waiter poured a deep red into a wineglass. The white-haired man started cutting into a chop. "A fine statesman. A visionary! The Lion of Jordan! And compassionate. Yet—you tell us—impossible to take seriously as royalty."

"I didn't put it like that. You know I didn't."

"But you just said a royal house must always be suspect. Wasn't that your word? Suspect?"

"Suspect? Why is that?" the woman to her left asked, lowering a wrist to the table.

The bearded man hunched over his plate as if trying to disappear. "Please—no deliberate misunderstandings. I wasn't even speaking of King H. I meant only that unchecked heads of state become corrupted. It's practically a law of physics. Royalty arrives at its power through lines of ascension, politics. Duress. Not some divine or superhuman decree—all myths notwithstanding." He put down his cutlery and placed his hands on the table. "After the royal house is installed, then comes economic and religious consolidation." He nodded toward the King at the head of the table. "In the ancient world that was the way it was done. Supposedly, we've put a finer spin on things in these modern times." After a moment, he picked up his knife and fork and resumed cutting his food. "In Israel, we elect our leaders—if nothing else," he added drily.

"Oh? The great democracy of Israel?" Now Eduardo sat forward, his midsection touching the tablecloth. "Democracy for themselves alone, as I understand it."

The bearded man's face lifted. "You would have us impose our style of government on those around us?"

"You already have," Eduardo rejoined. Amani looked at him.

"We'd settle for a modicum of justice and fair play." The white-haired man across the table sat back. "Instead of brutality."

"And *we'd* settle for being left in peace," the bearded man snapped. "Palestinians cry foul at every—any—perceived slight. If the day is overcast it's Israel's fault. Out come the rocket launchers. We survived the Holocaust only to find ourselves surrounded by terrorists and suicide bombers and hostile Arab nations."

A hush fell like a clap and emptied the air around them. Murmurs ran along the table. "Take care, when fighting monsters," the professor said in a quiet voice. "That one does not become the monster."

As if some electrical pulse had communicated itself, Hafez got to his feet, glass outraised, the other hand clutching his seatback. "In honor of the occasion of our beloved Royal Majesty's birthday, I think I speak for all present today when I wish you a hundred thousand more—in good health and joy. May the light of heaven shine down, protect, and elevate you, and may your guidance elevate all of us." He extended his glass toward several guests, ending with the bearded man across from Amani. "In particular, I'd like to welcome the King's special guest, the illustrious author Ben Sheltzer, who is one of the first to officially visit us from that exotic land to our north. Your presence here today shall help us inaugurate a beautiful friendship and spread peace throughout our nations."

Sheltzer nodded and raised his glass, though his thin shoulders and chest were still bowed. "May it be so," he said. The plates were cleared and replaced by chilled dishes of paper-fine radish, tomato, cucumber, and a satiny cheese. Amani picked up the chilled salad fork and glanced again in her uncle's direction, admiring his stealth and skill. He couldn't possibly have heard what they'd been discussing and yet he seemed to have an instinct for interceding at just the right moment.

"Do you know his work?" Eduardo asked quietly, barely nodding at the writer.

Her gaze shifted toward his; she shook her head.

"Nor I," he said genially. "I suppose we'll have to go buy his book now."

Guests were asked to move to an adjacent salon and were reseated at new banquet tables. Male servers entered, pushing trolleys with samovars of coffee and mint tea and platters of golden pastries. There was a many-tiered cake encased in white fondant beneath a cloud of balloons. The waiters tossed sugar confetti across the tabletops. The guests clapped as it drifted over their plates. As a server pushed in her chair, Amani felt the tension from the first table disperse. Hafez's toast had seemed like a sort of warning to the partygoers to behave. After a few bites of pastry, Ben Sheltzer wiped the napkin across his lips, laid it beside his plate, and stood. One, then another guest clinked spoons against their glasses. The writer slid his hand under his jacket and pulled out a folded paper. "Ladies and gentlemen," he said. "I am honored, humbled, to be among this illustrious company tonight on this momentous occasion. Life is filled with hurdles and markers. But turning sixty, I believe, is a particularly moving one. It is the moment where we finally begin to understand how much we love the world."

Amani noticed Eduardo's hand resting on the table between them, looking to her somehow like an invitation. She shifted her legs and her knee tapped his; she drew back, startled. He glanced at her.

"As I am but a young lad of fifty-nine"—Sheltzer paused for laughter—"I won't take up too much of your time with my chatter. Most of you have no idea who I am—which is as it should be. Let me just say, then, that I play with words. I'm afraid that has been my only vocation. I went from sticks and stones to words and never looked back. I am, quite honestly, overwhelmed to be a guest for the first time, not only in this palace, but in your splendid nation.

"In his honor, then, and with great humility, I'd like to offer this little scribble of mine. Please bear with me. I'm more of an essayist, and I hear there are actual poets present." His head dipped and Amani realized he'd nodded at her. She drew back in surprise. For a moment, eyes up and down the table moved to her. Hafez tapped the table with his hand. Crossing her arms, face burning, Amani realized she was starting to feel the alcohol. Her perceptions brightened, the room seemed to slide a few inches in one direction, then return to its proper place. Sheltzer unfolded the paper with some difficulty, shook it out, and cleared his voice.

It took a few moments to understand that he was reading a poem. It was a bit odd. Something about ways of looking at a king, something about night. He got to a section about an octopus:

> Hidden in the body, like the octopus' beak,
> The awareness of the passage. The whirl
> through time
>
> The octopus unfurls to grasp the currents
> Yet there is nothing there
> But the time we float upon in our dreams.
> Stay sleeping then, let his limbs unwind.

After a beat of silence the man lifted his eyes to the guests, glanced around, and smiled faintly. For a second, no one moved or spoke. Sheltzer fumbled the paper back into his pocket. His smile vanished and he said, "Well, thank you," and returned to his seat. Amani, who was still thinking about what she'd heard—*Octopus?*—looked around the room and suspected that this was not how one was meant to write about the King. She took a breath, then started clapping into the silence. Eduardo and her father joined in. "Yes! Wonderful!" Gabe coached the table. The King had started applauding.

Others joined them. Polite applause rippled along the table. Amani could see the relief lift from Sheltzer. He half rose, half bowed, then sank into his seat.

"They almost threw that guy to the lions," Eduardo muttered. "Maskeen." Poor fellow.

"I think he owes us one," Amani said with a half-smile. The salon was increasingly loud, warm with inebriation. She turned toward the writer and caught his eye, asking, "Did you write that specially for this occasion?"

He pressed his forehead with a linen napkin. "At this point I'm no longer sure *what* I was thinking."

She chuckled. "That's the best way to write something. Don't you think? I mean when you don't know what you're thinking about— you can sort of find it in the writing." She felt some presence then, like a pressure at the back of her hand, and lowered her glass of wine. "It's how the peace process should happen. Not that anyone's asking me." She smiled and sat back. "But no one's going to forget what's past—and I'm not sure if that's really such a great idea. You have to remember things if you want to move forward from it. Otherwise, you get really stuck—one holocaust turns into another kind of violence. Whether it's being done to you or you're doing it to someone else, everyone's still trapped."

"And yet some of us love our traps," he said wryly.

On the other side of the table, a woman stopped to introduce herself to Sheltzer, cutting him off from their conversation. But Eduardo moved incrementally closer to Amani, his shoulder seeming to edge the others out. "I like this—finding things in your writing."

Amani smiled at her plate. "It's like—we need to find another way of putting things. The Arabs and Israelis—I think they need to sort of write something new. Record their separate histories, claim their memories—acknowledge them. But also write the narrative of a different future."

"So your poetry—it's of remembrance?" Eduardo asked.

She took a bite of something airy and chocolate, then another, before she said, "When I was writing poetry, I was trying to hear myself, to learn what I sounded like. I think someone said that it takes a long time to sound like yourself. But more and more, I'd rather know what other people sound like. And I wanted to write about being here." She gestured toward the painted ceiling and chandeliers. "And all this beauty and history. I don't know. I guess I'm still finding my way."

"There's something both majestic and yet indirect about Jordanian culture."

She smiled because she had a sense of what he meant.

He took a sip of wine. "Will you read something to us as well? Of yours?"

She laughed at the suggestion. "Sorry. I don't carry my poems around with me."

"That's our loss then."

"Don't be so sure about that."

Shifting, Eduardo propped one arm on the back of his chair. "You are working on something new? Are you here, in Jordan, for literary inspiration?"

"Oh, well, I'm always working." She shook her head. "Am I finishing—that is the question." Studying the half-eaten pastry on the bone china, she turned it thoughtfully: it bore a sugar disk stamped with the Jordanian seal. "I'm not working," she said then, surprising herself with her own admission. "I've been fighting . . . to bring my mind into focus somehow—in the right way. Sometimes I really truly think I don't know how to write anymore. Really—I think I never did." She felt a flash of embarrassment.

Eduardo's light eyes rested on hers. "You know, there is something I tell my fencing students: Never fight. Only flow."

She looked back down at the sugar confetti: it was dusted with iridescence so it seemed to float above the tablecloth. "My mother has a saying like that."

"She must be a very wise woman." He smiled.

"It's a lesson I have to keep learning." Amani nudged a line of confetti with her fingertip into a more perfect swirl, then touched her fingertip to her tongue: vanilla. "Actually, I do have a little project. I have a letter—it talks about a place, here in Jordan, with a castle and a cemetery. I want to try to find it."

"A castle and a cemetery? Any other details?"

"I'm afraid not." Her chin lifted. "It was just a note in an old letter. But I'm going to do this. Find this place. It's become rather important to me."

Eduardo palmed the back of his neck, his eyes turning away from the table. He seemed to have forgotten about the party. "Castles—well. Jordan is overrun. We were invaded and occupied and rebuilt—too many times to count. Nabateans, Umayyads, the Romans. The Ottomans. And these days it's the land developers." He smirked. "All sorts of conquerors and would-be kings—all kinds of impressive leavings. I suppose the Crusader castles are the best known—scattered here and there. And plenty of cemeteries too." He shook his head. "I'm sorry, I'm afraid that doesn't help much."

AT THE END of the night, in the clamor of departure, Eduardo was surrounded by some of the young men in uniform. Amani rose hesitantly from the table—a waiter slid back her chair—but then several women gathered to ask her about her poetry—where could they find it? Were there books to buy? Lubna Waleeda, the woman who'd sat beside her, offered Amani a business card and asked if she might come to speak to her organization. When at last she freed herself, Amani found on her plate an ivory postcard stamped with a silver crown. Someone had written in blue ink: *I leave you to your admirers. Your company this evening was a pleasure. Call me please? Soon, inshallah. Yours, Edo.* With this was a business card, a tiny drawing of a fencer, one arm raised in a curl, the other thrusting a sword.

Amani turned it over: it bore Eduardo's name and the address of the Royal Pavilion and Sports Center.

SHE SCANNED the crowd for some glimpse of Eduardo, but the room was now packed with lingering dinner guests and newcomers arriving for the after-party. The room filled with laughter and perfumes. A beat of pain started in her right temple. She needed to get outside.

New activities had sprung up in other rooms as well: attendants set out card tables and backgammon sets. In a reception area, another orchestra with violins and qanoons began tuning their instruments. Guests waited before a raised stage. Gabe was nowhere to be seen and Amani wondered if she would ever get home. It was after one in the morning. She walked down the wrong corridors twice and had to be guided back. Passing the reception area, she saw her aunt Carole and uncle Hafez loitering near the stage, chatting with Lubna Waleeda. She was now twinkling, her hands sliding through the air. Amani noticed her aunt's face, something complicated in her expression. Amani watched them for a moment—realizing that her aunt hated this woman—then Hafez caught her eye and beckoned, but she only smiled and waved before moving on.

Amani found her father at the main entrance, ringed by a group of men in keffiyehs, most of whom held demitasses of coffee. His face bright, Gabe told her he would see her at home later. She put her hands on her hips and sighed, then said, "Oh fine."

She heard footsteps echo in the loud corridor, but when she turned around didn't see anyone coming toward her. Finally, she exited to the palace grand archway. The moon was cold, low and pointed, the stars crisp. A line of limousines waited in the circular drive at the base of the white steps, doors clipping open and shut. A driver in uniform emerged and trotted around to a passenger door. He held out his hand and Amani slipped inside, her senses steadier again. The car rolled away from the steps: beyond the windows the lights, the stars, the silhouetted trees melted together. She flashed on an old memory of lying stretched out on the backseat of her parents' car, watching lights stream together in strips, the sweetness of disorientation, of the night world. The city faded into the dark beyond the car and its soft turns, the street now so still and empty it had become another country. They passed a park like an island in the center of the street where children chased a ball, no adults in sight. She turned all the way in her seat, watching their small forms shining like reflections for as long as she could.

CHAPTER

9

THE BACK OF his wife's head whisked by, a well-sprayed wren's tail. It was the morning after the party and she was reassembling herself, one cosmetic at a time. Irritation drifted from Carole. How she'd changed! In the beginning, there'd been so much desire they couldn't keep away from each other. The memory made Hafez smile. Atom by atom, like a piece of wood petrified by stone, anger had displaced passion.

"How could you?" she was saying. "Really. How could you, Hafez? That horrible . . ."

"Hayati," he called her. My life. "But I had nothing to do with the invitations list."

She knew! Well, of course she did. She caught him every single time. There was so little to catch! Hafez didn't have affairs; he stole kisses. So innocent. He loved kisses, slow and luxurious and longing for more. But you couldn't have more, which was what made them devastating.

Last night at the King's dinner, Carole had drawn a bead on Mrs. Waleeda. Why, she wondered aloud, was this unknown seated nearer the head of the table than Hafez, or indeed, the wife of

Hafez? Who was she? Why was she seated next to Amani? What was the meaning of this? Hafez himself wasn't sure. Rafi and Mrs. Bosa had orchestrated the seating chart—with just a few incursions from Hafez. He didn't think he'd arranged to seat them together, but what an odd coincidence—especially for someone who didn't believe in coincidence. He wondered if some twist in his imagination, some imp of the perverse, had led to this arrangement. It was said that the guilty wish to be caught—the notion of acquiring a strict moral conscience appealed to him about as much as that of acquiring dementia.

Now Carole turned, hands on her hips, and speared him with her dark-blue look. "You may not do the seating charts, but you suggest. *Hayati.*" She threw the word back at him like a cheap ring. "You call up the social secretary and say, 'Invite my niece, my brother, and oh, how about that little number Madame X? In the painted-on dress?'"

Madame X? Madame X, he liked that.

"Ya wardi." Oh, my flower. "But you're so wrong. I would never, ever—" He followed her into the bathroom, where she was rubbing her face with a cream.

"Ya wardi," she muttered. "Hafez, you are wonderful at what you do, but you are always and forever looking for an angle. You attend the King's parties for favors. And networking." She ticked items off on her fingers. "And to see what the queen is wearing. But you. You won't even taste the soup unless there's some advantage to it."

"Is it lentil?"

"You invite your niece to show off; an Israeli to prove you're in support of the peace process. And if there's some little—little social climber that you can lean over and leer at—well, how could you resist?"

Now she was wiping the cream away with a hand towel. Why this exercise, with the cream and the towel and the more creams to come?

"But it wears on one, ya albi." My heart. "It gets old. I suppose your one redeeming virtue—if we can call it redeeming"—she splashed water over her face—"is that you're too self-absorbed to have an affair."

He snaked his arms around her from behind and peered shyly at her reflection over her shoulder. She didn't meet his eyes but let the water drip down into her pale-green dressing gown. "There is no one to fall for but you, my clementine."

A vertical line between her eyebrows. "Ha. Ha-ha."

"I've fallen down an entire staircase for you," he said. "I've broken every bone in my body. There is no more falling for anyone. There are no more bones."

She began brushing her hair with vigor. The bristles made a scraping sound. "Funny, funny Valentine." He watched her put down the brush and start rubbing some clear fluid into her skin. He kissed the side of her sticky cheek. She shot him a look. "Did you notice, by the way, your brother is looking quite a bit fitter than you or Farouq? Perhaps America isn't quite so barbaric after all."

He chuckled and stroked his stomach: he'd eaten two slices of birthday cake yesterday, necessitating more insulin, necessitating a late-late snack, resulting in heartburn for the remainder of the night. "That isn't saying much."

"Wouldn't it be funny," she said, putting down the lotion, "if you'd invited your brother to this duel and he beat the King? Imagine that." She walked out of his arms, wiped her hands on another towel. "That really would be funny."

Ah, still angry.

But leave it to Carole. Connecting all the dots, she finally worked out that Lubna Waleeda was at the dinner to stand in for the archbishop, who wasn't feeling well. Her connection to the archbishop— not to mention that Lubna's professional contacts, plus her wealth and old family name—gave her a superior ranking. Hafez wondered what Lubna and Amani had discussed. At one point in the evening, he thought he saw them looking in his direction. It was fortunate that Lubna was married—fortunate for everyone! Extra incentive for all involved parties to stay discreet. If their special relationship were discovered, it would go far worse for her.

Carole bent over the enamel jewelry box on her dresser, poking through it with her fingertips. "By the way. I gave Amani my necklace."

"Very good." He rolled back, crossed his arms comfortably. "Did I ever mention I think of her as my intellectual heir—"

"The Nefertiti. The one you gave me."

He uncrossed his arms.

"I didn't think you would mind," she said briskly, and swept out of the room.

SHE GAVE AWAY *that* necklace? His father, Munif, had given it to his mother, Natalia, when they married. It was part of Hafez's inheritance—what there was of it. To his knowledge, it was the only gift Munif had ever given his wife.

Back then, Munif Hamdan was tall and lean, with tumbling locks, a full mustache, eyes black and staring. *True Jordanian*, he called himself. Dissolute, lazy, and abusive toward the mother of his children. He was not, Hafez supposed, the most wonderful of fathers. And Munif's preference for his youngest son hadn't escaped Hafez. He'd named his eldest boy for a poet; number two, Farouq, for a king; but Gabriel—originally Jibreel—for a goddamn angel. Oh, he knew his father had always held Hafez in esteem. But esteem is not love. Sometimes it was even distaste. Hafez was too ambitious, too hungry—right from the start. He was a foreign element to his father. He remembered how Munif marveled at the teachers' reports, squinting and turning them over. But Jibreel—so playful, so quick to laugh—Munif wreathed in kisses.

"I am a true Jordanian!" Hafez hears.

"True Jordanian!" Munif bawling drunkenly, nearly flat on his back, sprawled on the thin cushions, one hand beating his chest.

When he was younger, Munif had panache, an insouciance, that Hafez found irresistible and tried to emulate. His father's eyes, penetrating, heavy-lidded, caught the imagination. He was able to recite verses of the pre-Islamic poets as he followed his sheep through night-filled fields.

But his mother. He blamed her for bringing Munif indoors. She hired Bedouin to tend the fields and animals. She would not be married to a nomad. She was a thinker, collector, tender of books. She'd grown up in Bethlehem, wearing good wool dresses and shoes her auntie sent her from Milan. She'd read Zola, Goethe, Epictetus, Longinus—some in translation to English, some in their original languages. In 1917, in the midst of the dissolution of the centuries-old Ottoman occupation, Natalia, her parents and two siblings, along with all their neighbors, had been driven from their homes by the retreating Turks. These soldiers, in a state of stunned desperation, walked through the streets, their jackets in tatters, boots broken, shooting men and children on sight, kidnapping women, stealing food and jewelry. Natalia's family were separated in the fleeing crowds. Her sister Intizar remained behind with her brother Khalil and their father: it would take the sisters twenty years to locate each other. Natalia and her mother boarded the Hijazi Rail line. From Amman, they walked twenty-three kilometers to the little town of Yara, where her mother had connections—the venerable Hamdan family.

When Natalia and her mother arrived at Munif's family home, her cotton stockings hung in shreds; she clung to an Arabic edition of *Grimm's Fairy Tales*. Their faces were streaked with grime and sweat. She was fourteen with dark, lovely, melancholy eyes. Munif was seventeen, the eldest of seven. They were legally joined within the year.

This was their marriage: Munif drank; after he got drunk, he walked the fields. Natalia read, cleaned, brooded. She told her children so many stories of lying on hillsides covered in greenery, floating in her books. When the Israelis moved into Palestine, she mixed them up with the Turks; she saw shadow-soldiers in fezzes, banded trousers, and bandoliers hiding in every corner of their venerable old house. Two of her babies died before Hafez was born, two more died after. He had a recollection of an infant, a small knot of fists at Natalia's chest. Little unnamed markers in the family cemetery. Girls, he supposed. Neighbors praised their family of all boys. A father's triumph. Natalia didn't live with them so much as she lived with her past—like all Palestinians—caught up in longing for their blessed history, unfaithful to their present. Munif's older sister, Lamise, would rant at her: why aren't the children fed? She'd pick up a frying pan and bang it with a metal spoon above Natalia's head as she stood over a tub of dishes. Wake up! Lamise called her kelbeh, haiwaneh, dog, animal, right in front of her own children, treated Natalia as if she were an incompetent servant. Once, Hafez saw his aunt strike his mother so hard her fingers left streaks on her face.

And what did Hafez do? He grew harder, a wafer of stone within his chest. He would be like his father, who watched it all in silence. Over the years, despite his drinking, Munif remained lean and elegant, his voice grew richer. Natalia grew squat, her back stooped by age forty, her eyes burning with memories. It was her fault, Hafez thought. Her fault that she'd lost all those children: she wasn't a natural mother or wife: she cared too much for her mind. She was a refugee. Sometimes he glimpsed his mother's face, gazing over his head, her expression never changing—as if she regretted her home, her husband, even her children. She stopped laughing. She was like all the Palestinians he'd come to know—scorning their new country. He'd seen it as a sign of weakness in his father that he'd married their mother: Hafez wished Munif had chosen better. Though, of course, then Hafez might not have been born at all. But he preferred to think he'd have been born a stronger version of himself, a better, purely Jordanian Hafez.

AN HOUR LATER, on his private mobile, his office door locked, he called and told Madame X that yes, decidedly yes, he'd started the wheels turning on securing that pardon and visa for her brother. It wasn't entirely an untruth. *Decidedly yes* might have been overstating the case. He hadn't actually done anything yet. There was no profit to be had in helping a journalist, but there had to be a way to keep her happy.

Wary at first, Madame X's voice began to defrost after he gave his assurances. The sooner my petition is dealt with, he'd added, the easier my mind will be, the sooner I can deal with your brother.

"Well it just . . . so . . . happens . . ." she said. "A little spot may have just opened in His Eminence's schedule today. Noon, in fact."

"Lunch?" His voice lifted. It was no problem for him to get an appointment with the archbishop, but Madame X sped things up ever so efficiently.

"You'd have to get in the car right now," she warned. "He's at a conference—it's down at Il Bahir. But this is a good chance to catch him. Otherwise, who knows. He's on the road a lot these days."

"No problem, my dear. The driver and I love an outing."

Before they hung up, she paused then said, "Your niece, by the way, is enchanting."

"Ya'ani," Well. "She is, isn't she?" he asked, stretching his neck and pleasurably scratching the underside of his chin.

It was early November, a fine day for a drive. They wound the soft curves of the King's Highway and Hafez let his mind wander over the memory of Madame X's bare shoulders at the birthday party. He recalled Carole's earlier comments with a twinge—she'd given away that necklace! Without even asking! He lowered the window and let the air rush over him. The stony earth turned to powder, a potion he inhaled through the open windows. *"Love Potion Number Ni-ee-ya—ee—ine. Love potion number nine."* He crooned softly in the backseat. Samir joined in for a few bars, but kept drumming out of sync on the steering wheel.

The archbishop was attending an ecclesiastical conference at the Dead Sea Mövenpick resort. A handful of clergy in black robes drifted through the dining room, murmuring and nodding to one another, carrying tiny cups and saucers. The reception hall signs announced panels on ministering to refugees; land rights and the Church; reconciling peace with justice. Hafez found Father Jacob at a table on the terrace overlooking the water. The air was sweet and limpid with turquoise light. Hafez stopped, bowed to the man; taking his spotted hand, he kissed his ring.

Jacob flicked his hand as if brushing away a fly. But he said, "Sit down. Sit. Sit." He sank his chin glumly on to the heel of his palm, folding his stiff gray beard forward. "So, you found me."

"How is your cold? Feeling better, I hope."

"My cold? Oh." He sniffed once. "Yes. Much better."

"Is this not a good time? Mrs. Waleeda told me—"

Again, the flitting gesture. "There is no good time, bad time. There is just time."

Holy men. No wonder the insides of churches made him itch. Hafez smiled. "I agree one thousand percent, Your Grace. And we mustn't waste a moment of it, which is why I come to you with potentially wonderful news."

"Potentially wonderful." The priest's smile was all but hidden by the wool of his beard. "Hafez, why do you so often make me feel I'm about to buy a really terrible car?"

Hafez chuckled—it was an obeisance, like kissing his ring. "I know you've been wanting to restore the chapel in Ma'an, correct? Isn't that the most historically significant site? While I can't offer to underwrite the entire thing, I'd like to be helpful."

The priest's heavy eyebrows lifted. He combed the backs of his fingers up from under his beard then back down through again. He didn't look at Hafez. "I'm listening."

Hafez had tried to mentally rehearse in the car, but now his stomach tightened. He took a breath. "There's a petition before you, for the disposition of an inheritance. Amer Amer, my cousin, Allah yerhamu," bless his soul, "left behind an estate, in land and cash, equivalent roughly to 275 million JDs."

The archbishop inhaled the steam from his tea, then replaced his cup with a small click.

"There was no will," Hafez said quietly. "And there's no imme-diate family. He lived with his mother—my grandfather's sister. When my great-auntie died, he was all alone. In fact," he added, "Amer Amer wasn't even Jordanian. His mother was second cousin to Natalia—Amer's parents from Gaza."

The bishop cleared his throat. "No siblings? First cousins?"

Hafez shook his head. "My mother was his closest relative—the property would all go to her house. And now, my brother Farouq and I are the only living relations. . . ." He picked an invisible crumb from his chest. "Also, it should be noted, I am firstborn."

The archbishop's eyes remained lowered.

"In our tradition, the Hamdan clan . . ."

"You have other siblings as I recall," the bishop interrupted.

Hafez sniffed. "Well. Two girls, and my second brother, Ra'ed, all died in infancy. . . ."

"Were you truly firstborn, Hafez?" The archbishop squinted at the windows. "It seems to me . . . I'm not sure."

His mind turned white. What did Jacob remember? Hafez collected himself: he filled his chest. There were so many lost children—who could keep track! Not so long ago, Amman was the size of a country village, the archbishop was merely Jacob and his family were distant poor relations to Hafez's family. While unlikely, perhaps it was possible Jacob remembered how many Hamdan brothers there had been. They were a Christian family in a Muslim country, so their land inheritance had to be studied and approved by the Church. Hafez needed the man's approval to be deeded the estate; he also needed to purchase Jacob's forgetfulness. He tried again. "In the Hamdan clan, the rule is that the firstborn son inher-its his father's property."

"But if, for whatever reason, there is no living firstborn son, the estate is then divided up among the remaining heirs," the archbishop said. His eyes framed by his beard seemed to Hafez intensified some-how, like those of women in hijab.

Hafez tipped his head to one side then the other: *Maybe, maybe not.*

The archbishop picked up his tea. "And isn't there another brother?"

Hafez put his hand on the table as if taking an oath. "Gabe. He lives in the States. But, you know—he converted, ages ago." Under the table, he crossed his legs, one foot bobbing.

"He said the Allah illahu?" Father Jacob's forehead lifted.

"In the military," Hafez said. The Church would disqualify a Muslim from inheriting what they deemed a Christian estate.

The archbishop picked up his cup. Hafez picked up his cup. He followed the man's gaze past the terrace to the gleam of water. He'd never liked the Dead Sea. Il Bahir didn't roar like a proper sea but laid there, buzzing, flat, magnetic, a tile glowing under the sun. He hated the way its water clung to the skin, how you had to shower right away after touching it or it dried into white mineral, shriveling the body. The last time he'd been made to go in the sea, it was because the King's aide-de-camp devised a team-building exercise for a meeting of diplomatic envoys and attachés. It was impossible to swim. Even to remain upright was a struggle. His posterior had bobbed up, then his stomach, like a cork. Afterward, he escaped to the shower the first moment he could, but he still caught whiffs of that sulfurous water for days.

"Neither of my brothers know anything of this, for obvious reasons," Hafez said, his gaze fixed on the far horizon. "It's a sensitive matter. Neither of them had anything to do with Amer, and there's no point to troubling them with this situation—at least until everything is settled."

Beyond the Dead Sea were the sage-and-almond-colored reaches of their country. Hafez sighed deeply, charged with reflection. Once upon a time, no one cared. Just a little neck of land, a corridor to cross between greater, older nations, called Trans-Jordan. Flyover zone. Set in place to buffer Syria, Egypt, Iraq, its borders stretching hither and yon, with no natural demarcation. A British concoction. "Winston Churchill's Sneeze," they called it. The Brits imported a king—the King's grandfather—from the Hijaz and kept in him in armies and under protection; they had to watch their backs since the French had helped themselves to Syria.

So much claiming and chopping, so many invaders, but this was homeland to Hafez—his breath and bread. This inheritance was the start of a long-overdue restoration. A making-whole. He'd eventually have to shave off bits to mollify and arrange cooperation—from Farouq, from the Archbishop, from a few secondary cousins. Most importantly, he was planning to offer Gabe a swap: land for a knife! A little spot near the water, in the graceful, fertile Ghor—the Jordan valley—to build a home. He saw the longing in Gabe's eyes—it had been a master stroke to bring him back. It was there in the way his brother had jogged out on that falconry field, his body light and fluid. He saw joy in his movements. Who could resist the delicious call of childhood?

"Hafez." The archbishop turned his teacup in his hand. Hafez noticed a jet-black rosary twined between the man's fingers. "You know that God sees everything you do. Not just what you profess."

Hafez glanced at the sky, a couple of clouds drifting in from the west. *Hafez, you could charm the angels from the trees*, his mother used to say, *but you don't fool me.* "All is well between me and my God," Hafez said.

"But what about *my* God?" The bishop replaced the cup. He moved the rosary beads with his thumb. After a moment, he said, with maddening persistence, "Truly, I'd thought there was another brother."

Hafez nodded slowly, uncertain if the holy man was toying with him or if he really couldn't remember. He took a risk: "Perhaps you're thinking of my cousin Musa?" He lowered his chin. "He vanished years ago. Around the time the Turks were in Jordan, taking boys for their army. Presumed dead. God rest his soul."

"Did he have no children?"

"No, no, none. He was taken so young." Hafez sighed heavily. He studied the man's eyes, so damp they looked almost gelled, their color of faded darkness. It wasn't right, he thought, to be led by those least able to enjoy the fruits of the world. Swaddled in his robes and acorn-shaped turban, the priest ignored the dish of chocolate and cake and white cream the waiter put before them. The thought of Madame X rose in Hafez, evoking her scent of almonds, evaporating in a trace of sugared smoke, fortifying him such that he declared again, almost happily, "But it's the law, isn't it? What can one do?"

The archbishop exhaled through his nose, the cushion creaking as he sat back, fingers tented, gazing at the silvery length of water in the window.

After a moment, Hafez said, "I . . . This is a very—draining—issue for me. But when all this paperwork is worked out, if the money is there, perhaps you and I could look at building a new chapel? Something near the sea? With a view—like this . . ." Tentatively at first, then with a growing sense of hope and urgency, of overcoming resistance through persuasion, Hafez pressed on. "It's essential for people to understand our country is not a Muslim monolith, that we embrace all identities. Christianity has educated and enriched the Middle East." Sitting back, he laced his fingers over his stomach and enumerated the wonders of Cordoba, Spain, its multicultural architecture and religious diversity; he spoke of the tenth-century Jewish Andalusian writer who advised his community, "Let Scripture be your Eden and the Arabs' books your paradise grove." He mentioned the great tradition of Muslims guarding Christian monuments: the Joudah family in Jerusalem, entrusted with the keys to the Church of the Holy Sepulchre, passing them down generation after generation.

Mystery, authority, and faith make the world go 'round. This inheritance could make many good things happen. Imagine, he thought, how a bequest might improve his youngest brother's life as well as that of his wife and daughter. Having lapsed into silence, Hafez studied the dwindling light in the windows—it was getting darker so much earlier these days. He nudged the plate toward Father Jacob. "The desserts here are outstanding—you really should have a taste."

The archbishop waved it away. "I must be getting back."

"Not one bite?"

The man touched the center of his chest. "Please have mine. *Sahtain*."

"Gladly. Though I do hate to rob the Church!" he joked. Hafez took a forkful from the near corner and said, "Fourteen hundred years ago or so, the Patriarch Sophronius entrusted the keys of Jerusalem to Umar ibn Khattab—a Muslim!" He took another bite.

The priest smiled and lifted his eyes. "An act of faith."

"Indeed. And it is the only way to get anything done—like the leap that precedes our own peace talks! Think what a monument to faith we could build, together. Think of what you could achieve with an extra 100,000 dunums of land. A chapel that could stand as tribute to peace itself. The Israelis—they see Muslims as troublemakers—well, let's speak openly: as terrorists. They see how Arabs in other countries suffer under their own leadership—the heart cries out for the Syrians, enduring Hafez Assad."

The archbishop shook his head. "Ya haram. May God have mercy."

"By enlarging the public profile of a healthy Christian community, we expand on our image as a country of both East and West. It instills confidence in the Israelis, a sense of fraternity—both of us people of the book."

"Well, yes. And the Muslims," the archbishop said. "They, too, venerate Abraham and Jesus."

"By helping the Church, we're actively helping the peace process—the King's greatest endeavor."

The archbishop didn't reply. He brushed at what might have been a dusting of dandruff down his front. He frowned, but didn't speak.

"Of course, we shouldn't forget—the Palace is continually on the lookout for resettlement lands—places to stash the refugees. Land like this, in transition—they declare it 'unassigned.' Neither of us can speak of this inheritance—not one word—or all the property will be in danger of confiscation." Hafez shifted his gaze out to the aluminum glow of the Dead Sea. Later, he would stop at the gift shop and buy lotions for his wife. She always said that the minerals of Il Bahir were the best for reviving the skin. "You and I both," he told the priest. "We could lose it all. And that would be a shame." He took another bite of the chocolate: it really was very good cake.

CHAPTER

10

SHE'D TOSSED, reawakening in the hours before dawn, then lain sleepless in bed, running her fingertip over the pendant on her chest, Nefertiti's tiny bas-relief features. She remembered the other night at the dinner party, Eduardo had asked what had drawn her father to fencing. "Honestly," she'd told him, "I didn't even know that he'd fenced until he got the invitation."

He'd smiled. "Fencers give nothing away."

The bedroom was cool in the early morning. Shivering, Amani finally threw back her covers. She sat up and rooted through the blankets for her T-shirt and jeans. Moving quietly through the kitchen, she made a cup of Nescafé and brought the steaming cup back upstairs. At her desk, she studied the letter: her grandmother's pen had left a faint impression on the paper. The dim lights of the city glowed in her window: three a.m., too early even for the first call to prayer. She reread a poem she'd been laboring over for weeks, pressed her lips together in frustration. Finally, she hit the X key over and over, then highlighted the whole thing and hit Delete. The office chair creaked as she rocked to her feet, to rummage through some of the books stacked on the floor—all found at the marketplace stalls around the town center: the translated works of Nawal El Saadawi, Liyana Badr, Adonis, Amos Oz, Hanan al-Shaykh. There were several works in Arabic that she couldn't read but loved for the way the covers were engraved with golden calligraphy—fairy tales, poetry, and legends, according to the booksellers, men in threadbare robes, their keffiyehs twisted in folds around their heads.

Amani once had an idea of what poetry was supposed to be. Something to do with language and compression and observation. She'd thought that one was meant to write fearlessly—as a book reviewer had said she had done in her collection. But she'd begun to lose faith. It seemed as if it wasn't worth so much to write fearlessly if you didn't know what to fear. She'd started to think maybe it was more courageous just to be afraid.

That afternoon, Omar came over and he, Gabe, and Amani took a cab to Hafez and Carole's house in Abdoun. They got out at busy Zaghloul Street, passed rows of ivory-colored buildings, then turned onto a lane lined with fragrant, dreamy eucalyptus. Hafez's house overlooked a glass-tile front courtyard and a splashing fountain. The white roof and surrounding treetops seemed to be sheared away by the low sun. It retreated behind distant clouds, and for a moment Amani felt loosened from things—lighter, as if she'd lost her bearings. Omar was scolding Gabe: the fencing match! This was not the time for drinking and feasting. "Amo, we should be at the gym right now," he said, walking backwards to frown at his uncle.

"It's just for show," Gabe repeated patiently. "Not a real match. Ninety percent sitting and talking, ten percent fencing."

They turned up the stone walkway: the sounds of laughter came through the door. Her father stopped on the front step. "There's a hefleh." A party. "He said it was just going to be a little get-together."

Omar bent to peer through one of the windows. "It's Hafez. This *is* a little get-together."

Amani glanced at the forms moving behind translucent curtain panels. She knocked and the door eased open. A commotion of greetings overtook them as they entered. Gabe and Omar accepted glasses of araq. Amani smiled a bit deliberately, moving her eyes around the room. She kept thinking about the woman at the party saying—*Ask your uncle*. Her lipsticked smile: *He knows where all the skeletons are buried.*

"Aha—people I'm actually happy to see!" Hafez declared, throwing his arms around Gabe, and several people laughed. There were great-uncles, second cousins, a few neighbors with adult children with their own small children. "Look at this. It's like Bedu at Wadi Rum and their ten thousand relations."

"He invites everyone then complains when they come." Carole put a glass of wine in Amani's hand. "This is my life. I don't know who half these people are. They just appear on the lawn." She waved a hand. "Meanwhile, you two . . ." She turned to Gabe. "I was starting to wonder what we'd have to do to bring you for a proper visit. It's like waiting for Italian movie stars."

Hafez steered Gabe to a gathering of men seated in a ring on chairs and couches in the main living area: a blue cloud of cigarette smoke floated over their heads. "Come, come. Let me play host. Did you know that in Arabic the word for 'host' and 'torturer' is the same thing?" He slapped Gabe's back with a laugh. "Look here—a roomful of power brokers, y'akhi—a bunch of desert sheikhs. These guys, they own all the well water." Gabe shot Amani an anxious backward glance as Hafez ushered him in.

She watched the two brothers together. Hafez was larger than her father, with an energy that seemed to swing just as easily toward menace as charisma. Something had shifted incrementally in her view of her uncle. Carole brought Amani to the parlor, where the women were deep in gossip, switching casually between Arabic and English. Several embraced Amani, kissing and pinching her cheeks as if she were twelve. After patting her legs and asking politely in English how she was and how was her father, they turned back to their conversation in Arabic. She sank into the couch, her eyelids heavy. After what seemed hours of drowsy listening, Amani was relieved when she saw Omar appear in the crowd of women.

"Omar, no, no." Carole stood. "Out. Please. Go back to the men. Dinner will be served in two minutes."

"I was telling Amani the other day about your pine-syrup drink— do you think we could have some?"

"Oh, that sounds interesting." Amani stood.

Annoyed, Carole tried again to dismiss Omar but he laced his hands together, pleading. "Aw, please. It's the best stuff—like delicious medicine. Auntie does all these syrups and spice mixes right here in the house."

Carole scowled but then her face softened. "Shu, Omar?" What now. She gestured toward the back of the house. "Go tell Mrs. Ward to give you some in the kitchen. Then Amani, promise you'll come to me—we can eat out on the terrace, where the younger set are." She put her hand on Amani's forearm.

In the kitchen, Sadia and Mrs. Ward hurried between the refrigerator, sink, and counters. Soros, the old landscaper, was washing dishes, a wrathful expression on his lined face. Mrs. Ward glanced at Amani but didn't stop moving. Sadia huffed and lifted big pots, making obvious circuits around Amani and Omar. They tried to move out of the way. "Thank you," Amani mumbled to her cousin.

But more relatives came into the kitchen. More kisses. Someone asked about her dear husband, and she said, oh he's fine. A great-uncle kept asking her questions in English about her "studies" while not understanding her answers. Carole walked through, announcing that anyone who wanted to eat mansaf with their hands would have to go to the side porch. "The rest of us will be given silverware at the table."

Eventually, Soros looked over from the sink and snapped at them in Arabic; Amani understood something about donkeys taking up space. She excused herself to go to the bathroom. On her way through the living room, Uncle Hafez himself approached her. "My dear one." He put an arm around her. "I'm so glad you're here. Are you enjoying yourself?"

She felt that momentary hitch. And he smiled and said, "Oh, of course you're not. I know, my dear."

They moved—or he drew them—around a corner, so they stood in a hallway. "The first weeks in a foreign country are terrible. You can be anywhere. Monaco to Zimbabwe. One always asks oneself, Now, exactly why am I *here*? It's even worse for you Americans, I think. You're so unused to travel."

Now Amani smiled. "That sounds more like a character failing than a reason for sympathy."

Hafez waved this away. "Not at all. Look at your poor dad. He grew up here and he seems absolutely paralyzed."

Amani tried to peer around the corner but saw only a crowd of men waving cigarettes.

"I wish we'd had more time together, when you were growing up," he said, a tenderness in his face. It was the very same thought she'd had as a child. It had always been so exciting—those rare occasions when Uncle Hafez suddenly appeared at their house, as if from a puff of smoke. "But you're here now—alhamdullilah! There are such places I'd like to show you."

"I'd love that," Amani said. "I've barely been outside of Amman. I hear I should see the Crusader Castles."

"This is an important time for you here, I think. Maybe more than a visit." Hafez's face was solemn. "This is your heritage, after all."

"Absolutely. And I'm so glad you managed to bring us over."

"Sometimes the mountain must come to Muhammad," he said with a chuckle.

"I think this is such an important trip too. I want to learn this place. I want to know about Natalia. My father never told me—just—much of anything."

Hafez's smile deepened, but there was something fixed about his eyes and she felt he wasn't quite looking at her. "Which doesn't surprise me."

"I used to ask, but he said he couldn't remember. He always says carpenters aren't paid to think."

"You can ask me anything you like, my dear," he said, opening his arms expansively.

"I just want to know who she was." Amani felt slightly breathless, the pressure of unformulated questions. "I have so little sense of her as a person."

"As a person? Oh, I think children have no idea who their parents are. If they're lucky. I can tell you that your grandmother was obsessed with reading and writing. She clung to these forms of escape. She was ruined by the loss of her original home and family, which led to raising a family that was . . . intensely challenged." He spoke in a blunt, matter-of-fact way.

Amani blinked, eyebrows lifting.

Her uncle placed one hand against his chest. "Honestly? Your grandmother was weak. A weak individual. I'm being totally candid with you. She was self-centered and not very interested in her kids. She wrote compulsively—to no end. She went a bit mad, I think. These are harsh things to say about one's mother. No matter how true. At a certain point, your father, and Farouq, and I were more or less left to raise ourselves."

Something shifted in Amani's face. "She went mad? But—Dad never—"

Hafez shook his head. "No, no, not raving. Nothing exciting. She went mad the way the Palestinians do: from a fatal obsession with what's lost."

One of the sheikhs emerged from a back room and called to Hafez. "Not to worry my dear," he told Amani. "Family first. We're built on that wonderful old Arab expression—what is it? 'Me against my brother, my brother and I against the stranger?'" He nodded at her briefly before excusing himself. "There is time," he said. "We will talk about everything." She looked after him. When she'd mentioned Natalia, Hafez's eyes had gone so still. It was one thing to invite questions, apparently, and quite another to have them asked. His answer was either very honest or very angry, she thought. And had also felt like a challenge.

Amani turned down the corridor, in search of the restroom. Always so many cups of tea at these things. The house was bigger than she'd remembered. The master and guest bedrooms were in the wing to the left, off the kitchen. To the right was another dim passage. Amani walked down the tile corridor, and the party noise dropped off as if muffled by a veil. Amani peered through the first open doorway; it was a small, plain bedroom, evidently for one of the staff. The next door was closed. She moved on and found a bathroom at the end of the hall, but then noticed that it was filled with someone's personal effects—soaps, razor, and medicines—clearly not for guests. She used it quickly, making sure to straighten the towels.

On her way back to the party, Amani stopped again to look at the closed door. It had an old-fashioned cut-glass knob on a bronze plate. She had the most uncanny sensation that there was someone in that room. Tipping her head to the door panel, she wondered if she heard breathing. Amani looked around, then squatted. Light shone through a large keyhole. She put her hands on the door and peered through the hole, then stood and rapped softly. After a moment, she turned the knob. There was no one there, just two narrow mattresses pressed against opposite walls, rough, polyester bedspreads on each, flat pillows, a single shared nightstand and lamp with a yellowing shade. She went in, looking around. On one side, the bedspread was iron-straight and tucked at the corners. The other bed was just a mattress covered with a fitted sheet. A few pieces of furniture were shrouded in drop cloths and the corner of a wooden armoire was visible. The walls were bare, aside from a single ornament hanging from a chain: a ceramic blue hand with an eye in the center of its palm.

She turned, her senses seeming to dilate; she saw each tiny fissure in the wall, the grain of the dust cloths. She heard the drum of her pulse in her ears, then froze at the sound of someone approaching. Omar appeared in the hallway and she felt a dizzy rush of breath. "Jesus. You scared me."

"Yo—this is, like, the servants' part of the house." He leaned inside the doorframe. "Those boys out there are getting wasted. If you're spying you better hurry. I think Sadia likes to sneak cigs back here when no one's watching."

"Yeah. I'd want a hideaway too." Amani touched the old armoire. It was small but well-made with panels and drawers with batwing pulls, decorative plates down the front. Her father would be able to take one look and say something like federal, or regency, or late French Renaissance.

"Cuz, I don't know about this." Omar still hung back in the doorway, looking over one shoulder as if expecting someone to appear. "I think I'm getting creeped out."

"Wait—wait." Amani noticed an open wooden box filled with old-fashioned costume jewelry—faux pearl bracelets and brooches. "So check this out."

"What the fuck." Omar came into the room and picked up a silver cuff. "What is all this?"

She took an earring with a big blue stone and held it up to her ear in the mirror. Settling on the side of the bed, she picked through the pieces—a pin covered with green rhinestones, a cameo, some gold chains.

Omar looked around the room. "What's in this thing?" He opened the big wooden armoire and there was a scent of cedar and eucalyptus and linen. Amani returned the jewelry to the wooden box and went to peer into the armoire. A few embroidered dresses hung from wooden hangers. There were painted ceramic plates, a shelf filled with classics: *Candide, Middlemarch, Wuthering Heights, Frankenstein, Don Quixote.* Under a lower row of unpainted shelves, she noticed a narrow drawer. Inside was an onionskin envelope.

Removing it, Amani sat back on the edge of the bed. The envelope was filled with scraps of blue paper and aerograms. They appeared to have been torn apart and crumpled, then carefully smoothed out. "This is Natalia's handwriting." She leaned over them, sifting through the pieces. "Some of it's in English. They look like poems.

Or meditations? Just—pieces of things, it looks like. Fits and starts." She read:

The wind blew up the scent of tea and saffron and these too were the creations of storybooks. Princess Rosemary walked the earth in her robes of green, her power of good and evil: to make you remember to never let go. Because magical power is like that—good and evil both.

Among the scraps, she found a small fragment of a black-and-white photograph: a teenaged boy sitting cross-legged. "Doesn't this look a little like my dad?" She showed it to Omar, who shrugged.

"Well, that's cool yet depressing," Omar said; he returned to the doorway and poked his head out. "What do you say, let's get out of here."

"I think this is all her stuff." Amani looked around. "Hafez must've taken it out of the old house in Yara."

"And stashed it here like the psycho he is," Omar said. "Like in a museum."

"Or a mausoleum," Amani muttered, turning the photograph in her fingers. She returned the picture to the onionskin envelope, which she slid into her shoulder bag.

"Excellent," Omar said. "Hang on to the evidence."

Someone appeared at the start of the corridor. "Hold up," Omar muttered. He went forward to intercept the person. She heard him launch into a cheerful volley of Arabic.

She left the room, quietly closing the door behind her. Breezing up the hallway, she passed Omar and another of their cousins, a woman with kohl-lined eyes whose name she'd forgotten. "Nope— that wasn't the guest bathroom," Amani said.

Her father was with a clutch of men sitting on cushions outside on the verandah. The air around them was sweet with the vapor rising from bottles of araq. She bent to his ear. "Want to get out of here?" She stood and waved to the others. "Sorry. Got to head out—poetry calls." Farouq was there holding a drink with both hands, his face puffy. "Ya bint!" he croaked at Amani. *Girl.* "Sit with us—have a drink. We're tired of each other." He slapped a seat.

It took Gabe a minute to unfold himself from the low cushion and push himself upright. "Okay, okay." He waved to the others as if they were far away. "Time to go now, bye-bye."

The others called after them, "Where are you going? Y'akhi. Come back!" Amani let her father lead her to the door, as if she needed the help. Omar took her opposite arm. Gabe waved without turning to look back.

CHAPTER

11

It's only sensible—anyone who wants to stay on top needs watchers on the bottom. Lamise's daughter, Abla, for instance. Sometimes he takes her to the café in Fuheis and she spills the family gossip. Yesterday, she saw his niece take a wrong turn down the rear wing of their house. She was there for at least several minutes, Abla reported. *At least.* Abla was going to check on her but Omar intervened. Hafez considered Amani: intelligence shining from her bold eyes, yet she often seemed younger than her age: snooping down the hall with her twenty-year-old cousin. So many questions about the family history—what was this about? A kitten batting at a shadow. Still though, she took after him, didn't she? She didn't accept the easy answers.

And what imagination, what delicacy he'd seen in her poetry. He'd reread her book. Then he looked up some of her essays. A mind like hers—she'd soon tire of family lore. He imagined a radiant future: he saw them working together, a government appointment for Amani, doing important work in the Ministry of Culture.

The boy brought coffee and a diamond of syruped namoura to the table.

The pastry was too wet. Hafez muttered under his breath as he put down his fork. He didn't feel right today. Not yesterday either. Perhaps he was coming down with a bad case of himself. He poured sugar into the thimble of coffee, stirring the black eye within its porcelain circle. He liked this coffeehouse for its anonymity, farther from the crowds of Rainbow Street. Women riffled by in their black shrouds as if afraid even to pause near the open doorway. The tiles of the old Husseini mosque were just visible to him through its side door. "Why not, why not, why not?" he muttered to himself. It was like a chant, a new mantra. Hafez put down the spoon and glared fiercely at the other customers—all men—the TV on the wall, filled with the head of a mullah, hands lifted. "Why not everything?"

Soros, his gardener, kitchen helper, and occasional fixer, who'd also noticed Amani using his bathroom, offered to question her "lightly." No, no light questions, Hafez told him.

How much would he share with her? Why not everything? Not even his wife knew the whole story.

Hafez re-stirred his coffee—tiny spoon ringing against the sides—deliberately sweeping the bitter grounds back into the liquid. His eyes roamed over the coffeehouse, the crowded, doll-like tables, the air thick with argileh smoke, a TV in the corner blaring a political rant, some sort of quasi-religio-political invective. Swimming through the static, the ghost of the mullah raised his arms and told them not to trust the American lies: that the devil came smiling in a beautiful dress, covered in a thousand points of light.

He wondered if his brother was prompting Amani. Gabe was becoming tiresome. At the King's reception, at family gatherings, the most inopportune times, his brother would corner him and ask: What happened? Don't you remember any of it?

Enough! Didn't Gabe have enough already? Was Hafez expected to be the guardian of family history just because he was a few years older? And why did Gabe always have that accusatory look? There were a few other unpleasantries he might raise with his younger brother.

THEY WERE ALL TOGETHER, a gang—all those international kids. Jordanians, yes. Also boys from Egypt and Turkey and Malta. Fredo and Claude, Nader, and that Irish kid? Horace? Mostly they dated American girls: back then, the Old World sent only their boys overseas. Pouring resources into (and giving liberties to) their girls was unthinkable. But with so many wonderful, inquisitive American coeds, one never felt a lack.

And the day he glimpsed Francesca. Oh. He still remembered. It was at that ice-cream shop where they all went. She had just come in and stood before the front window, adjusting her gloves. Her head was lowered so her hair spilled forward like a lampshade. Her lashes made tiny crescent shadows on her cheeks. She looked not quite American—her clothing not exactly fashionable, yet tasteful, too well made. Pearl, he thought. The light in the place turned crystalline, filtered by the snowfall outside. No wonder religions worship the untouched woman. He felt consecrated in her presence.

That boy, what was his name? A kid from the little village next door to Francesca's—he'd already claimed her. And she went along with it because that's just what the girls did, the good ones, they let the boys claim them. So she was claimed and chained—everyone knew it. Even Hafez, who accepted nothing, accepted this inevitability. Though, oh, how many nights he lay in bed thinking of those crescent shadows on her cheeks, the small pool of shadow beneath her lower lip.

Then that skinny Sicilian kid, he got really sick, pneumonia or meningitis, one of those things that tore through newcomers. He was stuck in the shared bed at the boardinghouse and Gabe slept on the floor so the Sicilian could have the bed. And all that time that Francesca spent at the side of the bed waiting, Gabe waited with her. Maybe at first it was for the sick boy, but after a few weeks, they waited with each other. The boy went back home, limp and half-dead, and Francesca stayed behind. And Gabe comforted her, even though Hafez saw her first. By that point Hafez had moved to his adviser's house in a faculty neighborhood on the other side of the Hill. He was given a guest room and the nicest bed he'd ever slept in, and his adviser's wife cooked him breakfast in the morning and brought him tea at night. These comforts distracted him from pursuing Francesca.

No one to blame but himself: he'd given away, yet again, what could have been his. Again to that brother, the troublesome, greedy, youngest. The beloved.

It was a Saturday, maybe six months after they'd arrived in America. Gabe worked through the weekends: he worked all the time, at restaurants mostly, washing dishes and cleaning tables and mopping floors. Upon arriving, his English had been practically nonexistent; he had no interest in attending college, but in the two months since meeting Francesca, he was showing a remarkable aptitude for languages.

For some reason, Gabe wasn't working on this day. It was a morning, in Hafez's memory, that glistened. He'd put on the warm parka, hat, and gloves that his adviser had given him and walked to Onondaga Lake. The sky glowed with milky light. He and his brother met on the lakeshore for a stroll, stealing a bit of time away from work and school—that's all there ever was for them in those days: work, work, work for Gabe, study, study, study for Hafez.

Surprise, she was there, she of the crescent shadows and billowy hair. He knew, of course, they all knew, those foreign kids—she'd fallen for Gabe. They were never apart. Hafez lost not only the girl but the brother, too, come to think of it. It was so bright and so cold on that day, the air so sharp, their breath coming in white puffs. It was so beautiful it hurt his heart. Everything did in those days. By then, their father was dead and their mother was three-

quarters mad, and they were alone on this fierce planet. The lake
was frozen hard—untouched in the early light, snow-dusted, skating with tiny rivulets of wind. Hafez crunched through the frozen
reeds and stalks at the water's edge. He laughed and said, "Look!
Look at this!" His first step onto solid ice was magical. A pure
moment. It lifted him as he went walking out onto the lake. The
wind rose, buoying him. He put out his arms for balance: he felt as
if the wind might cast him right into the sky. He looked over one
shoulder and saw Gabe at the edge, trying to follow him—just as
he'd done when they were at the opposite ends of childhood. But
Gabe didn't have the nerve that Hafez did. Gabe would look down:
the ice would crack. Hafez told him *no*, but he couldn't be heard in
all that wind.

His brother took a few cautious steps. Then Francesca walked
among the frozen reeds. And although she and Gabe had only
recently started holding hands they traded a look; she said something, and Gabe waved to him, gesturing, *Come back*, and turned
toward shore.

It felt like fire licking up the center of his chest. Gabe had followed
the girl—a total stranger—instead of his own brother! Infuriated,
Hafez walked out even farther, the surface making tiny crackling
sounds under the coating of snow. The wind whipped his hair and
iced his lungs. He thought he heard them calling to him. The air
drew tears from the corners of his eyes. He clenched his teeth in
a fierce grin. This girl had come to America, the United States of
Amnesia, so young she had no accent. She was just as spoiled as any
American-born—used to getting whatever she desired. And this felt
to Hafez like a day of forgetting—the air so icy and blue, it was obvious why this was called the New World. It was a day to make him
forget everything.

He'd been married a scant ten months by that time. Carole didn't
want children—not just yet, she kept saying. Their birth control
method—thick, desire-killing condoms. As such, he'd started to
question what the actual point of marriage in America might be,

without some family or church to appease. He was starting to suspect he'd been duped. He reminded himself of his significance: he was going to do important things in the world. He'd won a big fellowship to pursue Near Eastern Studies at Yale: he and Carole would be moving to New Haven in the spring. Certainly Carole would change her mind about children.

The trees on the hills looked frozen, their branches like shocked hands, finger bones outspread, the earth stark white. The ice changed color under his feet as he walked and slid, from white to black, which made him think of Ophelia in the river. He turned, taking in the open vista, the opal clouds. He was about fifty feet from the shore when he heard a moan from inside the ice—perhaps from the bottom of the lake. He stopped. The two figures on shore seemed more frightened than he, almost transfixed. He swiveled, took a step back, and there was a long black unmistakable crack. He looked for its source, the lake stretching beyond him like another country.

He took many careful, small steps back in the direction of shore, the crack following him. His brother and the girl waited, waving their arms; Gabe moved toward him among the reeds.

"Ta'al," Gabe was saying, "Ta'al houn. Hella." Come, come here. Now. "Yella. Imshee!" Hurry, let's go!

That was what did it. That *imshee*. Hurry. Fear bounced through Hafez like a sonar ping.

No longer walking on air, he looked down. He took an unbalanced step, tried to move the other foot to save himself, and both went out from under. He crashed flat on his posterior. He was wet. Soaked. And then, just like that, the ice was somehow around his ears, nothing under his feet. Cold-shocked, his skin and muscles, his bones ignited. He shrieked, his teeth and tongue and throat blistered by frigid lake water. He sank fast, looking up through blurry white forms, his body a white fire ejecting flames. He must've kicked, for he came back up and hands seized his sodden parka, hoisting and dragging. Gabe was pulling him through the smashed ice. There was a sound in the air, like a bright-red wire that seemed to be the sound of whatever had happened. He seemed to be broken somehow, limbs hanging, as his brother dragged him with fearsome strength. They took many steps. Gabe was pulling and sliding. The ice kept cracking underneath their weight, but they made it much closer in now. Gabe crashed through the surface, down to his knees, and he shouted and dragged, until finally they were on shore. Hafez was lying flat out on crushed snow and reeds, a thousand pounds of wet parka, gasping like a flounder, and at last he understood the thin red wire had been the sound of Francesca screaming.

Then it became so very, very quiet. That's how he remembered it. A wire of sound and then nothing but wind that was so far away it was like the wind on another planet. Francesca was holding his hand in both of hers. Her face was white. She was telling him, her voice juddering, his brother had run to get help. Hafez was too heavy to carry and he needed to get up now and move if he could. "If there is any way," she begged him.

He moved his head and water ran out of his ears, strangely warm against his skin. Then he could hear again—the wind mostly. He saw the awful treachery of this new planet, planet America, that would snap him in an instant. He wasn't really feeling the cold anymore. He was switched off. He tried to laugh and tell the girl he felt fine, but he wasn't sure if actual words were coming from his mouth, and she looked only more distraught and scanned the fields, apparently in the direction that Gabe had disappeared.

She was unbuttoning her coat then. It was a nice, long, woolen coat with a bit of fluff around the hood. He remembered resolving that if he lived he would get one just like it for that other girl— the one he was married to. He couldn't quite recall the other girl's name. It was right there—it'd been tucked away and it was just at the tip of his tongue. He tried to ask Francesca, "Now, what was her name again? The one I married?" This time he formed something more like words, but he might've spoken in Arabic and she was saying, "That's all right now. It's all right." She tugged off his parka, draped her coat over him, and from her neck unwound a long, knitted scarf which she used to encase his head. She was shaking, he could see that. Trying to smile, she said, "I don't know the right thing to do! I don't know if I should take off your wet things or leave them on! Oh my God, where is Gabe, where did he go? Oh, I really, really wish he hadn't gone." She wasn't exactly speaking to him. He wondered if he could somehow hear inside her head. It seemed something filmy powdered the surface of his eyes. He closed them and left them closed and his head bounced. Francesca was shaking him with tremendous force. "No!" she shouted; he could tell from the way the air vibrated and the shape of her mouth. "No sleeping! No sleeping! He'll come! He'll be here any minute now! Don't you dare sleep!"

She was angry, he thought. Her face looked like wax: it gleamed. Her eyes were cut away with light so he could see the gradient between the blackness of her pupils and the mahogany of her irises. It was an incredibly intimate thing. He felt surely that this was the girl, the woman he'd wedded. He smiled, and his arms lifted, and he cupped her face—which was already so near—and pulled her closer, passionately, ardently, and kissed her, a deep, melting kiss, her mouth was so warm. But there was a violent shake, a shout of disgust or anger—*stop it*—and then he let go and fell back against the snow, exhausted, thinking: Not the one I married.

Her eyes had looked so sharp to him—perhaps from wind or cold—but he thought it was from emotion. He'd often thought about that moment—the kiss they'd shared and her eyes lit with feeling. She must have realized she'd picked the wrong brother. Sometimes he liked to imagine that more had happened between them, in those private moments on the shore. He imagined it so frequently that sometimes he almost believed it had.

When Gabe finally reappeared, Hafez had started once again to dwindle, so he seemed to see all movement through dream curtains. Francesca stood a million miles away, watching from a stand of birch.

Blankets. Men. Stretcher. Waves of English and Arabic. Wet clothes stripped—at last! Carried through the air. Francesca's tiny

face telescoping away. "Carole!" he burst out. Surprised by the recollection as they loaded him into the ambulance. "It's Carole!"

"Right here, darling." A voice broke through the crowd. A hand
wrapped around his. "I'm right here," she said. "I'm not going
anywhere."

Was it possible that Gabe had ruined his life? Ma'oul, he thought.
Possible. Hafez had shown unusual tolerance toward his youngest
brother. It was common in the animal world, was it not, for older siblings to eat the younger? He'd read that somewhere and was struck
by recognition. Of course they did! Poor mothers. All the rest of his
life, Hafez had been nettled by that old memory—not by the kiss so
much (though there was that, yes) but the tears afterward. Francesca
seemed remote after he was released from the hospital. Whenever
greeting him socially, she stiffened in his embrace, turning her cheek
for contact-free kisses. He understood: this was how one learned to
live with mistakes.

He'd lived with his own mistake for the past forty years. He'd
learned to love her, even to cherish her, and most of the time to
remember her name. Carole was the one he was married to. Carole.

CHAPTER

12

SHE WALKED THROUGH a cloud of little schoolgirls, each wearing a green plaid jumper over blouses with Peter Pan collars. They parted and regrouped behind Amani in staring silence. Omar walked beside her with his loping gait, his face toward the sun. The Friday morning sky was a cold, silky blue. She felt hopeful.

Last night at a dinner for Great-Aunt Lamise, Amani said to Hafez that "a friend" had told her about an interesting cemetery. "Near a castle? He said it was well worth a visit, the cemetery."

He'd frowned and shook his head, a crease forming between his brows. "A cemetery—and a castle? Wouldn't you rather see the castle than a cemetery?"

"Well, it's just—I'd like to see both."

"Who was this friend who told you? Someone I know?" His eyes were so intent, as if he could see what she wasn't saying. But then Hafez sat back and jiggled the ice cubes in his drink. "Mm. That might be the Citadel downtown. There's a palace and such—it's is up on hill—just like this." He drew a finger in the air. "It *is* worth seeing. Great archeological interest. I can't get away just now or I'd take you myself. I'll have my driver take you."

"No need," Amani had said. "I like to walk."

"At least let me make you an itinerary," Hafez said. "The time is going too quickly! Only a few weeks left now, and I want you to see your country. There are things we should discuss, you and I. Your future. Everything."

A BOY ON A bicycle weaved by holding a tray covered in glasses and saucers on his head. Slowing, a driver rolled up alongside the cyclist and offered him a coin, which the still-pedaling child took with one hand, extending a cup with the other. Men in slacks and pullover sweaters stood on the corners. They flicked cigarettes cupped inside their palms, greeted Omar, and studied Amani. Across the street, four more women swathed in black looked over their shoulders at her.

"They can tell you're not from here," Omar said, his face smug.

"I pretty much got that."

He gave the women a jaunty salute. "So, are we supposed to see something special when we get up there?"

Amani pushed her hands into her pockets. The sun was bright but she wished she'd worn a warmer jacket. "I don't know. Maybe there'll be a grave? Or something? I just want to see what there is." Amani thought again of the blue letter, its words shifting to Arabic and back to English. She wondered again what exactly her grandmother had meant—was it "cemetery"? She'd started to feel as if the letter had been a private, imperative message, a commandment meant specifically for her.

Approaching the city center, they took the long sloping street downhill, then turned onto an access road without sidewalks. Cars blew past within inches. Omar directed her through a bank of shrubs that snagged on her jeans; stones slid underfoot. They went up five broken steps, crossed someone's courtyard, and squeezed through a fissure in a high rock wall. Emerging at the entrance to an open plaza on the top of a hill, Amani whacked at the dust and thorns on her clothes.

"You wanted the real Jordan, right?" Omar asked.

"Now I'm covered in it," she said.

Shielding her eyes, Amani looked around at stone ruins and etched statuary. Omar walked over to a column and found an informational placard written in Arabic. "So, like, this guy's Neolithic, Bronze Age, continuously inhabited, religious crossroads. Romans. That kind of stuff."

They walked through an array of immense footed columns that another placard said was the Temple of Hercules. The sun crested over Corinthian detail at the heads of the tallest columns, igniting the plaza and the pitted stone, and turned the dust yellow. After the columns, they came to an archaeological museum, its cases filled with what looked like undifferentiated rubble.

"This is, like, Greek and Roman. All that." Reading another card, Omar waved his hand over a vitrine. "Hafez loves this crap. No wonder he sent you here. He's got a secret pile of amphoras and really old vases and jugs and stuff—right in his house."

Amani studied what appeared to be a woman's hand in stone, broken off at the wrist, a ring on one of the smooth fingers. It rested palm-up in the case, fingers gracefully curved forward. "Where does he get them—his things?"

"People give them to him, I think. Baksheesh. This kind of ancient junk is all over the place here. People find, like, gold coins and pieces of Greek gods lying around in their backyards. It's totally illegal to keep, of course. That's all supposed to go to places like this, so other people can come and stare at it." As they exited, Omar pointed beyond the museum: "Over there, I think that's the castle. Kind of beat-up though."

They walked through shafts of light stirring with motes, then entered the arched doorway. The interior was filled with the same dusty light that glowed on a vaulted dome. Its carved columns and water-stained rock reminded her of a church chapel. "'Umayyad Palace,'" Omar read. "So those are the really, really old guys. I think the idea is like Jordan kind of started here. Or the city did. The Ammanites."

She took in the ancient building and the discordant, newer addition of the dome. The palace door had a sprawling view of Amman; its sun-blasted square buildings clustered and angled, packed together, filling every hillside. These were interspersed with construction cranes, a blue dome, another dome that looked like pure gold. A tiny, distant grove of olive trees shook its leaves, turning silver then green in the wind. Amani found a guard and asked if there was a cemetery nearby. He beckoned, led them around some construction scaffolding on the palace exterior, and pointed toward an opening in the rock wall. A new excavation, he explained as Omar translated.

"Do they know who's buried here?" she asked as they peered into the dank interior.

The guard said something and Omar told her, "It's so old nobody knows anymore."

It was a relief to move away from the dig with its earthy, sweetish scent. In the distance, a Jordanian flag flapped above a vista of pale stone buildings and clotheslines and birds cresting and swooping, changing with each turn like the olive trees from silver to shadow. On the way out, Amani approached an enormous round opening, encircled by a railing. Checking the placard, Omar explained that this was the Umayyad Cistern. "Seven thirty AD," he translated, then nodded. "More old stuff."

She smiled.

"You asked Hafez where to look? Did you show him the blue letter?"

She shook her head. "Not exactly. I just asked about the cemetery and castle. This was where he said to look."

"Hunh," Omar muttered.

Amani pushed her hair out of her face and knotted it behind her head. "What?"

"You know how he's so charming?" Omar spoke slowly, as if considering his words. "Hafez. He talks to you, asks questions, whatever—but did you ever notice he never actually sort of *looks* at you? It's like he's so into himself he can barely see anything."

"Sounds like a poet." Amani shielded her eyes again.

"Even my dad seems nervous around him sometimes—and my *dad*"—Omar shook his head—"for whatever reason, he usually isn't nervous about anything. Hafez acts like he's such a fun, regular guy, but then there's just huge amounts of stuff you can't talk about."

"Like their mother? The family?"

Omar shrugged, his hands still in his pockets. "I don't ask questions like that. I ask questions like *how*. Like, they're all nuts and *how* do I get out of this fucking place?"

"Where would you go?"

"Somewhere not here. I don't know. Somewhere cool. New York. L.A. would be cool. Somewhere where they're not constantly talking about politics and Israel and religion and not trying to marry you off or yelling about school or gossiping about your every move."

She considered Omar—olive-tan skin and dark eyes. He was half and half, like her, but the only sign of his American mother was his perfect English and clothes. "It's just, I'm not positive those other places would turn out to be as cool as you think."

"I know," he said. He leaned his forearms on the iron railing. "But look at your baba. He got himself out, you know? Isn't he happy?"

Amani rested on the railing beside him. "You know, I think he really is. But he also kind of found what he needed."

Omar turned so his back pressed against the railing and he faced the citadel. "I want to do things—I don't want to be scrambling around in my baba's shadow forever. I want to get my gym going. I've been thinking about this stuff since I was a kid. Like you did—I mean, with your poetry—right? Your parents didn't try to smother you to death. Didn't they encourage you to write?"

Amani smiled. It hadn't been her parents so much as Hafez who'd told her to follow her writing. "I'll encourage you," she promised.

"Right. Until you run away back to America."

Amani gave him a look. She leaned against the iron bar, gazing down into the cistern's round center—a big, stone excavation. The sky grew distant and paler and sounds lifted away as she felt the prickling sensation on her skin—a feeling she used to have in the days when ideas would come to her, and she could pick up a pen and begin. She kept staring, pressing her hands and ribs against the cold railing. She saw the closed room in Hafez's house, light filtering through its curtains. Peering into the opening, Amani tightened her grip on the railing, grime and rust flakes loosening against her palms, and she imagined the cistern as it once was, filled to its blue brim, a washing sound, a whisper like wavelets swaying back and forth. This wasn't the right place to look, she knew it. *The one.* Whatever she was looking for wasn't here. *Thrown away.*

She didn't think Hafez had deliberately sent her to the wrong place. He'd meant to help. He was the uncle who'd once told her she would do brilliant things. One year he'd sent her thirteen birthday candles made of gold from Singapore. Marvelous Uncle Hafez. She made herself look away from the dark eye of the well and a wave of vertigo swept over her. Again, her grip tightened on the metal rail. The clouds were blowing and she smelled rain and iron in the air. This wasn't the place; she knew that much. She remembered her uncle's fixed eyes and broad smile when she'd mentioned his mother, and she knew that he had been lying.

CHAPTER
13

• *The village of Yara, Jordan, 1951* •

GABE HEARD THE SCREAMING from every room in their house. He tried closing the door and hiding in the kitchen, but there was nowhere to not hear it.

It had gone on for weeks. Maybe months. Gabe had lost track. Farouq had moved out and Hafez was in the States. Gabe hadn't known it was possible for someone to scream like that, on and on. He was sixteen years old and he'd never seen anyone so sick, lingering in half-life, such intense suffering.

At first, before the screaming, his father was angry. "Soon," Munif had said. "No more. You'll be free of me. You'll forget I existed."

"No," Gabe had said. He was frightened when he saw his father's anger start to decay and break down. Soon Munif couldn't walk. He stayed in bed. One morning, his father woke and said, "Little pile of days. I stayed here for a little while. I disappear." Then the words rose and caught fire and there was nothing but screaming. Munif screamed even in his sleep.

Gabe ran to their kitchen. Rice and onions, yogurt sauce. He soaked it all in araq, 100 proof. Make him comfortable, the doctor had said. He hadn't told him this would be impossible.

Munif had screamed at his sister, Gabe's aunt Lamise, and she ran from the room howling, holding her face as if she'd been slapped. He'd screamed at his wife and slapped the plate from her hand. "You gave him away," he shrieked. "Felesteeni." Palestinian. Gabe didn't understand. She looked at her husband from a terrible height, and Gabe saw then that his mother was also changing.

Munif would eat only the plates of rice soaked in alcohol, from the hands of his youngest son. Only two bites. Then only one. Then none.

In his final hours, a thread of blood trickled from his nose. There were dark crusts in the corners of his mouth. His breath broke into pieces, bubbling as if he were underwater. He lifted his hand. "Bring," he gasped.

Gabe went to the box in the closet and brought out the velvet pouch. Every day of his adult life, his father had worn this knife. Munif had owned other knives, but this one was the favorite, the close one; he called it Il Saif. The knife. Some said it had belonged to one of the foster brothers of the Prophet, peace be upon him. Their father used to tell his young sons that this was the Prophet's ninth sword, Al Zulfiqar, the double-edged, the spine-splitter, stolen from heaven—supposedly given to the Prophet by the angel Gabriel, its two points an echo of the crescent moon, its presence enough to ward off the evil eye "But it isn't a sword," Hafez used to protest, ever the skeptic. "And it isn't double-edged." Munif always said, "Look more closely."

His mother came quietly into the room and stood beside Gabe. She took his arm. Gabe unrolled the velvet and gave the knife to his father. Munif held it for a trembling moment, his fingers a cage of bones, and Gabe saw he didn't have the strength to remove the blade from its sheath. "Take it," he whispered.

"Wait," his mother said. "No."

Gabe rolled it back into the velvet.

"Yours now," Munif said. "I give it."

"It's not meant for this one! Munif!" Her eyes were in tears. Munif gazed back at her, unmoved. "I forbid it," she cried. "Now *you* are giving him away. *Again.*"

Who? Gabe's breath caught in wonder, netted in the tops of his lungs. He thought of the araq. His father wasn't lucid. Gabe thought of his two older brothers: Hafez, far away, studying, destined to become important; Farouq at work, trying to make his store a success. They, too, would want Il Saif. It wasn't their fault they couldn't be here. He was the youngest, and he'd stayed by his father's side for these months because that was his duty. Farouq visited when he could; Hafez called from the States. Now Gabe's hands moved on the velvet: never had he wanted anything so much. But more than this, he wanted his father to live and he wanted him to claim Hafez. To love him. None of the brothers spoke of the way Munif rejected Hafez. Gabe wondered if some people weren't meant to be parents—if they'd been born without that capacity. There was nothing he could do about Munif's withholding, and yet because of it, in his father's final days, Gabe had grown increasingly angry.

"I won't," Gabe said, his voice shook. "It's yours. It belongs to you. And to Hafez."

"Nothing." His father cut him off with that rasp. There seemed to be blood in the back of his throat. "Yours. Alone. Don't you give this to your brothers! Swear to keep it. You must. Give it to your own son when it is time." His voice seized with pain. Gabe saw it in each tiny muscle, his lips trembling, the eyes rolling up. His breath became more like a gasp. A crimson thread rolled from the corner of his lips to his neck.

"Baba," Gabe cried through a rush of tears, his anger cracking in two. "I swear."

CHAPTER

14

• *Zarqa Governorate, Jordan, Tuesday, November 14, 1995* •

THE CITY LANDSCAPE shrank back and the street turned into a narrow road that curved into the hillside. There were white rocks and craggy, twisting bushes and a broadening sky. This was the fourth trip she'd made in four days. Omar tipped back in the passenger seat as Amani drove Farouq's loaner car. Her knuckles were pale on the steering wheel as they finally exited the city traffic.

For the past several days, Amani had bowed out of family dinners and events. Each time, her father looked at her doubtfully. "I thought you were here to meet everybody."

"I *have* met everyone. Twice." She patted his arm: her father didn't much want to make the rounds either. Amani felt sorry about abandoning him. Just another day or two, she promised: a couple more days of hunting and trying to decipher the blue letter. Then she'd go back to the parties with him. And to his match with the King on Sunday—not quite a week away now. Working from guidebooks, she'd made a list of castle sites, surprised by the number of Umayyad and Crusader ruins that dotted the countryside. She and Omar had driven from one outpost to the next, wandering around the ancient structures and looking for burial sites. The castles rose up from austere sand and rock plains, their domes and cracked arches and stone walls lacy with age. The structures looked swept clean, as if great invisible lungs had blown through them. There were variations in age and architectural style, but each seemed to Amani to have a similar frail, melancholy beauty.

Amani and Omar were driving to Qusayr Amra, another Umayyad bathhouse, referred to by one of the guidebooks as the "pleasure palace." It was an hour of empty, dusty miles into the desert. The parking lot and a small souvenir stand looked desolate. They walked around the perimeter of the fortress, searching for some sort of official entrance or guard, Omar cursing the shiftlessness of the local workforce. Amani returned to the front, pushed on the heavy stone door, and it eased open. After entering a main hall, they stopped, staring. Plaster frescoes of conquerors, naked men, and bathing women lined the walls. Omar strolled through planks of light and shadow, studying the scenes painted along the tops of the walls. He pointed to one depiction of a topless woman tipping out a wine jug. "In case you wonder how the pleasure palace got its name."

Amani went down a corridor peering into different chambers—changing room, caldarium, tepidarium—the vaulted rooms speckled with age. She was growing indifferent to castles—their weathered rock had started to feel repetitious. All castles were the same castle. She'd also started to feel sympathy for Omar, his frustration with his own country, the way it invited visitors in—*Ahlan! Welcome!* was like the national mantra, people shouting it nearly everywhere—and then shutting them out. *Ahlan* extended only so far before she encountered another silence. A kind of resistance that seemed almost a result of so much dust and bright, empty space.

After exploring the castle, Amani found herself back outside, hands on her hips, squinting into a yellow haze above the horizon. Not only would she fail to understand the private message of the blue letter, but she would also fail herself and her grandmother. Omar emerged from the castle. "Well? Anything?" He was hopeful for her, she knew that. But he was also humoring her.

Squinting, she noticed some figures emerging from a distant structure: a man and three dogs walking in their direction. The man seemed, even from far away, to be trained on Amani, his stare hard and unnerving. The yellow dogs trotted ahead and approached her with their doe eyes and waving tails. Omar greeted the man in Arabic. The stranger's face looked sun-cured, his lips nearly burned away, his features fixed in an expression like outrage. In his blue dishdasha and long white keffiyeh, he might have been anywhere from sixty to one hundred years old. He pulled a shred of his keffiyeh across his neck.

The wind gusted and long strands of hair lashed her face and lips. She pulled her hair back, anxious they'd been caught trespassing. "We—we were looking around. We just wanted to take a quick peek. Inside."

"Closed," the man said curtly. His hands made a finishing slash. "Open yowm el-jum'ah." Friday.

Omar said something in Arabic. He had a sly expression, as if sharing an inside joke.

The caretaker looked between Amani and Omar. "You Hamdan? Both?" His gaze fixed on Amani, studying her face. "You know Natalia Hamdan?"

Amani's jaw loosened. She put out her hands. "I'm her granddaughter." He took her hands in a startling, strong grip.

His name was Kurti; he was the castle caretaker, Omar translated. In 1918, when he was a young boy, he and his father had helped Natalia and her family cross from Palestine into Jordan.

He'd guided several families who were fleeing the Ottoman Army but had never forgotten the girl with the navy-black eyes. He was eight and she was maybe thirteen, fourteen. She'd told him she wanted to paint and write. He knew there would be no writing and painting for her in the village where she was headed. "Natalia, she is—" His voice trailed off in a question.

She shook her head. "She died before I was born."

Kurti's eyes seemed to soften for a moment. But then he turned to the fortress and lifted one hand. "My castle is beautiful?"

Amani smiled and nodded.

"She is much older than all of us," Omar translated as Kurti patted the side of the stone wall. "The caliph Walid put this here—he liked to have fun." Omar rolled his eyes. "In Islam, we venerate such ancient structures—they give us ibar—lessons, yes? To enjoy life before it blows away. But also they give ajab. . . ." Omar searched for the word in English, but Kurti interjected: "English says 'amazements,' or 'wonder.'"

The caretaker pointed to the stone archway. "Ajab means you feel God. Maybe when you see a leaf or a star. Maybe in old things or beautiful things. That's why we save the old things—they help us feel God." The man stared solemnly at the small stone castle. After another moment, he shuffled his feet and glanced at Amani. "I am eighty-five years old now, but I still see her—right here—" He moved his hand through the air before his own face. "When I look at you."

Amani lowered her eyes. She took the book out of her bag and produced the blue letter. It rattled in the wind as the man took it. "I found this. I'm trying to figure out what she was saying. What place she might be talking about."

Looking over his shoulder, Omar translated the note into Arabic. Kurti stared at it a few moments his fingers moving over the page, then held up one finger. "Not cemetery," he corrected in painstaking English. "This word—here?"

Omar looked again at the word the man pointed to. "Oh, yeah. Hunh." He and Kurti had a long discussion in Arabic. "That's true. It's more like—mmm, like a church or something, I think."

"A church?"

"Like a place where people go, like to hide away? To meditate and stuff?"

"*Sanctuary?*" she asked Omar. "All this time we've been looking for a cemetery."

"Dude, I don't know! *You* told me cemetery—I just took your word for it."

"Castle at Karak," the older man said to Amani, pointing to the paper. He switched back to Arabic and Omar translated: "It was outside of her town. There was a long trail. Very far. The castle is up on the hill and down below—that's the monastery. Not cemetery. Look for *monastery.*"

THE ROAD TURNED SOFTER, whitening as if scrubbed with briars and salt. They passed the southern outskirts of Amman, the city streets tapering into fields, semi-desert sand and knuckles of thorns and rocks. Amani's hair spiraled out the open window. She yawned, her eyes faintly red; she was tired yet perhaps also happy. Yesterday, she'd felt it in the center of her chest, a tap on the heart, hearing the caretaker say her grandmother's name.

"So okay, we're talking about the same guy?" Omar asked from the backseat. "He was, like, the youngest cousin? But he died, I thought."

Gabe's eyes cut to the rearview mirror, his nephew's face. When Amani told him about their encounter at the Amra castle, he decided to come along today. He told Amani he'd had a feeling for days that he might know who the note was referring to. "I never knew what happened to him," Gabe said quietly. "Musa. We played together. We were friends."

"Baba said you guys had a cousin who died when he was, like, really young or something," Omar persisted.

"Maybe. Our mother and her sister both lost babies. Before I was born. They're marked in the graveyard."

Amani slowed for a steep bend. She was getting used to driving the narrow highways. "I never heard you mention him."

They passed small children playing with sticks on the side of the road, dirty bare feet. They passed the stone streets and steeples of Madaba, then miles of crackling highway, Byzantine columns, valleys of juniper and scrub, high-tension wires and rows of trees that heaved away from the road as if shoved by an arm. Overhead, a hawk slanted through the light. The road narrowed and began to wind steeply upward. A sign in Arabic and English said they were entering the town of Karak. The castle lookout stood at the top of the road, high overhead. They pulled to the side of the road and bought bunches of round, dusty grapes from a boy pushing a handcart. The grapes burst between Amani's teeth with musky sweetness, and the boy gave her a water skin. Amani took a polite sip. Gabe held it high, pouring a stream into his mouth. Two men in keffiyehs and a woman wrapped in a thobe emerged from a shack along the roadside. Amani asked them about the monastery and they crowded around. They argued, then finally settled on the directions. It was farther down the road, a left, two rights to the deir. The convent. They insisted Amani and the others come to their homes for lunch; the woman tugged on Amani's hand, a gold tooth flashing in her smile, but Amani shook her head. "Another time, inshallah."

The convent was about a mile outside of town. Built of rough, yellow stone, etched with grime, the monastery had an imposing façade. There were cloverleaf windows set deeply into the stone, a gate of metal spears, a single dome, and a steeple with a belfry. They parked on swept dirt out front and it rose around them in small swirls as they walked to the convent; its doors shrieked as they entered. The three stood there a moment, letting their eyes adjust to the low light; from somewhere deeper within the building came a trickle of birdsong.

After a moment, a woman emerged from the back. She wore a dark habit, her head uncovered, hair bundled at the nape of her neck. She asked in French, then in fluent English, how she could help them. After a moment's hesitation, Amani said, "We are looking for someone."

The nun's brows lowered and she slowly shook her head when Gabe gave her his family name, but she asked them to please wait and clicked down the corridor. Moments later she returned with a leather-bound ledger.

Her father repeated, "We're looking for a Hamdan. Musa Hamdan, perhaps."

"A first cousin? From which side of the family?" The young nun—her name was Sister Sylvain—offered them curved cane chairs in the corridor while she paged through the records, her finger sliding down rows of the names of orphans and refugee families. Omar stood to one side, chatting in Arabic with two other nuns who'd appeared. They seemed to be intrigued, their faces turning in Amani's direction and then back again to Omar.

Gabe told Sister Sylvain he was four or so when this cousin had left their village.

The nun lifted her face.

"I know." Gabe turned his hands palms up. "Too young to really remember. But still I have these dreams. Sometimes they come a lot."

His cousin was a bit older. Gabe said he thought he remembered him. A sweet boy with a stick. No different from the kids they'd passed on their way into town. Her father shook his head as if he could stir his thoughts. Amani leaned forward. She hadn't known about his dreams. One of the younger nuns brought a pot of hot tea and a plate of butter cookies. Gabe's hand trembled as he held a cookie. Amani took the crook of his arm. "Dad, maybe it isn't the right place."

Gabe stared at the cookie.

There was a rustle of footsteps at the far end of the corridor—this nun was wearing a red cardigan buttoned over her habit and sneakers that squeaked on the linoleum. Her white hair was pulled into a bun on top of her head. "What's this?" she asked in Arabic. Shu? Shu? She sat on the other side of Gabe as if they were old friends, and took his hand. "Tell me the name, please," she said. "But say it loudly and slowly."

"Musa. He would have come here as a boy, in the late '30s. He was very—kind," he said carefully. "Very gentle. Not a—usual kind of person."

Her face filled with a look of such concentration the other nun lowered her ledger. The white-haired abbess, who introduced herself as Mother Philomene, rocked slightly. She took an audible breath, flattened her palms, and clasped them. "Musa. Could you be talking about Moses?"

The nuns' faces turned to Gabe.

"Ah," breathed the abbess. "Is that the one?" She pointed to an entry in Sylvain's ledger. "We didn't have his family name—he came to us without identification or any official records. We call him Moses. He has a lot of nicknames."

Amani stared at the old woman beside him. "He's still alive?" Startled, she felt as excited as if she'd known him herself. "Is he here? Now?"

"He doesn't stay with us, but he's not far." The white-haired nun nodded. "He told me. Ages ago. He'd had another name. He didn't remember it. But I know that he'd come from one of the villages, fifty or more years ago. He was still a boy when they brought him to us. I wasn't much older myself."

"That could be the right timeline," Amani said, sitting forward. "If he and Dad were kids together."

"Who brought him here?" Gabe asked.

Her face wrinkled with concentration, the skin fine and translucent, covered with a tracery of freckles. "I don't remember. They weren't his parents—I don't believe so. I was just a novitiate then. Musa was trouble for the nuns—whoever it was that first received him, I recall that much. He couldn't really even speak back then—not full words, just sort of broken pieces. Sounds. We worked with him quite a bit. Our Mother Superior tried to teach him to sleep in a bed, but he—" She chuckled and smoothed the hair at the nape of her neck. "He wandered. We'd have to go look for him. We'd find him sleeping in the fields, with the goats. In the end, we just let him be. He was very peaceful, always. Very dear."

"You—let him be?" Amani frowned. She felt pressure on her left side like a handprint.

"Really, he is alive?" her father asked. "Can we see him?"

The white-haired nun stood and gestured to them. Mother Philomene, Sister Sylvain, Amani, Gabe, and Omar took the corridor into a central courtyard filled with metal birdcages, canvas folding chairs, small tables, and a telescope. The outer wall was lined with illuminated alcoves containing colorful portraits and painted statues. They exited through an archway at the back of the stone wall that surrounded the property, emerging to briars and sharp-leafed weeds. A gravel footpath divided the field and twisted up and around a hillside, sometimes forking off into new trails. A hush came over the group, as if the trail were taking them into a forbidden place. Amani offered a hand to the white-haired nun, but the nuns were more agile than she.

They went single file, listening to the crunch of grit. Walking the stone path, the grinding, silty textures underfoot, Amani felt restored by the fresh air. She took in full breaths. After several long bends, they passed a ridge of white rocks that looked as if someone had tried to create a rudimentary railing. Beside the path, a curved and claw-formed tree with spiny needles bore a strip of cloth that flapped in the breeze. Vistas opened around them, valleys of honey-colored rock ledges strewn with pink oleander. The group stopped for a moment, the nuns smiling, their faces bright. Amani put her hands on her hips, breathing more heavily than she'd expected to. Her father bent over, resting his hands on his knees.

"It doesn't look that steep at first, does it?" Sister Sylvain asked.

They walked for nearly an hour. Near the top of the hillside, Amani saw what appeared to be a great pile of rubble but turned out to be a hillock of whitish stones heaped as high as her head. It looked runic and ancient, like a Nabatean monument. Philomene said, "Here we are." She stood at the foot of the rubble, cupped her mouth with both hands, and gave a warbling cry that rang over the valley. Amani jerked back, bumping into Omar.

After a few moments, she realized that what she'd thought was a shadow was actually a sort of opening beside the stone pile. She heard light footsteps on stones: someone was coming out. A man stood before them, blinking. He had strange dark, fir-green eyes in an earth-brown face. Dust webbed in his hair and eyebrows. For a moment, no one spoke.

The man gazed around, smiled, and embraced Philomene, then Sylvain. Her father cleared his throat softly and asked something in Arabic. Amani stared at the man, scarcely breathing. A pulse started in her head; she barely heard her father speak again, repeating, *Musa? Musa?*

At last, he smiled at Gabe, who came forward, tentatively touched his shoulder, then put his arms around the man. Amani thought she inhaled a soft, dry scent rising from his robe, like that of stone and air. Sister Sylvain put her hand over her mouth.

Omar and Amani came closer. She touched the man's arms, murmuring greetings.

Amani realized he was frozen, staring at her, mumbling something. Omar said, "He's asking—is it you? Like, he thinks he knows you."

It was as if she could feel him seeing someone else in her place—a face superimposed upon her own. "My name is Amani," she said. He stared a moment longer, then his eyes changed: he shook his head, waving his hand as if clearing a mist.

"Yeah, I'd be very freaking surprised if you two have met before," Omar commented.

Musa smiled more broadly. He spoke to the group, Omar translated, saying, "Will you stay? I invite you?" The man's voice was like a rusty hinge. Amani could hear that he spoke Arabic like the

Bedouin, with hard, formal consonants, lifted from the pages of the Qur'an. "Come to my house."

They followed him behind the stone hill. The nuns went first, without hesitation. The entryway was a narrow opening into a cave. "This is what he does," Sylvain explained as they walked, slightly stooped. "He fills in cracks and smooths his walls." The rock ceiling grazed their heads, but the place had a fresh scent of outdoors and rain. They put their hands out to make their way in the shadows, and Amani was surprised to feel the sides of the walls were soft and undulant. They'd been painted with whitewash. There was a turn, and then sunlight. They came into a clearing built into the side of the hill; the cave was wide open on this side, facing the purple valley. The earth floor of the cave had been pounded to a satiny finish, a small heap of charred wood and stone at the center, a metal pot on top. It was comfortable and surprisingly clean. The man disappeared into the shadows for a moment while Amani and the others stood, shielding their eyes, murmuring over the view. The man returned with cushions, black cotton ticking embroidered with designs of arrows and pentagons in red and white thread. He said something and Omar explained, "He saves these for special guests." He placed each one carefully in a circle around his fire.

"Musa sits only on the bare ground," Sylvain told Amani.

Gabe lowered himself to the cushion beside the man. Musa squatted and placed the flat of his hand on the earth, sliding it back and forth. Amani touched it as well; it felt as supple as human skin. Musa put his hand on Gabe's arm and said something that Amani picked up in slivers: "Welcome in my home." He looked pleased. "I live in here."

"Thank you," Gabe said. "We're happy to be here."

Musa nodded and rocked. He touched Gabe's face. "You are here." He stared at him quizzically for a few moments. Amani felt her throat tighten. She focused closely on his words, working to understand as much as possible. Musa started a fire with a piece of flint and some seedpods filled with white filaments. Squatting, he blew on the flame for a moment, then rubbed the top of his head with the back of his hand a bit frantically and rocked forward on his toes. He went to another corner, produced a paper bag of curling leaves. These he placed in the pot with brown lumps of sugar. From a jug, he spilled water into the pot.

"We bring him food and clothing. I wish he would take more," Mother Philomene said. "He could use our well, but he gets water from the spring up in the mountain."

"He takes only what he needs," Sylvain said. "Never more."

Amani looked at the man in shy glances. Gradually, fascination overcame her: she studied the robe gathered around Musa's shoulders that fell to his ankles, threadbare but relatively clean. His feet were well formed, his teeth square and white, his face and hands were strong, and she had no doubt that Musa could have carried them up the hillside two by two in his arms. She tried to imagine who this person might have been when he was still a child, part of the village. He must have had this animal stillness even then, a watchfulness that wasn't like that of other children, but more of nature—as if he'd had more in common with rocks and tree limbs than with boys. She felt something like happiness—a sweetness and calm—in his presence. Whoever he was. It was a pure sensation that, she realized as she sat with him, she hadn't felt in a long time. Amani leaned toward Musa from her cushion and said hesitantly in Arabic, "I'm his—Gabe's daughter." She touched her own shoulder.

Musa gazed at her and reached for her hand. There was such kindness in his face. She had an image, a little like a memory, of a boy who rarely got up to play; yet other children would have liked to be near him, touching his hair and the sides of his face. "Musa, Musa!" They clapped his hands together and he would have laughed and let them.

Omar left his cushion, squatted before Musa, and speaking slowly enough that Amani could understand, said, "So, I'm Farouq's kid. I'm the dumb one."

Musa touched the top of Omar's head and Omar beamed. Musa

got to his feet, rustled back in a corner, and came forward with a tin and a bowl. He poured cookies into the bowl, where they struck with pings. They were covered in sesame seeds. Then he went around the circle, crouching to offer a cookie to each guest. Her father tried one between his back molars. Amani sat with hers in her lap.

"We bring him little gifts," Sylvain was saying apologetically. "But some keep better than others."

"And the people in town, our local families . . ." Philomene gathered her loose sleeves around her arms. The nuns had refused the cookie. "They try to watch out for him. They bring things also. But I think we need Musa as much as he needs us," she said. Amani felt she understood: even the air around the man seemed gentler.

Musa had set aside the tin of cookies and was now squatting before the metal pot, stirring with a long spoon. The skin around his lips and fingers was deeply cracked, in places it seemed to have sloughed away in sheets. But when he smiled, his teeth all in a row in his wide face, he looked to Amani as though he might last forever. Her father touched the man's shoulder. "What can I do for you? I want to help you."

Musa shook his head. He turned his fine smile on him, then toward the sky, lifting his metal spoon. "Alhamdullilah," he said.

"Thanks be to God," Sylvain echoed in English. "Sometimes when I'm indoors praying, I think of Musa in this stone chapel."

"I can see it," Omar said. "Look at this guy—he doesn't need anything. He's got it all."

Philomene's forehead tightened. "I'm not so sure. We've found him half-dead from heat stroke or dehydration on more occasions than I can count. Humans aren't meant to live like wild animals," she said, but softly. "Certainly not all alone."

"I do think he is a marvel," Sylvain said, and she and Musa smiled at each other. "There are still cave dwellers in this region. Not many, certainly. The government discourages them. We don't know if he'll be able to remain here much longer. Lately, we're hearing they're going to clear these caves the way they did at Petra. They're considered squatters, but people have occupied these spaces"—she held her arm out—"for centuries."

Musa brought some small clay cups, which he filled by lifting and lowering the metal pot, pouring through steam. He had only four cups. Philomene refused any and Sylvain tried to refuse as well, but Musa pressed it on her silently, so she took a few sips and gave him the rest of hers. Amani and the others touched their cups together and Amani smelled something bitter and loamy as she sipped. Particles of twigs and brown herbs floated on its surface.

"Good stuff." Omar drained his cup. "Not for sissies."

Gabe turned to Musa, and Amani understood him asking, "Are you really all right? Do you like living here? Like this?"

Musa held his palms open like a book. "Kul shi tamaam," he said.

"Totally good," Omar translated.

He asked Gabe something that he didn't hear clearly. Then Omar caught it and told Amani, "Yeah, so he's asking, did you bring my mama?"

Gabe lifted his eyebrows. Touching Musa's knee, Amani said in her slow Arabic, "I'm—sorry. She isn't—she's not here."

Sylvain folded her hands together. "Whenever we've offered to relocate him, he always says that he's waiting—that his mother is going to come and get him."

"Waiting for Mama," Philomene murmured. "For fifty, sixty years."

"The nuns are my mama and baba," Musa said to Amani in Arabic, speaking so clearly she didn't need Omar's translation. "The goats are my brothers." He touched the ground with an index finger. "Here is my house. You are in my house. Welcome to here."

Again, he stood and went into the interior of his cave. He returned with something folded that might have once been an old T-shirt. Squatting, he spread it out on the floor, picked up a white stone near the fire, and began making long, firm strokes on the cloth. After a minute or so of this work, he stood and held it before Amani. She touched it: all she saw were white lines.

Philomene said, "He's showing you some of his special work. He rarely takes this out. He makes these and keeps them until they're in shreds."

"What is it, exactly?"

Omar leaned in to look at the rag. He said something to Musa, then translated, "He says it's the angel."

The group studied the piece of fabric in silence. Finally, Sister Philomene tucked a few strands behind her ear and said, "We think it's some form of creative expression. Possibly his way of compensating for so much solitude. A way to speak in isolation."

"I think they're rather beautiful," Sylvain said. "They have such a lovely shape. A sort of droplet."

Musa folded the rag and put it away.

The sun had diminished. Eventually, the visitors began to stretch; stiff from sitting on the ground, they dusted off their legs and looked at the light. Amani drained her cup. She lingered a moment. "You don't have to stay here, you know," Amani said, looking from Musa to Gabe. "Dad, tell him. I mean—are we really going to—just leave him here? All alone—in a cave?" Even without any proof of his identity, it seemed they couldn't just walk away. "Dad, please, tell him. We can take him back with us if he wants."

"Take him back? Where?" Omar said. "This guy? You going to dress him in a suit and take him to the office? I want him to take *me* back here."

"Dad, please, just tell him."

Gabe turned the cup in his fingertips. It was almost round, veined with cracks. "Do you want to come home with us?" he asked Musa. "We can take you."

"I am home," Musa said. But he didn't want them to leave. He had rice, he said. Dates. Yogurt. He would make dinner. Mother Philomene shook her head and said it was getting late. It was difficult to go down the hillside after dark.

Musa put his arms around Gabe then Amani and she felt the bands of strength in his embrace. They walked through the cave dwelling; once again, Amani inhaled its clean air. As they descended the hillside Musa stood at the opening, waving, calling Maa' salameh! Sylvain called back to Musa that she would return soon with clothing and cakes. Amani's lips trembled. She turned to the trail and began to notice the lowering sun filling the sides of the valley with a golden hum, as if ignited and set alive, the ridges like hammered gold, the hillsides mapped with desert flowers.

They watched the rock ledges, the needles and leaves transformed by the coming night. After what seemed a shorter walk than before, they reached the valley floor, the bell tower rising above them.

AMANI FOCUSED on the highway, the way dust blew in wraiths, snaking over the road and vanishing into the twilight. After a long silence, Omar pushed forward from the backseat. "That's how they do things, you know. Like, there's practically no choice. The lajeen." Refugees. "And the Bedouin. They have nothing, really. They can't feed all their kids. They can't even feed themselves. They have to hope the missionaries will care for them."

The headlights seemed to sway, intensifying as night fell. Her hands felt damp on the wheel. "I kind of can't believe we're just going to drive away like this and leave him there."

"The chance to take him back passed a long time ago," Gabe said.

"He shouldn't have been left there in the first place." Her voice tightened with anger.

"I agree."

"If Musa arrived at the convent in 1938 . . . Dad, you were, what? About four years old?"

"I don't remember," Gabe mumbled. "Yes, four or five."

"How is this even possible? Someone just left him there? And no one remembered him or even talked about him?"

"Ya'ani, he's *different*, cuz," Omar said. "It's haram, you know? Shame? Taboo. Those village rednecks. They hide people like that and everyone agrees not to notice."

Gabe made a soft huff in his throat. "And the village is gone anyways. There's no one to ask."

"My dad would've been, like, seven," Omar offered. "Maybe he remembers something? We should ask him. I mean, like, whose kid was he, Amo? Is he a second cousin, or where'd he even come from?"

Gabe shook his head silently.

Amani squinted into the circle of headlights. She watched dust flash over the highway, the sound of wind whirling behind.

CHAPTER

15

HE SITS SLOWLY DOWN. Slowly near the fire. Sometimes the bones move easily, full of air. Today the bones are hurting there is cold.

Today the angel came when the light made its bright edge. She checked his hands and feet and teeth and head. She checked his water. She brought the rice the onion the bread. They sat slowly sat near the fire and the bright edge opened and day poured out. The angel went back down the hill.

He boils tea and watches how the misting goes from his pot to circle the sky. The weather comes from his pot. He spends the standing up day smoothing the walls making them strong. That is what home is. The window is open for the day and the creeping things and the flying wings. They come to speak with him they touch his hands his feet all the standing up day while he works smoothing the walls making them strong.

He scrapes slowly his fingers in the dirt his neck bowed his back is soft over. The heat and light are on his head. He carries handfuls he places on the walls he makes the walls thicker. He sings the words that are sounds. When the shadow comes on his head he stops and goes to his mother place. He uses the cut stone to make sure the shape is right because she is inside the shape and he uses the white stone to make the marks of her face on the soft and then he will see her and she will whisper and tell him again soon she is coming. Ah, he misses her!

When the dark is in the air and he is lying down the smoothness on his cheek and his eyes closing and the dream pouring out.

CHAPTER

AN ENVELOPE WITH her name rested against the stone faun near the front door. She could just make it out in the cloudy evening light. Feeling some presentiment, Amani had picked it up before her father noticed: he was drained by their day and wasn't noticing much of anything. Later, in her office, she'd slid out a slim book of poetry and a note—from Eduardo. *I looked for Mr. Sheltzer's collection, but these poems made me think of you.*

The book was by the Palestinian poet Mahmoud Darwish. She flipped through it, finding phrases and details, a few emergent images, but her mind kept wandering. It had grown late and she'd just about decided to go to bed when there was a tap on her office door. She put aside the book and opened the door to see her father. "Can I ask you something?" He eased into a chair, holding a small parcel with both hands. "Not a question, a favor. . . ." He stopped and cleared his throat. After a moment, he started again. "I'm done with them."

Amani laced her fingers together, watching him. Her mouth opened slightly.

"All of them. This *family*." His voice was quiet. "I keep seeing him there—in that cave. How nice he made it." He faltered and Amani touched his arm. He didn't like to show anger—not openly. He straightened, wiping the heel of his palm against one cheek, then cleared his throat again. "I don't want this thing." He opened the velvet flaps and picked up the knife. The amber hilt, inlaid with a darker wood, the sheath etched with an intricate, nearly invisible design and lined on the inside with a thin, cracked leather. "Please— will you take it," he said, a bit insistently. "It's your heritage—it should go to you."

She blinked then dropped her eyes to the knife. He placed it in her hand. "Il Saif?" She looked into his face, watching him nod. Carefully, she turned the sheath, studying its lines. "Why would you give it away?" She slid the blade out: it stuck partway, then pulled free with a tug. She ran her finger over the inscription on the blade.

"I'm done, habeebti," he repeated. "I used to think it was—a good thing. A special kind of memory. No more." He rubbed the back of his neck. "I think there was something broken in my family. I don't understand it all the way." On the drive back from Karak, he'd told her and Omar he'd dreamed of lifting his arms, saying fawg— up—of being lifted. Again and again. Gabe admitted he'd tried to remember what Musa had been like, but could only recall sweetness and almost wild stillness, and then his own arms, his face tilted back, the up, up.

Now Amani looked at her father. "So, you brought the knife with you. All the way to Jordan. Does Mom know?"

He shook his head. "I wasn't sure I was really going to do it," he said. "There wasn't time to think it out. Hafez keeps asking if I have it, but he looks like—wild. Like he'll eat me. So I just tell him I forgot it."

She looked back to the knife.

"I decided after we found Musa," he said. "I know in my bones— I'm done."

Amani sheathed the blade. Shaking her head, she tried to give it back to him.

"Keep it," he said. "Or even don't keep it. You'll know what to do." He put his hand on hers. "You'll do better with it than I will. But please—just, you can't tell anyone."

"I can't tell?"

He held her gaze. "This family. They'll come—like those birds? Circling. Especially Hafez. The knife is worth something, I think, so don't tell about this. Be careful what you say and what you ask. Don't tell anyone."

ALONE NOW, Amani stared at the velvet wrapper. After a moment, she put it in the desk drawer, pushing it back as far as she could reach, and slid the drawer closed. She sank her face into her hands and tried to breathe; she could feel her pulse in the skin of her palms. When she finally lifted her head, her gaze fell back on Eduardo's gift. She sat back, then sighed and opened the book.

> *Out of jasmine the night's blood streams white. Your perfume,*
> *my weakness and your secret, follows me like a snakebite. And*
> *your hair*
> *is a tent of wind autumn in color.*

Flipping through, her concentration improving, she saw there were others like it. Your hair, your perfume. She hesitated. What had he said? I've never seen anything so beautiful come from a tent? Was that a compliment? *Strange beauty.* That's how her ex-husband, Bill, had once described her: *You have this strange beauty.* But she didn't want strange beauty: she wanted the ordinary kind with no qualifiers.

Amani was about to tuck Eduardo's note back in the book, then stopped, thinking of their conversation at the King's banquet table.

His speckled eyes, their focus on her. He'd left a voice message for her after that night, which she hadn't yet answered. Eduardo had told her he ran drills and practices every morning with his team at the Royal Pavilion. *We start quite early. Perhaps you'd like to come by?*

THURSDAY MORNING, it was still dark in the house when she left. The cold had cleared the air, threading it with strands of hyssop. The sky was a wash of blue and black. Amani wore a woven shawl she'd bought in a stall downtown. It smelled like spices from the souq with hints of something like hide. She looked up at the lighted apartment windows as she walked, the cars on Zahran Street quiet and sparse. Her nerves sped through her, not quite connected to her body, like currents of air. She thought of Musa again, the inky darkness of his cave, her surprising sense of closeness to the man, as if a match had been struck and flared in that cave, illuminating another world for half a second. She could still smell the herbs from that bitter tea, mint and wild thyme, the dust and pollen. Again, she saw the man as he first emerged, his gaze on her face. Amani wondered again if others in the family knew about Musa, if Omar was right and they had simply agreed never to speak of him.

The street climbed to the fourth circle—one of the main round-abouts that was nearly impassable with traffic at midday. Reaching the crest of the hill, she could see the strings of streetlights, traffic lights swinging on their cords, the narrowest sliver of moon still visible in the sunrise. Amani stopped and checked the address on Eduardo's card. There were no street signs. A cab honked, startling her, the driver leaning over the passenger seat to see if she wanted a ride. She showed him the card and he pointed to the top of a modern building a couple blocks away. "*Mashie,*" she said. Okay. "I'll walk."

The pavilion was cavernous and echoing, on one side a large, open gym filled with workout equipment, the other side lined with glass-fronted practice rooms. An attendant at a front desk heaped with towels pointed to the main salon. Inside, the floor was lined with slate-blue strips; a handful of men dressed in white stood around holding teacups on saucers. One put down his saucer and as he came closer, she saw it was Eduardo. Her breath leapt into her throat.

He laughed with surprise, took her hand, and bowed slightly, touching his forehead to her knuckles. "You came! We're just having a break."

"I'm sorry. It's so early—I'd hoped I might catch you before you started."

"We start at five a.m. Teatime is at seven." With his back to the windows, his eyes were very dark. Amani unwrapped her cloak. Her chest ached with some excitement or nervous energy. He escorted her into the room and asked a boy to bring another cup of tea. She took the moment to examine the room. A bank of windows lined the rear wall, brilliant with early sunlight.

He noticed her gaze. "A nice space, isn't it?" He positioned two plastic chairs together at one of the folding tables. "It's where I spend my days. I pretend I'm in an old Spanish salle with books and oil paintings with big gold frames."

"In your fantasy, is there also a sword and a windmill?" She smiled.

He laughed. "Yes, and I'm the donkey who think he's a stallion."

He wore white knickers and white shoes and a white jacket that zipped diagonally across the front and fastened high around the neck. There was a white mesh mask on the table beside him. Two men in similar outfits strolled past and nodded. They held masks cradled in their left arms, foils in their right. They scrutinized Amani, their gazes skating over her.

"They're from Bedouin families," Eduardo murmured. "Very traditional."

"They clearly don't approve of outsiders," Amani said.

"Of women," he said, faintly smiling. "In the practice area."

The child handed Amani a china cup filled with hot, yellow tea.

It smelled of bergamot and cardamom. "Women aren't allowed?" She blew on the cup.

"Oh, these fellows aren't representative of the sport. They're just being—I suppose, tribal. I personally believe men and women are well matched in fencing. You need coordination, balance, agility. Wits. Heart. Women outmatch the men. Look—" He stood, Amani following, and he handed her his foil. She lifted it, surprised by how light it felt in her hand. She passed it through the air, making it swish before handing it back. "It's sort of satisfying, isn't it?"

Eduardo's smile deepened. One of the men in white came to the strip and gestured to Eduardo. "Kasim is in training—would you like to watch?"

The two men spoke, then went to their places on the blue floor strip they called a piste. They lifted their foils to their masks and swiped them down to their sides. Eduardo took several steps, heel-first, foil raised; Kasim retreated, then bounded forward. Kasim's movements were quick but staccato; Eduardo was more fluid, crouching then lifting, his body narrowing and extending. Their actions intensified, moving in flashes. They shouted and lunged, jabbing so their blades curled. A loud buzzer went off repeatedly. The heat of their exertions seemed to warm the room and she felt the floor vibrate under their feet. She was struck by their precise sense of distance, the instinctive move toward and away; right foot forward, left back, knees bent, left arms slung back, wrists curved. Their movements were like electrical charges, the swords dashing out an inscription.

When the two men finally pushed back their masks, their faces were shining, their hair glittering with sweat. Eduardo dropped into the seat beside her, mopping his face with a towel. Her own pulse had bumped up during the display. "I can see why the King likes to fence." She sat back. "It's beautiful. A beautiful kind of combat."

Eduardo ran a towel over the back of his head. He unzipped his plastron, toweling himself off, his T-shirt damp. "You know he still trains, from time to time. His Majesty. Likes to keep his hand in."

Amani smiled. "I don't think Dad's fenced—well, at least since *I* was born. But the two of them—they aren't supposed to do any actual *fencing*-fencing—right? Dad says it's more of a demonstration, I guess."

"It's a little more than that," Eduardo said. "You know the Palace invited him to come practice with the King? Here—at the pavilion?"

"They did?"

"And your father said he'd try to come by, but that he had a lot of family engagements. That's what I was told."

"Oh, Dad." Amani curved the palm of her hand to her forehead and closed her eyes. "He never said a word to me. But yeah, that sounds like him. He doesn't like a lot of, like, flash and attention."

"He's channeling his inner old Bedouin," Eduardo said.

Amani laughed. "That must be it."

"Ya'ani, sometimes my inner old Bedouin shows itself—I try not to let it." Eduardo smiled as well. "Yella—come, please." He stood. "Let's not talk about old Bedouins. Now it's your turn." He handed the newly polished foil back to her. "Here—let me see how you hold this."

"Oh no. I can't." She hesitated, studying the foil, then stood. "I honestly have no idea how." Amani held it like a stick. Eduardo stood beside her and pointed out two fencers on the other side of the room who moved in rhythmic counterpoint across their strip. He showed her how to bounce softly on the balls of the feet. She tried to copy him, then swung the light blade back and forth, easing her weight between her front foot and back foot.

He watched her for a few moments, nodding. "Fencers like to say we're born to the sword." He leaned back as she angled the blade in his direction. "Yes, you've got it—in your hand, the position of your body. You have a feeling for this sport. You should try it out."

"Oh really—no, no." She noticed some of the men watching her hold the foil. "I don't know—I think we should try another time."

Following her eyes, Eduardo glanced at the men lounging against the walls, arms folded over chests. "This is the most perfect time." He nodded at Amani. "Come, please, this way." She tried to hang back, but he went out on to the strip and beckoned. They were bathed in light at the center of the room; she felt the men's gaze on her skin and the blood filled her face. Eduardo showed her where to stand, how to close her hand properly around the grip, how to lift her arms. "Shoulders down, please. A firm grip, but don't squeeze. Keep your elbow in line with the tip of your weapon." He moved behind her. "There. Have you ever taken dance lessons? There are foot positions also with this sport—first position, second position. Bend your knees—this foot back." He touched her hip and she felt her breath shift in her chest. She accidentally moved her right foot, then adjusted her left.

"Don't think. You just have to let the body speak. It's instinctive." He moved closer. "People have always fenced. Children fence with sticks. Did you know there are pictures of the old Egyptians fighting with blades? It's second nature—truly it is." He put his hand over hers, raising the foil. With his other hand, he guided her waist. His touch warmed her skin. Amani felt almost feverish. Her sense of the world beyond the piste softened. From behind her ear, he asked, "Imagine your opponent before you. Can you envision it?"

Amani smiled and said weakly, "Not really."

"Remember, your opponent may try to dissemble, fake a lunge. Then, perhaps, to intimidate. Attack left," he said quietly. "Parry riposte." His flat shoes took half steps behind hers. "Thrust right, parry left."

"I don't know what all that means," she said breathlessly, trying to follow his movements.

"Dance steps." He laughed. "Don't be worried—you have those old ways inside you. You're a natural fencer."

"Oh, Eduardo, come on." Still, she felt pleased despite herself and tried again, lifting her right foot, bringing it down in a lunge.

"Look at them! They can see it."

Amani realized the men were watching her move. She made a misstep and laughed, then waved to the onlookers, which seemed to disconcert them. Several looked away. One nodded. She was enjoying herself; it was good to do something that took her out of her thoughts. It had been so long since she'd felt someone's hands on her body—his touch assertive and direct. Inhaling, she attempted another lunge then felt a metal bump under her rib and pulled back.

Eduardo turned. "What happened?"

She tried to adjust herself and felt the bump again. "Ugh, you know what, let's stop." Amani's hand went to her lower hip and Eduardo's eyes followed. "I think that's enough for me for today." She handed him the foil. A drop of sweat slipped between her shoulder blades as she returned to the table and collected her scarf.

Eduardo glanced at the others. He placed the foil on the table. "I'll escort you home."

"No, no. . . ." She waved at him. "I can get home just fine."

He followed her out of the salle into the pavilion's main hall. It was dimly lit, echoing and empty. "I had the impression—when you first got here—"

She looked at him.

"You wanted to ask me something?" he said.

"Oh." She stopped. "Well, yes. Actually—" She'd nearly forgotten. She deliberated for a few moments, then looked around. She went to a quiet corner and Eduardo followed. Her hand slipped between the bottom of her shirt and the waistband of her jeans. She unclipped the knife and removed it. "It sort of slid out of place. When I was moving around."

Eduardo's eyes widened. She handed it to him. He turned it over and over, inspecting the sheath and handle, murmuring over its inlaid wood, running his fingers across the amber. He unsheathed it with a sharp tug and held up the blade. "Ya Allah," he murmured. "How extraordinary."

She smiled despite herself.

He moved the blade so it caught the light. "Damascus steel." He flicked his wrist, made digging movements through the air. He held it up on the flat of his palm, pointing out its balance; he tested its edge with his finger tip. "Not many repairs. This handle is maybe a hundred years old. The sheath—" He inspected its interior. "Looks like teak lining. The sheath maybe even two hundred years. But the blade—this is ancient." He lifted his eyes, the freckles in his irises. "Where did you get this?" His voice was low.

She nodded at it. "It was handed down. My father has held on to it—for years. Last night, he gave it to me. He calls it Il Saif."

"Il Saif?" Eduardo whistled quietly. "This is more than a treasure—it's a relic." He held it upright, turning the blade back and forth. "I've *heard* of your knife. Didn't it belong to Muhammad's family? There are stories. It's possible that Muhammad himself has touched it." They gazed at it together in silence. Finally, Eduardo sheathed the knife and handed it back to Amani with a nod. "Put this into a deposit box, straightaway. It's not a good idea to be walking around with it."

Amani clipped it to the waistband of her jeans, where she could feel the metal against the skin of her stomach. "I'm sure you're right," she said. "The thing makes me nervous."

"And better not to tell your uncle Hafez," he added.

She looked up at him quickly.

"Excuse me." He held out his hands. "That was inappropriate. I shouldn't have said that."

"Actually—" Amani broke off as a group of men walked past carrying gym bags, towels slung over their shoulders. She waited until their footsteps faded. "I hope you'll say exactly what you think. Whatever it is."

"Sometimes I say too much."

"No. I mean it." She waved one hand a little. "I'm sorry—I know you hardly know me. This whole visit has been so . . ."

"Frustrating?" he guessed.

She waited for a group carrying tennis racquets to pass. "Have you ever asked a question then felt sorry when you heard the answer? That's a little like what coming to Jordan has been like for me."

"You don't like what you're learning." He looked at her sympathetically. "A new country can be a shock."

"Ever since I got here—for a while now—" She pulled her wrapper closer. "I feel more—isolated? Almost like I'm being monitored. I go to these family gatherings and they all just *look* at me."

He chuckled and scratched the back of his head. "Ah, I can just imagine. We don't get that many Americans here."

"Well, they're supposedly my family. But there's no one I can really talk to." To her dismay, she felt her eyes start to burn. She'd tried to reach her mother a few times, but the connections were often echoing and broken, or Francesca had to rush to a meeting. Amani blotted her eye with the heel of her palm. "It scared me, about my dad—when he brought this to me. This knife is his prized possession." She looked at Eduardo, her vision brightened by tears. How hard it was to talk about this! "What does it mean," she asked at last, "for a person to give away something so special? I was shocked—when he did it, I mean. For him to hand Il Saif to me. I almost felt—it was like he was giving up."

"Giving up?" He narrowed his eyes. "By this you mean . . ."

"Like, everything. You should've seen his face. For a second he just seemed so defeated." She stared at Eduardo, at the pieces of black hair that fell across his forehead, the waiting patience in his eyes. "Like a surrender."

Eduardo inhaled and he shook his head. "I think for a man to give away something like this—if I may be so bold, more likely it means that he wants to be free."

17

HE WAS ANGRY with his family for their weakness, but Gabe
believed he was no better. He had failed to be brave.

Gabe's uncle Nader—his mother's younger brother—left
behind a village that had lost its name. He and his wife, Lutfi, and
several children came to Yara in 1948. His face was narrow and
pale with shock: he said they'd been awakened by neighbors banging on their doors and windows, screaming: *Get out*. There were
tanks and foreign soldiers moving in dust clouds through the village, shouting through bullhorns, the sound of Kalashnikov rifles
thudding in the distance. Nader and his family ran with only the
clothes on their backs. There were so many refugees arriving in
Yara at that time: without shoes, filthy, and starving. He saw how
the experience changed the children, turned them wary and feral.
Some of them always crying, others constantly fighting and hitting. Aunt Lutfi was said to be "backwards." He'd heard people
talking about her at the shared baker's oven. "Not backwards,"
his father's eldest sister, Lamise, had said, touching her temple.
"Crazy."

He tried to recall the face of the woman Uncle Nader had married, how she had looked to Gabe as if she were permanently crying. It was the way the lines in Aunt Lutfi's face were formed—deeply, vertically creased. It seemed her face was naturally shaped that way—that's what he'd told himself. The wells of her eyes were the shape of all the eyes of all refugees. When Aunt Lutfi died, he remembered they'd buried her with the old iron key to the house in their village in Palestine around her neck.

He remembered thinking his mother's laughter had a similar kind of softness, as if it were stained blue. He'd loved her fiercely, but this love was touched by a kind of longing—the awareness of imminent loss. She seemed always on the point of departure, as if they lived with only her echo. After his father died, his mother became eccentric. She wandered the house; she rarely ate or slept. He often saw her in her library, writing on her blue stationery. Sometimes she woke him in the night, breathless, her eyes roaming the dark of the room, to tell him that soldiers were coming. One night, he sat with her on the side of her bed, watching a red moon rise above the black rooftops, listening to her cry. When he'd asked, yemmah, what? What's the matter? She'd said: I want to go home.

But you are home.

The look she gave him: unblinking and frozen. My home is gone, she'd said.

Gabe believed she wasn't thinking clearly, yet he felt a chill like cold sparks along his vertebrae.

She said: Someone took my home and someone took your brother. You can't stay here or something will take you too. This place will suck the life from your lungs. Her pupils appeared to glint; her eyes looked silvery. Gabe held her hand; he squeezed her fingers. She was always a half step away, lost in thoughts, but how he'd loved the mother he'd once seen in glimpses. The possible-mother. She used to sit outside; she crossed her legs and stroked Gabe's head as it rested in her lap. Her hair was soft and loose. She brought glasses of tea to the Bedouin field hands; she knew all the stars; she read fortunes in the coffee grounds and the sand lines. She told him he would travel and meet a lovely woman and have a daughter like a pearl. "You will have a beautiful life," she'd said. "Treasure it."

"I will," he said. "I promise."

By the end of Gabe's two years of service, he moved back into the family house in Yara with his mother, but he missed the training and fencing. Everything felt close and small; the walls of the house pressed in on him. Aunt Lamise came every day, casting her gaze over the interior as if taking inventory. The servants had gone; only Mrs. Ward remained. His mother had withdrawn to her quiet recesses, her days spent over her pages. You must go, she told him at breakfast, and again before turning in for bed, rapping the back of his hand. I insist. I demand it. This place will swallow you up. Go, become whatever you will.

He'd tried to make jokes: But how would you manage without me?

Mrs. Ward will look after me, she'd said. When she looked at him, he felt the glance like a physical blow; a sense that there was some vital duty or obligation that he was failing to fulfill. Don't you dare use me as an excuse, she'd said. Don't you hide from your life.

One day, an Englishman stopped Gabe on the street to ask for directions—Gabe understood a little English and the stranger had rudimentary Arabic—after a few minutes of cobbled-together conversation, the man studied Gabe's face and inquired if he knew how to use a hammer. Who knew why the stranger had chosen him. Impossible, he'd thought. How can I leave? But the moment carried its own weight. He heard himself saying *yes*. Gabe was hired to help repair the interior carpentry and do other odd jobs aboard a steamship, the *Arabella*. He took a jolting, ten-hour bus ride to the Port of Beirut. They were in a hurry to set out and he agreed to work while underway. His employers gave him a sort of canvas sling from which he could hang outside the railing, shivering with ocean spume, spreading naval jelly over rust spots then repainting. He often had to work at night, to not alarm the passengers out on deck. It was a pleasure to work inside, even belowdecks, restoring cabinetry and floors. Once they'd docked at Porto di Napoli, the first captain recommended Gabe for another job, this time on an ocean liner bound for the United States. He had been guaranteed return passage home, but once they arrived in New York, Gabe was swept by the spreading green of that first harbor view, the expanse: the American trees and sky. He moved into a tiny, crowded apartment in Flushing. After he'd put in six months as a carpenter's assistant, Hafez called. "What are you doing, y'akhi? Get up here where you can breathe." He followed his brother Hafez north to Syracuse, delighted by the grassy valleys and the acres of trees. He wrote a letter to his mother on the bus ride up Route 81, listing in English the types of trees, pine, maple, birch, describing in Arabic the ones he didn't yet have names for: *oval leaves with jagged edges, a graceful trunk.*

At the time, he believed he was moving instinctively toward adventure. But he also understood he was leaving his mother behind. Deliberately and blindly. He ran.

CHAPTER

18

• *Aqaba, Jordan, still Thursday, November 16, 1995* •

"IF YOU SQUINT A LITTLE"—Hafez tapped on the tinted glass—
"you would think you were driving to Cannes. Maybe Biarritz."

"Mm. Maybe if you close your eyes all the way." Carole slouched
against the backseat, arms wrapped around her ribs.

Samir sent death-ray glances in the rearview mirror, a cigarette
stashed behind his left ear. Carole in the car meant no smoking. His
prayer beads on the mirror had been replaced by a fir tree.

They'd just wrapped camel and falconry exhibitions in Wadi
Rum and that nice troupe of children from—Romania?—doing
their dances with ribbons attached to long poles. His Majesty impec-
cable as always, standing to applaud, the ends of his white keffiyeh
twirling in the wind, his smile glowing. The desert wind had grown
overnight into a mistral and, upon release, the six thousand birthday
balloons whipped straight up into the dark. Today would be a motor-
cycle display along the water's edge, a grand parade down Al-Nahda
Street through Aqaba. Friday and Saturday, more banquets, more

performers—from Hong Kong and Mauritania and Luxembourg and who knows where else.

On Sunday, they would head to Petra for the fencing match. At last. His brother had been in Jordan for just a few weeks but the time had weighed on Hafez—the consciousness of Gabe's presence, his intrusive questions circulating among the family.

"No, I'm serious. We should have brought Amani with us. Her father fills her head with such nonsense. She has no idea what this country has to offer." He buzzed his window open so the car roared with warm, sandy air and Carole shrieked and flapped at her hair. "Sorry, sorry!" Buzzed back up. "Look—there. Nice little whitewashed buildings. The palm trees here are even better than in Cannes." Rows of waving fronds lined the street for blocks and blocks, shading the sweet, painted crosswalks, just like in France. Off to the right was the sparkling sea, filled with canopied motorboats, vendors walking the sand yoked with bags of magenta cotton candy, roasted nuts.

Earlier that morning, murmuring on his office phone, he'd talked with Madame X about—what? Nothing. Bêtises. Oh, well, there was still the unfinished matter of her brother Hassan Salhab, stuck in the clink, where, Hafez had learned, he'd begun tutoring prisoners in how to write testimonies and mount their own legal defenses. Busybody. Hafez had Mrs. Bosa collect a file of Salhab's columns—inflammatory, saber-rattling stuff: King H negotiates with the enemy and ignores his own people! King H undermines the Washington talks! Salhab was an instigator.

Of course, he mentioned none of this to Salhab's sister. In fact, they'd already planned their own quiet get-together. Madame X was also driving down to see the performances.

And then, this morning, Carole announced she thought she would join him at the seashore. She'd said merely, *It might be fun.*

She'd sniffed him out again. Hafez felt a slow smile form on his lips: his wife was a worthy opponent.

Well, Aqaba was marvelous, wasn't it? Even if the salt air had an occasional twang of garbage and shit—more Marseille than Cannes. But look at that sapphire sky! *Look, Amani,* he thought. *How beautiful your country is.*

The car swerved, executing a minor fishtail, righting itself. Samir shook his fist at some tourists daring to cross the street. At last, they pulled onto the tiled drive of the Four Seasons, its walls clean and white as sugar. Carole headed to the spa—Hafez returned her three-fingered wave. But the more he thought about Amani, the more he was dismayed, even vexed. She'd rejected his itineraries; he'd asked Samir to drive her to view the mosaic workshop in Madaba, the hot springs at Maan, the Mecca Super Mall, and each time she'd sent him back home. Instead, she went roaming all over the desert with her hopeless cousin.

And her father! Circling Hafez at parties, avoiding conversation, acting as though he were somehow frightened or suspicious of his own brother. Yesterday, he calls and asks out of the blue: What happened to our mother? What *really* happened to her, my brother. Do you know? *Now* he wants to know about their mother? Now?

He'd told Gabe: You want a mystery? The mystery is why haven't you come home in forty years. Not once. Nothing. The mystery is why you think you can pop up and start asking x, y, and zed. He sniffed, wrinkled his nose. That little flare of temper was unlike him. Emotions were the dance floor that one skipped across. He let out a long breath, relaxed his hands. He needed to shake this ghost. No dark thoughts at the Four Seasons. The concierge retrieved a folded slip of paper from beneath the counter and handed it over. Trailing behind the bellhop and luggage trolley, Hafez opened it: 528. That's all it said. It smelled of a rain-washed perfume. He drew it into his lungs—528—then crumpled the note and dropped it into a wicker trash bin beside the elevator.

Samir retrieved the cigarette from behind his ear and lit it. "I'll bring the car back tomorrow," he said to Hafez.

"Smoking is forbidden in the hotel. I'm sorry," a twenty-year-old bellhop said in English as he and Hafez boarded the elevator. His name tag said Serge. Under that, St. Petersburg.

Samir took a long, crackling hit on his Camel so the end glowed. "I'm sorry, I don't speak English," he told the boy in Arabic. Standing outside the elevator, he sent a rich exhale into the lift and waved, just before the doors closed. Hafez greedily drew in the secondhand smoke.

His room was 512. A bit close to that of his co-conspirator. Entering behind the bellhop, Hafez barely took in the terra-cotta walls, the basket of roses and other beastly flowers sent from the Lithuanians, the magnum of Champagne from the hotel, the plate of cookies, the cellophane-wrapped tray of Allah-knows-what, the three-window wall overlooking the water, the balcony beyond the glass. "Good, nice. Perfect." He tipped the boy ten piastres and left him to install their suitcases.

With a glance at his watch, he calculated. Carole would be wrapped in fluff, Dead Sea mud expensively spackled over her face. That took two hours. The beachside exhibition started in an hour and fifteen minutes. There was time. His mood lifted. He could grab a cig on the beach and still have a whole fifty minutes in 528.

Hafez reminded himself of how restored, new man–ized, he'd felt since the call from his attorney, Ahmad Zanzi, the other day. Zanzi had been in communication with the archbishop, and he said things were progressing. Progressing! Oh, 528! How good it felt to hope. The elevator doors slid open to the lobby and he headed toward the glass doors that glistened over the Tala Terrace. There, he encountered the ministers of health, education, and economics, as well as the dull-witted chief of staff, the royal valet, and the State Department spook, Abu-Khaider, all smoking and gossiping about this local warlord and that Saudi Prince and what to do with that saxophone player, Clinton. Hafez had taken maybe fifteen steps across the marble lobby when Rafi sailed up, wrists jutting above his cuffs, eyebrows pointed. "Can I just run down this agenda? With you?"

"I'm senior advisor, not senior party planner," Hafez grumped. Then he hesitated. Rafi could help cover for Hafez's little absences or he could report on his every move. Hafez could afford to alienate him only to a point. "Fine. Just be . . ." He twirled the first two fingers of his right hand. "Expeditious."

Rafi paged through his program. He reeled off the multistoried names of the desert rulers coming to pay their respects. He ticked his pen against the clipboard. He followed Hafez, speaking of events and times, asking questions all the way to the beachside celebration. The sliver of free time melted away—there would be no cigarette. Instead, there would be touring the motorcycles—a continuous array gleamingly parked on the sand—two of them birthday gifts from Sultan Qaboos. Their Majesties were late, again. So, it was up to Hafez and Abu-Khaider and long-suffering Prince H, the younger brother, to act as stand-ins, nodding at the chrome. Hafez cast a glance in the direction of 528.

After the motorcycles, he ran to the front desk to leave a message: *No time now. After lunch?*

Silent as a jinn, Carole materialized at his left shoulder. She glowed from minerals and rubbing and rinsing. Her blond hair was puffed and her eyes were ringed with some sort of blue frost. "Ana ju'aneh." I'm starving.

"I've been looking everywhere for you," he said in English. "I was about to organize a search party."

Carole rolled her eyes. A new shell-pink lipstick. There was some sort of necklace of stones and Dead Sea crystal around her throat that he was certain he'd never seen before. She threw her silk wrapper across one shoulder and led the way.

The sheikh's picnic involved all of Tala Bay Beach, extending from the Four Seasons to the Grand Hotel. Beyond the hotel, near the royal compound, steam rose from the King's favorite Alouette helicopter, its blades turning lazily in the wind. The royal couple had arrived at last. As the retinue made its way across the terrace, sunlight illuminated the sides of palm trees and shone over the infinity pools. Hafez shaded his eyes with one hand. In the bay, women in tiny bikinis bounded over the surf. Beside them, fully covered muhajjabat dragged black hijabs through the water. The ends of their garments twirled so they looked like human seaweed. Tourists pedaled pontoon boats, and farther out, freighters and cruise ships came up the Gulf of Aqaba from the Red Sea, the water glimmering as if painted on foil. Hafez slipped off his shoes and socks and carried them in his hands, hot sand pressing between his toes.

The sheikh's tent of white silk billowed and puffed and threatened to lift itself and everyone in it into the air. Hafez and Carole were given a cushioned divan. In the smaller adjoining tents, the guests were seated on pillows on the ground in the more traditional manner: it made Hafez's knees hurt just to look at them. He would be seventy next month: he had to keep reminding himself because he literally couldn't believe it. "Lovely," he said to the sheikh. "Bedouin seating for grown-ups."

The sheikh laughed and stroked his beard on one then the other side. Hafez heard him repeat the comment to other guests. There were two stiff-backed chairs wrapped in white at the top of the long, low table. Rafi came in, whispered to the sheikh, and the chairs were removed and replaced with another cushioned divan. "Imagine being so special," Hafez said to Carole, "you need someone following you around trying to make you seem less special."

Carole sucked in her cheeks. The sheer light magnified the lines on her face. It wasn't like him to say something joking in public about the King—even affectionately. He was somewhat giddy. He crossed his wrists in his lap.

"These little grapes are delightful," she said to their host. "Are they from the valley?"

"The Israeli side," the Sheikh boasted.

The sheikh's eldest son, Khaled, held up a grape: "Their fruit is wonderful, but where did the seeds come from? Where is their garden?" Abu-Khaider turned toward Marjit Conway, special envoy from Ireland, complaining about the policy restrictions that prevented Israeli officials from speaking with the PLO—which all but crippled open negotiations. "So we're stuck with covert tea parties in supposedly neutral places—like castles in Norway."

There were murmurs and laughter in the tent. An emissary from Cairo inhaled loudly. "Without Rabin, there is no more garden. No more tea."

"That remains to be seen, Abu-Sliman," Hafez tutted. The so-called Oslo peace talks between Palestine and Israel had been conducted by dilettantes, trying to show up the experts. The Palace had to learn about the Norwegian tea-party talks from Abu-Ammar himself—bilious old Arafat wheezing with laughter on the phone, "Truly, you had no idea?" The King had been furious: to be cut out of conversations that so intimately affected his kingdom. Hafez sympathized. He knew how it felt, to be nudged aside: he'd spent his childhood on study, good comportment, shiny shoes, and combed hair, only to be spurned by his own father.

Hafez had spoken with the organizers a few months after the fact, at a press conference announcing the new peace proposals. "We must have some form of reconciliation in order to move on to peace," the Norwegian organizer had said. "You politicians always forget that part. You must *agree* to forgive, *plan* to—even if you don't feel it."

Hafez had shaken his head. "What sort of peace is there without justice?"

"Yes, yes," the man had said, looking so tired, so stooped in his suit. "And how to effect justice without peace? The snake that bites its own tail. Someone always has to take the first step."

Men wearing salwar kameez offered a soft, resinous wine from Lebanon, goat cheeses in cylinders and cones and pyramids dusted with ash, pita with olive oil and rosemary blistered on an open fire. There were platters of fruit freshly plucked, bursting with ripeness. Servers brought forth whole roasted tiny ortolans on skewers: some of the diners placed napkins over their heads and began chirping—a tradition concerning the consumption of songbirds and the need to hide such an act from God. A poetic meal. Hafez wondered: Had Amani ever tasted the like? Perhaps she might write a verse about these grilled birds. She and her father had been invited to this event, but Gabe had left him a last-minute apology on voicemail: *We're bushed. And we've got to get ready for Petra.*

He noted that HRM 1 and 2 had finally taken their places, the King shining his youthful smile over the table, the Queen, more reserved yet lovely. Hafez accepted another refill. He imagined himself and his niece sitting beside the royalty, laughing. The glasses were so small and so good, impossible to keep track of how many one drank. "Like eating grapes."

"What was that?" Carole leaned forward, following his gaze.

"Like light. Don't you think Her Majesty looks like her name?" Hafez stared at her, then laughed. "Queen Sunshine is radiant. Get it? A bilingual pun."

"Her Majesty is always radiant," Carole said quietly. She smoothed back her hair and looked at Hafez. "Ya zowji." My husband. "Slow yourself down," she said sotto voce.

Still, he ate too much and managed a few more glassfuls of the Cabernet, his hair tossed by the dry wind. Deep into the banquet, between toasts and speeches, Hafez peered out the tent flaps and saw his driver, Samir, sitting with a ring of other drivers and a couple of the royal compound kitchen staff. They were cross-legged on the sand in their T-shirts and trainers, smoking cigarettes and drinking Bedouin coffee. Two men lay stretched out full-length, fast asleep. Another was cutting a cucumber in his palm. Hafez felt pierced by envy, a blade slicing him end to end. Oh, to be on one's own, without cares or responsibilities. To smoke and sleep on the sand. This was the sort of man he was meant to be.

The sheikh took out a small dagger with an emerald handle and began peeling an orange in one unbroken curl. "Ah, what a beauty," Abu-Khaider said. "Is that an heirloom?"

The sheikh laughed and jerked his chin upward, tch. "*This* is an heirloom." He removed a long, curving khanjar from his robes with a slicing sound. Heads turned. Hafez's breath stopped. The sheikh held the blade aloft, light winking on its sides. "A man requires a true knife. Don't you agree?" He looked at Hafez.

Hafez jumped at a sharp pinch on the back of his arm. Carole was leaning into him, whispering, "What's wrong with you?"

"What?"

"You should see your face."

"What's wrong with my face?"

Carole lifted her chin. "Are you worried about the fencing match?" She still didn't know about the inherited land or the knife. He turned away and took a gulp of wine.

Servers in floor-length robes covered the table with round trays of carved silver. The pots, carried two men at a time, were upended onto the trays. Mansaf, alternating lamb and goat on beds of rice and onion, appeared in plumes of steam. Hafez registered Carole frowning again in his peripheral vision. But Hafez felt moved now, inspired. He knew what he had to do: he saw it clearly, as if it were written on the tent. He would call Amani and tell her everything: unburden himself. For the first time in his life. He would share the truth of what he'd done to Musa. He would ask her to forgive him. Oh, he didn't expect redemption—he had no use for fairy tales. Still, he saw himself bowing before her, how she would place her hand on his head. Then and only then could he be made whole. Standing, he saluted hazily to the Mauritanian across the table, excused himself, and slipped out between flaps that weren't intended to be an exit. He heard Carole asking him something, but he couldn't stop.

He made his way past the gang of drivers and servants, saluting them as well. "Al fresco, very nice!" he called. He lifted his head and pulled in his stomach: if you can't walk straight, then stand straighter. Then he was at the glass doors, staring at a child with a wild profusion of silver balloons stamped with gold crowns. She bustled past. Entering the lobby, assailed by echoes and sunspots spinning over that slippery marble, Hafez put out his hand for balance. He could push off on one foot like he had that one winter day, on Onondaga Lake. When Francesca was there, all laughter, the snow powdering her hair. Hafez had wanted to kiss her, but his brother had claimed her: she and Gabe walking together, holding hands inside a single knitted mitten. They were children and Hafez the adult.

Hafez made it through the echoes and voices to the elevators. Confronting its panel of buttons, he stopped, staring at the rows of numbers, and then realized he'd forgotten what it was he had come here to do. He looked down and saw the emptied wastebasket, remembering that he'd dropped the room number there. Madame X was waiting!

He hit the elevator button and boarded, yet still felt bedeviled by uncertainty. Of course the number had vanished from his head. Everything smelled like air freshener. Room 628 or 526? He took the elevator to six and tried knocking on 628, then rattled the door handle. He tried several doors, up and down the hall, knocking, inserting his own key; he tried calling, "Helloo in there!"

At 648, a woman burst from the door, her hair a cloud of black frazzle. He was so startled he cried, "Oh, my dear!"

She slammed the door shut, startling him into a moment of clarity: 528.

Down one floor, he practically flew to the door, his head filled with the sound of his own hurrying footsteps. Raising a fist, he stopped and finger-combed his hair. He tried to check his breath with a cupped hand. He knocked.

Nothing.

He knocked some more. He tried the handle and called through the frame. He huffed, leaning against the door, hands in his pockets, playing with his worry beads. He knocked some more, as if by knocking he could conjure her up. Somewhere in the distance, he heard the chime of the elevator doors opening. "Ya Hafez!" Madame X called. "Stop. I can hear you all the way into the lift."

She opened her door and he hurried in behind her. "Where have you been?" he complained, suddenly aggrieved. "I've been waiting and waiting and waiting."

With a tug, she closed the curtains to three-quarters over the French doors. Her room wasn't as spacious as his. The windows overlooked a flowering courtyard instead of the beach. She dropped a notebook on to a stack of binders and folders on the table.

"What's all this?" He waved at the papers. "I thought you were here for me."

She sat in the chair near the table, not on the bedside. "I bring my work everywhere, my dear. This is the archbishop's calendar, his correspondence, requests and petitions . . ." She adjusted her pearl necklace. "Do you think I exist only for you?"

"You don't?" He smiled and sat in the chair across from her, impatient.

Madame X wiped both hands over her face, pushing it back so for a moment she looked less tired. Then she let go, the skin falling like a sigh. "I talked to my brother this morning."

"They let you talk to him?"

"His Grace has some pull. Maybe once every couple of months we can get a call through. Hassan said nothing's changed."

"Nothing?" Hafez did a good job of sounding surprised.

A wing of hair fell forward over one eye as she looked up, her eyes like magnetic weights. She tipped her face and Hafez thought of kissing the soft underside of her chin. "Have you done anything, Hafez? Anything at all?"

"For your brother?" Real indignation rose up, just as if he'd been laboring at this case for weeks. "I've called in favors, I've . . ."

"Who?"

"Excuse me?"

"Who? Who have you called, exactly? What favors?"

He inhaled deeply, reminding himself this was blood in exchange for land: a high-stakes negotiation. His laugh came from the center of his chest. "I am owed favors from very nearly everyone." He rolled forward in his chair. "You may not realize what a difficult case your brother is. Jordan does not have a free press. We can't afford one! *Most* countries cannot afford a free press. It was foolhardy—for your brother to raise such delicate questions of governance, of the King's most fundamental powers."

Her expression sharpened. "So, the idea is to humor the people with the appearance of a free press—like a little puppet show? Is that it?"

When had she become so irritating? Hafez's breath shortened. He didn't deserve this! He lifted a finger in warning. "Your brother was speaking of the King's death. He was demanding to know his successor!"

"Not demanding. Asking. Asking. As is the right and duty of any thinking citizen. We have the right to ask who we will be ruled by. We have the right to participate in that decision. We have the obligation to raise these questions!" She had also moved forward, her hands on the desk before her. "We are not children or puppets, no matter what the King thinks."

Hafez struggled against the impulse to get to his feet, but his voice lifted. "Have you any idea how many assassination attempts His Majesty has survived?"

"More than Rasputin, I'm sure."

"Seven to date. Seven. That's on record—who knows the actual total. He is surrounded by jackals and hyenas. There are the princes draining every drop out of Arabia! There is Assad crushing—never mind his enemies—do you know what he did to his own sons-in-law?"

Madame X pushed away from the desk. Rising, she went to the French doors and pulled the curtains all the way closed against the incoming afternoon.

"And Sadat! Gaddafi! And oh my God, Arafat! Never mind the Israelis! Never mind their systematic destruction—at least they *have* a system." He laughed too loudly and the room swayed: "Do you know what all these—terrorists—would do . . . if they caught even the faintest whiff of weakness from the king?"

Madame X leaned against one of the French doors so a piece of light poured in around her, dousing her features.

"They would tear him apart and then they would tear Jordan apart." He made the rending movement in the air with his hands. "Do you know what the Israelis call Jordan?" He suddenly felt very tired. "They call it 'Palestine.'" He laughed shortly. "We've become the holding tank." He was surprised to feel a surge of real grief. What was this? For a moment, he held still, breathing in traces of olives and garlic and the citronella aftershave he'd tapped on in that happy, far-far-away morning. Then so softly that at first, he thought he was imagining it, a hand touched his shoulder.

"But . . . you'll keep trying?"

He turned, gratitude blooming in his heart. "Oh, my dear. Oh, my world. Yes, of course. A hundred times, yes!" He felt that he actually meant it. That the risk was worth any of it and more. He folded her hands into his and kissed her knuckles, softly and ardently. She let her elbows bend and swayed into him.

She was pliant, like the stem of a plant. His hands slid around the inversion of her, the abundance of her hips, the globes of her buttocks. She did something with her hands behind her back and her black skirt slithered away with a crackle. Stepping out of it, she put her arms around his neck. Charmed, bewitched, he yanked off his jacket, tried to wrench his tie off, nearly strangling himself. It was nothing to lift her off the ground. Rather quickly, however, he had to drop her on the bed.

She laughed and peeled down the comforter—for a moment he felt a pang, some hesitation. But then they were together, under the sheets. A momentous occasion for Hafez, after so many years of technical fidelity: Madame X was charging ahead, leading him. She'd skinned off her panties, which appeared to be made of mostly lace and string. And now he was thinking—though he didn't wish to— of his wife's panties, which were somehow the very opposite of those of Madame X—big as a flag.

He wanted to say something about this, about the mysterious world of women's panties. Instead, he became fixated on the angle between the base of her neck and the top of her right shoulder. He focused on kissing her exactly there, on not saying anything at all. Carole said: *Sometimes one must be silent.* He moved down the length of her, marking her with a trail of kisses, dividing her full breasts that spilled apart from each other. He held and reunited them as he kissed. But then he and his hands were lower on her rib cage, then he tasted her navel. And then, oh marvels! He arrived at her nether region, which was mysteriously freed of nearly all hair. Carole still had this hair—or did the last time he looked—though hers was gray. He felt another pang, looking at Madame X's pudenda, naked to the world, too sacred to touch. But then he felt her guiding hands on the back of his head. And his tongue parted the innocent lower lips and he realized, with a soft ripple of fear and pure thrill, that she didn't taste like Carole.

He found he was watching himself, thinking that Carole had tasted of earth and salt, a trace of fish, an iota of something like thyme. He was no longer absolutely certain he wanted to be there, in that bed. Madame X smelled and tasted of a sort of chemical cherry nothingness, like hotel air freshener. This could not be him; this was someone else, praying for favors like a common prostitute. He thought back wistfully to long-ago weekends in bed. Once Carole had bit his shoulder so hard he'd cried out and there were teeth marks in his skin for days. He wished they were there still. This means you belong to me, she'd said. Twenty-four years old, skinny and crooked teeth and stringy hair, she claimed him.

He heard birdsong through the windows, and beyond that, applause, cheers, and off-key human song. Carole would be wondering about his whereabouts. His wife had dressed herself up. For him? Had he mentioned how lovely she looked? He remembered, unwillingly, his brother saying on the phone, *What aren't you telling me?* How he'd responded, *Why do you ask about things that don't concern you?* He sensed a gathering, an energetic field in the flesh beneath his tongue. Distracted, Hafez lapped with more vigor until her hands restrained him.

He wondered if it were true that there were secret cameras in these rooms. He began to feel a bit panicky, increasingly sure that this was not what he'd meant to do. It wasn't too late, was it, to raise a child? To make the life he'd intended? Not this, no. He imagined his niece's disgust upon seeing him there, abject, crouching between this woman's legs.

The situation was all wrong. Her fingers had begun to tighten on his scalp, but he sat up, his hands braced on her knees. "No, no, I can't. I mustn't."

Madame X opened her eyes, her expression nearly alarmed. "What?" she made a sound in between a laugh and hiccup. Then a groan of something like furious frustration. She screwed her eyes shut, scowling, and her hands moved under the bedsheet. She groaned again, then eventually gasped and sighed. After a moment, she too sat up, blinking.

"I'm sorry," he said. "It wasn't right."

She didn't respond but merely climbed out of bed and back into her clothes. A minute later, she was tidily refastening her blouse, combing her hair, splashing her face in the bathroom, straightening her string of pearls.

Hafez sank back down, turned onto his side—his shirt rumpled, half-buttoned. Aside from a few stirrings, his penis had drowsed through the whole event. "I am sorry," he repeated dolefully.

She was already leaning into the mirror, dotting on lipstick. She blotted with a piece of tissue. "Better get going. His Grace has a two o'clock with the Syrian ambassador."

Hafez rolled onto his back. His altered spirit trembled, hovered. He was warm and fragile. He stretched his bare feet, his shoes lost at sea on the burgundy carpet. Another swirl of birdsong beyond the glass. She hurried past, pulling up a zipper behind her waist. "What are you doing, Hafez? You've got to get out of here."

"You go on ahead. I might just—" He folded his arms under his head. What was this gloomy feeling? Was this what guilt felt like? Remorse?

"What? No, no, no. You can't stay in here! I've got a million things to do and you're not among them. You think no one's going to notice you just walked off your luncheon? If one word gets back to my husband, one *word* . . ."

"All right, my darling." Now, this was like Carole.

"Besides, how do you expect me to work on your inheritance, ya Hafez?" She winked at him in the mirror. "If you keep me all day in bed?"

"Ah." He swung his feet to the floor. He smiled. "You know what my petition is for."

She stopped stroking her hair. Her eyes seemed to go still in the mirror. Then she glanced at him. "Of course. I had to familiarize myself, if I was going to present your case."

"You read the document? You know what is involved?"

"All strictly confidential, naturally. The archbishop and I are the only ones who will know. Not another thought—I will make this happen." Madame X was standing at the door, peering out the peephole to the hotel corridor. "You go first. Be quick! Don't stop. Go straight to the elevator and get on. I'll have to wait at last ten minutes before I go. But I don't have ten minutes. Come on, imshee, yella!"

He thought of embracing her at the door, but she lifted her chin, smiling, nudging him out. "My brother is waiting. I'm trusting you now."

Then he was completely alone in the corridor of pale carpeting. He walked toward the elevators.

Freeing the brother, Hafez knew, was not an option. Madame X would certainly reveal the lengths she'd gone to in order to get him released. Or Salhab himself would ferret it out—the land, the church ruling—and make an example of Hafez, to prove he, a pure journalist, owed no allegiance to corrupt politicians. An exposé, starring Hafez Hamdan, in the paper would be disastrous. Amer's land, practically on the dividing line between Jordan and the West Bank, was in too sensitive a region. Crucial to border security. If they caught even a whiff of this freed-up property, the Crown would seize it. Especially when this much land was involved, worth nearly half a billion U.S. All land plots were titled and registered with the Land and Survey Department, and anything not titled as private property was considered government property. He'd had to pay an expensive visit to the office manager at the Land Department to assure that this estate took a long time to register.

Lost in thought, Hafez was brought up short when he reached the elevators. Rafi was there, waiting with the down button lit. "What are you doing here?" Hafez said.

"You walked out. In the middle of the luncheon." Rafi flattened his clipboard against his side. "I came to check on you."

"To check on me? You're my wife now?"

"Your wife was busy. She was talking with the Bahraini delegate."

"So now you check on me."

"Yes."

It was hot under his arms and shirtfront. "And what did you learn?"

Rafi looked at the floor. "I knocked on your door and you didn't answer."

"Right," Hafez said a little aggressively.

Rafi glanced at him. "Your room is down there." He pointed toward the water-view wing.

"So?"

"You just came from"—Rafi's eyes flicked—"over there."

Hafez didn't say anything. Did he hear footsteps? "I went to get ice," Hafez said loudly.

"You don't have an ice bucket."

Hafez felt as if his head might explode into flames. He definitely heard approaching footsteps. "They were out of ice!" he shouted.

"But—"

"Why haven't you pushed the elevator button?" He slapped the already-lit wall panel repeatedly. "Why are you just standing here like some sort of—"

Rafi stared as the elevator doors slid open. The two boarded in silence; all Hafez could hear was the sound of his heart walloping in his ears. His eyes shifted to Rafi's profile, then back to the numbers flashing over the elevator door. He felt off-kilter. *Get a grip, man.* He repeated it silently: *get a grip.* He put one hand against the wall and thought he saw Rafi flinch. He couldn't send Salhab to the West. Nothing strengthened a journalist like exile in Paris. But perhaps he might be extradited to one of their partners—prison in Algeria, say. Or Yemen. Yemen was interesting. He cleared his throat. Checked the position of his tie. When the doors opened, he sailed past Rafi and over the white ice of the lobby floor.

CHAPTER

19

• *Amman, Jordan, Friday, November 17, 1995* •

AMANI FELT QUIET, nearly bodiless, as she listened, watching the faces and the movements of hands—thirty women in sweaters, skirts, and boots holding glasses of white wine. On their shoulders were tags identifying names and cities. She'd agreed to appear at a holiday luncheon hosted by the British Women's Society at the Marriott. They'd started twenty years ago as a gathering for the homesick, but eventually branched into local politics and social activism. The black-haired woman at the King's dinner who'd sat on her left had called and asked Amani if she would give a talk to the group. "I think they'd be mad for you," Lubna Waleeda said.

At the podium, Amani cleared her throat and said the first thing that came to her: "I think I'm interested in what makes us who we are. What are the memories that, maybe, come through the land, to make a place into a country—like this one?" Then she nudged aside the podium and sat back onto the table. She hadn't prepared a talk ahead of time, assuming she could improvise. Now she wasn't so sure. "I like thinking about what it means—to be 'from' anywhere," she said slowly, uncertain what constituted too much information in Amman. Releasing a breath, she told them what she knew about her grandmother, Natalia. How she'd fled her childhood home, how they'd lost everything, how she'd ended up in a remote village. "I don't know much more than that," Amani said. "She died years ago—before I was born. But even so, I've often felt somehow we have a kind of relationship. When I came here, I thought if I couldn't know Natalia, I could try to know Jordan—at least a little bit—instead. If that doesn't sound too crazy."

A few women shook their heads, murmuring no, no. After a moment, one of them called, "If you want to be crazy, just marry a Jordanian."

The others laughed. A ripple seemed to go through the women. Amani leaned forward, crossing her legs. "I'd like to know what it's like for you here. People have this idea that women are totally oppressed in the Middle East."

"We are!" someone shouted from the back, followed by a rumble of laughter and voices.

One of the event organizers, a German woman named Renata, said, "We can tell you about this country all right. They think we're just a bunch of bored hausfrauen here. We do all kinds of outreach. We've been working on initiatives to educate girls and to teach literacy."

Another woman raised her hand. "The Arabs—they say they revere women. Yes, well, maybe they revere us, but they don't much like us."

The attendees started talking over one another, offering complaints: the cat-calling men, the bullying mothers-in-law, boys dominating their sisters; women stripped of their property, of custody of their children, of their reproductive rights. "Which is against Islam!" a woman in a glimmering blue veil declared, slapping the table. "Look in the Qu'ran—Islam protects women's rights. More than Christianity, even! But tell that to the Muslims."

One of the women said, "And if you want to know the Hamdan family? Be careful what you wish for."

Amani smiled uncertainly. "I'm finding that out."

"The Hamdans don't do women," the first veiled woman said. "They published a family tree a few years ago—it didn't contain any women. Not a one. Perhaps they spontaneously regenerate."

"Your uncle Farouq . . ." another trailed off contemptuously.

"He imports poisons!" the gray-haired woman stated. A number of people began speaking at the same time.

"Excuse me, but that's a bit of an overstatement." Muna, whose ID card said *Sri Lanka,* held up a finger. She said to Amani, "Farouq is a shareholder in Raghadan Inc. We keep an eye on them. One of their big moneymakers is an herbicide that contains Agent Orange. It's outlawed around the world. But they can get it here for pennies and the farmers send their kids into the fields to scatter the stuff. You see children with blood and skin disorders and leukemias."

Amani placed her hand on the table.

"And there's Hafez Hamdan."

Someone laughed. "Hafez, who has no enemies."

"Because they're all dead," another said.

"Oh, come now," the woman in the blue veil said. "Many of them are alive and well and tortured in secret prisons."

Amani felt her pulse in her ears; heat swam over her. "Wait. My uncle?"

The gray-haired woman said, "This is inappropriate. There's no definite evidence. Just rumors and wild tales."

"*Not* only rumors!" another woman called from the back of the table. "Hafez is part of the problem. They call him the King's bull-dog. Didn't you see? Just this morning he had an op-ed in the paper saying that we shouldn't have a free press. He said we needed to be protected from ourselves—like good slaves and subjects. We should leave the 'truth' up to him!"

A number of the women began shouting; someone slapped the table repeatedly.

"Khalas!" Stop. Renata stood and held out her arms. "Okay—okay, now. This is enough. We invited Amani here to speak to us, not to be roasted alive."

AFTER THE MEETING, Amani felt limp. Women had surrounded her, squeezing her shoulder or kissing her cheeks, and promised to find her book. A man in a trim, dark suit made his way through the departing women, and only then did she remember she was meeting Eduardo. He'd called that morning, wanting to see her again. When she'd told him she had to give a talk, he'd said, "Then it would be an honor to chauffeur you home." Now she stood with a little wave, collecting her things, tired and suddenly very grateful to see him. "You weren't waiting long? I had to let your fans have their turn," he said. He was helping Amani on with her coat when one more woman introduced herself. Nikki was very small with a pixie face and short, choppy hair. "Our families are related," she said. "There's lots of marriages between the Nawars and the Hamdans. My parents, I think, grew up in the same village as your grandparents. In Yara?"

"Yara. Yes. That's right." Amani raised her eyebrows at Eduardo, then turned back to Nikki. "Did they ever mention my grandparents to you?"

"I wish I could remember." Nikki looked apologetic. "They died—more than ten years ago. Even the village isn't there anymore. The younger people moved away—to England or to the city. I went to school in Beirut. My brothers and I didn't come back to Amman until we were adults."

"Ah." Amani released a breath. "Do you know—is anyone still around from the old village? I'd love to talk to someone who might have known my grandmother. It's been really just—frustrating. Trying to get any information. At all. Lately I've been wondering if she actually existed."

Pulling out a banquet chair, Nikki sat and produced a mobile phone. She squinted at the screen. "There maybe is someone. . . ." She dialed and put the phone to her ear.

While Nikki spoke in Arabic, Eduardo raised his eyebrows. "Ah. You've found a way forward, perhaps. A little key."

"Oh, I don't know," Amani said. "It could be nothing." But her hands were warm and she could hear her own pulse in her ears.

After a few moments, Nikki clicked the phone shut. She asked Amani, "What are you doing right now?"

"SHE SAYS SHE's one hundred years old, only I think she's been saying that for a few years," Nikki murmured. She crouched before the woman and kissed her hands then both her cheeks. Sitt Danya lived in a three-story limestone building above a pharmacy. It was in Dhiban, a tiny township on the Madaba Highway, a twenty-minute drive south of Amman. Nikki pointed across the highway when they parked and said, "Just over that way? That's where the old village— Yara—used to be. Where our parents grew up."

All Amani could see were open fields, sun-bleached dirt, and rubble and concrete powder. Some sharp-needled cypress trees bent in the wind as if shaking their fingers, the sky bone-white. Sitt Danya had the same view of the fields from her narrow balcony, though the windows were covered by mashrubat—screens of wooden beads that dappled her apartment with shadows. Nikki introduced Eduardo and Amani, and the old woman greeted Eduardo warmly but with a certain formality, inviting him to sit on a low cushioned chair with curved legs, as if he were a visiting dignitary. Then she reached for Amani with avid, knobby hands. She took her face in her palms and kissed her, smearing tears over her skin. Amani was startled and moved; she kissed the woman on her fragile cheeks.

"I tried to tell her who you are, but I'm not sure she understands," Nikki said. She spoke to Sitt Danya at greater length, patting Amani's shoulder and arm. She heard the words "Amreeka" and "Engleesi." The older woman didn't move her eyes from Amani's face. She had a map of creases across her cheeks, and her head

was wrapped in a floral band that was topped by a loose black veil.
Hala, her great-grand-niece, emerged from the kitchen with a tray
filled with bread, zaatar, and olives swimming in dark-green oil. Sitt
Danya said something to her and Hala looked at Amani, bemused.
"She thinks you're someone from the past." Hala said something
teasing to her aunt then turned to Amani. "She doesn't usually make
mistakes like that."

Nikki filled some tiny cups with coffee. "She keeps saying how
good it is to see you again."

"You were apparently close friends," Eduardo murmured, accept-
ing a cup.

Amani felt heat at the backs of her eyes and nodded. She leaned
forward to press the woman's hands. "Please tell her that it's wonderful to see her again as well."

Nikki told Amani, with some additions from Hala, that Sitt
Danya had never married or had children of her own. She knew
herbs and cupping and tinctures; she'd tended the sick and delivered
all the babies in Yara. She knew everyone in the village. The woman
smiled, her gaze on Amani. Amani nodded and said, "Would you
please ask her if she remembered—me—as being happy? What was
my life like?"

Nikki glanced at Amani for a moment before she turned to ask
the question. Sitt Danya bowed a bit, listening, and after Nikki finished, she didn't lift her head right away. She blinked, then she spoke
with her eyes lowered, and Nikki translated: "I think it was hard for
you, because you carried your old home inside. You never left it. You
were such a smart girl. I think your books and your animals saved
you." The old woman touched Amani's arm, speaking Arabic. Nikki
continued, "But you loved to laugh. You looked for ways to be happy.
You were always meant to be happy."

Amani's chest stiffened, but she was able to smile. "I think so too."

Eduardo took her hand. She held on for a moment, then slipped
out of his grasp.

They sipped coffee while Danya tried to recall what she could of life in the village. Childbirth was somehow a much easier process back then and the people seemed healthier, too, she thought, their bones were stronger. And their blood and teeth were better. "Not like now," Nikki translated while Hala looked ruefully down at her lap. Sitt Danya told stories about other families in the village, about the refugees who appeared suddenly, the tents, the undernourished children, their bowed legs. The little boy who sat alone, smiling in a beam of sunlight.

When the beaded shadows began to move through the apartment, Hala said her aunt would need her nap soon. Amani, Eduardo, and Nikki stood to go, though the old woman protested and clung to their wrists. "I'll come back again soon. I promise." Amani stooped before her. "But I did have just—one more thing. . . . Can you remember—how many children did I have?"

Even before Nikki translated, Sitt Danya seemed to understand, her eyes lifting toward the ceiling. She murmured, *wahad, teneen, talata, araba* . . . Finally, she said, "Saba'."

"Seven?"

Danya added something, which Nikki translated: "Three didn't survive."

Amani drew a breath. "She's sure it was three? I thought four babies died."

Nikki told her this and the older woman seemed startled; she looked at Amani as if seeing her more clearly. She said something and shook her head.

"Do you remember their names at all?"

Hala put a hand on her aunt's shoulder. "It's very hard—she delivered so many babies, and it was so long ago. She just isn't sure of the exact answers anymore."

As Eduardo opened the door, Sitt Danya tapped Amani's arm then drew her closer and said something, her eyes staring directly into Amani's. "Your first choice—if it was a choice—was not so good," Hala translated. Sitt Danya took Eduardo's hand in her left and Amani's in her right. "I'm very happy you found each other—

finally." She looked at Eduardo with great fondness and cupped his face.

"Oh, but, we aren't—" Amani stammered, her skin very hot. But Sitt Danya kept speaking, saying something more in Arabic.

Hala shook her head. "Oh. No, please—don't take that personally. She's just tired and a little confused."

"What did she say?" Amani asked.

Nikki glanced at Hala, then shrugged. "She said it's time for you to go home now."

"WE AREN'T WHAT?" Eduardo asked as they climbed in the car.

"Oh, come on—you know!" Amani said, waving to Nikki. "We aren't what Sitt Danya was—implying."

He smiled and pulled the car out onto the road. He chuckled.

It was fully dark when they pulled in front of the guesthouse. The thin, new trees in mid-sidewalk turned wicklike, shifting in the breeze, their leaves bouncing. The air was cold, the moon as sharp as scissors. The short white trees were nearly bare, their limbs like sparse hair. "Do you have time for a walk?" Eduardo asked. "It's dark, but perhaps not too late?"

She was tired, still her senses felt heightened and alert: she wasn't sure if it was from meeting with Sitt Danya or Eduardo's presence. "Which way?" she asked.

His eyes seemed to hold light; they glinted. There were long, vertical lines in his face. Looking at him, for a moment, she felt again the dizzy sense of being unmoored, the ground not in its proper place. Then it passed and it was good to be walking, out in the night and the cold. Her mind felt clearer.

They walked along the uneven sidewalk, having at times to walk in the street when the sidewalk ended. But there wasn't much traffic and she could almost convince herself that she and Eduardo were unseen and anonymous. Eduardo's knuckles brushed hers. They talked about Sitt Danya mistaking her for Natalia. He asked about the blue letter and her search. Then she told him about their discovery of Musa in his cave.

"I worry about him—alone in the cave. I don't know why I care so much. My father—he thinks Musa might be this cousin he used to play with when he was little. But who knows? Musa has no identification." She tried to make herself laugh. "He could be anyone, really."

"Blood is so little," he said. "It has little to do with who we actually love."

As they turned left at the Al-Abdali supermarket, the streetlights faded, the night in the small neighborhoods enveloping them. They walked back up Zemzem Street to her uncle's house and after that, the guesthouse, a pair of looming ghost buildings. Down the block, cats wailed their eerie, moonstruck voices. "Well," she said as they came to the tiled front steps. "That was fast."

"Ah. Here already," he said, stopping and looking around. "Probably I should go. We don't want to start all the neighbors talking."

She glanced from one house to the next, their darkened windows and balconies. Flapping, frantic, and low, something whizzed past and Amani flinched.

"Alkhafafish. Bats, that's all." He placed his hand on her arm.

She leaned just slightly into him, inhaling motes of his aftershave, the scent so faint she might have imagined it. She felt impulsive, unwilling to let the day end. "If you're not in a hurry—I might know a place we can stop. If you want. For a bit." She headed toward the next walk and he followed. The front door to the house on the left was propped open with a stone—she'd noticed the workers doing that. The door slid open through a layer of construction dust: the only light came from the moon through the windows.

"I thought that one—your house—was over there?"

"It is."

Eduardo hesitated, then followed as she went in and moved through the unlit rooms and out to the courtyard. Just next door was the south wall of Farouq's guesthouse where she was staying—there was the kitchen window, and above that was her office window, which seemed even now, with the lights out, to hold a residual glow.

In the semi-renovated house, she and Eduardo moved through the shadows to a rear door. The courtyard was half cement, half new marble tiles, and there in a tiled corner was the tile-layer's prayer rug. She shook it open: it was thick and soft and smelled of oranges. Amani spread the rug, sat, and looked up. Eduardo settled beside her on the ground, legs crossed. He was like a snake charmer, she thought, the way he looked at her. "This seems like the sort of place where a poet would live," he said.

"I'm afraid to ask what that means."

"Undone and beautiful—a little bit in pieces." He gestured at the walls. "Sheltered . . . exposed."

She sat back, resting on her elbows. "My uncle is remodeling this one." She lifted her chin. "He owns all these places. Guy's loaded." She sat back up, rubbing one hand along her arm. "Can I ask you something?"

"Now you sound serious."

She smiled. "Oh no. It's just that I keep thinking about what you said—how you didn't think blood had that much to do with who we loved. . . ."

He shook his head. "Please, ignore me. I'm apt to say all sorts of nonsense."

"No. I liked it—that you said it." She touched his arm. "You just seemed so—decided. Like you'd thought a lot about it. And that got me wondering."

"Why I feel so strongly?" Eduardo's eyes reflected the night air. He spread his hands on his knees for a moment, as if doing some slow calculation. "My mother," he said meditatively. "I didn't know who my mother was—or had started as—until I was eleven years old. Basically, up until that time, I knew her as Miriam Durreau—a French-Christian woman, born and raised in Marseille."

"But she wasn't?"

"It was a lie," Eduardo said, gazing at her. "Just this big story they'd told their children—for years. She was Jewish and Moroccan. Half-in, half-out. My father was Jordanian and Muslim. They met when he was stationed for a time in Fez. It wasn't accepted—marriage between a Muslim and Jew."

Amani drew her knees in toward her chest, wrapping her arms around them. "So, he left the army?"

"Ya'ani, no—not right away." His eyes turned. The night air was filling with mist, the courtyard lit with alternating stripes of shadow. "They tried to stay. For him, she disguised herself. She changed her name, and they both converted to the Orthodox Church. She left Morocco to live with him under an assumed identity. It was, as I understand it, quite an ordeal for them both. And when we were born they didn't tell their children. They said they'd done it for our protection—later on, when it all came out. They couldn't risk telling us the truth."

Amani rested her chin on the flat of her knee. She couldn't see much of him in the filmy light. "How did you learn the truth—about your mother?"

"They were discovered. Someone got suspicious and started snooping. Maybe one of the neighbors? I have no idea. But once it came out, my father had to resign his post. It was—well, it was a tremendous scandal. My mother saw strange cars parked outside the house at night; men started following them in the street. They finally moved us to France—to start over. Which was basically unsuccessful." He shook his head. "It was too much for them, the loss and indignity. My father reverted to Islam. They're still married, but it's not good." He shook his head again. "Things between them were broken."

The courtyard was a tiny box of night: all they could see were webs of stars, a black ridge of pistachio trees, and the farthest corner of the office window. Amani felt her breath move through her; she wanted to touch the slivers of his hair. "And you—none of you—have any idea about who the informer was? Not even your parents?"

Eduardo paused; he pushed a hand back into his hair. "My parents were fairly sure it was someone high up, like in government. Someone who could access things like old birth certificates. But several years back, my sister and I got some information that it was likely my father's younger brother. I barely knew him. It seems he was nursing some old grudge against my father. They all died ages ago." He shrugged. "There are always spies. We're surrounded by people who wish to tell us who we may and may not be. I want only to be myself—end of story. No embroideries, nothing hidden, ever. None of it matters anymore. I moved back to Amman when I was twenty-two. Jordan is my home now."

"After all that you came back." Amani sat up to cross her legs, her knee brushed his. "I'd think that would be kind of hard to do. Kind of scary."

He smiled. "I've lived in several countries. Some of the people I meet, they act like I'm this kind of impossible creature. Arab and Jew together. People always want me to pick one. As if it were up to me. It isn't perfect, but in terms of acceptance, Jordan has been the best of the lot. Or maybe it's just the most familiar sort of discrimination."

"But do you still—" She stopped. "Are you still careful?"

"Do I hide my identity?" His expression was faint in the darkness. "What I think is—there *is* no hiding. There are no secrets. If someone wants to know what I am, then that person will find out. The only way to be alive in the world is by claiming yourself. You take a deep breath and say, I am I. The rest will have to fall where it will fall."

"And I am I," she said. Now she did touch him, the top of his knuckles.

He took her hand and turned it, kissing the curve between her thumb and index finger. He cradled her hand for a moment. "I learned that blood is no guarantee of anything—not truth, not connection, not loyalty. It's because I grew up with layers. Everything

I thought I knew about myself and my family—all fake. But you know, even before our parents finally revealed the truth to us, my sister and I had already sensed it. I used to make up stories about my mother—that she was a lost princess, that her castle had been destroyed. It was an extraordinary thing to watch my mother's face when she thought no one was looking. Always so preoccupied."

"Well, she was still your mother, no matter what anyone said."

"But an elusive person."

Amani nodded. She felt a desire to defend Eduardo's mother. Men got to own themselves, but women constructed themselves in the mirror of the world. She looked at their hands, still joined together, and said, "You know when you said that I shouldn't tell my uncle—Hafez—about my father's knife. Why did you say that?"

"I felt protective. Of you." His voice was low, almost a whisper. "I'm sorry—that isn't very feminist, is it? I may be a throwback."

"That sounds pretty good to me."

Mist dotted their hair and shoulders. There were no sounds beyond the courtyard; the call to prayers, the traffic, the herds of goats, all held still. Amani thought of a story in her children's treasury, about how the animals and the things of the world all spoke to one another when the humans weren't listening and told stories about themselves.

Eduardo pulled gently on her hands, drawing her closer.

She'd gone on a few unremarkable dates since her divorce. But something about the way Eduardo touched her seemed to move under her skin. She barely knew him and yet she sensed that there could be no uncomplicated kiss with this man. She looked at their hands and said, "Edo, I'm only here for a little longer—not even two weeks left."

"Yes, well—that isn't enough."

She let him fold her in his arms. Her thoughts loosened, as if she were drawn by a current, and her eyes closed. They kissed till they were out of breath, a ragged plunge. He rolled back as they kissed pulling her on top of him, pushing his hands into her hair, one of her legs falling between his. She felt his exhalation on her ear, on the skin of her face. She broke off at last to catch her breath and look at him, finally sinking onto his chest, her arms around his neck, feeling his ribs through her shirt, his arms around her. She held still, moved only by the beat of her pulse.

The sky over the courtyard turned to the color of charcoal and hazy purple and the traffic noise had dwindled away. Powdery light glowed around the stars, touching the prayer carpet. In the distance came a faint bawling, the tinkle of goat bells, behind that, the shush of cars. She lifted her head, then laid it on his shoulder and they breathed together. "We should probably get out of here," she said after a while. "The workers will be coming back."

"Let them come. They would love this." His arms tightened for a moment. His eyes turned to hers. "You really are to return to the States? So soon?"

"Very, very soon."

His gaze held on to hers. "And what if someone were to ask you to stay?"

"In Jordan? To live?" The air was cold in her throat and lungs: a low fog was rolling into the courtyard. She sat up and he pushed himself upright beside her. "I'm an American, Eduardo. My whole life is over there. I couldn't even imagine it—staying here."

"But if you've said it, haven't you already partly imagined it?" He stroked a piece of hair off her forehead, but she smiled and stood and he followed her. She rolled the prayer rug and returned it to its corner while he watched, asking, "And isn't imagination very important to poetry?"

She avoided his gaze. "I'm not such a big poet as you think."

Again, they crossed the courtyard and stole through the empty house, furniture shrouded with sheets, looming against the wall. They opened the front door, and the street was erased by fog. Instinctively, Amani took Eduardo's hand as they moved out into it. A cypress loomed before them, a twisted trunk and green blades of foliage. She reached toward it, strumming her hand through the leaves as if through a stream of water. The fog thinned somewhat and Amani could make out the shapes of two-story square houses, and enclosed porches. They made their way to Zahran Street, where she said goodbye and released him. She watched him go in silence, and felt an ache in her chest, low and surprising, after he'd gone.

THE PHONE WOKE HER. Rosy sunlight filled the room and thoughts of the previous day—Eduardo's speckled irises—flickered once through her mind before Amani answered.

Sister Sylvain was speaking urgently, saying there was a situation.

Amani rubbed her eyes and felt for her watch. "A situation?"

It took several moments before she could put together what Sylvain was saying. Some sort of trouble for Musa. There was a new government initiative, the nun explained. They wanted to relocate cave and desert dwellers from sensitive historic areas and into official housing—as they'd done with the Bedu in Petra. Musa's cave was within twenty kilometers of a Crusader outpost. The convent had gotten word that scouts were combing the region, putting the so-called "squatters" on buses to dormitories, eighty kilometers away. "This would be ruinous for Musa," the nun said. "He's lived in his cave for over fifty years. He believes that someday his mother will come there to claim him."

"They can't do that! It's his home." Amani sat up in bed, holding the phone. "All he wants is that one little spot!"

"I know." She could hear a current of fatigue in the woman's voice. "I've been told there's concern the cave dwellers will encroach on historic sites. They seem to have no regard for the cave dwellers themselves—or the fact that they are *part* of the history. Muslims have always interacted and lived in their own sacred sites. But lately, the officials just want to sanitize everything—make it look 'authentic,' but not *too* authentic, so the tourists will come." She sighed. "Personally, I think they're worried about refugees pouring into Jordan and hiding in the hills. We've had such an influx from Iraq since the Gulf War." She explained Musa could be expelled at any time. It would be a matter of days at most before they took him. "They might try to pack him off to some sort of asylum. And we have no legal jurisdiction in this matter, no guardianship. He refuses to stay with us—though goodness knows we've offered."

"Yes, I'm sure you have."

"I believe your family—the Hamdans—have influence?" She spoke carefully. "I wouldn't ask if the situation weren't so grave. But I wondered if perhaps one of your relatives could intercede?"

Amani hunched on the edge of the bed; she rested her forehead in her palm, blinking. She inhaled. "Let me see what I can do."

Hafez would have the most power in the family. *Baksheesh* and *wastah*, Omar had said—bribery, connections. Hafez might be able to speak with the officials—they could make an exception for Musa. She considered the way he'd reacted to her questions about the family, his evident disapproval. She bit at the edge of her thumbnail then picked up her phone. Hafez's number rang without answer—she wasn't sure her signal was even getting through. A housekeeper answered at Farouq's house, but Amani's Arabic wasn't good enough to explain the situation. Her father was visiting relatives in Madaba.

She tried Hafez again.

CHAPTER
20

WINTER WAS IN THE AIR. Hafez held his cloak closed as he approached the edge of the rooftop. He'd found these robes in a cedar chest folded with dried palm fronds under layers of tissue paper. His father had worn robes like this every day for as far back as Hafez could remember—as had his grandfather and the grandfathers before that. Hafez felt as if he were playing dress-up each time he put them on.

The wind filled the folds of his robe like a bellows. The rooftop of the Mövenpick Resort had a good view of the crummy little town of Wadi Musa. Overhead, the stars were wrinkling, flirting, winking directly at him from their black velvet. He filled his lungs: he felt fine. Better than fine. Nearly whole. What a time. What a life. He'd been a professor in the political science department at the University of Jordan—local journalists loved him, his clever way of parlaying world news into bite-sized nuggets—for only seven years when the King's undersecretary called with an offer to quadruple his salary and shower him with prestige. Since then, he'd lived most of his adult lifetime in the shadow of the throne—a sweet shadow, indeed. And sometimes, like tonight, he seemed to inch closer to the light.

In the past, he'd often felt misunderstood. He'd heard the rumors: that he was egotistical, grandiose, overrated, ruthless, shallow, cunning. He'd heard it all—the wages of politics. This was what it meant to lead a people. He knew in his soul he was sweet, jazzy, generous, and charming: he had so much to give.

And he was ready, also, to receive. He felt the nearness of Il Saif. His body hummed. The whole drive up, from Aqaba to Petra, he'd sensed it coming toward him, the way a compass feels the pull of the north. Farouq had driven to Petra from Amman with his family. Gabe had come in a separate limo—Hafez had set it up—a limo for his youngest brother and his niece, it was the least he could do. Oh, Il Saif. It was as if the curtains had parted—just this once—and a voice had said, *Yes, you may. You will have the impossible.*

Amani called him this morning—the private line on his cell phone. No message, but the phone showed that she'd rung. The reception out here in the sticks was terrible. He supposed her father had mentioned Il Saif to her. Hafez meant to assure her: he would see to it that the knife would pass on to her. Then again, he might go pharaonic and require the knife be buried with him. Ho-ho, a neat trick. He wasn't ruling anything out.

The waiters moved around the rooftop behind him, setting up backgammon boards and stacking the argilehs, arranging the coals with tongs. Samir joined him at the railing with his delicious scent of a hundred cigarettes. He shook two out of the pack and gave one to his boss. "You should put more events here, ya ustaz." Sir. "This one's nice."

The driver lit the stick in Hafez's mouth. Hafez removed it with his own fingers and shook his head, exhaling smoke. "This is the last of it, alhamdullilah. This and the Ancient Sumerians display at the Sousin. Last birthday party till the King hits seventy, inshallah."

Hafez and his driver had viewed the world's treasures together. Samir knew a bit about Il Saif—it was unavoidable—he'd followed

Hafez through gold souqs and marketplaces from Majorca to Yemen, shopping for knives—cincals and daggers and khanjar—from scimitars with half-moon blades to Crusader weapons to one weirdly glimmering gold sword on the Zanzibar coast that the owner swore was the inspiration for the tale of Excalibur and the Lady of the Lake. Samir leaned his brown forearms against the railing and blew out a plume; ash fell to the ground, seven stories below. "So, tomorrow," he said.

Hafez couldn't help his smile. "There's going to be some warm-up fencing in the morning—Italy versus Jordan. Some Russians. Some French. Then the big exhibition."

Samir pulled till the end glowed then released a heavy sigh of smoke. At last, he said, "You and your brother—you're different, aren't you?"

"What makes you say that?" Hafez asked.

Samir shrugged, facing the distance. "He's an American."

"By now I'm sure he is. Thirty-seven years over there. Or thirty-nine? But that's nurture, not nature," he added in English.

"Too many words for me," Samir replied in Arabic. He studied the tip of his cigarette.

Hafez had called Gabe yesterday from Aqaba to run down tomorrow's schedule. The arrival, the warm-up acts, the backstage. *Do you have what you need? Are you ready?*

Gabe was quiet, his responses seemed disengaged, even curt.

Hafez felt pressure; it was inside his chest, rising like a fish to the surface—what was that feeling—pressing as if from just underneath the surface of the skin. *What's the matter, brother?* he'd asked. He needed to confirm that Gabe had brought the knife.

There was a long, unnerving pause. At last, Gabe had said, "Who is the man in the cave?"

Heat shot through Hafez's body. The pressure became a kind of hammering. He felt it in his ears, his hands, even his eyes. He knew who his brother was talking about, and yet it didn't seem possible. Musa was long dead. He had an uncanny sensation that Gabe had looked inside the dark hollow of his chest and seen Hafez himself: the tiny, hidden being that every person was meant to keep secreted away. He felt Gabe had looked upon that which was not meant for his eyes. This infuriated him. But he'd collected himself. At last, he'd said quietly, "What are you talking about?"

Gabe had said nothing.

He'd had time to recover since then. He was really feeling much better now, although perhaps it still felt like something was stuck in his chest, as if he had tried to swallow his own heart. Why should he be worried? The night was calm and balanced. He and his driver stared at the black sky for a while then he went in to bed.

THAT NIGHT, the temperature fell. A powerful haboob blew in from the eastern Sahara and by morning the air was pixilated with snow-flakes. Rafi walked around hugging his clip-boarded schedule of the day's events, exultant at the possibility of snow falling during the match. "Al Jazeera is sending a crew—if they ever get here. It will be very nice on camera." Rafi orbited behind Hafez, Carole, Gabe, Amani, Omar, Farouq, and Bella. "We might get on international news. Maybe they'll pick it up in the States!"

"Bad for the strip, though. All slippery," Gabe pointed out. "I thought this was going to be mostly talking. Not so much fencing."

"Oh, no, no," Rafi said. "We've got the amphitheater all set up with special surfaces and all kinds of equipment. The men will keep everything clear. It's going to be beautiful."

They were at the entrance to Petra, waiting for horses to be sad-dled. Hafez admired the ease with which his youngest brother mounted his roan. Hafez, Farouq, their wives, and Rafi climbed into one of the carriages. They'd barely settled on the wood planks when the horse began trotting over the stone ground, rattling every bone in his body.

The royal retinue was up ahead, their carriage bedecked in

streamers, Jordanian flags, and red Christmas tinsel. Someone had outfitted the horses—ragged, overworked beasts—with jingle bells, so the Muslims would ride in Christmas cheer. Rafi had seated himself perpendicular to Hafez on a small fold-out seat. "Now, please remind him—your brother should allow His Majesty to make the first move."

"Yes, yes," Hafez muttered. "As well as the last."

They passed a number of students and tourists on foot, and several groups of muhajjabat covered in black. Omar and Amani also walked and did not return his wave as Hafez's conveyance clattered by. "Rafi," Carole's voice rolled past Hafez's shoulder. He was surprised to hear her address the younger man—she was not known to be overly fond of the cultural affairs officer. "Have you noticed there seem to be more and more young women covering themselves these days?"

Rafi watched two veiled girls—barely teens—recede into the distance. "We've had so many more young Palestinians coming in," he said. "They have nothing to do—no work, nothing. Hamas gives them something to do."

"You're saying they're all Hamas?"

"Not all, no. But, you know, they pay girls at the university a stipend—in exchange for wearing the hijab."

"How grotesque." Carole wound the woolen blanket more tightly around herself. Hafez noticed she was wearing some sort of dark lipstick that made her mouth look grim. He reminded himself to tell her to discontinue.

"Do you think?" Rafi asked mildly. "It struck me as shrewd marketing."

Hafez grimaced into his chest as he pulled up his own blanket. He, Farouq, and Bella were all dying for cigarettes; no one dared pull them out around Carole.

"I was born in Amman," Rafi said. He wore only his suit, his narrow arms crossed tightly over his chest. The jolting carriage made his hair lift and fall. "In '54—six years after the Nakba—that's what the Palestinians called it—"

"God, Rafi, I've lived in this country nearly as long as you have," Carole said. "I'm familiar with the Nakba."

"I'm sorry, I never like to assume foreknowledge. Occupational hazard."

For a moment, Rafi and Carole looked at each other. Bella handed up another blanket from the back and Rafi offered it first to Carole: after a moment, her face softened. She insisted he keep it. Rafi wrapped it around his lap with as much dignity as he could manage. "That's just to say that when my parents got here, it was to the Zarqa camp. A canvas tent and dirt floor. By the time I was born—five years later—we were living in our own home in Jebel Hussein."

Hafez grunted. Yes, another refugee success story—but he rather admired the mad fortitude of those Palestinians who insisted on remaining in the camps, some even still in tents, adamant that they would someday return to their homes—despite all evidence to the contrary. "There's no loyalty like acquired loyalty, eh Rafi?" Hafez said.

Carole dug an elbow into his ribs. "What's that supposed to mean?" she hissed.

He didn't know, and then he felt sorry that he'd said it. His hands were shaking a little. He seemed to be saying all sorts of things this morning. Somehow, he could focus only on the tiniest of details, everything else skittered away. Rafi ignored him, lifting his blanket under his armpits. They passed through the narrow entrance of the monument, the *siq*—a long streak of rock face, striated with feldspar and quartz, and the pink and salmon and rose-colored sandstone from which Petra rose. Hafez was indifferent toward Petra: one of the world's wonders, sure, but such a dead thing—it felt secretive and forbidding—a windup clock without a key. There were thousands of steps, the whole place was one uphill staircase; always too hot or bone-numbingly cold. Like right now, the snow refusing to fall, just hanging crystalline and suspended, pricking the skin as they rode through it. The siq passageway was lined with its own secrets: there were ledges and caves that flickered with stone goddesses, sleeping

Bedouins, small fires. Two of the Bidul—a tribe evicted from Petra by the government—lounged on a rock staircase, waving to the royal carriage. At the end of the day, these men would walk by their own emptied caves to loud dormlike structures erected on the outskirts.

Who was the man in the cave? Hafez hunched forward, holding his knees. How could it be Musa? Musa vanished a million years ago.

At last, they reached the rose-colored gleam at the end of the *siq* and Hafez's spirits buoyed. He filled with optimism and squeezed his wife's hand. He felt good, his joints pliable. There was a buzz in the air. The driver snapped his reins and they veered right, past the camel lounging in the central square. The towers rose above them, glowing pink stone. Carved-out, rather than built—made not by addition but by taking away. He found the effect disturbing, unheimlich—those multistoried glories erupting from raw rock, the geometrical columns and sills and windows, the triangular ornamentations, gleaming like the porticos of Olympus. But enter one of the towers and inside was nothing but the dreariest chamber, four dull walls, with echoes and a whiff of pee. The so-called City of the Dead, rife with mausoleums. The original architects—the mysterious, extraterrestrial Nabateans—were said to value the dead over the living. Hafez felt a fluttering sensation along his spine, as if skeletal fingers plucked each vertebra.

The carriages stopped at the amphitheater. Rafi sprang to the ground and rushed to the royal carriage to round up handlers and early media. Official photographers, a reporter from *The Jordan Star*, a videographer, producer, sound guys, and two TV cameras fanned out as the King dismounted his carriage, ignoring the royal guard's gloved hand. He greeted the media with a radiant smile. Recently, Rafi had murmured that His Majesty was unhappy with the money being lavished on festivities. He'd canceled three banquets and one breakfast jubilee. Sensible. The King turned toward the carriage with his upright, Sandhurst bearing and helped Her Majesty dismount. There were even more applause and cries for her than him.

The Queen slipped one hand under her hair and swept out so it fell in a gossamer sheet over her coat collar. Hafez squinted in the frosted air, watching as the secret service whisked the royals backstage. Something flittered in his right eyelid.

He went to the theater's edge to take in the scene. Outlining the open-air amphitheater were tiny lights in the colors of the Jordanian flag—black, red, and green—but no one could see the black-painted bulbs, so it looked like more Christmas decoration. The risers sparkled with silver tinsel and an artificial tree stood in the entryway. Hafez caught the smug smile that Rafi telegraphed to Her Majesty. She had converted to Islam to marry the King, but she would love seeing the holiday displays of her youth. Rafi was always currying favor with Queen N, purring against her ankles. Hafez moved to whisper to Carole, but she was staring into the crowd. Hafez shielded his eyes: nearly half the royal court was already there, seated in the special box: the queen mother, the King's charming eldest boy, his twins, his tiresome younger brother. The prime minister stood on the sidelines, hands limp in his pockets. Hafez had heard, to his bemusement, that locals were betting on the royal duel: the Jordanians backing His Majesty, and the Palestinians were backing Gabe! Hafez squinted, trying to pinpoint what exactly Carole was gazing at so fixedly when Gabe appeared at his side; his eyes wide. "Y'akhi, you said it was going to be just a little show. I didn't know it would be so . . ." Gabe held out his hands. "Big. Big and—like this!"

"Big and like this, yes." Hafez put a hand on his brother's shoulder, but he wasn't looking at him. He had spotted the archbishop in a prime central seat. Beside him, in the seat designated for Father Jacob's sister Fedwa sat Madame X. She appeared to be staring at Hafez, her face impassive. This was not according to plan.

Even at this distance, he could see her lips looked very red; she wore some sort of crimson band in her hair. She looked cold, shiny, and luscious. Anxiety crept over him. He'd recently written an opinion piece for the *Jordan Times* concerning "moral journalism." In it, he made a case for journalists modifying their reporting in order to uphold "universal human values," including, most especially, "honoring and protecting the King." He stated it was not essential for the public to know "every single governmental foible and fluctuation," that it was, in fact, more important to shield people from their own unfounded fears and unnecessary panic. Finally, he decried the traitorousness of indiscreet journalists who wrote first and considered the ramifications second (or not at all). Hafez published such pieces regularly, to elucidate the position of the Crown. But this one he'd written out of a sense of indignation—a need to defend himself against the potential accusations of Hassan Salhab. He'd asked the paper to hold off publishing the piece for a few more weeks, until the business could be settled with the archbishop. To his dismay, it had appeared in the Friday-morning paper.

Publishing this article was not the same as transferring Madame X's brother to prison in Yemen, but if one wanted to see it that way, it might be interpreted as the first step.

"Are you listening?" Gabe asked. "I can't be in an actual bout with the *King*! I thought we were mostly going to tell stories. Maybe hold up foils. Click, clack, sit down."

Hafez patted him absently. "Come, it's nothing. A little swish with the swords. Why are you worrying? Remember—the King always wins. Right?" He laughed. His chuckle sounded weird.

Rafi elbowed between them, urging Hafez and the others through the stone archway to the side of the performance area. Through the walls he heard the Jordanian Youth Symphony snap open their cases on the orchestra floor and the cacophony of children warming up on instruments. Backstage was made up of a series of former Nabatean tombs, crumbling chambers connected by a series of archways. The central space, painted startling white and strung with Christmas lights, was dominated by a table covered with platters of mezze and rows of sliced vegetables and olives. The royal security detail helped members of the Bidul and Lathaynah tribes carry in platters of food. Hafez swiped a handful of wrinkled olives.

The King was over there, surrounded by media and handlers.

Across the room, Amani was standing rather too closely to that dark-haired, Sephardic-looking fencing instructor. What kind of Jordanian was named Eduardo? Farouq and his wife were stationed by the food, piling kabobs on plates. He'd lost track of Carole. Hafez retraced his steps through the linked chambers, listening to each step reverberate underfoot and cursing under his breath. This place. One great, caving-in funeral parlor. He'd heard Petra was being gradually swept away, grain by grain, leveled by the wind. Like Venice. Like all the decaying beauties. He'd wanted the match to take place at the modern Sports City. Petra was the Queen's idea—she was obsessed with all things quaintly traditional, old, and Jordanian. The more useless and antiquated the better.

He found his wife at last, positioned in the entry, still watching the crowd. He took her hand, he put his other hand on his chest—he was breathing a bit heavily. "I don't know why she's here, hayati. Truly. I had nothing to do with it."

Carole glanced at him. She took a cigarette from her purse. "Did you know, *hayati*, that pretty much all men are liars and cheaters? Weren't you the one who told me Petra was basically hidden from outsiders for a thousand years? Some jackass from—Germany? Or was it England? Johann something—dresses up like an Arab and tricks the locals into taking him here. It used to be this amazing secret city. Perfectly preserved. And this one jackass goes and wrecks the whole thing."

"The miserable colonialists," he said uncertainly. Hafez blinked at the cigarette. He tried to take her hand again, which she yanked back. "Honest, honest. I swear it to you," he said. "I have no idea why that woman—"

"Shut up, Hafez. For goodness' sakes. You give me such a headache." She used the unlit cigarette to point. "Who is that up there?"

Hafez assumed she was pointing at Madame X until he realized she was pointing to the left, in the upper rows. All morning, there had been special fencing displays; now crowds were pouring in for the main event. The organizers had installed cushions and carpeting in the two main tiers for the attendees. But someone was seated above the decorated section, up where the rows were in the worst condition, worn away by earthquake and flood and time. This individual sat alone, but seemed possessed by a special sort of solitude. Hafez removed his glasses from his jacket, wiped them on his sleeve, and squinted at the solitary figure. He felt the blood in his body slow down, then turn to sand.

CHAPTER

21

"Look—do you see? Way up in the third section—to the left of the center aisle?"

"Okay. Oh my God. I do see." Staring, Amani finally turned to Omar. "But why did you bring him *here*?"

Her cousin rubbed at the side of his neck. He'd just come from a public competition, testing himself against one of the club fencers. Dripping with sweat, he wiped his forehead with the back of his wrist. "It wasn't my choice, cuz. I called the housekeeper when Musa and I were driving back, to give her a heads-up. And she was like, Absolutely not, no way are you bringing this random guy in the house without your dad's permission. And by then it was already getting late." He mopped off his face with his towel. "So, we just came here. He crashed in my hotel room."

"Well, awesome. And what the hell are we going to do with him now?" She squinted at the still figure in the audience.

"Amani, I'm sorry but what can I tell you? At first, I couldn't even get him out of the cave. It wasn't until I said that Uncle Gabe was going to be in this big fight—*that* finally got his attention. Maybe he thought your dad needed help."

Amani lowered the hand shielding her eyes and turned toward her cousin. "Does he know he can't go back to his cave? Did you tell him?"

"Oh, I told him, yeah." Omar said. "But I don't think he gets it. Like, at all. Ya maskeen." Poor guy. "Jesus, you should've seen him getting into my car."

The air was turning wintry and sheer. She rubbed her hands together. They'd only been in Jordan a few weeks, but it was long enough for the clothes she'd packed to become inadequate. "Still, better we got him than the police," she murmured. She crossed her arms, trying to warm up. Where would they put him if Farouq said no? "We should tell my dad."

"Yeah, but after the match," Omar said. "Let's not freak out Gabe even more than he is."

To GET INTO the audience, Amani had to duck under the low stone archway and skirt the back of the curtained-off stage where she could hear men talking and warming up; their shouts as they charged at each other, then laughter, a coach correcting their form. She recognized some of the men from Eduardo's team, resting from a morning of exhibition fencing; a few nodded to her again. One lifted his foil. Eduardo came over to greet her, then kissed her rather closer to the jaw than her cheek, then placed another nearly on the neck. She felt a current down her back. "I thought about you," he murmured, "all night."

Her breath sped through her. She wanted to say so did I, but instead, she shook her head, smiling and pulling back. "Edo."

Omar slipped between them to introduce himself and gave Eduardo his card. "Hey, man. Like, maybe you want to bring someone in? Help strength-training your fencers? That's a specialty of mine. I hit nutrition, flexibility, balance, power. I'll give you an awesome rate."

Eduardo thanked him, then pointed to Amani as he was called away. "But later, yes?"

Out front, she waited for her breath to calm, then walked around the youth orchestra and started up one of the side steps into the crowded amphitheater seating. This was supposed to be an invitation-only event, but clearly no one had told the Bedouin. Men in jeans and T-shirts, women swathed in black, and wild-haired children had flooded in, filling the upper sections where there were no cushions, only bare, rock-carved rows. They visited with one another, passing around knives and fruit. Amani waded up into the third tier, trying not to step on picnic blankets, excusing herself as she shuffled in front of people—*afwan, afwan*—and managed to wedge herself in beside Musa. His face had been scrubbed clean; his hair appeared to be wet and channeled by a comb. He looked startled and years younger, as if he had no clear idea of how he'd come to be there. He looked at her fearfully before his features relaxed and she saw he recognized her.

"Hello, Musa?" she said gently. "Marhaba. Ahlain. Are you all right?" she asked, as clearly as she could in her simple Arabic. He smiled, his lips cracking, and said something she couldn't understand. "I'm so sorry—Ana asifa kteer!" she said. "You must be so confused. Your cave . . ." What was the Arabic for "cave"?

He gestured toward the performance area below, asking something in Arabic. He seemed to be focused on the events.

"Aboui oo il Malik," she said slowly, gesturing toward the dueling piste where the two men would appear. She wanted to explain what was happening, but struggled to think of the words. She started to say, *It's like a match*—then stopped mid-sentence when she realized she didn't know the Arabic for "duel" or "match."

"Mobaraza," the young man in front of them said, swishing his index finger in a sideways eight. His eyes appeared to be darkened with black liner and she could see a gold tooth at the back of his smile. Several of the people sitting nearby nodded and leaned closer. A woman, her face outlined by a headpiece and veil, laughed and said something to Musa, who nodded gravely.

Musa asked Amani something and the older man beside the first one said, "He wants to know if there is great danger."

"Laa'," Amani said to Musa. "Ma fi khatar!" She made a crossing-out motion with her hands. The others around them chimed in, patting Musa's arm or knee. "It's a just a show—a game," she said in English.

"La'beh," the young man translated for Amani. "Bas." A game only.

"Moubarat," the older man beside him said. A match.

Musa said something urgently to Amani. She understood the word "king" and nodded.

He settled back with a wide smile. There really was an unusual sort of sweetness in him, an untouched quality, in balance with the place itself. She looked past the edges of the amphitheater's horseshoe toward the prehistoric landscape—smoking mountains and the raw, marbled land, and above, the sky shocked blue without snow, clear and cold and flawless. She felt washed in it, in the cold light and the orchestral music. She realized the young musicians were playing "Take Me Home, Country Roads," which filled her with nostalgia and longing for her mother. And yet the beauty of this place was vast; it reached into her. She thought again of Eduardo's startling suggestion that she remain and shook her head as if to reassure herself.

Musa put a hand on her shoulder and said something in Arabic that she realized was *listen*. At first she thought he meant the music, but then she understood he heard something else. There was a ruffling sound to the wind, a high, distant surging sound, like that of waves. Amani heard him say the Arabic word for fifty. The people in front of them laughed and the woman said, "He thinks there's a khamseen. A windstorm."

Musa said something else and the young man said, "He says he can taste it." He argued with Musa for a moment, then told Amani, "He's dreaming. Khamseen mostly springtime. They say khamseen for fifty days of blowing."

Amani thought of the glimmering mist of the night before, how it had altered the things it touched. And it did seem to her now that there was a tint to the air like that of pollen, a yellow veil. She held Musa's hand, the wind steepening and washing through the pink canyons. There was a surge of applause for the orchestra. As soon as the musicians departed, stagehands rumbled out to clear the stage. Two of the Desert Patrol emerged in their long, khaki-colored uniforms, the tails of their keffiyehs flung back, bandoliers crossed over their chests. The fencing consultants—a young instructor, a Jordanian referee, and two foreign coaches—carefully unrolled the rubber piste, the white rectangle scuffed and scraped from the morning bouts. Two men on their hands and knees scrubbed at the mat, rose-colored Petra dust clinging to everything.

One of the Desert Patrol came to the center and welcomed them, though Amani couldn't hear him above the chattering audience.

Another man in a white jacket, knickers, and white socks walked out to the circular stage, his face open in an over-wide smile: it took her a moment to recognize her father.

CHAPTER

22

THEY WALKED, SINGLE-FILE, through the backstage chambers toward the performance area. The French fencing master sat in the corner, a stack of notes under his chair. He insisted to the guy with the clipboard that he was supposed to lecture on the history of fencing in Jordan while Gabe and the King demonstrated moves. The schedule kept changing. Gabe didn't know if Hafez was responsible, or there had been popular demand, or it came by order of the King himself, but apparently they were actually going to duel. The Italian master, who would also be a judge, was going over the rules—just two bouts, three minutes each or four hits, whichever came first. One minute in between. Or possibly a few minutes. Depending. And the official guy with the clipboard and a beard shadow across his lower face kept patrolling and issuing instructions: The King goes first, then you—make sure to bow—then you, you . . . No. *You* come first. His Majesty will emerge after . . . Nothing rough, remember . . . we finish in seven minutes. . . . Then will be time for discussion, Q and A, some instructional background . . .

Then the handlers were herding them out, and where was his daughter? And there was so much noise, so loud, Gabe thought there was some sort of waterfall nearby. After a moment he realized it was applause. The audience—so many people!—were on their feet. And Gabe was panting: he couldn't feel his arms or legs, yet somehow, he moved. His nephew Omar was there saying things that Gabe couldn't make out, so Gabe just imitated everything he did, touching his toes, jogging in place, rolling his head, his shoulders . . . Glove on, a foil was placed in his hand. His face mask pushed down into place. He gulped air, his ears as full of breath as if he were scuba diving. He wasn't ready for this. The King emerged in his whites, his mask lowered, arms lifted. The crowd roared. They moved into position. Facing him across the line, behind the mask and uniform, Gabe's opponent could have been anyone. The audience shouted and ululated.

At a sign from the Italian coach, Gabe tentatively lifted the hilt of the foil to his lips, extended the silver point to the referee, the audience, to the King. His Majesty did the same.

Someone cried, "Fence!"

With that, a rush and scramble of feet, a flash of silver, the tip streaking past. Gabe's instinct was purely defensive, scrambling backwards, very nearly—but not quite—landing on his backside, saving himself, arms wheeling. He was so startled, he didn't register his opponent's hit, a chalk mark on his inner right shoulder, the King silent as he struck. Gabe barely heard the crowd as they shouted. The judges' hands went up, counting the strike. He was slow and disoriented.

But then his muscles did begin to remember, as Omar had predicted—the shape of the game started to form. It came back to him—all those years ago, how they'd practiced, sometimes three or four hours a day—a patch of dirt behind the barracks, under the sun. They were young men together, buddies. But there was always that sense of being outmatched when he fenced with the King, always a hesitation, the whisper that the King always wins. Gabe was still strong; he'd spent the past decades lifting wood, hammers, and saws, but His Majesty seemed strong and spry and commanding—he remembered his old coach's words: the King does everything like a taller man. Like a giant. Now they were sixty-year-olds, with cracking joints and not as much give in the knees. The King still smoked. Once again, he heard Sr. Cavelli remind him: "Distanza, velocità e scelta di tempo," listing the three variables of fencing, always admonishing Gabe: Choose your time!"

They returned to their marks and this time when the King sprang forward, Gabe decided he too could pretend to be young and agile: he hugged in his rib cage, lifted his chin. The King's tip sailed past Gabe's stomach by a breath and Gabe parried with a singing swipe, missing as well. He remembered this, the conversation with one's opponent, how there was small talk with feints and jabs then sudden plunges and heated flurries of back and forth. Gabe risked a full lunge and landed heavily, leaving himself open: the King whacked the outside of his waist. Another three points.

Three minutes were already up: First bout to His Majesty. One bout to go. There was a pause while a boy brought them bottles of water. Gabe drained his, the mask pushed back on his head. Omar gave him a towel and he mopped sweat from his eyes. His body was glowing hot. The King paced around, shaking out his limbs, mask pushed back to the top of his head. "This is amazing, Amo. You are *the man*," Omar hissed. "You're owning it."

"Really? I look okay?" Gabe was panting.

"So, so much better than I thought," Omar said. "But he is crafty, dude—he snuck in that first point when you weren't looking. He's psyching you out. Just—try not to think about who you're playing," he added. "Don't let him inside your head. You're the man."

"The man maybe." He mopped his face again. "But he is king."

Across the strip, the King pointed at Gabe, nodding.

"Well, don't forget who you are either, Amo!"

"Ha-ha. Why? Who am I?" Still panting, Gabe slid his mask back down.

"Come *on*—you're Zorro! Remember?" His nephew swiped the big Z, left, right, left! in the air like a child with a plastic sword.

Gabe laughed and shook his head. He walked back to his mark. Facing off, he looked for the King's eyes behind the mask.

"Y'akhi—you all right?" the King asked, but gently. Gabe nodded, lifted his hilt again, then saluted to the blurry distance.

At a signal, the King jumped forward and Gabe's legs nearly tangled as he cross-stepped back, barely jerking out of the way. He remembered some rule about the rear leg not crossing the fore, but no one called him on it and then the King did it as well. As if in slow motion, he watched the King thrust at him straight-armed, then half-stepped backward with a quarter turn. Gabe deflected the blade with a swat to the right, jumping back slowly, so he felt himself hover then land, all his joints flexing and bringing him into position. He felt forty years lift from his body. The King made a false attack, which Gabe fell for, parrying; he made a solid riposte on a lunge, the King catching the side of his blade with his own, sliding its full length to strike Gabe at his sternum. Gabe laughed, surprised, and jumped in reverse. Crafty indeed.

His Majesty circled on bent legs, turning just his wrist, swirling his foil around Gabe's—a coupé—a taunt. The foil thrust and swished past the bottom of his mask, under the chin. Gabe gulped air. *Take the risk.* He deliberately stamped once, loudly; the King started. Gabe opened one arm wide: a single riposte, he just missed the King. But His Majesty was distracted; it was his chance. Gabe hesitated for a bare moment, then lunged with a cry, and struck the King above his solar plexus, near the center of his heart, bending the foil nearly in two. The King yelled, "Touché!" Shouts went up from the audience. A judge raised his hand. They called the second bout for Gabriel Hamdan.

"They're cheering for you!" Omar cried.

Startled, Gabe lifted his eyes.

He looked out at a sea of faces, streamers, and lights; he heard their cheers. The sense of this great, watching public poured into him. People did love El Zorro—defender of the little guy. His mother took him into town to see the movies on the rare occasion that a new one came; he remembered how she sat with him for showing after showing of *The Mark of Zorro*. She never said no. How she would have loved this day. One of the referees came out to the playing surface dressed in black pants and shirt, gray hair loose in the wind. Holding up both their hands, he announced to the crowd that the judges had deliberated, assessed their performances, and decided to declare the King was the winner.

Gabe smiled and swayed, trying to absorb the applause; the noise shook the bones in his head. Why was he so happy? A little girl with black hair bouncing down her back came out with armloads of roses and presented bouquets to both Gabe and the King. The King lifted Gabe's hand and presented him to the crowd. "*Imshee!* Walk around. Arms up. Let them cheer you." Gabe felt his mind step outside of itself; his legs carried him from one side of the arena to the other, arms lifted. He felt an airiness in his body. He looked for his daughter. He looked at the stage. The King's jacket, knickers, and mask were smeared with rose-colored dust: a swatch of red extended from the top of his head to the lower right edge of his neck. A handler was trying to brush him clean with a towel. The King took Gabe's hands sideways in both of his. "We did it, y'akhi!"

"We did?" Gabe croaked. "Alhamdullilah."

THE KING WENT backstage for a few minutes before he reemerged in his desert robes. He grabbed Gabe's shoulder and shook him, just as if they were brothers, then hugged him tightly. There was laughter from the audience. Someone tossed a rose that fell at Gabe's feet. Gabe bent and tucked it behind his ear. His body was still catching up with the exhilaration. His eyes stung with sweat. He couldn't stand straight, so he sat. A little boy had carried out folding chairs for him and the King, side by side. He was running on momentum. Tomorrow, Gabe knew, he would be aching and covered in bruises. For a few seconds he had flown.

Other former fencing partners crowded the arena while the Desert Patrol tried to shove the audience back. They had to get rid of the chairs. There were shouts and unruliness. Everyone wanted to stand up with the King, posing for cameras, chests puffed, chins raised. Gabe was tugged at, pulled this way and that: he wanted to tell the crowd that His Majesty had always been the superior fencer; that he was in all ways, the better man. But the mic was gone; some of the men were telling one another drinking stories from their days in the army. Gabe looked over and saw the King's eyes light with humor; for a moment, just one of the guys.

His mother. Looking like a lovely young woman, hair in black scrolls against the wind. Her smile fresh and wide. Like the stories from her childhood, how she swam in the wild herbs that grew on their hill, how she outran the boys, ran till she couldn't feel her legs beneath her.

And the boy.

The two of them reunited. Sitting in the audience. Right there, *there.*

Hands at his sides, Hafez stood fixed to his spot beside the arena. His heart pounded. He watched them talking, leaning toward each other.

"Yemmah," he said.

Someone brushed by. A guard, a group of men in white knickers. He looked back, staring; his eyes burned with not blinking. He watched his mother lift her hands, clapping. He saw her shift in his direction and turn into his niece, Amani.

The boy beside her was now an old man.

CHAPTER

24

HE PICKED UP his gym bag and went out to the street behind the arena; it was quiet and empty. The crowd was still inside listening to the King. For a moment, he stood motionless, taking in the way temples and columns seemed to float over the gold rock. A falcon with a wide, horizontal fan of feathers wafted overhead, looking like the drawing on an Egyptian tomb. One of the desert patrol had told Gabe that English tourists with binoculars routinely came to Petra only to stare at birds. They were situated on a great migratory passage.

"Wonderful match."

Gabe lowered his gaze to see a large man shadowed by late-afternoon sun walking toward him. He was holding some silver foils with enamel hilts. "A gift from His Majesty—to show our gratitude. You ran off before we could present it to you."

Gabe took a step back as his brother's face emerged in the light. "A gift," Gabe said. He smiled at Hafez but didn't reach for the foils.

"These were commissioned by the Palace," Hafez said. "Hand-forged in Italy. I approved the design myself. I know how you like things made by hand. You'll never find any as nice anywhere."

For just a moment, Gabe looked away from his brother, his center filling with heaviness. He felt tired and done and now he just wanted to go home.

"You don't like them?"

Gabe's brother's face appeared at that moment to be filled with tenderness and a kind of hope. It seemed so genuine. "I don't have it," Gabe said.

Something shifted in Hafez's eyes.

"I don't. I'm telling you the truth. I used to, of course, for years and years. I hid it away—and I'm sorry about that. But I don't have it anymore."

Hafez was still smiling. "Where is it?"

Gabe shook his head.

"You really don't have it?"

"Really."

"You're lying," Hafez said.

"I'm not."

"Then where is it?"

"I gave it away."

"Why would you do that?" His voice dropped. "Who did you give it to?"

Again, Gabe shook his head. "I threw it away. I threw it in the river."

"What river? There is no river." Hafez reached for Gabe's bag. "Let me see."

Gabe backed away again, clutching his bag. "What are you doing?"

"What am I doing?" Hafez seemed to truly ask himself. "You've taken everything else." Hafez looked unearthly, his face and voice flattened. It occurred to Gabe that something was not right with his brother, that he was somehow ill. "What's left?" He tossed the foils at Gabe's feet. "Come. Just give it to me. You know I was supposed to have it. You know that. You brought it—why? Just to taunt me?"

Gabe took another step back.

"It won't be so simple for you to just walk away with it anymore. I can tell that you brought it, y'akhi. Your face always gives you away.

Did you bring it to mock me? If you try to leave the country with a valuable Jordanian artifact, you'll be stopped at customs and it will be confiscated. You might even be prosecuted. They could hold you here."

A shiver started in the bones of his legs. Staring at his brother, Gabe tore open the gym bag, showing its black interior; a towel and empty water bottle tumbled out. He flung the bag to the ground between them. "*Il Saif mish houn! Il Saif!* I gave it away. To the King. Yes. I gave it to him. Just now! On the piste. What—didn't you see? Weren't you looking? Didn't you say you wanted him to have it? His voice rose into a shout. Didn't you say it was for our king? For his birthday present? Go get it from your precious king!" A group of young men came drifting over, Bedouins in dusty trousers, cigarettes between their fingers. They stood watching.

"I said nothing!" Hafez barked. His balance was tipping. "I said? I said what? I said nothing." He brought his face too close: Gabe could feel his breath. He saw a red tendril of vein in his brother's left eye. A tremor at the corner of his mouth. With both hands Hafez shoved Gabe so hard he staggered backward. "I said nothing."

For some reason, this filled Gabe with anger. His lungs stretched with air. "*Everything you say is nothing!*" he roared.

One of the young men watching clapped loudly. "*Ai-wah!*" Yes. "*All of it is nothing!*"

Hafez walked over the foils on the ground and swung wildly at Gabe. Gabe yelped and jumped back. "Zero," Hafez hissed between his teeth. "Who are you? You think you deserve to come here and fight the King? Why would you think that? Do you know what that man has done? He's led a kingdom. What have you done? Fled. You make boxes from wood. That's what you do."

"*Sah,*" Gabe said. Correct. "Did I ever say anything different?" But something in his stance loosened then. His arms fell to his sides. "Hafez. You talk to the Israelis. You say you make peace but, y'akhi, it's like there's no peace inside you. We're too old for this. The more you live the more you lose. What if we just let go of it now?"

Hafez's eyes grew as if he no longer saw Gabe. "Fight!" He

shrieked and shoved Gabe again. "Fight. Or I'll kill you right now."
He swung again at Gabe's face, just missing.

Falling back, caught from behind by onlookers, Gabe heard other
voices urging him forward. Hands slapping at his shoulders. "*Ya rab,
imshee,*" someone said. You better run. More people had gathered.
Gabe turned away and Hafez smacked the back of his neck as if
knighting him. Stumbling, he gasped and grabbed his neck.

Someone in the gathering shouted *andale!* Gabe felt his ribs swell.
He turned. Hafez nodded, his face distorted, nearly unrecognizable.
Gabe laughed with fear.

Hafez gave a wild yell and charged at Gabe. Gabe jumped back
and stumbled again, tripping over his own heels. A voice shouted
in Arabic, *I'm coming.* Gabe tumbled to the earth, hitting his tail-
bone and elbows, Hafez toppling over him. From their sprawl on
the ground, head ringing, Gabe turned from his brother to see Musa
charging between people to jump on top of him and Hafez.

Amani's voice rose in the distance, calling Musa's name.

Desert Patrol came from both sides of the street: their khaki skirts
and bandoliers flapping; one had a gun in his hand. It seemed to
Gabe that thirty men descended on them—later, he heard it was five.
Hafez gasped, flailing. Someone—the young fencing instructor—
pulled Gabe away. The guards immediately decided on barefooted,
wild-eyed Musa as the trouble and half-dragged him off. Shaking
himself loose, Hafez ran after them. He yelled, "Wait! Wait for me!"
A few people clapped.

Another guard offered his hand and asked Gabe if he was quite
all right.

Gabe stood slowly. There was a searing pain in his low back,
and his head rang with a metallic, anvil-struck peal. He swayed.
"That's—that other man is my cousin," he gasped. A firm hand
held Gabe's upper arm, helping him stand upright, which he wasn't
sure he was ready to do. Eduardo gripped his shoulders and stooped,
peering into Gabe's eyes like a doctor. "You're okay? Your hand is
laid open."

"Oh God. Oh, Dad." Amani was there, her arm around her father; he left himself shift some weight onto her. "Look at your hand!"

Eduardo got a roll of bandages from the medic. Stripping out tape, he wrapped Gabe's knuckles snugly. Omar appeared and squatted beside Eduardo. "Well, it's official—Hafez is out of his fucking mind."

"Please—that man . . ." Gabe tried to point out to the remaining officers where the patrol had hustled Musa away. "That's Musa, my cousin. Don't let them hurt him."

One officer turned to look, but they had disappeared into the crowd.

"Dad," Amani said. "He's not your cousin."

CHAPTER

25

HIS HANDS SHOOK and danced along the steering wheel. Hafez wasn't used to driving. His hands and neck felt clammy. Was that a symptom of something? Was it a symptom of kidnapping someone? Once he'd separated Musa from the security detail—with a thousand reassurances ("He's a distant relative . . . completely harmless . . . very simple . . .") plus fifty dinars *rashwa* per guard—then took him by rattling carriage through the siq, and loaded him in the back of the car. . . well, uncertainty had set in. It seemed he'd lost a bit of control over the situation.

Hafez wished he could've brought Samir, but he needed the time alone to think. It was terribly awkward: Musa seemed not to know what a car was. So thin yet wiry, curved into a hunch, he balked at the door, climbing in with difficulty. "So, my friend," Hafez said. Always begin with friend. "So, hello to you again. It has been such a long time, hasn't it."

Musa, I am Musa, the man in the backseat kept saying. In the mirror, Hafez saw the strong jaw bone, the chin. A family face. The man stared out the windows, unfamiliar with highways or car radios. The mouth. The long face. The placid, nearly infuriating stillness in his eyes. The way he gazed, the broad purple land opening across his retinas.

How had Musa come to be there? Hafez felt darts of panic. Had he been found out somehow, had word of the inheritance had made its way to Musa in the nuthouse? Musa with the eyes of a prophet— Musa who'd risen from the supposed-to-be-dead. Had he come to lay claim? He was just as grimy as he'd been in childhood, as if he hadn't bathed a day, almost certainly leaving smudges all over the upholstery. Hafez could only steal glimpses in the mirror. He watched the late-afternoon light turning, running bands over the man's face.

"This isn't the way to my house," Musa said. "We aren't going to my house."

Hafez watched him, his thoughts unspooling. "Why did you come? What were you doing there?" But the man remained blank as paper, mesmerized. This was the boy Hafez remembered. He knew it was him. The situation was almost geometrical in its completion— Musa sitting in the audience, gazing out with that indescribable face: those eyes that looked through one's soul and saw what was written on the far side.

"It's strange," Hafez said to the air, placing his fingers on top of the steering wheel. "You think—oh, it seems as if you work and work, always 'eyes on the prize.'" He made air quotes. "Like they say. Whatever the prize is—a promotion or a house. Whatever. You work. And when you finally get it—it is so very wonderful." He sighed again with a tiny whistle through his nostrils. He knew Musa didn't understand English. "So amazing. And you think: After this, my life is now different. I am changed. Forever. It'll never go back. Like you're a great actor—you're Marlon Brando! You're a star, and you think: That's it—this is my new life. And it is. But then a little time goes by and after a while no one but you remembers being a star.

"You think: Once I make full professor, once I get appointed to the cabinet, once I broker the peace talks . . . *then*, then! I was at

Madrid, did you know? *Before* Oslo. I walked into that bullring, so to speak." He smirked. "That was me. I went in there with lousy George Bush, that sidewinder. Me and His Majesty. The Palestinians—those boys, they were actually scared to sit at the table with the Israelis. One of them asked us if they really had horns." He snorted and adjusted his sun visor. "A grown man. Lived all their lives around each other—no idea who the other one was. The Israelis called Arafat's men 'the terrorists.' Openly, like that was their actual name. The terrorists. Yeah." He rubbed the heel of his palm against an eyebrow. "I sat in between them. Palestinians on that side, Israelis on that side. Me and Il Malik. We got them to talk. Jackals, all of them." He squinted at the road. "I was on the evening news— in the States. Dan Rather. Not Walter Cronkite. Not as good. But not bad. Not bad. It's the kind of thing you think, Now everything will be like this. From now on. You start to think anything's possible. You think, Now it's time. What was meant for me will be given me. Did you know our mother gave Il Saif away to Gabe? You must get to a point, you know—it just eventually . . ." He fell silent, staring at the navy bands of the horizon. "But then, well, one gets old, of course. And young is not interested in old. And Jordan is so young!"

During the duel, from near the backstage area, Hafez had watched Musa out of the corner of his eye, the arc of his back, the intent shape of his gaze, the claylike skin of his arms, hands, and feet—which Hafez realized only now, were bare. When he'd seen him talking to Amani like they'd known each other all their lives, Amani had looked so much like his mother, Hafez had felt actual fear. Natalia, an intelligent, broken woman, had believed in demons and jinns. Natalia's belief system was filled with symbols, "energies," and spirits. And despite his inborn horror of primitive beliefs, Hafez felt an icy finger trace his spine, sensing that this creature gazing up at him from the backseat was a jinn. He was here to punish Hafez for his desire for—well, for anything. His mother used to say Hafez had been born with a devil inside—"a clever, naughty, troublesome demon" who would get his way. Not like Gabe. Where Hafez had to charm and dance his way through life, there was some magical property in Gabe that dissolved all resistance. They'd named him for the angel—a malak—so near the Arabic word for king.

Hafez glanced at him again in the rearview mirror and saw Musa watching the desert highway with an unnerving intensity, a yellow light in his eyes. He wouldn't have been surprised if, at any moment, the man unfurled a fiery tongue. Or perhaps this man, too, was an angel, because Hafez could no longer tell the difference. He was tired and dizzy, his vision mottled with sunspots; his ears buzzed. He flicked on the windshield wipers. "Can't see a damned thing," he groused. "All this damned dust."

"Khamseen," Musa said.

HAFEZ NEVER ONCE saw him in shoes. Wrapped in a loose woolen robe, more creature than child, at night Musa had slept outdoors with the goats. There were twigs in the boy's hair, leaves, weeds. He preferred sitting to playing, walking to running. He sang tuneless things, smiled, and rarely spoke. Babies stopped crying when he held them. He lived with his head in their mother's lap, playing with her necklace like an infant when she sat underneath the walnut trees. He brought bird nests into the house, rocks, scorpions, beetles. Once, Hafez was painfully bitten by a centipede in his shoe: he knew where it had come from.

Natalia said Musa was goodness personified. She said he wasn't of this world. He hadn't wanted to be born, she said. When Natalia was ten months pregnant, Sitt Danya had to plead with the unborn baby: *Yella, imshee!* Time to let go! He was limp and gray when he was finally pulled free. The midwife rubbed his back, held him on her lap and tried to rock life back into his body; she blew into his nose, then into his mouth; she lifted him by his ankles. There was no cry: he'd started breathing only when she touched a drop of honey to his lips and his skin bloomed pink.

Hafez had loved Musa, in the vague, self-centered way of children, until he was eight and had gone into town with Munif and
the men were calling his father Abu-Musa—Father of Musa—and
he saw how his father's face hardened against it. It was supposed
to be an honor—parents were nicknamed after their first child.
But Musa couldn't attend school, couldn't read or write, couldn't do
much more than sit on the ground, laughing, watching the other
children, tracing the flight of birds with his fingers. Sometimes he
soiled himself; when their mother tried to bathe him, he wailed
loudly enough to be heard by the neighbors. For years he refused
to wear clothing.

Damaged, fugitive, embarrassing: Just like a refugee. Natalia
wasn't pregnant with him when she'd fled her country, but Hafez
had long sensed that Musa was a result of that flight all the same.
Her terror and loss passed down in genetic memory like broken
strands of DNA.

Their father was ashamed of Musa. Dashing, jaunty Munif had
sired this bizarre boy, this changeling. He pretended his firstborn
didn't exist. Hafez knew what the village all understood: Musa was
too much for them—he was unpredictable—increasingly so as he
grew older. He made strange sounds when visitors came to the house.
The neighbors murmured he was unnatural; they were afraid he
would follow their daughters. Natalia was Musa's protector—the one
who kept him fed and sheltered. Once, Hafez saw them sitting on
the ground, Musa leaning against Natalia, the two of them laughing
and covered in small blue butterflies.

At times it seemed his father had no use for Hafez either—but he
was better than dim-witted Musa. Hafez caught a glimmer of advantage. Usually there was little benefit to being a second son. Everyone
knew the rule of the firstborn: eldest boy takes all, lands, money,
titles. The first becomes sheikh, he becomes malik. Sometimes the
firstborn, after coming into inheritance, distributes it, equally or
unequally, among his siblings—or just to his brothers, or possibly
to no one at all. It would be a disaster, Hafez knew, if Musa were to

inherit anything—he'd lose it in a twinkling! The villagers would descend: Hafez could see a thousand hands extended. His brother had no idea of who was family and who was imposter. Who was deserving and who a thief.

In 1938, a few months after Hafez turned thirteen, during an ocean of unseasonable heat, his mother's elder sister Intizar arrived with her children. A year earlier, her home had been seized in the night by soldiers, her husband was shot as they ran. She and her children had been hiding and starving up in the hills, eating wild herbs and little else for weeks, having fled their country on foot. Their family, smelling of goat manure, clothes hanging in strips, crowded into Munif's house. Seeing those grubby children, Hafez had felt shame like a physical mark. He felt exposed. For all their boasts of education and culture, their dismissal of Jordanians as goatherds and nomads, the Palestinians were still the dispossessed, crammed into those grim cement structures and tents, no electricity or water, open sewers in the alleys.

Natalia never entirely forgot her childhood terrors of twenty years earlier when their family had run from the tumult of the Arab Revolt against the Ottomans. There had been famine in the Levant: the Ottoman Army—what was left of it—had trampled the fields, seizing the crops. They'd dragged away women and screaming children, bayonetting, pillaging. Hollow-eyed soldiers set fire to houses and orchards out of sheer spite, in the wrathful spirit of lashing out even as one is dying. Natalia's old fears sometimes rattled her sleep. Once, she whispered to Hafez she thought she saw a soldier hiding in the curtains, his wrapped legs and dusty boots emerging from under the fringes.

Hafez had awakened on a night late in November 1938 when the heat made lying on a mattress almost unbearable. He heard his mother and aunt's voices rooms away, reminiscing over their beautiful, lost childhood, their evanescent Nazareth. He heard Aunt Intizar ask his mother, "Do you remember our old tea service?"

His mother sighed. "Yes, and teatime. And those terrible gloves Mama made us wear? I tried to hide in the orchard to escape."

"She always said you'd never be a mother. And yet here you are."

Natalia laughed her curious laugh. "Yes, they caught me at last." After a long moment, his mother asked in a new, lower voice, "You said it was soldiers who came—that night?"

"We don't know who they were. They kicked in our door. We were sleeping." Her voice snagged.

"Were they Turks?" At this, Hafez felt a river of chills through his blood. The other day, his aunt's eldest boy, Cyrus, had commented that he'd heard the Turks were taking boys around Musa's age to rebuild their army.

Another long pause, then his aunt murmured, "It might have been."

It came to him in a surge: he sat upright from the force of it: he knew what to do.

THE NEXT DAY, his mother and aunt were rolling grape leaves in the kitchen, entwined in conversation, when Hafez burst into the room, his pulse leaping in his veins, hair plastered to his forehead. All afternoon, he'd gone over it in his head, whispering and pacing. When he thought he was ready he'd gone to the neighbors—the ones in town, the ones in the marketplace, telling his story to anyone who would listen. Practicing. Serving it. Sowing it like a seed. Telling and retelling until no one could remember how the story had started. The people he told looked at each other—their eyes wide, their hands opened. They began to back away as fear took hold; gratings rolled down over the shops. The schoolmistress dismissed her class. Shutters slammed. When he ran back into his own house, he believed every word.

"The Turks are coming!" he burst out.

The sisters both stood: Natalia beckoned Hafez over, wrapping him in her arms. He was shaking. "What is it, child?" she asked. "Tell me what is happening."

He told them, breathlessly, about the Turkish infantry spotted out-side of town, in places like Madaba and al Khadra and Zuwayza—far enough away to be difficult to check, near enough to be frightening. People were saying the Ottomans were reconstructing their army, going from town to town, taking the biggest, strongest sons from each family and bearing them away to training grounds on the Bos-phorus. "If they come here . . ." He trailed off, his voice quaking. Into the air rose the specter of soldiers dragging off helpless Musa. Hafez was enthralled by the power of his lie—a lie he hadn't even had to tell completely. "It's impossible! I'd go in his place, if I could, if they'd take me . . ." At thirteen, Hafez looked like a skinny ten-year-old. Only two years older, Musa could have passed for an adult.

Natalia sent Farouq to get Munif. Gabe played on the floor with a leaf. Natalia made Hafez repeat his story to Munif: he did, add-ing details as he went—the number of soldiers, their ferocity. Munif frowned at the floor, nodding as Hafez spoke. He asked where he'd gotten this information. Hafez told him about the schoolteacher and the barber, a gathering on the street corner: the way the shopkeeper rolled down his iron grate. He thought perhaps his father looked at him a beat too long, but then Munif said, "We will do whatever is necessary to make Musa safe."

His father went into town. When he returned hours later, he confirmed the stories. They had spread from neighbor to neighbor, grown with flourishes. In fact, Hafez's idea was supported by a well-spring of longstanding rumors and village gossip. Yara and all the villages around it had a communal terror of the people they called "the Turks." Stories about the Ottomans still circulated: the slaughter of Armenians, the death marches through the Syrian Badia. Even though the empire had collapsed in the wake of World War I, the entire village of Yara was prepared to believe—expecting, in fact—that the Ottomans would rise up one day and reassume their former power and brutality. Now people claimed to have seen the soldiers themselves. The shopkeeper had repeatedly slapped his own face and chest for selling cigarettes to a Turk—someone with a long, red face and blue eyes. That night, they bundled Musa in two robes. Hafez, his father, and Musa in his bare feet, walked seventeen kilometers in the dark to al Daraja, where they paid a goatherd to take Musa the rest of the way—to a convent, another thirty-six kilometers away. It was a place his father had heard of. The nuns there were said to accept anyone who needed sanctuary. They would hide him there, "just for now," Munif had assured his wife. "Till the Turks are gone."

Hafez had cried a little when they handed Musa over to the goatherd, surprised at his own grief. His father had nodded with approval. After they left Musa—blinking, soundless, staring after them, Hafez didn't feel the walk back. There was a bit of emptiness where he'd held his older brother's hand, as if he'd lost a little bag of coins. They were hungry that morning, with another long walk ahead. It was a strange, ghostly sort of hunger. His father caught and killed a rabbit in the fields, Il Saif neatly slitting through the pink meat. Before they'd eaten, Munif had looked at his son, and it seemed to Hafez that his father was looking through him. Like a sleepwalker, Munif put his thumb to the bloody remains then drew it down the side of his son's face. "So you are a man now."

HAFEZ'S YOUNGER BROTHERS were upset when Musa didn't return, but after some anxious questions about Musa's whereabouts, seven-year-old Farouq seemed to accept the change. Gabe, the youngest, normally so placid, had cried for weeks after Musa had left, inconsolable and pleading to be lifted. He wandered the house with his arms outstretched.

Only the housekeeper stared at Hafez with her implacable eyes, her hands folded at the waist.

Some of the other families also sent their sons into hiding: all returned after a few weeks. Not Musa. If only his mother could have accepted it. Hafez listened at his parents' door: he heard Natalia sobbing, begging her husband to find the boy. Munif told her not yet: it wasn't safe. He pleaded with her: *Leave it be.* He shouted: Ya Allah! It's better this way, the nuns know best how to care for him. One day, after he had been gone for months, their mother wasn't there at dinnertime. No one knew where she was. That evening, Munif and two of the field workers rode out on horses, and Aunt Lamise with her hard face, her hands like tree bark, put the children to bed. Munif came home in the morning with Natalia on the back of his horse, her face streaked with tears and grime, the bottom of her dress and her shoes sodden with mud. She didn't speak for days.

That was perhaps the worst of it. Hafez realized he'd hoped their mother would somehow return with Musa. There was still time, then, to erase the terrible thing. He asked her, not long after she'd come back, if they could please search for him again. The look she gave him could have sent a forest up in flames. "No, Hafez. Your father says Musa is safer this way." She wasn't crying and yet tears leaked from the corners of her eyes.

Hafez might have said then, *I made it all up.* But he couldn't do it.

His father went on, apparently unfazed: though he seemed to mistrust Hafez more than ever. Yes: it was Hafez's fault that Musa had been taken from their family. But it was his father who'd made it possible, and his father who had somehow made sure that he wouldn't return, convincing himself that they weren't qualified or able to care for their own son.

Even his mother had played a role, because hadn't she given in to Munif? Hadn't she, too, eventually given up?

The blame shifted. It transformed over time. There were whispers for years to come across the village of the impending Turks, and frequent reports of soldiers and spies. His mother was altered in ways that took a longer time to see—as if a fissure, just a hairline at first, had appeared in her foundation. Eventually, gradually, it would yawn open. She stared at soldiers, any man in uniform, wherever he might be—in the streets, in any public place. Hafez and his younger brothers had grown up, gone to school, to the military, to work, overseas. But Musa remained behind, pinned to childhood like a moth to a display. Hafez felt something moving, as if memory had changed into water. Open one eye and there were three boys, open the other and there were four.

Hafez couldn't believe how easy it had been—this thing he'd dreamed of for years—to simply become the eldest.

&

"I TRIED TO RECLAIM Il Saif today." Hafez spoke out loud, facing straight ahead. "That didn't happen." He checked Musa's face. "I didn't think it through. Rather impulsive." He squeezed the steering wheel and twisted to glance over the seat. "I would keep it for the both of us you know. You and me. The point is to bring it home. Sah? This is where it's supposed to be." He punched the steering wheel with the side of his hand hard enough to hurt himself. "*Wallahi*. Damn me. Damn it all."

"Home." Musa said.

"Home. Right. Here we go. Walak. I'm taking you there. Isn't that so lovely?" They passed a road sign with the figure of a camel on it. Xing. "Do you know if you hit a camel in your car it's like driving into a brick wall? That's what they say. We're not going back to your little hole. We're driving to your real home, yes? We're going back to Yara."

He saw awareness flutter like pain over the man's features. Uncertainty.

"And that woman you were sitting next to in the audience? Did you know her?"

Musa murmured something inaudible.

Hafez said. "Amani. She said she would meet you here."

Hafez hadn't known what he would do until he'd seen the mountain ridges, pale with distance, coming nearer, not as rosy as Petra. Here the columns of rock were streaked saffron, tangerine, gold, shifting with the sun and clouds, shadow-split, rising from earth. Wadi Rum: Valley of Mountains, Valley of the Moon. They were entering the true palace of the dominion. Here was the seat of power, here in the desert, house of the Bedouin, where armies were defeated, where mysterious kingdoms rose and fell and nothing lasted.

Musa studied the rock faces, eyes lifting. Hafez watched him in the mirror. He followed the parched dirt road to its end, its surface like burned skin. The visitors' offices were closed up. It was cold, wind striking the sand into ribbons. Already, the sun dipped behind the rocks, casting a frigid shadow. Hafez put the car in park, folded his hands over the wheel, and rested his head on his knuckles for a minute. "We're here," he said without turning to face the man. When he got done, he thought, it might be nice to go on a little vacation. Istanbul was supposed to be lovely in the snow: like an ice palace. He would woo Carole back after her Madame X sighting; give Madame X a little time to cool down after that op-ed. After a moment, Hafez sniffed deeply and straightened. "We made it!" He tried to sound hearty and cheerful. He pointed toward the west. "There's your home, Musa. That way."

After a moment, the man said, "It is home?"

"Yes." He drew out the word dreamily, as one might with a child. "Your true home, y'akhi. The first one. Yara. The real one. Where our mother and father and family lived together. Do you remember? Where you started?" He smiled and looked over the seat back, then pushed open the car door with his shoulder and flinched at the icy air. Almost winter. His feet on the ground. "You were a special problem—an artifact of exile." He searched the sky, the sunset coming now in slicks of pink above the rocks. "Our mother was broken, like you—before any of us knew her. Like the others. It's what happened to those people, whether they stayed or ran away—all of them, like this—" He put his fists next to each other, then snapped an invisible stick. "You and all the refugees, you make peace impossible because you are the only ones who know exactly what happened. And the only way to create peace is to forget."

Musa was sitting with the back of his head against the seat, his face illuminated by the bands of pink and blue over the evening horizon. Hafez felt, for an instant, that the two of them had been caught in a dream together. Lifting his head, Musa asked, "My mother? She is here?"

Hafez pulled himself to his feet and opened the man's door. *Me against my brother.* "Over there," he pointed to the farthest mountains, a blue shadow. It would be cold tonight. The sand on the hilltops ruffled with wind. "If you start walking right now and you don't stop, you will be there by morning." The wind filled Hafez's jacket, belling his sleeves. He watched as Musa took a few steps toward the dunes, then stopped.

"Home is there? Our house is?"

Hafez nodded. *My brother and me against the stranger.* "And your mother. Just keep going."

Musa entered the fields and began to trudge into the sand. Hafez was shaking. He shouted, calling him back. When Musa returned, Hafez hesitated for a long, tormented moment, then gave him a bottle of water and an orange from his glove box. Musa held them, gazing at Hafez, then turned back toward the desert. Hafez supported himself against the car and watched the silhouette walking toward the red dunes. Time was not an arrow but a bellows, expanding and contracting. Would Hafez really make the same decision now as he had almost sixty years ago? The wind flung sand against his face and eyes. He watched until the stars emerged against a royal-blue field.

He could have left Musa back in Petra, he supposed. Could've let the Mukhabarat have their way with him, put him in prison. But everything might have been discovered. Perhaps there was a birth certificate for Musa hidden in an ancient office. There were still so many documents to be signed. Too many variables, as the Americans say.

But then again, grown-up Musa had turned out to be so docile, so feeble-minded, Hafez realized, that he might've simply convinced the man to sign everything over to himself—it all could have come to him cleanly as a gift. He might have earmarked some of the money to care for his brother. He waved a hand before his face, dashing away thoughts. If the family learned about Musa, they would reex-amine every detail of the inheritance, each demanding a share.

No, Hafez thought, Musa had survived exile as a child and he would certainly make it as a tough old man. The Bedu tribes here knew every inch of Wadi Rum. They would find and rescue him. He who belongs to none belongs to all. Musa would become prince of the wasteland. Venerated. King of dust.

CHAPTER

26

• *Tuesday, November 21, 1995, Amman to Karak, Jordan* •

IT WAS EARLY; pillars of dust-spun light filled the room when
Amani left the guesthouse. At the big stone house next door, she'd
reached between the scrolls of iron work and rapped on her cousin's window. Omar was doing push-ups, his hair shiny with sweat.
He met her at the side of the house. His mother was out in her car
and Aunt Lamise had taken the loaner. Gesturing to his cousin, he
slipped into the garage with the spare key to Farouq's Mercedes. The
driver appeared, scolding vigorously—red-checked keffiyeh knotted
around his shoulders and a loaf of pita in one hand—and shooed
them away.

They walked from the house to Zahran Street and tried to nego-
tiate with the cabbies who pulled up, but none would make the trip
for less than fifty dinars. Omar clicked his tongue in annoyance. "It's
a long way—they can't afford the petrol."

From there, they'd walked fifteen blocks into Hafez's leafy neighborhood. The house looked closed-up. Samir was in front polish-

ing the silver sedan, a filterless cigarette between his fingers, another behind an ear.

"Hey man." Omar leaned against the car. "Hafez come back?"

Samir clicked his tongue, flicking his chin up—no. Gone. Impatiently, he waved Omar away from the car.

Amani touched Omar's shoulder and said to Samir in English, "We'd really be grateful if you could help us. It's kind of urgent."

With a sigh, Samir lowered his cloth, his eyes shaded under the brim of his baseball cap.

They wanted to go to Karak, Amani explained. She and Omar had twenty-seven dinars between the two of them, but Omar could get more if they could stop at the ATM in Abdoun Circle. Samir turned away, said he had to stick around in case Hafez needed him.

"But Hafez isn't actually here, is he?" Amani asked, glancing at the house. The big iron shutters were closed on the front windows. She'd left several messages on his phone. "Has he called or anything? Is Carole here?"

The driver shook his head. He didn't look at them. He fingered the edge of his ear, then jerked his head toward the car. "Come, come." He took their twenty-seven dinars. "It's enough. Yella." Samir opened the backseat doors. Once they were all in, he rolled down the long drive and turned the wrong direction on to Zahran Street.

"Wait." Amani leaned into the front seat. "It's south! We need to go south." She and Omar glanced at each other as Samir rounded another corner, bumping a yellow-and-black striped curb. They passed a construction site—the grounds broken up with cement, rebar, orange flags—made two more turns, and pulled in front of the stone faun. Omar said something in Arabic about Karak, which Samir ignored. Amani tossed a hand up, exasperated. "What's going on?"

"We don't go without the baba." Samir bounced his fist against the center of the wheel, horn bleating.

"He's asleep!" Amani protested.

"Samir policy," the driver said.

Gabe's face appeared in the upstairs window. Moments later, he emerged in shorts, T-shirt, and sandals, put a hand on the top of the car and bent to peer in. Amani saw pouches under his eyes. "Yella." He climbed in front. "Any word from Musa?"

"Nothing," Amani slumped back against her seat. "I kept calling the Petra Desert Patrol. The last guy I talked to acted like he didn't even know who I was talking about. I started thinking maybe Musa found a way back to Karak."

"Inshallah," Omar said.

"So that's where we're going. No one answers at the convent number. And no Hafez either," Amani added. "We went to his house."

"No, I know," Gabe said. "Hafez is gone. Like the Phantom."

The late light burnished the interior of the car and created an aura through the top of Samir's hair. Samir glanced at Amani in the mirror; he looked anxious. He whistled as he drove, his fingers drumming on the wheel. They spoke little.

On Sunday, Amani and Gabe had waited for hours at the visitor's center in Petra, expecting someone would release Musa. The officers avoided them. A deputy sheriff finally sat across from them in the lobby and informed them that, apparently, Musa and Hafez had left.

"*Apparently?*" Carole's forehead lifted. "Left where?"

No one seemed to have any idea where they had gotten to—or if they did, they weren't telling. Samir reported the car was gone. Carole alternated between fury and panic. "What has that idiot done?" she ranted, pacing through the center lobby, twisting her shawl around her shoulders. "He goes off without a word. I honestly don't think he's in his right mind. He's been acting so—so *bizarre*—for days now! I couldn't get him to sit still. I never can. He doesn't drive, either. I don't even know if his license is still good. That man must've driven! Do you think that man kidnapped my husband?"

The police assured her this was unlikely. One of the palace officials had offered her and Samir a ride back to Amman, but Carole decided to wait for Hafez at the hotel. Eduardo wanted to stay with Gabe and Amani, but the officer encouraged them to head back home: there was nothing they could do in Petra. He promised to call immediately if they heard anything. Amani thought her father looked drawn, his face nearly gray with fatigue.

Now Gabe spoke into the silence of the car as Samir drove. "Things will be okay."

She knew he wanted to believe Farouq, who had made inquiries of his own. One of his sources claimed that the Palace had quietly arranged to send Musa to a facility, a nice place, where he was being examined and tended to. Practically a spa, Farouq said, very modern, with doctors. They just want to check him out, make sure he was all right on his own . . .

Gabe sighed through his nose.

This morning, Amani had called the Royal Hashemite Court Office, then police headquarters downtown: she dialed a number one of the police had given her for a Mukhabarat agent, and then a security specialist with the American embassy who asked where she'd gotten his number, then suggested she try the court office. After that, she'd tried contacting hospitals and mental-health facilities in Amman, then in Beirut, Damascus, Jerusalem. No one had information on Musa, though everyone seemed reluctant to disappoint her, and she was given more names and numbers—all dead ends. She called the convent in Karak repeatedly. Were the nuns no longer there?

The highway was lined with ragged billboards and structures of pitted concrete block. The land stretched out. They drove past fruit stands, herds of sheep, camels decorated with tasseled bridles, and parched miles of pavement, before pulling into Karak. The convent's carved doors were propped open; the young nun, Sylvain, rested on an entryway bench in a band of light, a pair of worn work gloves and two geraniums in ceramic pots beside her. Rising, she put her arms around Amani, Gabe, then Omar, and brought them into the office. "I'm so sorry we missed your calls," she told Amani. "The day was so beautiful, I'm afraid we all went outside to work in the dirt." She looked from Amani to Gabe as they sat down, her eyes almost transparent in the watery light. A cedar crucifix and a cross of palm fronds hung on the back wall above her chair. "Is Musa not with you?"

"He's not here?" Amani sat nearest the nun. "We were hoping somehow he might have found his way back home."

But Sister Sylvain had no information: there had been no word from Musa. And when last they'd heard, the government scouts had come through and sealed off his cave. "Come, come—we'll check the cave." The nun stood and Amani, Gabe, and Omar followed her out.

Sylvain led the group back up the ridge to Musa's cave. Strands of police tape blocked the opening. With swift, impatient movements, Sylvain tore away the tape. The place was desolate; gray cinders covered the fireplace. His burned pot was on the sand floor. Beside it, a plate with a cracked glaze and blue rim, the image of a faded gazelle at the center. A withered T-shirt. The place smelled of cypress and crushed herbs. Amani rubbed her hands over her arms and surveyed the folding purple hills, the serpentine road in the distance. Omar stooped near the fireplace and tipped the little pot; water swirled in the bottom. "I forgot—he was making tea when I came for him," he said, replacing it. "He expected to be right back."

"Dammit," Amani said. "Where is he?" She surveyed the ground beside the knife, the pot, and the cold ashes, the air swaying and soft inside the bowl of the open cave. It seemed almost possible that Musa would be back at any moment. She muttered, "Where is he?"

Within the cave, she noticed a bit of fabric poking out of a chest and tugged it free. It was like the one that Musa had shown them on their visit, covered with chalky white strokes. She picked up the cloth, folded it carefully, and put it in her bag beside the onionskin envelope with the scraps of blue letters. Touching the inner wall of the cave, smooth as one of her father's planed boxes, Amani took a last look before they departed.

BACK AT THE CONVENT, Sylvain said, "You will let us know if you hear of anything?" She wrote her personal phone number on the back of a receipt. "I'll do the same."

Amani nodded.

The nun walked them to the car: Samir was still outside, wiping down Hafez's silver Mercedes, talking with the gardener, who wore canvas gloves, a trowel under one arm. "Oh, your driver! I would have invited him in for tea," Sylvain took a rosary of olive-wood beads from her pocket and gave them to Samir, saying, "To keep you safe on the job." She patted his arm. "May you be protected and guided."

Amani saw the driver look surprised. He laid his hand on his chest in thanks. "Isn't Samir Muslim?" she asked Omar quietly.

Sylvain said, "My beads are nondenominational."

AFTER THEY DROVE OUT of Karak and pulled onto the highway, Omar said, "Well, that was a bust."

"And where is Hafez?" Gabe asked darkly, arms still folded over his chest. "That's what I want to know."

"If he's with Musa, I have to believe they're both okay," Amani said. "I mean—it's Uncle *Hafez*, right? He wouldn't let anything happen—I mean, he's a big official, he—"

Samir's head jerked, his focus shifted in the mirror. "He took the *car.*"

Omar looked at Amani, eyebrows lifted.

"He doesn't stop to tell me. He just *goes* and he *takes* it." Samir's voice was low and terse. "The car—it's *my* job. *My* responsibility." Samir took a long breath and Amani sensed something giving way in the driver. "Do you know he never even lets me inside of his house? He said because of Mrs. Carole. But I don't think that's true."

In the backseat, Amani noticed the prayer beads wrapped around his wrist. After a moment, she sat forward. "You've worked for Hafez for a long time, I guess."

Samir didn't meet her eyes in the mirror; his gaze shifted back and forth over the highway, as if tracking thoughts. Finally, he said, "You're looking for that one—the one the desert guards stopped?"

Amani glanced at her father. Beside her, Omar sat up, but Amani made a settling gesture. "That's right," she said. "Musa."

"Hafez took him, you know. He put him in the back of the car. I saw it. I saw everything. They were gone for maybe three, four hours. When he comes back to Petra—no Musa."

Amani put her fingers over her mouth. Gabe's head turned toward the driver. He and Omar began to speak at the same time. "Do you know where they went?" Gabe asked. Omar held the back of Gabe's seat.

Samir made the hard clicking sound, *no*. "The guards tell me in secret. They give him to Hafez. He bribed them. A lot of rashwa. They tell me this later while we're waiting for the boss. Miss Carole, screaming where is Hafez? Could be anywhere. But the car— covered in sand when he got it back. There was a *khamseen* starting in Petra. Hafez told her he took him to the tabeeb. For checkup. All I know is no Musa. Only Hafez, and he doesn't say anything, only that Musa is majnoon." He tapped his temple. "That he needs all kinds of doctors."

Scarcely breathing, Amani glanced at her cousin: she felt a growing unease. Up front, Gabe muttered what sounded like a string of curses. "*Kelb*." Dog. "He did something. What did he do?"

"What doctors? Where?" Omar asked. "Did he take him to Amman?"

Amani asked Samir to pull onto the side of the road.

"You really don't know where Hafez is now?" Gabe asked Samir.

The driver shook his head. "I drove them home from Petra last night. This morning, he and Mrs. Carole are going on vacation. Maybe Turkey, he says. Maybe to the Gulf. Missus wants to go to France. They take two suitcases to the airport." He gave a short whistle between his teeth and lip, dipped his fingers through the air. "All gone."

"Are there, like, any hospitals around Petra?" Omar asked.

Amani said, "I've called clinics and medical facilities all over the place. Petra, Amman, Zarqa, Aqaba. No record of Musa anywhere."

"Musa's not in a hospital," Gabe said. "I know it."

"For years—for so many years I'm working for your brother," Samir said to Gabe, his face darkening. "I was a boy when he takes me from school. He tells us he is the best boss because he doesn't whip us. I think maybe it's true. But I think he has beat the house girls. Last year I want to get married to a nice girl—the boss says no. I must not. He says I don't make enough to support a family. He says now I'm married to him. I listened to him. I don't know why."

"Dude does that to people," Omar said. "He can tell you that you're eating ice cream when he's feeding you khara." Shit.

"Khara," Gabe muttered.

"You said when he came back, the car was covered in sand?" Amani asked.

"It took me all day to polish it. Still dull."

"Was it just like the sand from Petra? Like he'd just been driving around town?"

Samir's eyes stopped, his face narrowing. He opened the car door and got out, Amani and the others following. Samir stooped, running his finger along the headlights, the undercarriage. Gabe joined in, checking under the door handle, the grille, the neck of the rear-view mirrors.

"I wasn't looking so closely yesterday when I polished. But my whole family are Bedu—I know what Petra dust is. If I can see it again, I would tell you." Samir fingered the license plate.

"There's nothing left," Omar said, wiping a palm along the sleek cartop. "It's like a skating rink."

"Wait." Samir opened the driver's door and squatted. He scanned the floorboards; after a moment he shook his head and stood to close the door. Then stopped and crouched again. There was a thin ridge of powder between the door and the interior carpet. The powder was almost the same color as the carpet.

"I didn't have a chance to vacuum this side yet." He pressed his index finger into the powder and brought up a bright fingertip. "Petra dust is softer, more like sunlight. You see this? Hard, red?" He squinted up at them. "This is Wadi Rum."

CHAPTER

27

OMAR SAID, "You know guys, Wadi Rum is massive, right? To try to find one person? Shouldn't we, like, call the police or the American embassy or somebody?" They'd turned the car around and driven due south. It would take another three hours to get there.

"Police like the ones at Petra?" Gabe asked. "The ones who lost him in the first place?" He had tried calling Hafez's mobile again: a message answered that the voicemail at this number was full.

Samir said something in Arabic, shaking his head.

"But I mean—he isn't *lost*," Amani said. "Hafez had to have taken him somewhere. We just have to figure out where they went."

Still, she felt urgency in her gut, in her bones. She told herself that Hafez wouldn't let anything happen to him, but she kept imagining Musa's body buried in the desert or picked apart by raptors, the bones carried away. She let her head tip against the seat back and fell into an overheated doze, the words *raptor, rapt, enraptured,* vibrating in her thoughts. When she woke, the car windows were blazing. Sun-struck mountains rippled across her vision, so close they seemed about to spill into the car. They had turned off the highway. Her father offered her a bottle of water and a shawarma sandwich rolled up in pita: they'd stopped for gas and food while she'd slept. She gulped down the water then devoured the sandwich, licking the garlicky sauce from her fingers, staring out the windows. The ground looked like coppery satin. Horsetails of sand flickered before the car and a sound like ticking needles sprayed across the windshield. Samir cursed and turned on the wipers, clearing waves in the film that instantly filled in.

They came to a small compound of concrete and sandstone bricks, a sign overhead in English and Arabic: *Wadi Rum Visitor's Center.* Drivers leaned against a row of jeeps; in the distance, Bedouins with wrapped heads led camels across the stony earth. Stepping out into the wind, Amani held the side of the car and surveyed the palatial rocks and crimson sand. The wind dashed shrouds of dust off the mountains, currents of it twisted into the sky like immense ghosts.

The entry area listed different prices for Jordanians and foreigners. A man in white trousers, blazer, and a waist-length keffiyeh trimmed with white tassels sat at a ticket counter. Gabe spoke with him; at first, the man scowled fiercely, shaking his head. He seemed to be trying to dismiss them. Then Samir started speaking, touching his sternum, and the man's eyes lifted. He nodded several times, glancing at Amani and Gabe. Amani realized that Samir and the man—who said his name was Daleel—were comparing family trees. Omar leaned over and whispered: *This guy knows something.* The man turned to Gabe and said in English, "I didn't think you are Hamdan family. My mother's sister is married to Toufik Hamdan."

Gabe nodded, "Sure—I know Toufik!"

"Second cousins," Omar murmured to Amani. "And that's how it's done."

Daleel hesitated, as if about to say something when another man joined them: he wore an ankle-length dishdasha and a red keffiyeh wound like a turban around his head. Gabe and Omar spoke to him in rapid Arabic, moving their hands. Amani could hear them describing Hafez and Musa, but the second man clicked his tongue. "No one here like that," he said in American-accented English. "We

can check the registry, but we know everyone who comes in or out."
Amani saw the first man look at her, then away. Four then five others drifted over, conferring in Arabic, shaking their heads; a few of
them held cups of tea. They offered tea to Gabe and Amani, who
declined. Two desert officers joined the group. "They have no record
of these people. When do you think they come?" one asked.

"Someone would have seen them," another said.

"Probably they have gone home already."

Gabe and Amani gave as much information as they had. The officers disagreed with the ticket merchants, saying that someone coming after the ticket office closed could enter the monument fairly
easily. "Only the stars are watching then," one officer said, pointing
to the deepening blue light in the sky. "And scorpions." The other
officer smoothed his mustache with the flat of his thumb.

A man holding a demitasse cup gestured with it to the sky.
"There's supposed to be another windstorm coming. They're not letting tourists in right now anyway."

They asked where Gabe and Amani were from, who these missing people were, why they were missing. They had a lot of questions, but offered very little information—just theories and more idle
speculation. After a while, Amani wandered away from the group,
almost certain they were withholding something. She walked into
the center courtyard, ringed by souvenir shops selling bright scarves,
embroidered linens, and pottery. The wind had settled for a moment
and the air looked gauzy. Holding both hands to her forehead like a
visor, she squinted at a rock formation in the distance that reminded
her of smokestacks.

"That one is the Seven Pillars of Wisdom." It was Daleel, the first
man they'd met at the ticket counter. Daleel's face was so tanned and
etched it looked like dried leather; his mouth had a thin, bitter curve.
He stared at the red-rock mountain.

"I only see five," Amani said, again shielding her eyes, deliberately
not looking at him. She felt as though she were trying not to frighten
off something wild.

"That's right," he said. Then his gaze ticked back: she could feel him studying the side of her face. "You remind me by someone," he said at last. "Very much." After a few moments, he murmured, "There is people here I think who will know more."

She turned toward him, uncertain. "I—I'm sorry, I don't have any money."

He put one hand on his chest and lifted the fingers of the other as if taking an oath and Amani felt embarrassed for having mentioned payment. "You wait here. If you're ready now, I can bring you." The man trotted to the line of parked vehicles and brought around a jeep with only a windshield and bars where a roof would be. Amani stopped at the door, looking back over her shoulder.

"We must go—right away. I'll be in trouble if anyone sees I help you." The man gestured vigorously.

"Let me just run and tell my father."

The man made a slashing movement with his hand. "No—no! The others will see. I'm sorry—it has to be now. You have to go with me. Or I can't help."

There was a lift in his eyes like a promise that she thought she could trust. She felt braver in Jordan—there was less crime in Amman than in the little college town where she lived. If this man was her only chance to find Musa, she was going to take it. "I'll just be a second. I can—" Amani craned to look back over one shoulder, but felt the jeep begin to roll. "Wait! Fuck!" She jumped in and the man accelerated, looking around anxiously. "Where are we going?" she asked. He shouted something, but she didn't catch it over the rush of wind, her hair whipping back.

They rumbled by strings of camels, a child walking before a herd of horses, a small group of men squatting together above a campfire. Approaching a compound of concrete buildings bordered by faded red walls, the driver shouted that this was Rum Village—the source of tour guides, drivers, and camp cooks. Amani saw disemboweled cars and flapping laundry. A camel nosing a bag on the ground. The road turned to powdery sand tracks. They drove around a rock tower, the jeep's engine pulsed, stones pinging and banging against the undercarriage. A boy stood outside a row of tidy striped tents with flat tops, waving as they passed. Once they'd slowed enough to hear each other, Daleel said over the car's roar that he'd heard someone had been found in the wilderness area the other day: he would take her to some guides who knew where he was.

"Why is it such a secret?" Amani asked, lifting her voice.

"They are protecting him. It's their culture—the guest is higher above all others. And the authorities are not trusted." He brought his fingertips together with one hand, steering with the other, and shouted, Stenna. Wait. Almost there.

They drove into deeper sand and the engine noise became a low churning. The sun had gone beneath the horizon and the temperature dropped. Amani wrapped her arms around her ribs. The driver reached into the back and gave her a long cloak. She was grateful for its warmth. Her thoughts swung back and forth: she wondered if she should feel afraid.

The jeep rounded another imposing Mesozoic rock and pulled up to an encampment hidden at the base of the massif. The tents made a clapping sound in the wind. Light glowed through the stitched, woven panels. The cold air smelled like juniper and stone, as if the mountain had exhaled. Daleel called out as they walked to the encampment, then he bent to the tent flap and pulled it back, revealing a small table with a kerosene lamp, men huddled around a card game. Two of them stooped to come outside: they murmured with Daleel, casting evaluative glances at Amani, and again she wondered if she'd acted too rashly. It felt as if they were very far from other people. Finally, the men approached: one wore a skull cap, the other a keffiyeh that he wore folded in a tail down his back. Amani pulled her hair behind her shoulders, feeling exposed and uncertain. One of them beckoned. "We'll go to their horses," Daleel said.

They followed the two men along the foot of the rock until they reached a crevice in the rockface. They gestured for Amani and Daleel to continue. Amani followed Daleel, turning sideways

to squeeze through the rock opening into a wide canyon. Swallows
darted through the air, snatching insects. It was hard to see, the evening rapidly darkening. Amani's feet slid over the dimpled sand
and she felt residual warmth through the soles of her sneakers. She
touched the side of the butte for balance, it was cool and rough. In
the distance, a voice seemed to rise out of the rocks; the wind had
grown into a rumble and the song was so faint it might have been
imagined, but then Daleel sang along for a few bars. He glanced at
her with a quick flash of a smile. The men had moved ahead and
vanished around a corner. Daleel was many paces ahead too, but she
hung back, startled and distracted by the sky.

Overhead, stars had already started to emerge; they were impos-
sibly close and so bold and so many, the night was crowded with
them, shooting and pulsating, like nothing Amani had ever seen
before. Arrested by the dial of constellations, she stopped to stare,
stepping back, turning, eyes lifted. She craned, looking all the way
up, and the depths enveloped her. "My God, just—just *look* at that,"
she whispered, spellbound. "My God." She watched a star appear to
flash red and streak across the sky. "It's all so much closer here." She
stared and lifted her fingers to the refracting light as if she might
actually touch it. "God, I wish my mother could see this." She trailed
her fingers back and forth. "I wish . . ." She stopped then, listening.
She lowered her eyes. "Daleel?"

Turning slowly in a circle, she realized she was all alone.

CHAPTER
28

AMANI STOOD STILL. Her eyes filled with night. "Daleel!" She looked in the direction where she'd last seen her guide and hurried that way for a few minutes, calling to him. Then she stopped, suddenly uncertain. Wasn't the tent just behind her? The starlight seemed to reach only halfway down the rock towers; the desert was erased, unlit as an ocean floor. She cried, "Hello? Anyone?" The wind on the sand made a continual oceanic boom and it was hard to hear her own voice. She took several more steps and stopped again. She could barely see her hand in front of her face. "Daleel?" She called. She felt a tremor in her chest. Her heart rate sped up. Now she shouted, "Daleel! Hey. Where are you?" Her voice bounced back in blurry echoes. "Oh, for God's sake," she cried, somehow both frightened and exasperated. The words came back to her: *Oh . . . God's . . . sake . . .*

She thought she heard a man's voice calling, first in one direction, then another—it, too, repeated, seeming to ricochet off the rock walls. It was surprisingly far away.

She headed toward the voice, its last location, jogging, trying to catch up to it, her feet digging into the sand. After several minutes, she stopped again, hands on her hips, breathing heavily, then called out. She could see nothing. No sign of the tent anywhere. Again, she seemed to hear a scrap of voice, this time behind her. She inhaled deeply, squinting, looking around. The guide must have realized she wasn't there and started looking for her, but now she wasn't sure where he'd left her. Which, she realized, was stupid of her—wasn't that the first rule for children, if they lose track of their minder—to stay still? She tried to reassure herself that certainly he would know where to look. This sort of thing must happen out here all the time. At any moment, she'd hear him calling—though she could hear almost nothing over the sand rumble. He would come tap her on the shoulder. Wouldn't he? She could just imagine the relief of it. She smiled at herself, though it didn't feel quite convincing. She shouted again.

She stayed still for a few minutes, waiting. She waited longer. She kept calling out. He would come. She waited until she thought twenty minutes had passed. Maybe longer.

He'd walked off in this direction; she was certain. Maybe she would take just a few more steps . . . this way. He was just over here. She called out. For a moment she thought she heard a car engine, then a flash of a high beam or search light in the dark. She cupped her mouth, crying out as loudly as she could but the light extinguished as quickly as it had appeared.

The wind seemed to have picked up; she swayed a bit, feeling vertiginous. The desert horizon beyond the great rocks seemed to stretch, following the curve of the Earth. She stared and waited and after a while it felt as if she were becoming aware of the surface of the planet, its existence as a minuscule object hanging in space. It seemed like a good idea then to sit down, so she did, though then she felt gusts of crystalline sand, hissing against her skin. She pulled the cloak more tightly around her shoulders and over her head, shielding herself from the sand.

Amani thought about her father and the others, their worry when they realized she wasn't in the visitor's center. Would they start to look for her right away? And where? She and Daleel had driven at least thirty minutes into the desert. It would be bad for her father— not knowing what had happened to her. At least she knew where she was. She managed to smirk at this. When the guide had pulled up in his jeep, he was in such a rush, there'd been no time to consider. She'd seen how warily the other guides had looked at her when they first arrived: they were outsiders. Daleel had taken a risk in bringing her here—perhaps just as much as she had in going along with him. And she'd gotten distracted and wandered off all on her own and now she was going to die the stupidest death imaginable. For a moment, her vision blurred with tears. She lifted a hand, but the wind had already dried her eyes. Now she laughed out loud at this self-pity. Daleel was only a few steps away, she was certain. Pretty sure. She started to shiver. Using one hand, she stood again and looked around more determinedly. She was too cold to be lost. "I'm too cold to be lost," she said out loud. She thought she heard something, a kind of hiss or shush, and held still for a moment, listening.

"Hello!" she shouted. "Anyone?" There was nothing. She tried clapping. As her eyes adapted, she picked out the contours of tire tracks in the sand and felt a surge of hope. She began following them, clapping and singing. She would just get on with it—she was certain the track would lead to Daleel's jeep. Or to one of the guides, or their camp. There were Bedouins out here—she'd seen tents and lanterns as they'd driven past. If she kept following the tracks, eventually she'd find them.

Amani walked and shouted, then walked in silence. After a long while, she stopped and hunched, hands balled into fists at her sides: she shouted very loudly, as loud as she could, realizing as she did she could hardly hear herself over the wind. She walked and sang some more, losing her sense of time. Her voice began to scrape; her throat felt raw. She banged a couple of rocks together, but one of the rocks shattered after a few strikes. Bending to pick up a white rock, she saw something race out, glossy in the starlight: two outstretched claws and a curving tail. Amani shrieked and dropped the rocks.

There was no sign of anyone. The tracks seemed to vanish in places, but then she'd pick them up again. She wondered if she should turn back. She wondered if she should stay in one place and wait to be found—was that the wisest course? But waiting passively as the night drew on seemed unbearable. She told herself, *This doesn't actually happen in real life. People don't die in the desert anymore. This is something from the movies. Like wandering into quicksand.* Then she remembered she was in another country where she wasn't sure of the rules.

She went on. Her running shoes filled with sand. She took plodding half steps, sinking slightly with each on. At first, she stopped to empty her sneakers; after a while she realized there was no point. Panic shot across her skin, but as long as she kept walking she found she could push the panic to the outside. She berated herself: look what she'd done. In what way had she helped Musa, dragging him from his cave, getting herself lost in the desert? She couldn't let herself cry—she had to preserve every drop of fluid. She knew that much. The moon and stars had shifted in the sky. Her legs became heavy and the back of her neck hurt. It occurred to her that she hadn't had anything to eat or drink since the bottle of water and sandwich in the car. She was thirsty, her lips desiccated, and she could feel the start of a headache. Her fingertips, even the palms of her hands felt stiff and dry. Her face was stiff. She stopped, shaking with doubt. She started walking again; there was no turning back.

Her right shoulder had started to ache and she realized her small canvas purse was full of sand, its strap weighing down the side of her neck. She dumped it out and considered leaving it behind—the mobile was useless here, as was her wallet. But deliberately leaving her bag felt too much like surrender. Instead, she took out her wallet and every twenty or forty feet or so she left a piece of identification behind, like a trail of crumbs—her library card, business card, school ID, insurance card—placing a stone on top of each, hoping someone might come across her leavings. She kept her driver's license for some means of identification, but eventually she dropped her wallet too, just a few dinars inside.

There were no Bedu, no camps, no lanterns. Sometimes she heard chittering or unearthly warbling sounds; she thought she saw something like mice scrabbling over the sand. But the longer she walked, the quieter the earth became; gradually, she heard only a continuous whisk of sand over sand. The darkness was total, like a concentration of night, and even the massing rock formations in the distance disappeared. She began to slow down. She had no idea how far she'd walked. She wouldn't think about her mother. But then she remembered her mother's principle of things: Don't struggle against the tide, let it carry you. Reaching a long, flat piece of rock, Amani sank to her knees then onto her heels in the sand beside it. She was still. She would be carried. At some point earlier in the night her fear had lifted. Now she only felt how absurd she was for being here. She could see the pale vapor of her breath, but she didn't feel cold. *I'm sorry*, she thought. The words formed in her mind like a written message. *I'm sorry. Please forgive me.* She tried to write some of this with a stick in the sand, which was immediately blown away. Then she started trying to form words with rocks, but remembered the hidden scorpion. What use was writing anything? The stars had pulled farther back into the pitch-black, just a few glinted as if through layers of transparencies. Gazing toward the darkest band over the horizon, she thought about the onionskin envelope, all those fragments of her grandmother's voice—a record of interruption. There hadn't been time to show it to her father. She hoped he would find it. Then she pushed away this thought, which made it seem as if she were already dead.

IT WASN'T SLEEP but a softening. The moon turned into a white haze and cast tiny shadows. Her consciousness seemed to shiver, like a shuddering old film reel. She focused on her breath, the thread of her pulse. She waited, listening. When at last the sky lifted with a touch of gray, Amani slowly pushed herself upright, then back to her feet. She could feel the cold easing. Her throat felt swollen. It occurred to her that she had to find some kind of shelter or shade before the sun was fully risen.

She tried to continue in the same direction, but there were no markers to guide her. Predawn sifted into the sky as the landscape came into relief, gradually revealing a featureless plain. She thought she heard birdsong, though she couldn't see birds or any trees. There appeared to be a rock ridge but it was so far away she might have been dreaming. She tried to remember how mirages worked, but she couldn't hold on to thoughts very well. They ran through her body like minnows.

The sun edged over the earth, pinkening the sky, turning the earth a vivid garnet color. Amani lifted her forearm and bent her head before a sheet of dawn light. At first, she walked lightly, following the dashes that remained of the tire treads, energized by the brief rest. And by hope: she was tired yet she'd made it through the night. The air was softer and easier and she was making progress. But was there such a thing as progress when you didn't know where you were going? She tried not to return to the thought that she didn't have food or water. As she walked, she noticed a large, hull-shaped rock emerging in the middle distance. Its substance seemed reassuring and solid on the glowing sand.

Her slowing happened so incrementally she barely noticed anything more than a slight shift in the shadows on the ground. Then she began to feel the warmth. The change was subtle at first, slowly intensifying. All the freshness dried out of the air; the birdsong evaporated. Her throat began to ache with thirst and the headache came back, banging in her temples, rocking her vision. There was a thickening sensation all around, as if the sky were starting to gel.

As the morning advanced, her legs became increasingly heavy, laden with a kind of dream weight. She felt she was churning through mud. The bottoms of her feet were hot and she wondered if she had started to wear through the soles of her running shoes. She kept putting one foot in front of the other, but it seemed maddeningly as if she weren't moving. The hull-shaped rock didn't appear to get any closer; at times it actually seemed to sink away from her. The more she walked, the more it seemed to recede.

She tied the guide's long cloak over her head: its weight was smothering, but it blocked the sun. Rivulets of sweat crept through her hair and evaporated before reaching her face. She wasn't sweating as much as yesterday—was that a sign of something? Heat stroke?

There were no borders and no limitations here. Her body would break down, fall away, into the murmuring. *Hello, I'm back.* She understood, perhaps for the first time, that no one knew where she was. No one was coming.

The heat became too much then. She didn't raise her eyes for fear of burning them. The sun boiled overhead, cutting through everything. Heat waves warped the air. She heard a harsh buzz or rustle, like that of insects, but drier, as if the sand itself were rattling. Her vision swam and she wouldn't let herself think, for she was afraid that even the energy of thought might impede her in some way. She had to stay in her body now, in the lifting of one foot, then the other, then the other, then the other.

Still, the air became progressively heavier, more turbulent. She began to hear a thrumming behind her: sand brushed past her in sharp whirls, lifting and bouncing. When she turned to look back, she saw a vaporous orange curtain rolling toward her. The wind rose, lifting the clothes on her body. She hacked. Her lungs felt gritty. Amani moved the wrapper so it covered her head and face and she peered through its weave. The drumming sound intensified, becoming thunderous, booming. The remnants of the tire trail were swept clean. She wanted to crouch, to cinch into a knot. But some instinct drove her forward, a certainty that stopping would be obliteration, and she hadn't accepted that. Through the wrapper, she seemed to see the sand floor rise, crumpling around her, as if some great hand had reached under the earth, seizing and ruffling its surface like a carpet. Sand levitated straight into the air and she was in the thick of the storm.

It howled in her ears; there was sand in her lashes and mouth, but she didn't stop. Sand crusted between her teeth: that sensation of grit made her feel somehow stronger, as if she were deriving some kind of energy from the storm itself. She dragged each foot, one after the other, as wind spun around her, sometimes propelling her forward, sometimes knocking her sideways. She could see nothing but the orange haze and felt nothing but stinging sand, the ground sliding and wobbling beneath her. Just when she'd decided that she wouldn't make it to the rock, that it was just some vision that she'd conjured, she realized she was getting closer. It rose directly out of the flat ground, prehistoric, jagged, pounded by wind currents. She reached toward it and felt how her body was trembling, how she seemed to be falling forward. Her palm made contact, the rock grainy and hot.

Struggling against the wind, hair uncovered, whipping fiercely, she managed to snag the wrap's weave on the rough rock face and extend the rest of it to the ground, scraping up handfuls of stone to hold it in place. She sat huddled against the rock while the shawl bellowed with the winds, snapping against her body, the wind screeching and demonic. She would have wept, but her eyes produced no tears.

Her lids closed: for long minutes she saw flashing lights, faces, broken pieces of memories and poetry. She supposed she was hallucinating. She curled into herself. She'd failed them—she saw it now. *I am done, Natalia.* She'd failed to risk herself, to take the sort of leaps her grandmother had taken, to love so deeply, the way her grandmother had loved her family—especially Musa—to risk releasing that which she loved the most. Amani had tried to keep herself locked up: she'd made herself so small, a cipher—to others and to herself. She thought then of kissing Eduardo, the sweetness of the memory filling her, and she realized that one kiss had moved her more than the years she'd spent in her marriage. If only she had let herself feel it. It was possible, she thought, that she loved him. The wrapper surged with wind and nearly tore loose; if it did, she decided she would let it go. Even in the roaring sand and the night, she felt how much she loved this world, how it had waited inside her all along, to break her open.

Her lips were crusted together. Even closed, her eyes burned.

Time dissolved away. She gave herself up to it. To the beautiful dissolving.

CHAPTER

29

• *Wadi Rum, Jordan* •

SHE BECAME AWARE of a sweet, blooming smell. Sage, perhaps. Silence. Herbs and flowers. Light shimmered through her lashes. A voice.

There was a child. On a donkey.

His brown face was caked with sand, his hair a mass of wild black curls. No more than nine or ten. Possibly he was older, just physically small. She had the oddest feeling that he looked like her. Behind him the sunrise was breaking in long, red rays, setting the tops of the mountains on fire. He was holding her wallet. There was no sign of the storm, though she still seemed to feel its quailing vibrations in her bones. The wrapper was gone, but she had made it through another night on the sand. Staring at the boy, she thought she was still dreaming. After a moment of shocked staring, he quickly climbed down and gave her a round leather canteen covered with Smurfs stickers. As she drank she felt her thirst awaken and she tipped back her head, filling her throat. She sat up. With his help, she tried to stand, shaking with the shock of surviving, of being found. Instantly, she fell back to the ground. Clicking his tongue and toeing the earth, the boy managed to bring the donkey to Amani's side, then down to its knees and belly in the sand.

He helped her creep onto his donkey, who shifted and complained in low grunts but allowed her to slide on. It brayed as it stood and staggered slightly, then found its footing. The boy tried to give the wallet to her, but she didn't have the strength to hold it, so he tucked it in a saddle bag. She thought the boy was saying he would bring her to his mother. There was no actual saddle, so she clung to the tufts of hair along the donkey's neck. The boy turned the donkey and they seemed to be walking slowly back in the direction that Amani thought she'd come from. She had no bearings and no sense of orientation. There was no sign of the jeep tracks she'd followed, and now, slumped over the donkey, she saw she might have simply been following contours in the sand. As the sun reached the desert floor, the warmth was again gradual but steady. The boy sang and occasionally flicked a stick against the donkey's side. After a few hours of walking, the boy suggested they could shelter under some low, spreading trees growing in a clump near a rock tower. She realized he was doing this for her and she wanted to protest that she was all right to continue, but instead she said, "Mumtaz." Great.

From the shade, she watched slivers of clouds dissolve high overhead. They were surrounded by canyons of wind-carved rock, notched and inscribed as the walls of cathedrals. "Ismi Zedi." The boy said his name was Zedi and that he'd been returning from bringing goats to his grandfather when he found her nearly buried red library card, then her. He gave her the rest of his water from a second canteen and suggested politely that they continue. Amani lifted herself onto the donkey, who briefly nuzzled her face before groaning and beginning. Reaching the back edge of the canyon, the child led the donkey into a chasm in the rock and the temperature dropped. There was a sweetness in the air, an echoing drip. A set of rudimentary stairs cut into the rock led down to a clear, shallow pool.

They drank and waded in together with the donkey and refilled the canteens. Amani splashed handfuls over her head and face, her lips cracking and bleeding when she smiled. Zedi laughed and splashed water at his donkey, who shook like a dog, spraying droplets.

When they emerged, Amani felt the moisture on her skin and clothes evaporate.

It's not much farther, Zedi said.

Alhamdullilah, she said.

They left the canyon and headed toward a vast folded rock in the distance—though, as with the other rock, it seemed the farther they walked, the more the rock shrank away, as if distance had no logical meaning here. Every now and then, the donkey would simply stop and noisily blow air through its lips and ignore the child's efforts to motivate it—flicking at its side, pulling at its lead or pushing on its hindquarters. Amani became more adept at getting off and walking for a bit, at which point the donkey would start moving again. After a few steps, she would get back on again and the donkey would continue. She saw rocks that looked pyramidal, striated as the sphinx itself. There were archways, cairns, and stone ledges, and at one point, the child pointed out hieroglyphic inscriptions in the rock that looked like camels and humans and lines of words similar to Arabic. "Very, very old," Zedi told her.

As they walked, she noticed something black at the base of a rock wall that blurred then gradually became a cluster of tents. Amani thought again she was dreaming. She had started to feel that this was now where she would always be, climbing on and off a donkey. When Zedi ran ahead, calling, his feet beating over the earth, Amani's first impulse was to cry out, "Don't leave me!"

Just moments later, two women emerged from the tent. They ran to her and helped her down from the donkey, Amani collapsing into their arms. They brought her to their tent. Out front, there was a small rock circle for fire, a metal teakettle, two jerry cans of water. They sat her on a broad, flat rock and poured panfuls of cool water directly over her head and back then dried her and stroked a fragrant balm over her arms. The older woman asked her name, what she'd been doing in the middle of nowhere. Amani didn't have the words to fully explain herself, but Kamaria—the mother—didn't seem to expect her to. They brought her inside the tent, which felt as cool and luxurious to her as any hotel. There were a few cushions, a low table holding dishes, a coffeepot, a cutting board, and what appeared to be some sort of radio with an antenna. The floor was covered with flat, woven carpets. A curtain hung down the center of the tent. Kamaria's daughter, Mina, took her into the back half of the tent and turned away while Amani removed her shredded clothes and put on a plain cotton shift. Mina helped her onto a row of cushions against the tent wall.

The bed was wonderfully comfortable. The women gave her sweet tea and dates and wrapped her in a blanket. Amani nibbled on the dates. She listened to the women talking about her on the other side of the curtain and realized that at some point, somehow her mind had fallen into the rhythms of Arabic—as if some last bit of resistance or hesitation had finally given way to comprehension. And then, for what felt like the first time in days, very quickly, she was asleep.

WHEN SHE WOKE, someone was holding her hand. She heard her father say her name and she looked up at him, his good, dear face, his brown eyes and soft, round nose, and graying hair even in his eyebrows. He bent and gathered her to him so tightly she felt tears against her neck. She could see through the tent weave that night had fallen.

They'd looked without stopping, he said. As soon as they realized Amani wasn't out in the courtyard or visitor's center, they began to hunt. Someone reported that Daleel's jeep was gone. Gabe, Omar, and Samir, along with the guides and several Desert Patrol officers drove to Rum Village, then the tourist camps, and finally into the desert, searching with flashlights and dogs.

Daleel, the guide she'd left with, hadn't returned to the center—certainly, they said, he was afraid of being punished for losing her. For taking her out in the first place. The desert police filed a report, but Gabe learned there were no official search-and-rescue operations in the area, and the nearest PSD helicopter couldn't be brought up from Aqaba until the next morning. They'd had to rely on the Bedouin trackers to help search for her. Kamaria's son Zedi had found Amani deep in the wilderness area. She'd walked in just the wrong direction—far from any of the encampments and villages. Once they'd gotten word of her whereabouts, Omar and Samir had to stay behind: the driver explained he was able to take Gabe only. The sand was deep where they were going and too much passenger weight would sink the jeep.

Amani told him and the women about her first night—as much as she could remember—Mina translated for Zedi and her mother. Amani tried to explain the pale light she'd seen in the sky, the way the stars shone and turned blue, how she'd felt something take hold of her in the night, and the murmur she'd heard beneath her head, coming up from the earth. The mother agreed, telling her daughter, "I've heard that too."

Gabe nodded and asked questions, but it seemed that all her father could really take in was the relief of finding her. "Hayati, hayati," he repeated. My life.

The women's call had come to the visitor's center around five o'clock that evening, and it had taken over an hour and a half of four-wheel drive to reach their tent.

Kamaria placed cushions in front of the tent and they gathered around the fire along with Gabe's guide from the visitor's center. While Amani and her father talked, Mina slowly scraped sand from Amani's hair with a wide-toothed plastic comb. Zedi brought out plates of olives, bread, and cheese, zaatar and oil, sliced eggs and salt. Kamaria said her husband worked in the Rum guesthouse with their two older children, and she saw him only on Sundays. Kamaria and Mina apologized repeatedly for not having a goat to butcher, but

Amani felt queasy after just a few olives and some bread. She sipped her tea slowly.

Gabe shook Zedi's hand and said he was a hero. He thanked the family profusely and repeatedly. He tried to stuff dinars into Zedi's pockets, but the child refused. Zedi did however ask if he might keep Amani's bright-red library card, which he'd found not far from her wallet. She gave it gratefully and gave her sandy jeans and T-shirt to Mina in exchange for the plain cotton thobe she was wearing. She gave her digital Timex to Kamaria, who put it on and kissed her on both cheeks.

Gabe's driver, Ben, offered to take them back to the Rum clinic and have a doctor look at Amani, but she refused. "I'm fine," she said. "I actually feel good." Her feet and ankles burned, her back ached, and the interior of her throat felt peeled away. But her mind was clear. She was light, scoured clean. Everything looked and smelled and tasted beautiful. "The worst part was in the beginning—just not knowing what would happen," she said. "When I tried to feel hopeful . . ." She shook her head. "It was terrible. After a while, I gave up on trying to control any of it. That helped."

Her father smiled for the first time. "For me the worst part was all of it," he said, once again holding her hand, unwilling to let go. He peered at her a moment, adding, "And next, we should get you back home."

She squeezed his hand. "We still haven't found him."

THEY HEARD the whine of motorbikes. Some of Kamaria's neighbors had come by to see her amazing visitors. The women brought out more food and tea. Zedi put down additional cushions. Two men and a woman with a tattooed chin, their faces furrowed and sun-blackened, squatted near the fire, and asked about her ordeal. The tattooed woman asked how Amani had known what to do.

"I had no idea what to do!" she said. She told them about the scorpion under the rock and they laughed. Kamaria said it was an omen. They murmured at her leaving her cards and bits of ID on the sand—though she couldn't tell if they approved or found it foolish. Then Amani remembered something. When she was still in the desert, searching her bag for anything else she could leave behind, Amani had felt the balled-up fabric from Musa's cave. She'd smoothed the cloth over her jeans, trying to make out the chalk markings at the center. There was something familiar about the shape of the fabric. Turning and holding it up with both hands, she'd realized she was looking at a double-pointed teardrop. Then she'd seen it: the chalk marks at the center formed the rough silhouette of a face. Amani had touched the pendant hanging from her neck: *Queen Nefertiti.*

She found her bag beside the cushions in back and brought it out. Producing the crumpled fabric, she flattened it on the ground before her father. "Look," she said. "Do you remember? Musa's artwork?"

Everyone shifted around to look. Amani unfastened her pendant and laid it on the ground beside the fabric. Gabe looked from one to the other. He touched the piece of cloth, then picked it up. "Ya Allah," he murmured. "He was drawing my mother's necklace."

She described Musa to her hosts and the visitors—how he'd disappeared, and why they'd come to Wadi Rum. "I believe he's here," Amani said. "Somewhere. Daleel was going to take me to him."

She saw the others exchanging glances. "Daleel was foolish. Not a bad man. But irresponsible," one of the others said at last. Kamaria nodded. She studied the necklace and the cloth drawing, comparing them closely.

The men wanted to drive back to a larger encampment for meat and rice; they wanted to make a party in honor of their visitors. But Amani shook her head, pleading exhaustion. They invited Gabe and Amani to come back to their tents, which they said were larger and more comfortable. There was some argument between Kamaria and the others, and Amani heard her father promising that they would try to visit them soon, inshallah. At last, the neighbors left on their motorbikes and the women put Amani back on her cushions against the rear of the tent. Gabe would sleep in the front section of the tent. Kamaria and her children would sleep on the carpet.

"You are quite certain that your uncle is in Wadi Rum?" Kamaria said lightly. She was squatting over a cup of tea, swirling and studying its interior.

Amani stared at the top of the tent, moving with the wind. "I am. I feel that he's here," she said.

"You're welcome to stay here as long as you like," Mina said to Amani, pulling a thin quilt up to her chin, as if she were a child. "As long as it takes. Longer even."

Amani looked at the daughter, then her mother sitting on the carpet beside them. "Do you know where he is?" she asked.

The two women glanced at each other.

Amani sat up, the quilt sliding to her waist. "The man we're searching for—he's a very special person. He's the reason I was out there—in the desert. If he's still alive—or not—I need to know. If you know anything at all. This means everything to me."

Mina put her hand on her mother's. Finally, Kamaria said, "There is a possibility."

CHAPTER

30

THE VEHICLE WAS waiting outside when Amani and her father woke in the morning. Like the other guide jeeps, it had no sides; there was a makeshift roof constructed of a bedsheet wrapped around the roll bars. Kamaria's cousin Jasim lived in an encampment on the other side of the valley and he had brought the jeep in the night. A tall man with a narrow, sun-weathered face like Kamaria's, he bowed quickly, touching his forehead to the back of Amani's hand. Jasim said only that he was going to drive them.

Amani felt steadier today. Gabe helped her into the back of the car. He sat up front beside Jasim. There was some discussion of which roads would best support their weight. Kamaria and the children waved and stepped back as the jeep rolled away, picking up momentum on what looked to Amani like a swath of sand inside of more sand, but which Jasim called the road. They flew into the desert, the rooftop buzzing and humming above them. The sun came up, transforming the earth into a hammered golden sheet as they wound through the valley. When they slowed, about a half hour later, near the base of a coral-colored massif, Amani thought they were taking another break. They climbed out and Jasim gestured to Amani and

Gabe to follow. They climbed a powdery slope to the rock face, their feet sliding back with each step. As they reached the top, a small tent appeared. Jasim stopped a few feet from the opening and called out.

At first, the only sound was the wind beating against the sides of the rock. Amani shielded her face, looking out over the desert floor stippled with weeds, turning pink in the early morning. Just when she began to wonder if anyone would answer, a veiled woman ducked out of the tent. She was small and sturdy, her hair hidden under a black scarf. She crossed her arms over her chest, her back to the sun. The driver spoke to her and she shook her head, making brisk cutting motions with her hands. Their voices rose and fell, he pointed at Amani repeatedly. A girl of about ten or eleven came out of the tent and approached Amani. "You are America?" she asked shyly. "I'm study America."

The woman sent the child back to the tent, then stood scowling at them, her hands on her hips. Amani looked from her to Jasim. No one explained what was going on, but she sensed that this woman knew what had happened to Musa and that she placed the blame and responsibility squarely on them. "She is doctor," Jasim finally said. "Bedouin-style doctor. She is the one decides."

He explained that this tabeeba was an authority held in the highest esteem among the tribespeople. This was not a place for outsiders.

Amani kept her eyes lowered as she introduced herself and her father. She told her they were searching for someone who may have become lost in Wadi Rum.

The doctor studied Amani's face and Amani met her eyes: the doctor had dark lines like Kamaria's, tattooed from her lower lip down her chin, and her eyes were thickly outlined in kohl, giving her face a stark, commanding appearance. After a long moment she said, "I see you've also been in the desert." She took Amani's hands and studied her palms, then turned back to her face. Gabe waited silently behind her. The doctor's gaze shifted to Amani's neck. "Al Jamila," she said. "Queen Nefertiti. The beautiful one."

Amani put her fingers over her pendant. "From my grand-mother," she said.

The doctor nodded. "It's good you wear her. A good protector." She cupped the side of Amani's face for a moment, then bent and drew open the tent flap. Entering, she gestured for them to follow her.

Inside, it smelled of fresh air and sage. There was a mat tucked against the far wall and a form lay stretched full-length under a sheet. As they approached, she saw the face was dark as cinders and a crown of tiny green leaves and yellow flowers was woven through the hair. The form was so still, Amani wasn't sure if he was alive or dead. Several children sat beside him; one held his hand, another suddenly stopped singing to stare at them. In the silence, the man turned toward the newcomers and Amani felt the bones in her legs weaken. His smile was very white. Gabe was the first to go to him. He sat up with Gabe's help and the two men wrapped their arms around each other. Amani heard her father saying something, over and over. She crouched beside the bed and also put her arms around Musa. Her father was saying, "I never forgot you, Musa."

"Fawg, fawg," Musa said, smiling.

Gabe nodded. "Up."

A COUPLE OF the Zalabiya Bedu had found Musa, the doctor said, walking north and west of Rum Village, in the belly of the desert, miles from any outpost. He was barefoot, the children said. Dehy-drated. He'd had almost no food or water for two days, though he was holding an empty water bottle. He didn't have any head cover-ing. See? One little boy said, pointing to Musa's face: his eyelids were scorched, as well as his nose and lips, and the tops of his scalp and ears, and his shoulders and hands.

"He's remarkably strong," the doctor said. She spoke with a Brit-ish accent. She stood beside him, running her hand over his closely cropped hair. "He survived as well as any of the Bedu would have.

Better, I think." She showed Amani how she soaked pieces of a shrub called *sheeh* in oil, then ground it in a mortar to make a paste. "The medicine will keep his skin from falling in sheets. He should make a very good recovery."

"It looks painful." Amani's throat still hurt from her own time in the desert.

"He doesn't complain, but he doesn't know why he's here. He keeps saying he is going home."

Gabe sat with crossed legs beside the mattress. "I like your crown," he said in Arabic. Musa smiled and touched his head. Then he looked with a sort of wonder at Amani and said in Arabic, "The man brought me. He said I was going home." He gazed around the small tent, then at Amani and Gabe. "I am home now?"

Gabe took his hand and said, "You're close."

The doctor hadn't told the park officials about Musa, nor did she trust the clinic doctor in Rum Village. Musa, she believed, required extra protection. "Sometimes the Bedu bring in tourists, different people—they fly here from all around the world, come to the desert and get stranded or lost. Sometimes on purpose. The Bedu, they find climbers stuck up on the high rocks. Often, they find just bones. But this time was different. He is not only lost." Musa had told her about the man who'd brought him and turned him loose in the desert, and the doctor suspected someone had tried to kill him. She sat beside Amani on the edge of the mat and touched Musa's forehead. "There's something about this one. The children took to him—you see?" She stroked a white salve that smelled like mint tea just above his brow and temples. "One extraordinary thing— even though he had no compass or instruments—he was walking in a straight line. Everyone lost out on the desert floor—they go in orbits. Not this one. Straight, as if he knew just where he was going."

Amani nodded. "He did maybe."

"Do you know of anyone who would want to hurt him?" she asked, turning from Gabe to Amani.

Amani raised her eyebrows at her father. "He's safe now," Gabe said. He patted Musa's hand and sighed.

The young girl who had first greeted Amani brought them a lunch of lentil soup, bread, and yogurt. This was followed by small cups of coffee. Gabe tried again to pay Jasim for his help. There was extensive arguing before they would accept a few dinars to help cover the cost of the gasoline. He insisted on staying until Gabe and his daughter were ready to go. Amani refused to leave Wadi Rum without Musa. And the doctor needed to tend to several patients before deciding what to do about him.

"This could take a while," Gabe warned Jasim.

"Everything takes what it takes," Jasim said.

A number of patients arrived to consult with the doctor. A man asked the tabeeba about a rash on his leg. She made a sticky paste in a mortar and told him to use it twice a day until it was gone. An elderly man came in with his wife who was too timid to speak or to let the doctor examine her under her robe, so the man described her symptoms while his wife listened in silence. The doctor looked at the woman's teeth, tongue, wrists, and palms, and recommended she fast during the day for four weeks. Another woman came in and gave the doctor a clucking chicken to thank her for curing her baby's cough.

While patients came in and out, Amani and Gabe stayed with Musa, drinking the sharply bitter coffee, and waiting. After a few hours, the tabeeba returned to take another look at Musa. "I'd prefer to keep him here longer, but he does seem eager to be off." She checked his tongue, his eyes, and his hands, and wrapped his head in a white keffiyeh. "The real medicine is inside the mind, of course." She sighed deeply. "We will miss this one. Do you suppose you're ready to travel again?" she asked him in Arabic. "But no more strolls in the desert." He nodded solemnly.

The doctor prepared a few jars of ointments and released Musa to Gabe and Amani. "Please be careful with him," she said. Musa took a small orange from the floor at the side of the bed. Jasim drove them the two hours back to the guesthouse in Rum Village, where they reunited with Omar and Samir.

Late in the afternoon, they headed north while Amani and the others tried to convince Musa to come to Amman with them. He shook his head. "Home," he said again. "I'm going home." They took him to the little al-Karak Hospital, where Musa sat on a padded table, craning his head as if dazzled by the lights and instruments. The doctor wore a spotless coat, *Dr. Afaf* embroidered in English beneath one shoulder. After his exam, he switched off the lamp, shook his head, and told them that Musa was really quite healthy. "Right." He patted Musa's shoulder. "The burns on his head are already starting to heal. I see no evidence of heat stress. No disorientation. Though he does seem a bit . . . dissociated, is it?"

"Yeah. No, that's just how he is," Omar said.

The doctor wanted to keep him in the hospital for the night, but Musa repeated, "I'm going home," and stared at the wall.

"He's not used to being away," Amani said. "It'll probably be more trouble than it's worth to try to keep him here."

Like the tabeeba in Wadi Rum, Dr. Afaf looked unhappy yet unsurprised, as if he were already familiar with this sort of recalcitrance. Musa was released with more ointments and bottles of a pale-green drink that Omar sniffed and identified as Gatorade. Amani called Sister Sylvain at the convent to tell her they were coming, and the nun's voice had risen with relief. "Of course. Bring him back," she said. "He has to be in his place. We'll watch over him. If the officials come after him, we'll find another cave. We will do whatever we must."

They discussed it further in the car. "Everyone totally watches for everyone here," Omar tried to reassure Amani. "One thing Jordanians know how to do is get up in each other's business."

"It's not like in the States," her father said.

"No, I guess it isn't, is it?" she said.

Musa rode between Amani and Omar on the drive to the convent. He held the orange in his lap. Amani asked in Arabic, "That orange—from Wadi Rum?" He nodded and smiled as if seeing it for the first time.

"You just gonna carry it around?" Omar asked.

Musa said something more in Arabic: Amani realized he'd said he was saving it for his mother, and touched his shoulder. He stared at the fruit in his lap for a long moment, then looked at Amani. "Or maybe you would like to have it?" he asked her in Arabic and handed it to her.

Amani peeled the orange, its sweet incense filling the car. She offered sections. After watching Amani eat a section, Musa accepted one as well. When they pulled into the dusty parking area, a tall nun holding a basket of allium stopped in her tracks, dropping and spilling purple flowers on the ground. She ran to him, helping him out of the car, kissing his hands, and hurried him inside. A moment later, Sylvain pushed through the wooden convent doors, "Oh he's home." Her arms opened. "Alhamdullilah."

CHAPTER

31

• *Tuesday, November 28, Amman, Jordan* •

"IT IS TRUE THEN," he said.

She let her eyes rest on the weapon in the glass case just a beat longer, its lilting shape, a tilde. Then she turned to see Eduardo. He wore a soft gray suit. She hadn't seen him since the day of the duel in Petra. There were many messages from him on her phone asking her to call, each slightly more imperative than the one before.

"You really did go into the desert. Your cousin told me what happened. But I almost think I can see it myself—just looking at you."

Eduardo appeared the same to her, yet somehow more pronounced: the speckles in his eyes, the arc of his posture, each part of him seemed so well formed. Still. She hung back, unable to tell him about how the desert had walked into her. She couldn't explain the night when the lines between herself and the world had seemed to waver for a moment. Or the way she'd thought about him. Yet she was altered. Not even a week ago, she huddled against the earth in a sandstorm, but her memory of her time in Wadi Rum seemed to be drifting away from her—remarkable but already a dream. She'd tried to describe the experience to Omar, but it was like trying to approach the rocks in the desert—the way they receded when she tried to come near.

She'd almost skipped this event—a reception and exhibition of Islamic Arms and Armor—she was tired of weaponry and old things. But this reception was the conclusion of the royal birthday celebrations, and Amani wanted to take in these last moments. And she'd thought Eduardo might come. Ever since she'd returned, she felt an outline, a sense like anticipation, of what might happen between them—the imaginary promise of what was possible. In another life. His face, his eyes, the hum of his voice had come to her so many times while she'd walked through Wadi Rum. Though now she was afraid to look at it too directly. It was dangerous, this sort of conjuring. She didn't let herself call him though; it wasn't fair to either of them—to imagine more between them. She had lain awake for the past few nights, gazing out at the old stars through the curtains. She and her father would fly home soon—Gabe had opted to stay home and pack tonight—and their time in Jordan would also fade, lovely and ephemeral. She had to go back, certainly, but when she thought of returning to her life in the States, she had the sensation of trying to squeeze herself into a shrinking tunnel.

She turned to the display case, in part to hide her face. "You're right—I was changed by it," she said. "I really was." The sword was mounted and spot-lit under glass. It was one of the many artifacts in the Sousin Foundation's display. The card underneath said in English and Arabic:

"AL ABIAD / THE WHITE"

Ancient Sumerian. According to folklore, a lesser sword of the prophet Muhammad. Passed to Alexander the Great. Materials: pewter and silver. From the collection of Ferensa Modani.

She touched the glass. "I'm getting the impression that the Prophet owned an awful lot of weapons."

"Scimitars, swords, daggers, and knives. They were the treasures of their age." Eduardo stood near her to gaze upon the object in its vitrine. His hand touched the glass beside hers. "Look where it ends up."

"Well, that seems kind of sad," she said, and moved away slightly to ask a server for a glass of water. "I guess no one really gets to keep anything. Not forever."

"But don't you think it's freeing? Not even our bodies go with us—we don't even own those. And they don't own us." Eduardo smiled and the skin folded around his eyes. "If we lived forever, our lives would be worthless."

"Then it's better not to hang on to things—just—just have the moment." She felt a quiet pressure across her body, some gravity drawing her. Perhaps he had walked into her too, along with the desert. Perhaps she wasn't as inclined to keep him out. She moved toward a different display case.

"Exactly," he said, trailing after her. "For example, I didn't know for certain that you would be here today."

"But you thought I might be."

"So, I took the risk," Eduardo said, lowering his chin. "Which is challenging. And necessary. To me, it's always worth it—win or lose. For example, right now, just seeing you . . ." He tapped his chest. "Risk."

She touched the edge of the glass case before she realized she was leaving fingerprints. "Eduardo. I fly home the day after tomorrow. Me and Dad."

When he didn't respond, she looked up at him. His eyes were light against the depth of his skin. "And you did, too, didn't you?"

"What did I do?" she said. A small group of American embassy officials in dark suits moved between them, glancing at Amani.

"Took the risk. Yes?" He moved forward after the group passed. "Knowing I might be here."

"Well, knowing and hoping are different," she said slyly.

"And here we are, all the same." He laughed, which made her smile, but Amani paused then and said softly, "Edo. This isn't my home. I wish it wasn't like this, I swear. But I can't stay."

"Home is not in a place. It's what's between people." He held one hand in the air. "Here is home. Here, right now."

Amani studied his face. He was disorienting—like a good-bad angel. Enchanting. Again, she felt off-balance. She placed her fingers experimentally on the edge of his sleeve. Smoke from the lamp's spout. His smile deepened. He looked around the now-empty room and slowly pulled her into a kiss. Her arms crossed around the back of his neck and she felt their kiss all the way to her knees. If kisses could change minds, she thought, this would do it.

He broke from their kiss and murmured, "You *can* stay, Amani."

She pressed her face against the side of his neck and said, "I wish."

CHAPTER
32

• *December 7, 1995, Syracuse, New York* •

FRANCESCA WAS WORKING at the kitchen table. Before her was a stack of bills: mortgage, electric, water, and now this new invader, the cell phone. She wore a pair of glasses that had belonged to her grandmother—little lenses that cast crescents on her cheekbones. Her lopped-off hair startled Gabe yet again. She'd cut it while he was in Jordan. Now her hair glowed like a black corona and he'd discovered the back of her beautiful neck. When he first saw her hair so short, he'd felt it like the loss of a limb, and though he'd been back for a week, Gabe still wasn't used to it.

She told him the stylist had braided and cut it off—and the braid almost made it worse for him—giving the loss form. But the banded braid kept the hair in one neat piece and she'd donated it to the people who make wigs for children. He recalled then she'd undergone a similar denuding about five years earlier, and also five years before that. Soon, she'd be dragging him in to give blood—that happened twice a year. And their driver's licenses checked every box—that upon their deaths the doctors should feel free to come and dismantle their bodies for spare parts. Their neighbor, Mrs. Winslow, swore this meant they'd let you expire on the spot if you ever dared show your face at the hospital.

But this was the point of being alive, according to Francesca—to give yourself away. Whatever physical resource you had—blood, bones, hair—was meant to be plowed back into the shared planet. The only way to be truly alive was to let go of yourself. Smile and let go.

Gabe sat across from her in the terrible, uneven chair that he was going to fix—soon! And she looked at him, all lit up in the midday sun, Our Lady of Invoices. He went into the refrigerator, looking for lunch, pulling out bowls of cold things, half-things—leftover tabbouleh, hummus, some cheese and bread. He hummed as he assembled the food.

He'd told his wife two things after he got off the plane—two things that had been worrying him all the way across the water. First about Il Saif. When she learned he'd taken the knife to Jordan without telling her and given it to Amani, she had gone quiet for a moment. Then she'd said, "She'll know what to do with it." The other was something that Hafez had said to him on the day of the duel, while they'd waited in the backstage area in Petra. He'd told Gabe that he'd stolen Francesca away from him, that she had loved Hafez first, and that it was likely, he'd added with a shrug, that she loved him still.

Francesca was driving them home. She with her astounding new hair and neck. She'd placed her hand flat on her sternum and looked at Gabe. "He said that? Hafez did?"

Gabe, not trusting his voice, merely nodded, his chest aching.

She released her silvery laugh then, the magical one that made people fall in love with her, three notes, high and low. So like his mother's. Light as water. "He said that?" She wiped tears away. "Oh my God. That guy. Will wonders never cease. You didn't believe him? Oh, tell me you didn't!"

His throat melted and his breath fell back into his lungs and his rib cage expanded and for what felt like the first time in a month, he was laughing too. "Of course not," he said. "Never."

"Oh my God, your brother!"

Now he was washing the lunch dishes, little puffs of suds clinging to his elbows, when Francesca came in with the mail. On top of the usual stack of flyers was a creamy oversized envelope, carefully sealed, stamped by a courier service. It said: *Mr. Gabriel Hamdan*, in English and Arabic.

He used the paring knife to open it. Inside, wrapped in an overleaf of tissue paper, there was an 8 × 10 photograph of two men and a handwritten letter in blue ink on fine stationery. He read:

ON BEHALF OF HIS MAJESTY, KING H OF JORDAN:

> *We would like to express our deepest gratitude, for the time,*
> *courage, and skill that you so generously contributed to the*
> *Jordanian cultural trust. The palace library will include*
> *narrated video recordings of your exhibition bout in Petra and*
> *we will be pleased to send you a copy when they are completed.*
>
> *On a personal note, I would like to reintroduce myself.*
> *We met on the day of the fencing match, though in the*
> *day's flurry of excitement, I doubt you would remember.*
> *I am the King's cultural affairs officer and one of his*
> *personal secretaries. In this capacity, I oversee a wide array*
> *of planned events and also deal with all sorts of unexpected*
> *occurrences. I wear many hats in my position and sometimes*
> *I find myself working with the unlikeliest partners.*
>
> *Such was the case on the afternoon of November 19,*
> *1995, not long after the conclusion of the match. As you*
> *know, your relation, Mr. Musa Hamdan, had unfortunately*
> *become entangled in a situation outside the Petra*
> *Nabataean Theatre and was subsequently intercepted by*
> *security detail.*

Mr. Hamdan was then released to the custody of your brother and my colleague, Hafez Hamdan. As Mr. Hafez was already exhausted by the weeks of planning and activity, I had grave misgivings as to the wisdom of this decision. When security informed me that your daughter was searching for Mr. Musa, I contacted private investigators.

From them, we learned that Mr. Hafez had escorted Mr. Musa to Wadi Rum—a UNESCO World Heritage site—perhaps so he might enjoy a late-day hike in those pristine surroundings. However, he inadvertently neglected to provide Mr. Musa with water or head covering. I was greatly relieved to hear that Mr. Musa was intercepted by local tribesmen while trekking through the protected wilderness area.

Our investigators eventually located Mr. Musa back at his home in the foothills behind St. Elias Monastery in Karak.

His Royal Majesty, King H, has expressed particular concern over Mr. Musa's plight and I'm pleased to tell you that the Crown has created an exemption to grant him permanent residency above the St. Elias Sanctuary, and has started construction of a private dwelling for Mr. Musa, adjacent to his cave, with a view of the valley floor. In addition, the Crown has provided Mr. Musa new furnishings, as well as an excellent woolen Anatolian kilim. If you peruse the enclosed photograph, you'll note that Mr. Musa has nicely positioned the furnishings about his cave. The sisters of St. Elias inform us that he has also moved two goats and several sheep into the construction area.

Finally, you are no doubt aware that Mr. Hafez has decided to step down from his governmental duties and enjoy a well-earned retirement.

His Majesty and I once again offer you more heartfelt thanks for all you've given us. Whether here or abroad, Jordanians like yourself are at the heart of our beloved

country. If we can ever offer you any assistance in turn, we
hope you will not hesitate to call upon us.

> *With admiration,*
> *Very truly yours,*

> *Rafi Bustani*

Gabe picked up the photograph again—it wasn't black-and-white, yet it retained an old-fashioned, almost sepia-toned quality. Propped on a carved wooden chair, one foot cantilevered against the opposite knee, was Musa. He gazed into the camera with his open face but Gabe could tell someone had posed him in that chair. His hand touched a tray of silver cups and a coffeepot that rested on a camp table with brass fittings and bamboo legs. A brass lamp hung from the ceiling. Putting the oversized photo to one side, Gabe removed the fragment of photograph from his wallet—Amani had taken it from an onionskin envelope filled with scraps of blue paper and given it to him just before he left Amman. He compared the boy's face to that of the man in the cave. When he'd returned from Jordan, he'd pulled out his family photograph, the one with the missing corner, and found that the fragment fit exactly into that corner: at last, his three-year old hand closed around the fingers of an older sibling. Now as he compared the boy's face in the fragment to the newer image, fifty-six years melted away. His breath shook inside his body. How to reclaim a childhood—how to reclaim a brother?

SOMETIMES THE COLD woke him. Even in winter, Francesca liked to keep the heat turned low at night—a frugal old habit. They had a comforter, buoyant with goose down; it usually slid off the bed and the cold wound in through his sleep. He opened his eyes in the still darkness, wondering. He tried to recall more clearly this Rafi

Bustani who'd signed the note. A pale, nearly featureless face hovered in his thoughts.

Gabe fell back to sleep, then woke later with new sunlight. His dreams had been quiet. *"Fawg." Up,* he murmured, Francesca still asleep beside him. She'd been doing this lately on weekends. Would they live long enough to ever retire and let the weeks soften into new shapes? He lay with his face against his pillow. He felt it again, Musa running into the street in Petra to save him from Hafez. He thought of how Musa had vanished from their family the first time. He considered the rules of inheritance. No. Hafez was capable of many terrible things but not murder. Gabe would not let himself imagine such a thing. The next time Gabe returned to Jordan, he thought, he would go to the cave with gifts—he would bring Musa a good warm jacket; the nights must be terribly cold in a cave—especially at his age.

He had to hurry and get dressed. It was just January, but already he was getting orders for decks and new windows and painted cabinets for springtime kitchen renovations. Still, he stayed in bed a moment longer, watching the way the light strayed across Francesca's ankles. He tugged the comforter back over her feet. He wanted to brush the short fan of hair away from her face, but that might disturb her. There was time enough for waking. When her eyes opened, he would put his arms around her. It was strange, how you could live with someone for so long that you nearly stopped seeing them.

Other times, though, you might suddenly catch a glimpse, and then it was like seeing a waterfall. You might tell yourself that this person is like gold to you, melted gold, running through your arms, lovely and ungraspable.

When she woke, he would hold her: he would remember how infinitely precious she was. He would try to remember to do that every day and every hour—because they were limited, he knew all too well, the hours and the days.

CHAPTER
33

• *December 18, 1995, Karak to Amman, Jordan* •

THE STREETS WERE WET with ice and rain when Omar pulled up in front of the guesthouse. He honked twice.

"I thought we were going by cab." Amani climbed in and swung the door closed.

"Well, it's a miracle, cuz," he said, drumming lightly on the steering wheel. "I was halfway out the door and Baba asks where I'm going. And I guess he liked whatever I said, 'cause then he says lately he's been thinking, like, I might be worth something after all." Omar grinned. "Who knows why, but he did. Anyway, he must've been in some kind of major good mood, because he told me to take the car!"

"Take it today or take it forever?" Amani gave him a sidelong glance.

"I can dream, right?" Her cousin swung the visor down: a pair of sunglasses fell into his lap and he put them on. "They're shipping him a new car from Germany—it's on the boat now. If I don't say anything, he might forget about this one."

It was cold outside, but the sun climbed over their heads as they took the hairpin curves on the King's Highway. They were on their way to the convent. Amani buzzed down the glass, taking in the dark hills like ocean waves. She inhaled the air that even in winter smelled somehow so specific to Jordan, with traces of sesame and olive.

A FEW WEEKS AGO, Amani opened her eyes in the guesthouse, her hand touching the Nefertiti necklace. She'd dreamed about the desert again, that she'd flown over tents and seen underwater currents in the sky, and she woke smiling. She and Gabe were supposed to fly home that day. But sitting up in bed, she'd known she wouldn't go back to the States. When she told her father she was going to remain behind, he'd laughed, then stared. He hadn't believed her. She rode in the cab with him to the airport and told him she didn't have specific plans yet and she didn't know how long she would stay. He shook his head repeatedly as if trying to clear it. When their flight was called, he stood up holding his carry-on bag, once again staring at her. "You really are sure of this?"

"As much as I can be."

He walked toward the jetway, then stopped. He looked at her, aghast. "Your mother."

She hugged him and kissed his cheek. "Tell her I might even be happy."

"Then good," he said, and kissed her head. "Your grandmother said 'love and fear never eat from the same plate.'"

And she had started writing again. Not poetry now; this was something between fiction and journalism. She transcribed to her computer all the bits of writing she'd found in her grandmother's envelope, piecing them together as best she could.

Amani knew what the paper scraps were—a writer's false starts, the beginnings and ends and partial pieces, and the tearing and crumpling that accompany the fight to translate ideas into words. Mrs. Ward had saved them. She told Amani that before Hafez had moved back to Jordan, she had lived with and cared for Natalia during the final years of her life in the rear wing of the house. The jewelry box, and the books, clothes, and writing that Amani had found in the armoire had all belonged to her grandmother. There were nineteen fragments of work, which had become for Amani the openings of nineteen chapters. They were her inspiration and jumping-off points, the beginning of a conversation between herself and Natalia. She was writing about a girl, raised in one place, uprooted, moved to another, married too young, left to hardship, who tried to restore herself in books. Amani had started to talk to people who might have known Natalia, or might have understood her loss. She met again with Sitt Danya, and with the guard at the pleasure palace, and she talked with other refugees and visited the camps, walking between the rows of cement-colored tents, Mostly, though, Amani read the blue letter and Natalia's fragments and imagined her grandmother's life. She needed only focus, only the slimmest light— a trail from desk to fingers. Her mind felt supple; the writing had begun.

Farouq had lent her the guesthouse for as long as she wanted. She emailed a brief, forthright letter of resignation to her university. The Sousin Arts Foundation gave her studio space and a stipend in exchange for opening and running its small café in the mornings. Both Farouq and Bella had argued against her taking such lowly, public work. Her uncle offered to place her in his investment company headquarters—or to connect her with people in almost any professional field in Jordan.

And then there was the letter from Hafez, addressed to Farouq, who'd read it aloud:

Abu Dhabi, they say, is lovely this time of year. But it's not as lovely as you might think. The taxis are worse than ours: one senses the imminent possibility of murder just beneath the surface. I think longingly of my little buggy. Our hosts have taken us to the gold market, to the tallest building on Earth, to shopping malls where German tourists scuba dive behind vast plate-glass windows. They are very hospitable here—there are approximately 20 "guest workers" for every 1 Abu Dhabian: life here is for the lucky.

We're visiting my old college chums Odeh and Manal Malouf. Odeh is—according to Odeh—making a killing in pharmaceuticals and pesticides—the two go hand in hand, he says with his smile, like love and marriage. I expect you'd know something about that, Farouq.

Farouq snorted. "He goes on—still obsessed with the damned knife. Amer's land. It's going to be claimed by the government. Surprise, surprise. He says he's so disappointed for all of us. Ha-ha. I'm sure he was planning to take us all to Disneyland." He looked at Amani, adding, "He says he wants to get you a job in the ministry of culture."

Rafi assures me that the king will not be angry for long; he tells me that all is mostly forgiven: His Highness understands I wasn't trying to hide the land from him, that I didn't appreciate the political sensitivity of its location. Always more refugees to accommodate.

We will remount the peace process—though I no longer quite the confidence I did before. I do feel, I'll admit, somewhat diminished these days. Peace does not come easily to some: we must learn to embrace it. When last we spoke, Shimon Peres assured me that we will move forward, that Rabin's assassination will not destroy the treaties, that the warmongers will settle down, the militants will lose interest. He will establish the Peres Center for Peace. He says the Internet will make war obsolete. I would choose to believe him, but I myself am not a man of peace—as our brother once so wisely observed. I am more familiar with our enemy, which is as they say, oneself. What I know of the enemy, therefore, does not bode well.

Do I fault myself? There are certain things I should have done differently. I try never to feel guilt or pride: but this a cold way to be, so separate from oneself. To paraphrase the airlines: Be kind to yourself before being kind to the person next to you.

FOR NOW, the café was what Amani needed. She liked the twist of expectations—deliberately trading a professorship for a job waiting tables. She really did feel happier, more lined up with herself. Amani no longer wanted a drink—she hadn't in while. Her thoughts grew sharper, clear as instrument strings. She looked forward to the scent of brewed coffee, the early quiet hours there before she opened. First, she tied on an apron, then straightened the tabletops and started the silver espresso machine. Placed croissants, fruit, and biscotti in the case. When business was slow, she'd take her notebook and a coffee to the table near the windows and let her thoughts unspool. She found her natural pace. Mrs. Ward, who now cooked for Farouq and Bella, told her Natalia had liked to say Al-`ajala min al-shaytan. Hurrying is from the devil.

IN KARAK, Amani and Omar climbed Musa's hill, the sky a bowl of blue smoke. Musa came out and took their hands and led them into his cave. On the ground was a flat, woven carpet of brilliant colors and over this a smaller Persian carpet that shone like water, the surface of its fibers silvery. Musa squatted on the carpets and patted two leather hassocks for Omar and Amani to sit. He said something that Amani didn't catch, and Omar laughed. "He says he's too old to learn how to sit on a chair." Musa gestured: there were new pots in a glass-fronted cabinet, a brass-topped table, a silver tray, a tapestry of a gazelle, even a new coffeepot. He got to his feet and gestured toward the cave's other opening: there was the start of construction, some cinder blocks and the wooden frame of a floor and a door. "He says the King is building him a house," Omar said.

Amani nodded and ran her hand over the tapestries, the layered textures of wool and silk. As Musa bent over his dented saucepan filled with twigs, she noticed a glint at his side: the knife tucked into a piece of fabric tied around his waist. He poured them cups of tea, then chuckled and said in Arabic, "No cookie today." Removing the knife, he carefully pared an orange in one continuous peel, and handed segments to each of them. He wiped both sides of the knife on his robe and replaced it in his belt. Settling his cup on the brass table, Musa went still for a moment; his face lifting to hers looked like that of someone awakening.

IT HAD STARTED to snow while she and Omar sat with Musa: the night was dawning purple, white flakes coming down so gradually, so brightly, it seemed possible to see each crystalline fractal as they turned in the air. They picked their way back down the hill carefully, skidding on wet patches. A powerline in town had fallen under the weight of the snow and the convent had lost electricity. Along the walkway and on each step leading into the building the nuns had placed lighted pillar candles, glowing against the early nightfall.

Sister Sylvain offered them dinner, but Amani was tired and ready to get home. The two embraced tightly.

They drove back to Amman in silence, into a starry night that turned as if on a dial. She slept in the passenger's seat for a bit and woke, then slept again.

When Omar pulled up in front of the guesthouse, she glanced out the window to see a man unfolding from the front steps under the porch light. Amani inhaled sharply. She hadn't yet told Eduardo she was staying. She hadn't meant to avoid him, but once she'd decided to remain she couldn't think of a way to talk to him about it that seemed natural. She didn't want the fact that she was staying to feel like pressure or expectation. And then the longer she waited, the stranger and more complicated it seemed. She turned in the car and gave Omar a swift, fierce look.

"What?" He held up his hands. "Someone had to tell him. Maskeen. I didn't know what you were waiting for."

"For the right time!"

"Pff. What even is that?" His hands dropped. "This is Amman, cuz. Three hours is a very, *very* long time for someone here not to know something, never mind three weeks."

"Two and a half weeks," Amani snapped. She climbed out and slammed the door.

Eduardo waved at Omar, who flashed a peace sign before pulling away, then waited as Amani walked toward him. "So your cousin called me," he said. "I had to come see for myself. I've been rather at loose ends, you know."

Her skin felt hot. "I've wanted to call you—every day. I am sorry—I should have. I wanted to. But. I didn't want me being here to mean more than it needed to." She held her left shoulder with her right hand, as if she could still feel the old talon marks. Her throat felt constricted. "I don't know. I'm so bad at—this sort of thing."

After a moment, he lowered his head and nodded. "I think, perhaps, you had your guard up. It's wise—to shield oneself. But at some point—"

"I know." She nodded. "It's supposed to come down."

He followed her just inside and stood in the open door; his hands holding the doorframe. The streetlamp behind him cast its glow into the entryway. "So, may I ask you something?"

It was difficult to make out his backlit features, but she didn't want to turn on the lights. "Please."

"Is your guard still—" He put one hand on his chest. "Up here?"

She let go of her shoulder. Her mind felt clear, as it had since her nights in the desert, as if she'd put down something heavy and walked away. She moved toward Eduardo. Reaching around him, she pushed the door shut. Amani slid her arms under his. Their kiss was private and soft, like a message passed in secret. She began to pull out of it but he bent to her with more urgency and she felt a shivering current through her body. When they stopped, he was looking at her. "Truly—you're not going."

"Not right now, I'm not." She put a hand on the side of his face.

He seemed to wait, to study her a moment longer. Finally, he said, "All right. If that's what it is." Outside the uncovered windows, the clouds looked low and moonlit. "I think . . ." he said, considering his words. "I think you may have to help me find my footing. I'm not sure where we are."

"I'm not either," she said quietly. "That's okay. Let's not know."

They held each other in the unlit house. Closing her eyes, Amani listened to the wave of breath in his chest. Her thoughts went from the cave to the little room in her uncle's house. She saw it—not just a room but a space held against disappearance. It was too easy to believe so much in promises, in things, she thought, in the created world: keys, letters, knives, even land. Better to look a bit farther, behind the things. It seemed to her as they stood there, in the bare light from the street, that the invisible world was the only one that mattered.

"All right," he said at last. "I suppose I can do that."

The street light dimmed in the windows; a mosaic of snow had once again appeared, patterning the night.

With her finger, she dashed a Z across his chest and he smiled and said, "The mark of the brave."

ACKNOWLEDGMENTS

I OWE A GREAT DEBT of gratitude to my grandparents, aunts, uncles, cousins, and extended family for their tales and inspiration. I'm from a tribe of poets, dreamers, and storytellers, and I'm proud to help carry on the family tradition. I'm especially grateful to my mother, Patricia, and sisters, Suzanne and Monica, for encouraging my work and believing in the value of my stories.

In addition, I'd like to especially mention Camellia Angel, Elias Majlaton, and Kathy Sullivan for their expert opinions and guidance. Thanks to Bassam Frangieh for his generous expertise in Arabic. And special shout-outs to my cousins Nasser Abu-Jaber and Hamoudeh Abu-Jaber, for their exemplary cultural guidance; to my much-loved Aida Dabbas and Claudio Cimino; to my good friend Bo Haroutunian; and to the fabulous Alain McNamara and the Fulbright Commission, which is a global treasure.

I'd like to thank my wonderful writing friends, including Jake Cline, David Hayes, Ana Veciana-Suarez, Andie Viele, Aaron Curtis, Lauren Doyle Owens, and Andrea Gollin, for their invaluable support and wisdom.

I'd like to thank Joanna Sutherland, Rachel Franklin Gordillo, Whitney Otto, John Riley, Lorraine Mercer, Carey McKearnan, Ana Menendez, Kathleen Cohn, Stephanie Pacheco, and Jose Pacheco Silva, for your laughter and the grace of your friendship.

I'd like to offer special thanks to Deborah Sharp, Kerry Sanders, Debbie Stokes, and Mike Stokes, for helping us to keep our heads and hearts up and navigate the waters of these extraordinary times.

And as always, always, to the outstanding professionals and wizards who I have had the great good fortune to work with—sometimes for decades (!!) and who have become cherished friends: Alane Salierno Mason, Joy Harris, Erin Lovett, Mo Crist, Adam Reed, and Mitchell Kaplan.

Most of all, I'd like to thank Scott, Grace, and Hobie, for every single bit of it.